The Goulep

by

Stella Atrium

FIRST EDITION

Copyright 1997, by Star Hall
Library of Congress Catalog Card No: 95-90802
ISBN: 1-56002-617-0

UNIVERSITY EDITIONS, Inc.
59 Oak Lane, Spring Valley
Huntington, West Virginia 25704

Cover by Mark Grosskopf

Dedication

To Daddy,
who taught me deductive reasoning,
for his childlike delight in nature.

Part One

Chapter One

I had been on Cicero twelve hours and I knew the bad news. My travel number for the jump back to Earth wouldn't become active for eighteen months. Ricardo called from his office at Stargate Junction near the worm hole and suggested I fill the time with this new work as administrator.

"Brian Miller?" a receptionist asked from behind me. She bowed deeply. "The Regent asks that you wait a few moments." She bowed again and returned to her desk behind a Chinese screen decorated with the image of a twisted and angry dragon.

Regent Sim Chareon's office was located in the biosphere, an oasis of Earth culture on technically backward Cicero, one of four inhabitable worlds in the tri-star system of the quadrant's Westend.

I stared at the Company logo embossed on the wall, an off-black and eggshell white image of the long-extinct Chinese giant panda roundly sitting with one paw on its knee, superimposed over a circle of mandarin yellow rimmed with royal purple.

I was tired of Westend duty, tired of transport food. Grab a fortune in the outlands and jump back with enough capital to raise horses in Montana, that was my plan. I hadn't seen a horse in seven years. Montana seemed like a dream, snow-laden mountains with the *aurora borealis* across the winter's night.

I squinted at the security camera trained on me with its reflective eye. I knew they watched me. I knew what they thought. I wasn't mandarin enough, not detached from duty with their rigid cynicism.

Sim Chareon studied the image of their visitor on his office security screen. "How long has Brian Miller worked in Westend?" he asked.

"Four years. His tour of duty just ended," answered Daniel Chin, executive secretary.

"Brian Miller is moody, hermetic and unorthodox," Chang Lin claimed with a hard look at the young Manchurian. "Isn't there someone else Ricardo can get for this venture?"

"The mining operation Brian Miller just completed had no labor unrest," offered Daniel Chin while he studied the dossier.

"How did he accomplish that?" the regent asked.

"He gave the conscripts one day in seven to rest provided their quota for that period remained the same."

"That's certainly unorthodox," Sim Chareon said with humor in his voice. "Is that why Ricardo Menenous requested him?"

"That and linguistics," Daniel Chin said. "He picks up native dialects easily."

"And Ricardo?"

"Originally from Bolivia," Daniel Chin offered, then switched to another file folder. "Exports to Earth Consortium goods that have favorable exchange rates. This new venture, called Brittany Mill, includes a monopoly on local textile manufacture. Ricardo hopes to test the Westend market by weaving Chinese designs into the durable linen used by Dolviet tribeswomen."

"Brian Miller's too sympathetic with natives," Chang Lin interrupted. "He doesn't maintain military distance."

"Brittany Mill isn't a military operation," Sim Chareon lightly returned.

In reception the high style of one long-past fashion season in Beijing was locked in time. The slight and manicured women, their hair braided down their backs, came and went with the rustle of layered satin robes. Air in the brightly-lit room was heavy with their flowery perfume. I felt like a conscript in my sturdy field uniform and heavy boots.

Hamish Nordhagan exited the elevator and handed a sealed file to the receptionist. He was a big Scottish man with graying hair in a non-regulation tail at his neck. One of the old guard who knew supply routes, Hamish trained Consortium administrators. He could afford to be cavalier concerning regulations. The Company needed him and men like him.

Hamish joined me for a moment, appraising my clean-shaven, too blond looks that belied my years of experience. "Sim Chareon called you here?"

"I can't jump back for eighteen months."

"Throw you a bone, huh?"

"Oxygen-suckers," I complained under my breath.

"But you're their man."

"Three options."

Hamish softly chuckled. "I saw your name on the shuttle register. We'll travel together."

"You'll disembark on Dolvia?"

"Transport duty. Upgrade their communications with the new chip. See you at the shuttle launch." The receptionist looked

6

up when we shook hands, not their official gesture.

Four kinds of men served in Westend. Chinese descent officers of the autocratic Company held all the real power. Technical men who came adventuring and stayed for the money did administration. This group included many of the old guard like Hamish who didn't jump back to Earth after extended tours. In a way I felt sorry for Hamish, perhaps afraid I would end the same. He enjoyed the camaraderie of the young administrators, but they understood him very little. Stand to the duty was all an old soldier had.

Colonists from many worlds comprised the third group, mostly tradesmen with families who signed away futures on their time for a fresh start on the frontier. Single destination resale licenses allowed families to travel as colonists. And they disembarked only on planets such as Dolvia designated by the Consortium government as needing the goods and services.

The fourth group who worked in Westend were conscripts, criminals and third generation offworld born with few opportunities to improve their station. Conscripts depended on the Company for lodging, food and medicine. Even the air.

It was discovered recently that life support systems supplied more oxygen to Company areas than to labor quarters. Company explanations claimed the rich mixture was needed for clear-headed thinking in a culture where everyone wore pungent perfumes. One conscript organized a revolt from outrage at the iniquity. The movement was quickly disbursed, and the leader separated from his group. For several hours he held hostage a highly-placed Company official. Company enforcers explained his situation, that he must lay down his weapon.

"I have three options," he called out in a clear voice. "I can shoot myself. I can shoot my hostage. Or I can shoot him first and then me." He was terminated.

After the Oxygen Incident, labor quarters security was tightened and all privileges suspended. The stark clarity of three options became a slogan in conscript slang known as freightate.

I was glad Ricardo offered me ground duty. I wasn't required to implement the repressive Company measures to control conscripts who outnumbered them seven to one.

Jump back was also a freightate term. After the Consortium completed Stargate Junction and signed trade agreements with the Company, travel through the worm hole was mostly one way for decades, importing hardware and armaments to subdue the native work force. Recently the trip through the worm hole to Earth's solar system was booked years in advance. Exports of ore and crude plus artifacts and inexpensive native goods clogged the stretched trade routes, making travel possible only at Company convenience.

"The Regent will see you now, Mr. Miller," the receptionist

murmured. I was ushered into a waiting room where an ancient Chinese vase was showcased under glass and lights. I caught myself computing the weight, the bulkiness of special packing, the insurance premiums and the distance in light years the vase had traveled for this ostentatious display.

Two thin panels silently slid back to reveal an ornately decorated business office. Whole rooms of the Forbidden City must have been dismantled to gather that much real teak. I greeted Regent Sim Chareon, his favorite advisor Chang Lin, and a secretary whom I didn't know.

Company men were slightly built with fineboned hands. Their eyes slanted neither up nor down but seemed to pull back into slits like a dozing cat. They wore dark suits of the richest silken material, tailored to their trim forms. Their crisp, white shirts sported round collars that put me in mind of the Jesuits who had guided my early education.

Sim Chareon was an older man, silent and without mannerisms. Of Mongolian descent with a round face and fat fingers, he sat on the couch and allowed the young businessmen to talk while he played the pensioner role, a retired colonel expert with arcane weapons.

Chang Lin, who sat behind the desk in a winged chair, was Han-Chinese. His reputation as an unbending arbitrator held that the code directives were more important than the fates of the people he judged.

"You're aware of the position being offered?" the secretary, one Daniel Chin, asked from where he stood behind Chang Lin with my dossier in hand.

"I read the Brittany Mill prospectus."

"Are you familiar with the situation in Dolvia?" Daniel Chin asked.

"I have been out of range of the comtechs."

"The transport library has dossiers on major tribal players," Daniel Chin said. "Plus language tapes, university research whitepapers and land surveys. Unfortunately, our knowledge of tribal custom is sketchy."

"There was an incident there a short time ago," Chang Lin explained. "Administrators and conscripts from a mining subsidiary were massacred for burying one of their own after an explosion in the mine. They were not aware burials violated tribal taboo. We prefer to avoid disruptive incidents."

I shifted in my seat and addressed Sim Chareon. "It was my understanding that Brittany Mill was independent. My agreement is with Ricardo."

"Ricardo Menenous' export businesses use Company trade routes," Chang Lin quickly insisted. "We ask only for reciprocity."

"Monthly reports?" I asked.

"Plus timely communications about developing situations," Chang Lin added.

Reciprocity, an elegant word. Snitch was more correct. After my meeting with Regent Chareon and friends, I wandered down to the promenade mall. Company women in brightly colored brocade robes shuffled past the shop windows on high stilted shoes. After my three years quartered on transports that orbited frigid asteroids, where assets were hard won and harder to keep, the colorful abundance of goods displayed in the mall windows seemed sinful. I even saw a table cream pitcher in the shape of a dairy cow. Who spent time producing such trifles?

I sat for a short time over Irish coffee in a promenade pastry shop. A female Chinese newscaster delivered the Company line with unctuous authority from the ceiling mounted comtech. The commentator with bobbed hair and modulated voice most likely had not reported the Oxygen Incident, the Dolvia massacre, or any news that made the Company lose face.

I made my way through security checks to the lower deck crew quarters near the shuttle launch pads. There the comtech volume was muffled by thick material packed around the monitor speakers. A few shops in the Commons offered resale and repair services. Two bakeries displayed soft bread specialties filled with apricot or raspberry.

Two young Asian women with rich hair braided down their backs suspiciously looked up at my entrance, then returned to their conversation. Most likely on a break from work, they wore the ribbed pullovers and multiple-pocket dungarees tucked into round-toed boots that were standard issue for work detail.

There was a row of pleasure suites along one side of the Commons. After experience in the virtual reality pleasure cubicles of long distance transports, travelers highly prized contact with a real woman. Prostitutes from exotic worlds waited outside individual rooms decorated after their cultures and the pleasures they offered. My shuttle to the transport wasn't due to leave for sixteen hours. I entered the third suite where incense filled my senses and erased traces of Company perfume.

Chapter Two

The next day I slept during the eighty minute shuttle ride to the transport. Hamish Nordhagan roughly shook my shoulder. "Get up. You smell like a warthog." I yawned and rubbed my eyes, then grabbed my carryon pack and followed him into customs.

Westend transports came in all sizes and shapes. This one made the run between Cicero and Dolvia to supply Company mining subsidiaries and export ore and crude. Actually three structures locked together, it looked like a legless and misshapen red ant. A cargo hold called midship was the largest section with no portals except four docking bays. The labor quarters bulkhead was attached by two causeways. Neither had engine or guidance equipment separate from the mothership. The much smaller Company ship was of military design, well maintained with many armaments and exterior cameras for security.

Hamish and I flashed our panda logo badges and were passed through customs while other passengers had their gear searched and papers inspected. We entered the stifling and badly-lit promenade of midship.

A wallmounted comtech lent blue overtones to the narrow room. Along both sides cramped shops with iron bars on their windows offered repair and resale services. The six long benches, clustered just outside the customs office, would be overcrowded in four days with colonists waiting to disembark on the same shuttle for which I had tickets to Cylay, the capital of Dolvia.

Two men in black field uniforms with silver insignia loitered by the labor section entrance. Their round collared loose tunics fastened down the right side in Manchu style. Their flat-heeled boots over loose pantaloons indicated they were Consortium Blackshirts recruited in Westend. Hamish nodded to them then falsely grinned at me. We ran the security gauntlet and passed through the hydraulic doors to the Company mothership, immaculate and well-lit with the panda logo and directional decals along the walls.

"Guest quarters are down this corridor," Hamish said. "I'll see you at dinner in VCC-2."

"Dinner?" I asked.

"You have been in the outlands. The two hour meal each night is part of service. For Company and administrators only. Keeps us in mind of who's in charge here."

"And the families?"

"There are lunchrooms in midship. Plus restaurants that cater."

"So crew families live at their own expense?"

"Welcome to the Westend," Hamish grinned. "And take an airbath."

My quarters included a bed, a table and chair, plus an efficiency bathroom. A library screen and extra-atmosphere modem, called an EAM, waited on the table. My luggage was delivered by the time I bathed and changed clothes. I entered my code into the EAM and called up messages. A note from Ricardo said I should keep an appointment next week with one Martin Sumuki at the Tri-City Bank Corp in Somule, the second largest city on Dolvia.

I called up geography menus on the library screen and rambled through the choices. Over the next several hours, I absorbed what I could find about my interim home. I began with the land surveys written by Company surveyors.

A small planet with two moons, Dolvia had a ring of rain forests at its equator. Near desert Somule the mantle crust was thin and volatile with hydro-thermal geysers and bubbling mud pools. With a dry season and a rainy season, the region produced enough grain and vegetables for Dolviets to live simply on their local produce.

The quiet and trickling stream Dolviets called a river swelled its banks two weeks before clouds formed in the sky. The cold water from northern mountain thaw mixed with the hot springs that dotted the landscape. The waterjets left bacteria and algae residue ranging from lavender to deep green and luminescent orange. For shock value and towering majesty, the geysers from that exchange of water temperature were not matched anywhere in Westend.

Reports supported by satellite readings of the surface and sub-surface water temperature claimed the initial exchange of mountain thaw and old subterranean water was vital for the eight week rainy season. Without the cooling mountain thaw, the sub-surface water and unremitting desert temperatures would create a brackish wasteland in which no life, certainly not the fragile bacteria and plankton on which the food chain depended, could survive.

Land survey reports concentrated on the flats of Arim, twelve miles west of Somule. Created a hundred thousand years ago by a collapsed volcano basin called a caldera, the flats were the center of two-thirds of the hydro-thermal geyser activity.

On one section of the flats, terraces of geyserite and deep pools of mineral-rich water emptied into a heated, meandering stream. Other cooler springs drew microscopic bacteria from the underground activity and displayed a variety of colorful algae growth.

Below the flats a monumental butte stood vigil, towering over the dry savannah. The muddy stream lumbered between it and a high plateau then west to the ocean. The high and craggy walls of many savannah plateaus faced off solid buttes. They had, in fact, formed when the shifting mantle rubbed against the bedrock of the buttes that were rooted as deeply underground as they rose in the air. The mantle broke and lifted like an iceberg forming sheer cliff walls with sloping backs.

There were four main tribes in the region; the Mekucoo, the Putuki which included Martin Sumuki, the Cylahi and the Arrivi. The Mekucoo were known as Ketiwhelp killers. Fourlegged furbearing omnivores with a head most like a fox and a lion's broad feet with retractable claws, Ketiwhelps traveled as well on two legs as on four, day or night. In disposition they resembled the grisly bear, not because they were solitary and irascible, but because once angered, they hunted to kill men.

Once Ketiwhelps had traveled in packs and massacred entire unguarded villages. When cattle were domesticated, the tribes hunted Ketiwhelps almost to extinction. The few that remained lived in solitary family dens on the high savannah and hunted mostly at night. Females raised usually two whelps without assistance from the male and were vulnerable after the bountiful rains when they needed to hunt to feed their young.

The most populous regional tribe were the Arrivi who covered their women from head to foot with light and colorful body veils. Arrivi women showed themselves to only one man in a lifetime. If their leader called Rabbenu entered the home, only the faces of the wives of Rabbenu's financial equals were uncovered in his presence.

I decided to learn more about the tribespeople and accessed personnel files from the Company records. A head shot of Martin Sumuki plus his visual statistics came onscreen. He was five feet, nine inches tall and weighed 215 pounds. He had blue-black skin and no jewel in his wide nose above thick lips. Martin Sumuki had managed the Tri-City Bank Corp for the past five years. He held a university degree in finance, was a tribal Council member and spokesperson for the Putuki tribe. Married with two infant daughters, he had been an assassin's target during tribal unrest seven years earlier.

The screen prompted me to call up dossiers for known associates. I selected Oriika, the holy woman. She was a ponderous woman from a northern tribe, chocolate brown with nappy hair cut close to her head. Only 32 years old and decked out in colorful skirts and showy jewelry, Oriika was unmarried, held no title or tribal status and was a known agitator at the Company limestone quarries on Arrivi land.

I reviewed the file on a Mekucoo warrior named Cyrus, also a known associate. He was five feet, six inches tall and weighed 145 pounds. His straight, dark hair was tied back at his neck, and he could easily pass for white. His face was disfigured with a broken nose, uneven jawline and cauliflower ears. He had led an insurrection against a Blackshirt garrison in Somule eight years earlier and was captured. He was held for interrogation but released when the garrison was disbanded and Company forces were transferred to Cylay.

Held for interrogation. Must be how he got those scars.

Released when the garrison was disbanded. The insurrection must have succeeded. Information was a dangerous thing to have laying around, sometimes for what it didn't say.

I had no feel for the rhythm of time without the passage of a sun. Evenings I played pinochle with crew members from Hamish's shift, but mostly I spent the next three days reviewing Dolviet language tapes. I sat back and rubbed my face, depending on the EAM to log how many hours I studied.

I must not have been paying attention. On the day of disembarkment when I came through security with my pack, I was stopped before I reached customs. In the midship promenade Company Blackshirts in riot suits and hard plastic shields pushed back angry colonists slated for this launch. While their frightened wives and children waited in a cluster, colonists shook their fists in the air and shouted at being bumped for different cargo.

A detachment of slim and elite Chinese Blackshirts, carrying weapons of choice and packs displaying the panda logo, boarded the shuttle. They looked back at the angry crowd with contempt and offered no assistance.

Hamish signaled crew officers to pass me through to customs. The waiting colonists with their sturdy clothes and canvas toolbags shouted at me and crowded the line of transport Blackshirts. "What the hell, Hamish?" I impatiently said when I reached his position.

"Colonists have hocked everything for passage," Hamish called out above the din. "If there's an extended delay for the shuttle's return, they can't afford lodgings."

"They'll become conscript?"

"They can sell a percentage of their licenses."

"And become midshippers in partnership with the Company."

"Not all of us are offered ground duty at tour's end," Hamish answered, his eyes flashing with cynicism.

"Can you get me onboard?" I asked.

"That's easy enough," Hamish said. "You have mandarin yellow all down your back."

I pushed my way to the causeway and boarded the shuttle, glad to escape the orbiting transport. I nodded to the well-fed and manicured Blackshirts. The two across from me squinted when they saw my eyes wander to their polished weapons.

On Dolvia the train from Cylay to Somule was first class down to brass accouterments and white gloves on the coachmen. The train jerked and stopped, then slowly glided into the station. I entered a Company-issued round and ribbed prefab metal hangar with air-conditioning and bad acoustics, decorated with the ever-present giant panda logo. Barefoot native children clamored to carry my bags. A dirty street vendor offered a warm and murky drink.

I passed through the revolving doors onto an open platform made of imported wood with a clay tile roof that extended to several adjacent businesses. A shimmering wall of heat obscured my view of the hotels above winding sidewalks and narrow bazaars. The grim reality of ground travel without technical support was debilitating. I sat on a wooden bench in the narrow shade and took quick, shallow breaths before I could walk two blocks to the hotel.

Somule was a boom town due to limestone quarries on nearby Rabbenu land and the Company hotel investment. The need for additional construction had prompted the Company to send transport conscript gangs. Barefoot and bald men in loose tunics and baggy pants worked on the upper floors and back entrance of the hotel. As if to punish conscripts for breathing fresh air and enjoying the sunlight on their necks, the Blackshirt detachment who oversaw their work kept them in the squalid hotel basement without adequate food or sanitary facilities.

These Blackshirts were mercenaries or former conscripts who had gained status through service. They wore the same uniform and insignia as the elite guard. Without adequate education and track records, they were excluded from administrator privileges and had none of the Chinese haughty and eloquent manners.

I waited in the hotel lobby, apparently their first guest. A blue-black Putuki man behind the desk struggled to find the correct forms to sign and the room key.

One Blackshirt addressed as Lt. Lebowitz, a burly and sunburned man with eyes set too close together, watched me with a hateful look. He took pleasure in using the leather switch that other Blackshirts carried more for show than discipline. He turned the whizzing switch on a laboring conscript without provocation, mostly for my benefit. The Putuki man who served me stiffened, then hid his resentment.

I stayed at the hotel two days and took short walks until I

could step outside without feeling my lungs wither and my legs turn to rubber. I ate in the Chinese restaurant decorated in Manchu style that offered imported delicacies. The Putuki women in service seemed indifferent to the impatient demands of the Han-Chinese manager who insisted the chef's dishes be delivered at just the right temperature. Since I was their only guest, to spare the tribeswomen this torture, I bought native dates and bread at the street bazaars and ate in my room except for the evening meal.

One afternoon when I came in from a short walk, I saw several Han-Chinese Blackshirts waiting at the hotel entrance and in the lobby. Two women dressed in layers of kimonos and white and red make-up entered the lobby from the restaurant. An Arrivi woman accompanied them wearing an imported high-collared and belted dress and a mantilla of intricate lace. Her peridot jewelry was expensive and overdone, competing with the long strands of coral beads that were required adornment for Company women. The Chinese women bowed slightly to me when they passed. They left the hotel and entered one of the waiting ECCAVs, or enclosed cross-country air-conditioned vehicles. The Blackshirt guards disdainfully looked around then left in the second ECCAV.

"Who are they?" I asked the Putuki clerk.

"The regent's daughters and Julia Le of the family of Rabbenu."

"Arrivi women no longer wear body veils?" I asked. He glanced at me then sourly turned back to his work.

On the third day I decided I could tolerate exposure long enough to get through the appointment with Martin Sumuki. The cool and bright high-ceiling lobby of Tri-City Bank Corp was a pleasant surprise.

Martin Sumuki came out of his office and bowed to me as was their custom of greeting. He wore a rumpled, cream-colored linen suit and looked like his dossier picture only heavier. He was pleased with my appreciation of the bank building. "It's native adobe, and we imported the ceiling fans. We keep air-conditioned rooms for those who don't care to acclimate. My office is similar to this room if you feel comfortable with that."

Martin's office was painted gray and apricot with cane chairs and a ceiling fan. Sunlight filtered through the slats of the interior shutters. He switched off the single lamp on his small apricot-colored desk that was really a plank over two sets of drawers. His books were locked in the only expensive piece of furniture. I saw the luminous dial of a dehumidifier inside the leaded glass cabinet doors.

Martin asked if I smoke, and I shook my head. We settled into the cane chairs and he lit a thin aromatic cigarette, an act that classed him as groundborn.

"So," he began offhandedly. "We secured the buildings, and I studied delivery schedules. But these aren't your real problem."

"Ricardo wants the factory operational in three months."

He confidentially leaned forward. "Your statistics on the labor force are outdated."

"I saw conscript gangs at the hotel."

"A dirty business," he said with a squint. "At first the Company used tribesmen for construction, but the skills are different. Now tribesmen have left or been taken to fight. There's an insurrection in the northern mountains."

"Will there be fighting there?"

He shrugged. "At Tri-City ours is a small operation, underwritten as a developing venture. Ricardo has more at stake. And you are his point man."

I smiled, wondering at his ambivalence. "Ricardo mentioned the possibility of employing the women."

He gestured expansively. "For the Cylahi perhaps. And the Mekucoo, but there are few of them here."

"And the Arrivi?" I asked.

"There's a harem mentality among them. I thought you'd want to see for yourself. There's a wedding tomorrow, Haku Rabbe Murd and Karima Le of Arim. But it's outdoors, early before the heat of the day and maybe three hours long. Are you up to it?" We smiled together again, very cordial. Of course his demeanor spoke of accommodation to all. The land separated the doers from the players.

Back at the hotel, I ate several patties of the tasteless and salty native bread. I turned off the air-conditioner in my room and opened the doors to the small balcony. I was determined to spend the remainder of the afternoon and evening in the open air.

Sweating and lightheaded, I managed to set up my briefcase screen with a coolant unit in the growing shade on the balcony. I locked in the EAM and waited for my code to clear at the transport library. Presently the screen read, "Brian Miller, good di."

I indicated I wanted to communicate in Arrivi. The screen blinked and read, "Rabbenu Miller, hiki." Rabbenu was a title of high honor. Rightfully I should have been addressed as Brian Rabbe Miller. At least the gender was correct. Had the EAM assumed I was a woman, I would have seen the diminutive form, Brian Le.

Every six hours the EAM signed off for forty minutes while the transport's orbit dropped below my location's horizon. With an open-ended dialogue, it automatically came back with my geographic time of day and the accumulated cost of the call. Then I saw the familiar greeting, "Rabbenu Miller, hiki."

During the break I looked out over the balcony rail and

realized it was night. Except for the well-lit hotel entrance and restaurant, the yawning blackness was deep as though nothing was there. I heard the hotel generator and workmen hammering in the railstation where an engine was being repaired overnight. I knew that away from the buildings I would hear the nightbirds and rustle of the trees while predators too smart to hunt during the day were out.

The screen came back on, "25:367 amk. 3418.420. Rabbenu Miller, hiki. Parle hai Rabbenu Menenous?" I felt a cold chill run down my back. I had felt safe from surface peeping-toms but had forgotten the transport was wire heaven. Ricardo could have tracked the wanderings of my mind for hours. And for all I knew, had a conference call with Martin the whole time. I knew instantly I wouldn't depend on the EAM again. I typed in, "Rabbenu Menenous, hiki."

A facsimile of his round and balding head came onscreen. He moved a dial. "I can't see you, Brian," said his electronic voice.

I typed in, "This is an EAM-50."

His image nodded. "Did you contact Martin?" said the electronic voice.

"Today at the bank," I typed, and after a pause added, "Good man, Martin."

But Ricardo was onto business. "There was a puncture in the cargo hold. The loom was frozen clear through. Under gravity it will crack like peanut brittle. I want you to occupy the buildings, set up everything else. I may be able to get a local replacement. How are your landlegs?"

"So, so," I typed. "I have a couple questions about the labor situation."

Immediately I heard, "Yeah, yeah. We'll talk. See you then."

I exited the screen and powered down the EAM. I laid on the bed in the humid night to get what little rest I could with a salted stomach, then thought about the need to go bald.

There had been a popular novel some years back about a paranoid personality who dreamed his head was wired. He refused services and ranted about his need to go bald until he was terminated as a recalcitrant.

For fieldmen, going bald was a real possibility. Survival training was basic second level. My only bald assignment had been seven years ago, before I knew space travel. In those days we were sent out in groups and regularly monitored.

I got up very late and went out onto the balcony. The air was cooler but dry. I heard the call of the nightbird and rustling bushes beyond the brownout hotels. Where was the balance on Dolvia? How much did the land test your mettle? How much the mettle of a bald outlander?

17

Chapter Three

The next day I waited outside the hotel lobby wearing my lightest administrator's uniform. Martin arrived driving an ECCAV. He saw the question on my face and quickly offered, "It's Ricardo's. He won't acclimate, you know. If we have, why not use?"

We drove away from Somule, a cluster of low adobe buildings with two hotel towers reflecting the early sun. Martin pointed out the windowless Company compound built into a rise just west of town.

"Actually it's a quadrangle," Martin explained. "Interior windows face a traditional Chinese garden. Truly. Caged birds and bubbling ponds stocked with fancy goldfish."

"They imported goldfish through the worm hole?"

Martin shrugged. "Kariom are gray."

Kariom were mudfish who hibernated most of the year, then with the first rains sprang forth to breed in pools on the savannah. They were netted and dried by tribesmen, and served as a year-round Dolviet staple.

We drove due west toward the towering butte that faced off a high plateau below the flats of Arim. I watched the red sandy savannah with infrequent stunted shrubs speed past the ECCAV window. At the site, a wedding tent and smaller family tent were erected in the early morning shadow of the monumental butte.

The real surprise was the arrival of two more ECCAVs. Four Company men wearing dark suits stepped into the oppressive heat. "My God, Martin. Is all of Westend coming?" I asked.

He laughed out loud. "Haku Rabbe Murd is the strongest voice of the largest body of the cheapest labor in Westend. Ricardo isn't the only one who noticed."

Martin bowed low to three tribesmen then guided me into the tent. Our seats were near several seated Arrivi families who faced a podium and semicircle of cane chairs prepared for members of the wedding party. The Arrivi were careful to keep their honored Softcheeks guests visible to all but separate from each other. Martin looked across the way and bowed slightly to the Company men who nodded. Two young Arrivi men served them damp cloths and salted olives. They ate to be polite and refused the cloths to be manly.

"They must be dying in those suits," I whispered to Martin.

"Actually they gain respect for personal stamina, even with the acclimation pill," he answered. "I wonder how many years they suffer from liver damage."

Olive-skinned Arrivi boys in tunics and loose-fitting linen trousers offered us cool cloths and a plate of olives, dried dates and fish on a bread patty. I reached for a second piece of fish, and Martin grabbed my wrist. "You'll be sorry for two days."

To our right stood the invited Cylahi women and children who, in honor of the day, wore clothing over the essential parts. Mostly I was impressed with their hand wrought gold jewelry and bright paint.

In the back stood three Mekucoo warriors in short, sleeveless ponchos and carrying decorated shields. "Take a note of these clothes. Ricardo wants the patterns."

Martin saw my look and shrugged. "Ricardo wants everything."

Rabbenu Penli, the tribal leader, entered the tent and greeted families and guests. A rotund man with a full head of curly hair, he wore a richly patterned silk caftan and rings on every finger, plus a jewel-studded stiff and square hat of the same pattern.

Rabbenu Penli bowed slightly to each of us and carefully pronounced my name, then moved onto the next group. "This is your last chance to get some air," Martin whispered. "When he sits, nobody leaves."

I thanked Martin and almost ran from the tent while I felt my stomach churn. I relieved myself by the ECCAVs that quickly heated, even in the butte's shade. I mopped my face and kicked some dirt over my shame. About 20 yards away, a group of Arrivi women appeared to be arguing, as well as one could tell from watching patterned tentlike veils.

Two of them curtly walked away and joined the wedding party. Of the four who remained, one seemed to be taking blows all around. The others pulled her veil and let it fall to the ground. They laughed and high-stepped over it, then left to join the gathering.

She was a lovely girl standing there alone, no more than 17 with olive skin and a jewel in her nose. I had read that Arrivi women wore their hair in long braids, but this girl's curly hair was short and clung to her temples in the heat. She wore a loose hand-stitched domestic gown with panels that crossed her bodice and tied behind her back. The generous skirt hung to her ankles over open Arrivi sandals.

My stomach acted up again. When I stood, the young girl

waited beside me with her veil placed on her shoulders like a shawl. She held its edge over her mouth and nose with one hand and extended a cool native cloth toward me with the other. With sheer delight I mopped my face with the cloth while I kicked more dirt over my shame.

Music came from the tent, and the murmuring grew more intense. She asked in Arrivi if I wanted the acclimation pill. I shook my head and answered in her dialect, "In time I will grow strong."

She shyly smiled. "I will show you a thing."

She guided me toward the much smaller family tent where a natural spring bubbled in the ground with no landmark and no apparent cause. She knelt before the spring and touched the fingertips of her left hand to her forehead then her lips. "If you soak the cloth then wear it under your collar, the ceremony won't seem so long."

A few minutes later we walked back to the wedding tent and crossed the path of a silent Mekucoo warrior. The girl pulled the edge of her veil/shawl in front of her face. She bowed her head and shoulders and held her free hand high, palm toward him.

"Melinga, Cara," she said. The warrior glanced at us while she bowed again. Then he looked across the savannah as though he were alone.

The music stopped, and everyone shifted in the heat. I walked briskly to my seat next to Martin then turned in surprise to see the girl next to me. She held the veil over part of her face and greeted Martin. He smiled and answered, "Kyle Rabbe Arim, hiki." From under the veils near us somebody giggled. Kyle Le immediately sat on the ground to Martin's right.

"Why do you address her as a man?" I quietly asked Martin in his dialect. He shook his head slightly. Then Kyle Le also spoke in Martin's dialect. "Where is the other one?"

Martin looked at me and shrugged. Kyle Le asked again, "There are three of you. Where is the other one?"

There came a low chuckling noise from under two veils. Someone tugged at the edge of Kyle Le's shawl. She stared at the ground and murmured, "I apologize. I must be mistaken."

So these were the alluring Arrivi women. It was unnerving to sit in their veiled midst. They were watchful through the facial panels and vocal, even censorious.

I counted six women in the crowd who wore the designs of Arrivi but no veils. They were older women except the one who was decked out in a weighty, ostentatious display of jewels. She was Oriika, I recognized her from the Company dossier photo.

I looked around in the oppressive heat. Besides the men of the Company and ourselves, the only ones in foreign dress were a young Arrivi couple of some importance in the tribe. He wore the most fashionably cut white linen suit and too many pieces of jewelry. I recognized the wife as Julia Le, the one who had lunched with the regent's daughters. She wore an imported long dress and a mantilla. The beige lace veil drew murmurs of appreciation from guests who didn't know its original purpose.

We sat in the heat and dust while instruments played and Rabbenu officiated. At one point, the groom gave his bride one end of a bright ribbon. The bride held the ribbon on top of her veiled head while he slowly walked around her four times in widening circles unrolling its full length. Then the groom nonchalantly held the ribbon's end while the bride walked toward him in tight circles allowing the ribbon to wrap around her body several times. In this way, they said that although the man chooses the woman, the woman binds herself to him.

The ceremony ended. The groom bowed to each man while his veiled bride stood behind his shoulder. I was presented to Haku Rabbe Murd who had married one Karima Le, and we chatted for a moment. I had no impression of her through the facial panel, of course, but he seemed stout and oddly bloated with deeply-cut laughlines and full cheeks and lips under high cheekbones.

The bride stood near Kyle Le and gently touched her while we talked. A clucking started from under several veils, and the couple quickly moved away.

They worked their way through the gathering and greeted the other Softcheeks while the modern couple approached us. Martin introduced me to Dillan Rabbe Penli and his wife Julia Le. Martin's eyes grew wide when she spoke first. "We don't use those old names. My husband is Dillan Penli. He has attended Company business seminars on Cicero. My legal name is Julia Luria-Penli. Isn't that so much nicer?"

Martin actually hesitated, then stretched his face into a smile. There was no clucking.

Martin was steamed while we walked to the ECCAV. "Uppity cow," he complained. "Imagine, evoking the names of the last and present Rabbenu as though that insured they would be next. The office of Rabbenu has always gone to popular leaders."

He would have said more except the Company men standing by their ECCAVs bowed slightly to him. The stretched smile appeared again on Martin's face while he bowed to them before they entered the cool interior.

We heard a loud complaining among a tight group of veiled women. The bride and two others stood talking with Kyle Le. One of them lovingly pulled Kyle Le's veil/shawl closer to her face. Julia Luria-Penli left her group of friends and authoritatively walked to Kyle Le. With one jerk she pulled Kyle Le's shawl to the ground.

The bride moved between them and argued through her

facial panel with Julia Luria-Penli. Before they could indulge in more body blows, Oriika stepped forward. She picked up Kyle Le's veil and casually draped it over her own shoulder. She brazenly stared into Julia Le's face, then stepped to Kyle Le who stood behind the bride with her face averted.

Oriika patted Kyle Le's cheek with a bejeweled hand, and then coaxed her to hold her chin high. Oriika took off a long gold chain with medallion and put it on Kyle Le with one gesture over her head. Oriika did not give back the veil. Julia Luria-Penli spoke the most indiscreet Arrivi words and pressed forward but was blocked by the three friends.

To my astonishment, Oriika then knelt and tossed several fistfuls of the gritty dirt over her own head. There was a sharp intake of breath from several veiled women in the crowd. Still kneeling, Oriika threw two fistfuls of dirt onto Kyle Le's dress, then stood. She evenly and deliberately poured more dirt over Kyle Le's head and shoulders.

The three friends seemed jubilant, as well as one could tell from their movements under the veils. Julia Le and several others in the crowd curtly turned and walked away.

Martin controlled his look of satisfaction and got into the ECCAV. Once we were away from the gathering, a broad smile took residence on his dark and glistening face.

"So much for the mysterious Arrivi women," I said.

He chuckled then began to laugh. I laughed with him, glad for relief from the tension. "How well do you know the Arrivi?" I asked.

"Twelve Arrivi men sit in assembly, and some have dealings with the bank, including that young cock and his cow, Julia Le."

"Why do you address her in the feminine but refer to Kyle Le as a man?"

Martin drove on for several minutes before he answered. "It's a long story," he confessed. "Kyle Rabbe Arim owns land. Her father is dead. She has no brothers, and she hasn't given her mantel to any man. I negotiated the mortgage on her land. To avoid awkward assumptions, I address her as I would anyone who does business at the bank."

"Arrivi women bestow their mantel at her age?" I asked.

With frank surprise, Martin looked at me then chuckled again. "Kyle Rabbe Arim is twenty. That she's so lovely only adds to the myth of what they must be hiding by the custom of veiling."

"So why do the women take her veil?"

"Kyle Rabbe Arim is goulep."

Chapter Four

We offloaded equipment and upgraded the Brittany Mill buildings, thick adobe structures with dirt floors and rounded windows. We hired the long-haired colonist tradesmen to whitewash the interior walls and install covered runners for electrical wiring. Alongside the automated loom, rows of long tables held stainless steel electric sewing machines. Manual iron sewing machines mounted on their own stands waited in crates in the back storage area, Ricardo's back-up in case the generator gave out.

In the sunlit front building with display windows that faced the street, I set up a retail outer office for shipping and receiving. My quarters were directly behind, surprisingly cool under the clay tile roof and thick walls.

The buildings were far west of the railhead with the street of shops in between. Ricardo had bought them because infra-red transport photos revealed they were situated on bedrock and not vulnerable to geyser activity.

In the next block, north of Tri-City Bank Corp, was the old Company garrison with four long dormitories currently used by colonists while they served out their indentureships. Next to the garrison, colonists had built their own municipal building and a church.

I sat through a series of meetings in the hotel stateroom with executives who Ricardo sent from Stargate Junction. We revised plans to develop Arrivi linen for lightweight Chinese robes. A computer program instructed the loom to twine thread with special strokes that automatically added traditional dragon, butterfly and crane images in bas-relief.

The locally procured loom was a constant headache. I traveled to Cylay three times to get a continuance of regulation concerning its use. Finally, Martin sent over two Putuki men who were creative mechanics and brought the multi-functional loom up to standard.

I had on payroll four Mekucoo men which was impressive

even though each was maimed from Ketiwhelp hunting or some previous mercenary employment. They weren't a friendly group even with each other but came to meetings with adequate progress reports.

Each day I walked around the millhouse floor, and the women briskly bowed to me. Putuki women quickly mastered the electric sewing machines especially one Fumi, an older woman, blue-black and wrinkled. I demonstrated how the computer screen images instructed the loom to weave special designs into the cloth. She scratched herself and sucked on her remaining teeth, but soon ran the computer menu without assistance.

One day Fumi offered some opaque paste in a narrow round container like a shoe polish can. She indicated I should rub some on my skin and in my hair. I assumed she offered the goo because my blond complexion had turned ruddy under Dolvia's sun. I bowed and accepted the gift but never got around to using the sticky paste.

Tribeswomen rejected the uniforms we issued at the mill. Cylahi women complained the pants chafed their thighs. As the season grew drier, fiber in the air would break up ultrafine and scar workers' lungs. I issued surgical masks which the women loved and took them all home. Then Fumi pieced together a hood that covered the hair, lower face and neck. I asked her to design a uniform the tribeswomen would accept. She made a simple caftan that fastened down the right side in Manchu style and had three-quarter length sleeves. The women who worked at the sewing machines wore sleeve protectors from the needle arm and flywheel action.

On the whole my first twelve weeks on Dolvia were smooth and productive. There were a couple unpleasant moments, the first during Ricardo Menenous' visit with the marketing executives. He held a dinner at the hotel that resembled a victory party. Rotund and high from the acclimation pill, he was pleased with himself for securing the second loom. This was before we knew it was substandard. When the wives and prudes, as he called them, went home, Ricardo invited ten of us into another room for drinks.

Presently ten women covered in prototype imitation Arrivi body veils entered to music and gathered together for an undulating dance. Most of us stared without knowing what we saw. Martin was immediately angered and approached Ricardo with an active and red face. "What is the meaning of this?"

Ricardo was too calm. "They're hired Cylahi dancers. Makes it better knowing what's available under the veil. Um, delicious."

"This is intolerable," Martin said. He jerked the nearest dancer's veil, uncovering a nude and frankly sensual dark-skinned beauty who quickly moved to make her jewelry sparkle and jangle. The men joyously applauded and reached to uncover the others.

Martin dropped the veil and left. I followed him out but missed him in the lobby. When we met a couple weeks later, he made no mention of that night.

The second disturbing event was the death of Rabbenu Penli by natural causes. I put ashes on my forehead and handfuls of dirt over my administrator's uniform, then joined Martin in the slow and winding procession.

A simple affair and very moving, the funeral included a blazing fire in the low mist that comes before the rains, sad chanting from under many patterned veils, an old man's high and plaintive voice reciting an ancient and indecipherable prayer. All these touched a quiet place in my soul, and I felt adrift.

Three Arrivi men stepped before the fire. Each in turn bared his chest, drew his beltknife and inflicted deep and wicked cuts on his arms and upper chest. The men were already scarred. The oldest was very scarred. There was a swaying and a low moaning from the women's group. I had the impression that under the veils they participated in the same ritual.

Dillan Rabbe Penli stood at the funeral pyre of his father in a dusted dark Company suit with his foreign dressed and partially veiled wife. One man who bled freely on his arms and chest approached him with a large knife. Dillan glanced at the knife, then stared into the mist beyond the fire. He spoke clearly as if to make an announcement. "Mutilating grief is a useless custom for women and old men. It brings us nothing."

Oriika loudly spoke from behind me. "The law is all we have to protect us from forces Dolvia has allowed."

Dillan looked into the old man's pleading eyes then knocked the knife to the ground. A huge Murmurey bird which resembles a vulture flew above the mist with wings flapping and a soulful, plaintive cry. Disapproving clucking came from under several veils.

"Superstitious children!" Dillan Rabbe Penli shouted at them. He threw a fistful of dirt onto the fire and walked in broad steps from the company followed by his flustered wife.

People threw handfuls of dirt onto the now smoky fire and left in groups. When she came forward, Oriika's bodice was stained red. Her usually shiny jewelry was dull from caked blood and dirt. She picked up the knife and gave it to the old man. Tear streaks made obvious paths on his face. Perhaps it was the misty scene or the chanting or the bloodletting, but the image of Oriika and the old tribesman stayed with me for a considerable time after that day.

I met Martin at the bank soon after the funeral. When I arrived, he was standing outside his office with Kyle Le who I had not seen since the wedding. I thought I must thank her for her kindness by the spring.

I approached them perhaps too hurriedly. Kyle Le pulled her veil that she wore as a shawl in front of her face and moved as if to hide behind Martin. Customers and bank personnel stopped their work and stared. Martin's look was angry and protective when he bowed to me. He presented Kyle Rabbe Arim, indicating I should incline my head in the curt gesture of greeting among men of business. The people turned back to their own concerns.

"Where is the other one?" Kyle Le quietly asked.

It was the same question she had asked at the wedding. Martin shrugged. "What have you seen?"

She turned up her face with a smile. "A manatee."

We both chuckled then stopped short, aware of the public place. Kyle Le pulled the shawl to her cheek, passed between us and left the building. Martin guided me into his office before I could further embarrass him.

Inside the cool office Martin asked if I cared for a drink. He poured one for each of us and lit a slender cigarette, a habit I still found jarring. Then he leaned back in his big chair and rubbed his face with one hand. "Would you still like to hire Arrivi women?"

He didn't wait for my answer. "Dillan Rabbe Penli is seduced by the Company lifestyle. He dishonored himself at his father's funeral. Many won't follow him just when the region is threatened by war." He sighed sadly, then glanced my way. "Kyle Rabbe Arim asked what defense she has against him. I could offer her nothing.

"You should have seen her face when I said no," he continued. "There has never been a man to protect her since her father died. Because she's goulep, no Arrivi man can be concerned with veiling her. Equally, they cannot be concerned with who uses her body. That's why it's so shameful to be unveiled."

"Can Ricardo speak to her in public?" I asked.

Martin blinked at me. "She doesn't know Ricardo."

"But she saw a manatee."

"You thought of him too?" Martin quickly asked. The idiotic grin on Ricardo's flabby face after he swallowed a couple acclimation pills resembled the frozen smile of the manatee.

"But if she doesn't know Ricardo, then how?" I asked.

"Kyle Le has second sight."

Martin saw my look and quickly explained. "I know. Many among the tribes claim to see. Just as there are astrologers and witch doctors everywhere. But Kyle Le has a track record that dates back more than ten years. She served her father and Rabbenu Luria then Rabbenu Penli which is how she secured the pension. But she won't serve Dillan Rabbe Penli."

"Does Rabbenu have the power to negate a legal deed?" I

asked.

"What's legal? Even if the government doesn't collapse, Dillan can take away her livelihood so she defaults on the mortgage."

"Can she work at the Mill?" I asked.

Martin's eyebrows went up with interest. "She would have to be in debt to you but not to Ricardo who would use her. She cannot sell her land but has full use of its benefits. There's a section with hot water flats that's sacred to her people."

Martin waited two beats while he inspected his hand. "You could buy, say, twelve percent interest in the water rights and put it out that you plan to bottle and export the water."

I was getting the picture. "And if she wants to invest in water export but has no capital, she can work for me and have part of her wages set aside. You're good at this, Martin. Except for one thing. She'll never let me take the water."

"People have short memories. Once you can know the persona Kyle Rabbe Arim and work with her every day, people will forget how it started. But you must win her trust."

"I can't even talk to her!"

"I can't do everything for you."

"Why doesn't she set up shop and make them pay for her insights?"

"By tribal law an Arrivi woman with second sight may serve only Arrivi men or her mate with her gift."

"But as goulep she's outside the law."

Martin shrugged. "Kyle Le's a purist."

Chapter Five

No handbook or library whitepaper prepared me for Dolvia's rainy season. There were similar seasonal changes on many planets, but for sheer sustained incapacitating deluge, the interminable weeks of rain tried everyone's patience.

One day the sky clouded over, and it rained for two hours in the late afternoon. Tribeswomen gathered everything including non-flying fowl into the huts. Most families kept semi-tame mongooses on leashes inside the family circle.

Just when I thought I could live with the rumbling and surprise of geysers, it rained all day every day for three weeks. My quarters became waterlogged and seeped. I went to sleep to the sound of pelting rain and woke with the feeling that ten minutes had not passed. The sound of the rain was as constant as when I had drifted off.

The loom creaked and rusted as did the iron sewing machines. I closed shop and sent everyone home except the Mekucoo men who shrugged and claimed the millhouse was their home. Insofar as they kept mongooses and practiced their hunting skills on migrant squatters of all descriptions, I decided Ricardo's enterprise could tolerate their presence.

Just when I thought I could live out the remaining weeks of rain, the insects came. All varieties from flying and biting to crawling and biting to nesting and biting seemed to step out of the woodwork. They nested and laid eggs, then died within a few weeks.

With the insects came the birds, rodents and snakes. The area I had casually thought of as mine was overrun by a teeming mass in an unending struggle to eat and be eaten. What I had written up as valuable raw material became a compost heap which we moved into the deluge proper by the second week of the rain.

And just when I told myself I could see the end of it, I discovered my body was a breeding ground for fungus and a colony of mites who turned a simple cut into an open and angry sore. I couldn't scratch the fungus for fear of breaking the skin. I couldn't apply the ointment I ordered from the transport that discouraged mites for fear of inflaming the fungus. I became the same as the smelly and disintegrating mass of fibers in my backyard.

Just when I was at my wits' end and ready to petition Ricardo for escape to the orbiting transport no matter the loss of face, the clouds broke. A few warm, drying rays of sun reached my window. My feeling of salvation was as ancient as Gilgamesh.

Tribal myth claimed the ancestors and the land were one. I assumed the jubilation that rested on me was the same spirit that coaxed Dolviets outside dancing and singing in that first, brief patch of sunlight.

Preoccupied as I was with my discomfort, I didn't recognize until the savannah was dry again that the early growth of forces shaping our lives began in that dank and depressing season. These were the events as nearly chronological as I remember them, the first being the arrival of Quentin, the renowned wrestler and healer.

I saw him only twice although he stayed with the Arrivi during the idle time. A tall, chocolate-brown Putuki man, Quentin was well proportioned with soft hands and a shaved head. I first encountered him when he gave a performance in Somule.

A simple boxing ring with bleachers was erected in the Council building, and men from all tribes gathered for the event. Quentin challenged and defeated two imposing men who traveled with him. Then he dared men from the audience to come into the ring. Surprisingly, several young men who were hopelessly outmatched in size and skill took up the challenge.

Quentin played embarrassing and increasingly brutal tricks on various victims. One man became a mongoose in heat when Quentin snapped his fingers. Another strutted and clucked like a chicken.

It soon became clear that he held these men in hypnotic trances that began during his planned exhibitions. He held sway over several audience members including myself.

No wonder women were excluded from the performance. They were spared the sight of their men displaying animal characteristics on demand. Plus by their absence tribeswomen could not be enticed to similar indiscreet gestures.

Then Oriika entered the gathering with a rustle of dry skirts and a clatter of jewelry. Oriika never wore a veil but often covered herself with dirt. That night she was clean and glowing without dirt or sweat or moisture in her clothes. It was just as though dryness was her covering. It had been so long since anything I owned was dry, I enjoyed the sweet though nearly inaudible sound of dry linen against dry linen.

The men looked around, surprised she interrupted a meeting

that excluded women. She didn't acknowledge Quentin but shook a long strand of Ketiwhelp claws and chanted four unfamiliar words while she slowly rotated in a circle where she stood. "Netta, kari, cylay, om. Netta, kari, cylay, om."

The crowd had been tense in the humidity, intent on Quentin's movements. Oriika's chant seemed to break the spell. Men relaxed and easily chatted with benchmates who they had not before acknowledged. Quentin took immediate offense and spoke a stream of maligning words to the holy woman. But his hold on the crowd was gone.

Quentin had gained strength with each challenger in the ring, grew more powerful with each humiliation, caused them to point and laugh at the discomfort of friends and relatives. But now they jeered at him.

One man who had been a mongoose ten minutes earlier loudly called to him, "If you really want to help us, why don't you come in time for the cattle drive instead of two weeks later when there's no work?"

The men laughed and slapped their knees and each other's shoulders with manic energy. Another man called out, "And why do you leave just when it's time to hunt the Ketiwhelp?"

Without thinking about it, I moved to where Oriika stood. I remember I needed to ask her how I could have dry clothes. Quentin raised one arm and snapped his fingers. I looked up, startled with eyes wide open. I instantly knew he controlled my will. I wanted to run from the assembly. But I stared at him without blinking as eight men before me had. The thought of humiliation in front of them sickened me and my throat contracted as though I wanted to throw up. But at the same time I found his look, his stature, his fluid movements and deep eyes above the malicious grin to be riveting.

I heard the men laugh and realized I was undressing before Oriika in a most coquettish way. My awareness of what I was doing made me feel faint. I knelt before her in an aggravated state of shame and remorse only to realize that I also exposed my private member in a rigid position of readiness.

The men stopped laughing and stared at my disgrace. There was no excuse even under Quentin's spell even for an outlander to show a private thing to a holy woman. I felt my heart sink to my tailbone. I began to weep while I went through the degrading motions. One man nudged Oriika as if to coax her to make me stop. She looked directly into my contorted and tearsoaked face. "You will be saved by what you see," she whispered.

I wanted to shout I saw nothing but my shame. But I couldn't speak between the sobs while my hand motions became more frantic. I closed my eyes in despair and saw the image that had stayed with me after Rabbenu Penli's funeral. I saw the old man whose arms and chest were cut and bleeding. And Oriika whose clothes and jewelry were caked that day with dirt and dried blood. The old man received from her the knife that Dillan Rabbe Penli had refused. I seemed to stare into his tear-streaked face until I saw in his anguished eyes a reflection of my anguish that moment in the assembly.

I became that old man, and received the knife from Oriika's hand. He became me and took on my dread and shame. I collapsed onto the floor at Oriika's feet soaked in my own sweat and tears. Oriika shook the long strand of Ketiwhelp claws over me three times. She looked at Quentin with sheer hatred, then turned on her heel and left the company of men.

I awoke on my soggy bed wearing my pants and with no idea how much time had passed. Two Mekucoo employees, who I knew as Lam and Dak, loitered at the door smoking some aromatic root. I tried to sit up, but felt a crushing pain in my head.

Lam came to my side and pushed me back onto the pillow. He said in the guttural speech of his dialect that the pain in my head and chest would last three days. He made me swallow from a bottle of strong native drink, then forced me to drink again. The burning liquid made my stomach contract. I drifted off to sleep and didn't awaken until the middle of the next day.

Rain pelted the roof and windows of my room. I sat up in the close air and filtered light from a single lamp on the table. I reached for the bedstand but misjudged the distance and knocked it over. Lam immediately entered and pushed me back onto the bed with an angry shove. He repeated his instructions from the day before with a tone in his voice that said I was a foolish Softcheeks who refused to listen. I pushed away the drink he offered. He held my nose and poured it into my throat and face.

When I awoke again, I was packed down with wet and vermin-filled clumps of dirt. Mites crawled over my skin and the patches of fungus screamed to be scratched. I pushed away the offensive filth and sat up, only to bang my forehead on what felt like an invisible wall of concrete suspended eight inches above my head. I black out and came around again, I'm told, three days later.

Martin sat beside me. I opened my eyes and enjoyed the languid calm in my limbs that I had experienced once before when I was knocked out. The air smelled fresh. I felt no tension or drive to get something done. Martin looked at me with his implacable face. "Don't sit up."

"Is the wall still there?" I asked.

"What do you mean?"

"The one over my head."

Martin chuckled in his sad way. "The Mekucoo chased Quentin out of the region two nights ago. It's a tribute to you, even the women know."

"They know what I did?"

"Probably better than you," Martin calmly answered. "You're infested with mites. Why didn't you use the salve Fumi gave you?"

"That paste for my hair?" I complained. "And what was the syrup Lam made me drink?"

"Just rest," Martin said. "I'll explain one day over a bottle of Kiam gin. I brought you a nurse. We waited for you to come around just to be safe. But the spirits are calm now. Come forward."

And then I saw Kyle Le's smile, that special mischievous smile I had thought was reserved for Martin Sumuki.

Kyle Le rubbed Fumi's sticky paste on my skin and into my hair to chase away the insects. She spoke wholesome words with gestures of encouragement, but I stared at her from someplace deep inside. I knew what she said and what she did. I couldn't come up with a reason to answer.

I was lethargic for some time after that. Events swirled around without my notice. Kyle Le tended me daily, but I had no will to respond. The Mekucoo turned away with disappointment. Two left from shame, I think, that they had accepted me as their employer. The Softcheeks who had defied Quentin was an old woman ridden with fungi and drooling in his food.

Kyle Le gently explained that my soul had turned during the trance but that kari would come back to me in time. Another day she said my spirit had turned from my face and looked into itself. She brought baby mongooses to handle and a cacophony of tropical flowers. She released into the room a couple dozen orange and yellow butterflies the Mekucoo had netted. She brought cool spring water in a dried gourd and the feathers of the egret, peacock and Murmurey birds.

The mongooses bit me, the flowers withered and the butterflies all died. Her gifts seemed temporary and essentially sad. So Kyle Le set up the EAM-50 and covered it with the coolant unit. I idly watched the screen flicker with a permanent static line across the monitor's left side. "What is that?" Kyle Le asked, pointing at the static.

"There's no defense against the putrid, insidious, oppressive rot of the rainy season," I shouted. The next day Kyle Le brought a small section of netta.

We analyzed it later as a symbiotic balance of sulfur over silica, superheated for decades by subterranean geysers and spewed out the vents before the cooling rains. Later it was synthetically produced and used in industry throughout Westend. But at the time, netta was a swatch of cloth that resembled burlap, dry but filmy to the touch.

With a smile Kyle Le showed it to me, then placed a one

inch square on the EAM inside the coolant unit. She securely wrapped a piece over the angry growth of fungus on my elbow, and another on my lower left back where she said the fungus sought a favorite organ.

I didn't understand or care about her nursing. I was resigned to my degenerate state even after Martin explained the fungus attacked my joints where it sought the bone marrow and once there would stay with me year round until my skeleton collapsed.

I swallowed a spoonful of the thick syrup she offered and turned my face to the wall. But when I awoke, I was lying in a dry bed in dry clothes. My tongue felt scratchy, even flaky. I rubbed my hands against my clothes and looked at them to verify the material was free of moisture.

I went to the window and opened the interior shutters to look out at the end of the rain. Mist crowded against the window ledge. Branches dripped with blossoms and water and insects. Rain on the breeze spattered against the window announcing the entrance of another day of deluge.

If the rain hadn't stopped, then why was I dry? My mouth throbbed and my lips stretched to crack. I was more than dry, desert dry, in need of moisture for balance.

I touched the interior shutters that were swollen with moisture. The imprint of my fingertip repelled surface moisture on the waterlogged wood. I switched on the EAM, and the screen lit up with the clear and static-free resolution I expected during the dry season. I punched in my code and waited for clearance. My mouth was intolerably dry. Where was Kyle Le?

I peered into the outer office. I realized suddenly that I had not been out of my quarters since my encounter with Quentin. How could I have been so negligent? I switched off the EAM and walked through the dark office.

I heard a mongoose scurry and pounce and felt shivers at the thought of concealed deadly snakes. I walked to the millhouse floor where the monumental and worthless loom still housed a squatter population. Beyond its spines Kyle Le stood with Lam and Dak in a tight circle engaged in an animated discussion in Mekucoo.

They were arguing about why netta had no effect on the steel sewing machines beyond drying the materials and flywheel. They stopped in mid-sentence when I approached. A small piece of burlap was placed on the machine. All moisture receded around the burlap, but most of the steel surface glistened in the humid air.

I began to laugh. They looked at each other, then at me. I reassuringly put my hand on Lam's shoulder and kept laughing. How could I explain the alloy of steel was valuable to us because it didn't rust? It followed in my head that the native cure for rust and rot had little effect on a rustless surface. Oh, what wonders Dolvia provided to delight us.

They were alarmed by my high spirits. Lam and Kyle Le led me back to my quarters while Dak left to find Martin. When Martin arrived forty-five minutes later, I had washed and shaved and changed clothes and eaten. Martin gratefully sighed and sat with me. "Your spirit is in your face again."

"Martin, do you know about netta?" I asked.

He looked sharply at Kyle Le. "You have netta here? Where did you get it?" With her eyes averted she served him fruit and tea.

"Show me," Martin said to me.

I showed him the section on my elbow and explained, "I woke up insect and fungus free and dying of thirst." I showed him the EAM and dry coolant unit.

He turned back to Kyle Le. "Where did you get this netta?"

She looked up almost flirtatiously, "Goulep knowledge."

"Don't you start with me," he harshly complained. "This is Martin you're talking to. You can't hide with me." Kyle Le smiled and shrugged. Martin stepped to the office door and called for Lam who immediately appeared in their anticipatory way.

"Bring Oriika here," Martin ordered. Lam looked past Martin's shoulder to me. I looked at Kyle Le who signaled that he should go. Martin was steamed.

"Who's in charge here, anyway?" he asked when Lam was gone. "I sent her here as an employee. Now she gives orders to Mekucoo? You're coming clean with me, young lady. No more secrets. There isn't anything so sacred or so shocking that I can't know it."

She serenely responded, "Goulep knowledge."

Arrivi women were taught to read and write. They studied the sacred books and the law. But they were not given reading material concerning matters outside Arrivi tradition. Many Arrivi women spoke but did not read other dialects. Their oral tradition was transferred mostly in family circles, mostly by the men.

Kyle Le had been instructed by Oriika who spoke manly words and communed with spiritual forces that existed alongside the law. But what Kyle Le knew was necessarily goulep knowledge. No honorable man listened to her.

Oriika didn't arrive for a couple hours. Martin pumped Kyle Le for more information. She sat silent and sullen, then offered to serve him in any manner he requested. Finally anger flashed in her eyes, and she made the first motions of disrobing, evoking the law that he could be desirous of only one thing. Martin curtly slapped both of her hands then ignored her and the question of netta while we sat at the table.

To fill the time I asked Martin what happened during the episode with Quentin. "Quentin is seduced by his gift," Martin explained. "Like an addict he looses the spirits for the intoxication of their presence. He seldom destroys property, but does spiritual harm.

"With Oriika's help, you defied him," Martin continued. "Lam didn't know what to do. He made you drink the medicine and covered you with dirt. They smoked kari root until Dak developed a sore on his lip. While your spirit was turned, Quentin had a foothold here. But now you're back."

"If there was a danger, why did you bring Kyle Le?" I asked.

"Oriika suggested it. The only surprise was your selfpity."

"Why did Lam and Dak stay?"

"I didn't tell you this before," Martin said. "They're assigned to you by Cyrus."

Kyle Le moved slightly, and Martin cleared his throat. "I got word the other day that Cyrus will attend the Ketiwhelp hunt."

Kyle Le went to the stove and heated water for another pot of tea. I don't pretend I ever learned to read any of them, but the mention of Cyrus' name made Kyle Le restless.

Oriika arrived finally. She inspected me like a hospital chief of staff. She probed my elbow under the netta, then pushed me forward and poked at my back. "Kari, cylay," she abruptly asked, to which Kyle Le answered, "Netta."

Oriika pushed me back in the chair and lifted my eyelid. She stuck her finger into my mouth. Martin cleared his throat.

Oriika sat with us and spent a full minute adjusting her jewelry. Kyle Le served her then returned to the stove. "So," Oriika began, aware of her advantage. "Martin Sumuki and Brian Rabbe Miller, what would you learn from goulep?"

Martin's guns were loaded. "Kyle Rabbe Arim has mortgaged his land at the Tri-City Bank Corp. I am the administrator of the mortgage."

Oriika raised her eyebrows. "Kyle Rabbe Arim has full use of the benefits of his land."

"Kyle Rabbe Arim has entered into a contract with Brian Rabbe Miller," Martin countered, "concerning the water rights on the flats of Arim. By law he must disclose the potential earnings of Brian's interest."

Oriika smiled at me. "Netta, om?" she asked.

"On his elbow," Kyle Le answered.

Oriika chuckled and blatantly looked into Martin's eyes. "Goulep says Brian Rabbe Miller wears his twelve percent. For more, you and he will have to pay."

Chapter Six

Pay we did, all of us and dearly. I suspected the story about my relief from the fungus got out through Lam. We opened the mill office toward the end of the rainy season to accommodate the steady stream of petitions and gifts that anticipated the distribution of netta.

Kyle Le did not serve in the office as an act of charity, sparing orthodox and sensitive Dolviets contact with goulep. Her three sisters were hired by my twelve percent interest that also paid for temporary use of Ricardo's place of business.

It was Martin who noticed that Arrivi women did not queue up with gifts. He badgered Kyle Le again and with increasing force to which she irritably answered, "Goulep knowledge." I began to wonder about these two who had once had so tender a friendship. I didn't know Martin's situation because it had not occurred to me to ask about his family. But one day they, too, came by the mill office.

Martin Sumuki's wife was a lovely, blue-black and amply proportioned woman whose broad feet were bare under bowed legs. She stood silent and embarrassed with two daughters under age six.

Kyle Le's veiled sisters interrupted their work with the other petitioners and led Martin's family into another room. I can't say what happened. It's unmanly to ask what the women do together. But Kyle Le said to Oriika within my hearing that Martin had forbidden them to come. He had relented only when the fungus appeared on his daughter's ear and eyelid. Karima Le saved the girl's life that day. I never learned the price except in loss of face for Martin.

My lethargy slowly dissipated, chiseled away by the bustle of activity in the office. One day I thought about Oriika's perfunctory examination of my fungus. I realized her questions and Kyle Le's answers used the four words Oriika had spoken to Quentin.

I went to the EAM and typed in my code. I accessed the

transport library and asked to communicate in Arrivi. I had forgotten the pleasures of open-ended dialogue with the screen. I stared into it for hours, rambling through the library files more impressed with the steady progression of words on the luminous screen than with their content.

I was aware that Kyle Le served me, but the heavy cloud of inertia still slowed my judgment. More than once Kyle Le stood over my shoulder and remained in the room longer than her duties required. When I looked up, she busied herself with some task.

"Would you like to know the EAM?" I asked. Shyly she nodded.

"I can pay," she eagerly added.

"My part of netta will make me rich. I want something else."

She hung her head. "As goulep I cannot refuse you."

It was a knee-jerk reaction with her. Men either wanted the benefit of her land which was now translated into money or the use of her body. Such was her wounded self-esteem that she didn't offer friendship. She didn't count it as negotiable goods.

Kyle Le was childishly proud of her new wealth. She wore a different patterned gown each day and had six gold-fringed veils. She wore finely crafted peridot jewelry on her arms and fingers. She proudly displayed the gold chain and medallion Oriika had given her and often tied her shawl so the medallion was visible in public. She kept her hair short and had several pairs of peridot earbobs and various jewels for her nose. But her pride was innocent and easily bruised. She had too much the heart of a servant to be truly arrogant.

On the millhouse floor, Kyle Le helped Fumi draw Arrivi symbols on the computer screen to be weaved in bas-relief patterns into the linen. She ordered extra bolts of the fine cloth woven with the open, structured Arrivi patterns, then sewed it into domestic gowns and veils. She paid for afterhours time on the loom computer and experimented with a sturdier weave to produce the rugged linen worn by Arrivi men. Plus she was eager to learn the EAM.

I typed in the four words Oriika had spoken. Kyle Le stared at the screen. "I have searched the library," I said in Arrivi. "I can find no definitions for these words."

"Which Arrivi man did you ask?" She was as naive in my world as I was in hers. I turned off the screen, and the light went out of her face. We sat at the table, and I explained about the transport, what a library was, the need for information. "You mean, as we learn more about Dolvia's gifts, our service to Her increases," Kyle Le summarized.

"Yes," I nodded. "I want to learn these words of power that exist alongside the law. And don't say goulep knowledge or I won't boot the EAM."

She pointed at the EAM. "Teach me."

I taught her my code and how to access the library. She easily communicated in Arrivi and Putuki but became frustrated when several technical terms didn't translate. There were no equivalents in her dialect. On impulse I switched to the visual aids and called up the transport camera's image of Dolvia.

She stared like a child at the circus. She didn't accept that was a complete picture of Dolvia. I showed her the moons and sun and other planets. She asked to see a moon again. When the picture came up, she wanted to talk to the people there. "Nobody lives there," I explained. "It's frozen with no atmosphere."

"What is atmosphere?"

I brought back photos of Dolvia and pointed at the blue aura and cloud cover. "The air we breathe brings the mist and covers Dolvia for ten miles straight up."

She looked at me with tears standing in her eyes. "Atmosphere?"

She stood and left the room. I had not thought the lesson was so shocking. I didn't see her for two days and finally asked Lam where she was. His look was dark and suspicious, but then it always was. He said to look in the millhouse.

I found her wearily sitting at an iron sewing machine that was operational through the miracle of netta. A family of mongooses lazed at her feet. She looked up with swollen cheeks and teary eyes.

There were only two ways to approach Kyle Le. I chose the wholesome one. "Kyle Rabbe Arim, I have been patient. You have not honored your part of the agreement. I will know the definitions of the four words."

She sadly smiled. "I knew you would come. You will be the first to see them." She held up a patternless but richly woven, sky-blue veil with a white fringed edge. She turned it over to display a lighter blue underside. "These are for my sisters. You are the only man except Haku Rabbe Murd to see the inside."

"But I thought the designs protected you from spirits."

She held her chin high. "My sisters will be veiled as Dolvia veils Herself. They will gain grace from their alignment with Her."

And that day I came to know the true heart of Kyle Le, a woman I had thought was secretive and hoarding, but who stored knowledge the way my people were encouraged to store sexual energy. Kyle Le expected nothing from others and did not seek our approval. She acted on what she learned in the purest sense. She expressed her increased knowledge in service and reverence to Dolvia, Mother Earth.

"Kyle Le, why don't Arrivi women come to receive netta?"

She carefully folded the veil and released the other material from the machine. "Why should they wait for something that is already theirs?"

"But how is it the men don't know?"

"It's an indiscreet matter," she sadly claimed. "Netta sends away moisture. All moisture. A woman's body makes a lubricant for her husband's passion. If she wore netta when he came to her, she would appear ungrateful for his interest."

"By why don't Arrivi women share the secret?"

"Our men have chosen to veil us. What we do under the veil is our business."

"How many sources are there for netta?" I asked lightly, taking advantage of her willingness to share precious secrets.

"It is as Dolvia provides," she coyly said. "Perhaps the hot springs before the rain where the land turns green and orange. If you soak a natural fiber in the geyser water then let it dry in the sun, sometimes netta occurs. Not often, but sometimes."

"And the geysers with green and orange sediment are on the flats of your land."

"They are where Dolvia brings them forth. One geyser came outside Martin's office window this year. Another was in the street by the Council building. Oriika said to ignore them, and we prayed that no judgment should come from the waste. We stayed on the flats and worked every day with the burlap because we had no courage to give reverence in Somule. We are only women and goulep."

She stowed the material and instruments then added, "Karima Le delivers our tithe each week to Julia Luria-Penli. As we prosper Rabbenu is made rich."

"How do you feel about that?"

"Rabbenu died in the days of my father. All that is left is . . ." She hesitated and sighed. "Only the words are left," she concluded.

"And what do the words mean?" Now we were getting somewhere.

"Netta is for neutral, the balance that's in the desert. Kari is a stirring of spirits, a new growth. Cylay is a spreading out of forces so they aren't dependent upon the source. Like a plant gives leaves and blossoms, fruit and seed. All these hold the essence of the plant within them."

"And om?"

The sadness in her eyes was very like Martin's sad look. "Om is the end. A completion, perhaps a success. Maybe only an ending before the new beginning. Om is the best where you learn Dolvia's purpose, but it's also very sad."

"So when Oriika looked at my fungus, she asked you, 'kari, cylay,'" I said.

"Yes, how serious was the spread? And I answered 'netta,' a dry balance. She looked into your eyes and mouth for damage from the dryness."

"And when she negotiated the sell of netta, Oriika said, 'netta, om,'" I said.

"She asked only what I saw, like you would say, 'What's going on here? Advise me.' We had agreed while we worked the flats to use the benefits of my land."

"On what other matters did you agree?"

The mischievous smile appeared on her face. "That Kyle Rabbe Arim works for Brian Rabbe Miller. We were afraid you would desert us after you met Quentin."

I blushed and looked away. "Can't they put Quentin in jail or something?"

"Quentin's gift is very real. He'll see himself one day and put his powers into service."

"And until then?"

"Om is upon us before we begin. Don't wish it speed."

My curiosity had returned, but my heart was still heavy. "Kyle Le, why weren't the words in the transport library?"

"They are originally Mekucoo."

Chapter Seven

Gifts of prior appreciation filled the office and my living area before a break in the rain. The office hung with parcels of herbs and meat. The shelves, constructed to hold inventory files, overflowed with bolts of fine cloth, bags of grain, dates and olives. The sisters asked that fowl be brought in alive because there were more than could be consumed in a time. The birds' chatter drove me to distraction. I insisted that part of the wealth be moved to Karima Le's house. They were gone the next day.

Then netta was dispensed according to need and ability to pay. It was a tribal matter. Kyle Le's sisters were even-handed and generous, almost servile, deferring to each other's judgment.

Kyle Le brought a large and glassy amber topaz and asked if I wanted it set into a ring. I blinked and looked up at her. "In exchange for the birds," she explained. "We didn't realize you had no use for them."

"Are there more jewels like this?"

"For now there's more of everything."

With Fumi and her good friend Rose, I reviewed the weave of the sturdier Arrivi linen on the loom computer. Fumi listened to my instructions and nodded, but grew frustrated when her designs looked differently in the cloth than on the screen.

I asked Fumi to fashion clothes for me from the new Arrivi linen. I showed Fumi a pair of dungarees worn for work detail on the transport and requested a similar cut for the trousers instead of the baggy tribesman cut. We agreed on a simple pullover shirt of light material that was full in the shoulders and sleeves. We discussed making a sleeveless tunic with flaps that crossed in the front and tied together at the lower back. Fumi and Rose experimented with several patterns for the pants and tunic before we settled on a hybrid of Company and native workclothes.

One day I tried on the new products. I threaded the tie of the tunic through the sheath of my Mekucoo beltknife and tucked the dungarees into my round-toed boots. I inspected my

41

new look in the mirror. My hair, forehead and arms were stained from Fumi's paste. My blue eyes peered out from a tribesman's face, thin and menacing, no longer the Aryan outland administrator. At least these clothes didn't include the hated panda logo.

I had Fumi make several sets of dungarees and tunics for my personal wear. Karima Le giggled from under the veil and ordered dungarees for Haku and his uncle. Later a market sprang up among colonists, and we started a domestic trade that, along with the millhood, delivered eighteen percent of our gross.

I regained my strength and threw myself into the mill business. I wondered occasionally how I could have been listless for so long. I was surprised at the changes in Somule when I visited the street of shops.

By chance one day I stood with Lam and Dak across from the railway station. I saw a squad of Chinese Blackshirts disembark, hard and lethal men who brought their weapons of choice and looked around with cunning and disdain.

"One day they will learn we are blacker than they," Lam darkly claimed.

Increasing numbers of colonists called Hardhands disembarked with import licenses and toolbags and no return tickets. They viewed Dolvia as their new homeland with opportunities for freedom, to build something, to raise their families with dignity. Bakeries lined the street of shops, and the colonists began commerce with tribespeople for soft bread laced with sugar and baked from imported staples. Plus the Hardhands brought pigs.

Some were successful, in particular one Heather Osborn who had flaming red hair and whose husband ran a toolmaking shop with contracts for offworld trade. I watched Heather's progress with interest. She opened a household goods store on the street of shops and welcomed all visitors, even the sisters of Arim. From under the veil, the second sister, Katelupe Le, negotiated with Heather for the right to sell millmade tunics and dungarees in the back of her shop.

I made excuse occasionally to pass Heather's shop and inspect the many imported goods in the display window. Tribeswomen pointed at me and clucked disapprovingly. The gaucho Softcheeks was making unseemly advances to this married woman with two children.

Most new colonists were of a religious sect that honored the divinity of the Virgin. They followed strict religious imperatives. For instance, no Cylahi woman was touched by the Hardhand men whose religion prevented them from looking upon, let alone tasting, the flesh that was so freely offered.

But to their credit Hardhands improved their community. They remodeled the barracks area and built municipal buildings of their own, not willing to enter Dolviet civic activity. And they had the church. Every Sunday the women and some of the men sang together and listened to the dry and timid priest who had disembarked with them.

Cylahi women loved the church. They couldn't believe their luck when they learned Hardhands used this building for only a few hours one day a week. When Sunday services ended and Hardhands left to spend the afternoon with their families, the Cylahi women filed into the church and occupied the pews for what they considered would be a week's stay.

The priest misunderstood their presence and began a Mass for them. They stared and murmured the words. They touched his gown and whispered in awe at the statues and many sparkly and gold-laden goods he kept near him. They grew bored long before the service ended. They talked among themselves and began the activity of the evening meal complete with cooking fires and privies.

The Cylahi women dutifully vacated the church each Sunday morning with their children and goods and the pigs gained in trade. They returned that evening in time for Mass that was still offered until a course of action was determined.

Hardhands met in their municipal building to discuss the problem. Tribesmen met in the Council building to guess what the Hardhands discussed. Finally one Sunday evening when the Cylahi returned to their weekly domicile, they were met by Hardhand men, some who never attended church, who blocked the entrance and sheltered the priest.

The Cylahi tried to go around the men, then through the group so little was their understanding of Hardhand ways. With the butt of his gun, one Hardhand struck a naked but richly painted Cylahi woman across the jaw. And so the women returned to the abandoned huts by the railhead. They did not approach the church again until they became sick from eating the poorly cooked fatty meat of pigs.

Kari was wicked and prankish in its season, or perhaps only in my mind because I associated it with the character of Quentin. The men gathered in Somule to hunt the Ketiwhelp before they brought the cattle down from the north grazeland. To kill a female Ketiwhelp within the next few weeks ensured the death of her young. Perhaps it was the assembly of men that began the politics. Perhaps it was the shoring up of courage for the hunt. Perhaps it was the presence of Cyrus.

Events descended in a single day, the day I made plans to reopen the mill. I went to the outer office to discuss with Kyle Rabbe Arim the need to move her enterprise to another location. Two sisters of Arim in body veils idly sat over closed account books. They bowed and offered whatever the Softcheeks may want from the overflowing goods.

"Where is everybody?" I asked.

"Needs have been met," one explained through her facial panel.

"All this must be moved now. The mill opens next week." They immediately stood and packed goods into large and already full baskets.

I went to the millhouse floor where Kyle Le and Karima Le were teaching two Cyhali women how to sew linen dungarees on the rust-free iron machines. In the back four Mekucoo men stood engaged in an occupation that looked like sharpening tools with hand grinders.

"Kyle Rabbe Arim," I called out. "It's time to move the netta business. And clear this area. The mill opens next week."

Dak put down his work and left. Lam and Cyrus handed their tools to the other warrior who I recognized as Cara, the one who had attended Karima Le's wedding. When Cyrus approached, Karima Le bowed her head and shoulders holding high her outstretched palm. "Melinga Cyrus."

Square and muscular, Cyrus stood five-seven with energy centered in his abdomen. He wore only the brief loincloth and leggings of a warrior, plus the sheathed Mekucoo beltknife. Wicked and mesmerizing scars covered his back, arms and legs. Decisive and lethal, he displayed none of the gamesmanship that had been Quentin's signature.

Karima Le moved in front of Kyle Le as if to shield her. The two Cylahi women sat motionless, eyes averted. Cyrus didn't acknowledge Karima Le's greeting or any of the women. He looked at me appraising and cagey, then allowed a smile to flicker across his face.

Karima Le intently watched Cyrus through the facial panel of her veil. At his change of expression, she signaled the Cylahi to leave then cleared a place at the end of a long worktable.

Cyrus and I sat across from each other, straight-backed with feet planted wide apart, and communed for the first time in complete silence. Karima Le served tea, fruit and fish.

Kyle Le could serve me as an employee, but didn't dare approach Cyrus. With slow and measured movements as though she was weighed down by a world of concerns, Kyle Le released the material from the machines, folded it into piles, and gathered the utensils the women had been using. She made several trips to remove the materials from the mill area.

The first to arrive was Haku Rabbe Murd who owed me nothing. He made a good wage from the Company limestone quarry on Rabbenu's land. I paid his wife from my twelve percent on top of what she received from her sister. Haku Rabbe Murd gave no greeting but stood square and proud behind my left shoulder. Cyrus evenly looked at him, entertained by his choice. More men arrived and chose sides, standing behind Cyrus or me in silent statements of allegiance.

Dillan Rabbe Penli hurriedly entered with four others and his fully veiled wife, Julia Le. Three stood behind Cyrus. The other hesitantly walked to stand next to Haku. Dillan Rabbe Penli seemed in doubt.

There was a shuffling of feet and Dillan grew tense. He sat at Cyrus' elbow on the bench of the long table, the first of the crowd to sit down. Cyrus didn't acknowledge him. But when Julia Le also sat, Cyrus directed his gaze past Dillan, staring directly into her facial panel. Julia Le couldn't withstand his look and joined the other women in the doorway.

Martin Sumuki entered alone and stood at the head of the table. Karima Le brought a chair and a third cup for tea. She poured for Cyrus, Martin and me but ignored Dillan's presence at the table.

Martin confidentially leaned forward. "We have a labor situation here, Brian. The men wait to hunt the Ketiwhelp. The full price for netta that their wives received has not been paid. If you open the mill now, they must work to pay the debt instead of hunt or bring back the cattle."

"The mill should have been operational ten days ago," I said. "Deliveries are scheduled this week. Ricardo arrives in less than a month."

"If they don't hunt the Ketiwhelp, they will be hunted by it," Martin claimed.

I met Cyrus' gaze. "Ketiwhelp no longer threaten the cattle."

Cyrus squinted, and Martin spoke quickly to soften the tension between us. "It's more than a predator. It's . . ." He sighed and looked away.

"Manhood will be tested soon enough in war," I pronounced in loud and clear Arrivi words. "I'm trying to build something here."

Dillan Rabbe Penli interjected. "Just delay the opening a few days. That's all."

Nobody looked at him. Curiosity came into Cyrus' eyes. But my position was clear. "I have been closed for more than two months. That's excessive."

In exasperation Dillan Rabbe Penli slapped his hand on the table. Cyrus glanced at him cool and expressionless. Martin put two fingers on his ample lips and sat pensively for a moment. He spoke without asking counsel.

"Mekucoo and Arrivi men have no debt to netta," he began. "They can bring the cattle down. If the hunt begins tonight, five to seven days are spent."

Cyrus looked at Martin, then back at me. Martin slowly continued, speaking courageous words into the silent crowd. "What are the essentials to begin operations? Clean the area, inventory of goods. This is work for the women."

"I have open employment," I said before the crowd. "For Arrivi women as well."

"The Arrivi are not in your debt," Martin answered.

"Indebtedness is not my primary concern. I will hire Arrivi women for wages."

Dillan Rabbe Penli moved in his seat and gestured toward me. Before he could speak, Haku Rabbe Murd assented, "Hai."

Assent was spoken three more times from men in the crowd. "Hai. Hai, hai."

A new look flickered across Cyrus' face. He pursed his lips and stared ahead. Dillan Rabbe Penli withdrew his hand and looked at Cyrus cold and hard as though it was all Cyrus' fault. Martin's voice was full of humor. "It's settled then. The hunt begins tonight."

I stood and offered my hand to Cyrus. I don't know if the gesture existed before in his culture, but it did in mine. Cyrus stood also and shook my hand. A shout went up. With the silence broken, the men amiably greeted each other and filed out in groups.

I asked Martin in Putuki, "Where does Cyrus live?"

"For now he lives here."

"Is it correct to invite him for a meal in my quarters?"

"Who will serve?"

"My employees," I said as if to question why he asked.

"Cyrus will bring a second, probably Cara."

"There's plenty."

Martin was pleased. "It's a rightful gesture for those who have no women for the night."

Tribesmen entered their family circles with the solemnity of a night before battle. Mekucoo warriors had made peace with their women who lived far north. They joined the single men around a communal fire until the time of departure. Tribespeople provided food, and the Mekucoo were served by boys too young to hunt.

Our meal was like a state dinner, an organizational feat considering the communal fire was served outside my office door. My dry living area was swept and scoured. Dinner was prepared from freshly slaughtered meat and daily picked fruit. Haku Rabbe Murd joined us and Karima Le oversaw the serving. The men took ritual baths, and the women gathered wearing new gowns. The sisters wore their sky-blue veils.

Cyrus, Cara, Haku Rabbe Murd and I entered my quarters and removed our shoes before we sat at the prepared table. Karima Le put a pot of tea before us. Haku reached to pour from it.

Cyrus grabbed his wrist. "Haku Rabbe Murd, why do you insult me? Am I a trespasser that you veil your women in the house?"

Haku put both hands on the table's edge. "This is not my home."

Cyrus turned to me. "Why do you diminish these ones?"

I looked at him and shrugged. Cyrus turned back to Haku. "With Brian Rabbe Miller's permission, may we know the spirit of your wife?"

Haku swayed back and forth glowing with pleasure. Karima Le stood behind him and slowly lifted the tentlike veil. The two sisters received it from her and carefully folded it. She stared at the ground with her hand on Haku's shoulder. He sat quiet but emotional while we gazed upon the face of his wife.

Karima Le had olive skin like Kyle Le's, bigboned and demure. She looked to be no more than 23, but I mentally added a few years assuming youthful looks were a family trait. She wore her long hair coiled and secured at her neck. Karima Le lifted a liquid and self-assured gaze to Cyrus who appreciatively smiled, "Hiki May."

Her greeting was melodic and calming. "Cyrus. Cara. We are honored, Brian Rabbe Miller."

This was my house, and I was the host. I disliked these surprises. I was led by Cyrus to lend undue influence to Haku, implying that he was my financial and influential equal by the act of gazing upon the face of his unveiled wife.

Cyrus wasn't satisfied. "May, I was a guest in your father's house and knew the spirits of your sisters as children before their beauty required the veil. What have I done to forfeit this honor?"

Karima Le looked at Cara. "It's the Eve of the Hunt," she murmured.

Cyrus' eyebrows went up. "He has four children by a Mekucoo princess who's said to be the most beautiful woman on Dolvia."

May glanced at me but, after the honor awarded to her husband, could not withhold honor. She led one sister forward to stand behind Haku. May steadied the girl and turned her to us. "As you know, we are orphans of no estate. This is the second born, Katelupe Le." May lifted her sister's veil. Terry was athletic and surprisingly tan with forest green eyes. She wore her hair in short, clinging curls much like Kyle Le's hair.

"Hiki Terry." Cyrus gently said. She quickly glanced at him and nodded, then stared at the floor.

May removed the veil of the second sister and presented her. "This is Klistina Le, the youngest." She was young and truly lovely. My appetite for food vanished. I felt a sharp pain in my gut and was glad there were no more beauties to be presented. Cyrus was gentle, almost fatherly. "Hiki Tina," he whispered. She giggled and hurried to the stove followed by Terry.

Cyrus didn't seem hungry either. "May, I knew you and

Haku before you were married. I witnessed the signing of the deed to his land. Why do you lie to me on the Eve of the Hunt?"

Haku stood up, livid and trembling, a shocking mass of insulted spirit who had glowed with honor minutes before. Cyrus didn't flinch. "Sit down, Haku. On the night of ritual all may be known. Brian Miller, you have one in your employ who is with us tonight but who does not serve. What have we done that you chose to insult us?"

Haku sank into his seat. The two young women turned back to the stove. May looked at Cyrus and sighed, weary and heartfelt.

Kyle Le sat next to the stove with her back to us and her hands folded. As goulep she could not serve or touch anything that passed to the men. Cyrus included her without breaking the law by using the avenue Martin and I employed. I spoke clearly, "Kyle Rabbe Arim, where is my tea?"

Kyle Le approached the table without looking at anyone. Cyrus' look changed. "Karima Le, why do you allow the youngest to dress like Cylahi?"

May gave Cyrus a level look. "Kyle Rabbe Arim is my employer. It is not right for me to correct him."

Cara put one elbow in the table and covered his mouth with his hand. He couldn't keep humor from his eyes. Cyrus glanced at Kyle Le, and I remember the thought came into my mind that these two had history. Cyrus stared at a spot on Cara's shoulder. "Only Cylahi whores wear wealth of their own making."

Kyle Le answered evenly, staring at the floor. "Any woman who gets wealth wears it."

I felt like Cara's brother. I gritted my teeth and rubbed my chin with one hand. Cyrus looked away. "Take those off and serve us here."

Kyle Le loosened the first ties of her gown, evoking the law that he could want only one thing. Cyrus slammed her wrist onto the table. "On the Eve of the Hunt, what could Mekucoo need?" he hotly asked.

"What does Mekucoo ever need from goulep?"

Cyrus held her arm. His look didn't waver. "Goulep is as dead as Rabbenu."

"Then I honor the Dead."

He released her arm that was red from his grasp. "Leave us," he commanded. She left the room without looking up. She had looked at nobody except Cyrus.

During the silent and tedious meal, Cyrus stared at a thin scar on Cara's arm. The tracks of his actions came clear in my mind. He had honored the family for the right to know Kyle Le. But she had not lent her mantel to him. Cyrus was not often bested. After so many steps to get there, to receive nothing was galling. It would have been distasteful even from a man.

The night of surprises was not over. A knock came at the door. Haku answered it and greeted Lam who whispered that Dillan Rabbe Penli would arrive. Cyrus joined them. "Bring Kyle Rula, by her hair if necessary."

Karima Le and her sisters reached to put on their veils. "Nu delaya," Cyrus spoke quickly. He intended to lose no more ground.

Kyle Le entered just ahead of Dillan. Cyrus grabbed her wrist and drew her to his side. Dillan entered with his partially veiled wife, Julia Le. It greatly pleased me that Julia Le was the only veiled woman in the room. She could not be uncovered without formal introduction to Cara, but none was offered.

Dillan sat in Cyrus' chair. "What I have to say is for the men."

"Then why did you bring your wife?" Haku quietly asked.

Dillan spread his hands in a conciliatory manner. He couldn't suggest the women leave without including Julia Le and Kyle Le in the same group. He glanced at Kyle Le, then noticed she was being restrained. "Of course, the privilege is yours," he murmured to Cyrus.

Cara stood and put his hand on the hilt of his beltknife. Cyrus smiled. "If you were on the land of my ancestors, you would be dead where you sit."

Cyrus pulled Kyle Le's arm, drawing her directly in front of him. "Kyle Rabbe Arim was just telling us of the deep honor he receives from the right to tithe the proceeds of netta to Rabbenu."

"All Arrivi honor Rabbenu," Dillan said then paused, smelling a trap. "Will he hunt the Ketiwhelp?"

"Since he herds no cattle, Kyle Rabbe Arim's estate is not threatened by Ketiwhelp," Cyrus claimed.

My respect for Cyrus grew each minute. I wanted to see him in action with Oriika. He casually added, "Kyle Rabbe Arim honors the hunt by providing for the single men outside. He also honors Cara and myself at the table of his business associate."

"Do you have business with him?" Dillan asked.

Cyrus' face didn't change when he asked, "With whom?" If Dillan Rabbe Penli spoke Kyle Le's official name, then he could not with honor ignore the mortgaged land or the former pension.

Kyle Le had made Dillan rich as she had most of the people in the room. Julia Le wore a full necklace of peridot gems of the same quality as the topaz Kyle Le had given me. But Dillan was not big enough to give up the past. Rabbenu choked and died that night when Dillan Rabbe Penli could not bring himself to acknowledge the substantial tithe of a tribal member. Haku hung his head with shame.

Dillan had reached the peak of his wealth. None would stand behind him again with their might or their tithe. And in this way

Cyrus took the loyalty of the Arrivi men as I had taken the loyalty of the Arrivi women to work in the mill. It was right that Dillan's wife should be veiled. He was in the company of his betters.

We heard the unmistakable thudding sound of a spearhead into wood and outbursts of men's voices. Haku opened the door while the sisters quickly donned their veils.

Dillan and his wife left through the office followed by Cara, Lam and Dak, Cyrus and Haku. The women crowded out until Kyle Le and I stood alone in the room. I gestured that she should go first. She wrapped the blue veil around her head and shoulders and joined the others ahead of me.

Before the assembled tribesmen and their families, the men who had been my dinner guests stood on one side and the women on the other. There was no sign of the drama that had taken place at my table. But I knew who was under the veils and responded to each veiled mound as I would to the spirit of the person. How ignorant I had been.

Quentin waited in the assembly, ready with a new challenge. Oriika and many others waited. But the one who I saw was Quentin. The distribution of netta was the big event of the season. Quentin competed with it for attention.

He stood over one square foot of dirt that was dry, sandy dry. He strutted around it and walked away from it and allowed people to bury their sweaty hands in the desert sand. It remained dry, by force of his will, desert dry.

I looked into the tribesmen's faces, but they treated Quentin's trick as simple entertainment. Oriika confidently walked to the square and spat into it. The square gathered moisture around the spittle. Slowly and visibly, moisture entered the square so that it appeared soaked from the inside out.

The men chuckled and gathered their weapons and shields. They prepared to leave without acknowledging Quentin. They were more impressed with netta, a simple balance of chemicals found in nature and acting by natural forces, than by the paranormal powers of Quentin the healer.

The young men sounded the drums and began a low and growling but joyous chant. Spear shafts rhythmically pounded the ground and hands slapped against thighs. The air stirred with anticipation. Chanting and fairly dancing to the rhythm, the men picked up their simple gear and confidently walked into the darkness.

Cyrus and Cara were the last men who stood by the fire. Cyrus looked deliberately at Kyle Le. She stood expressionless amid whispers and clucking from under the veils. How could he signify her if she didn't respond?

Cara waited by the firelight's edge. Cyrus turned and walked past him. With both hands, Cara held his spear high in the air and shouted once. The chanting instantly stopped. Not even the rustle of underbrush lingered.

The women chattered under their veils while they left in groups. Some looked back at Kyle Le who stared at the spot where Cyrus had disappeared into the night. I realized she had acknowledged him and defied custom. There was no submissive bearing in her gestures. She had not averted her eyes or held out a hand in supplication.

Chapter Eight

I wasn't invited to hunt with the men. They were still wary of me, not impressed with my friendship with goulep.

The hunt had ended and the cattle returned by the time Ricardo visited. He waited with Chang Lin and four Chinese Blackshirts who stood stoically at the entrance of the hotel conference room. Chang Lin stood in the blast of cold air from the window air-conditioning ducts. On the wide and polished table, I displayed bolts of fine cloth with interwoven Chinese symbols.

Ricardo pushed them aside. "Show me netta," he said.

"Ricardo, look at the quality of this weave," I insisted.

"Fine, fine," Ricardo said. "Hire two more designers, and I'll get another loom computer. We'll make twelve bolts of several patterns, then track which ones sell. Martin will secure another building, one we can use year round. Now show me netta."

I abandoned the bolts of cloth and sat across from Ricardo. I was more than a little successful as administrator. I had accomplishments to show off. A full labor force, exclusive designs, profits to reinvest. Ricardo swallowed it whole and was onto something new. Chang Lin watched me with a smirk then gazed out the window.

"Netta isn't mine to sell," I said.

"Come on, man," Ricardo said. "I know you have some."

I gave him the limp piece I carried. It's potency was gone, stained with medicine and body oils. Ricardo focused on me, hard and unbelieving. The truth sounded like a weak excuse. "Netta is seasonal," I explained. "They don't store it."

Chang Lin stepped over to the table and felt the burlap. "I'm told you have taught this native girl how to operate the loom computer and the EAM," he said.

"Several tribeswomen work in shifts at the loom computer," I defended.

"Do they each pay time-sharing charges to develop their own market among Hardhands in competition with Ricardo?" he

52

countered.

"I asked Fumi, our designer, to make the clothes I'm wearing now. There's a local market among Hardhands for similar workclothes."

"And do the colonists wear dark blue and light blue together?"

"Those are hand-stitched veils."

"Are they? I want to meet her."

"Who?"

"Don't be tedious," Ricardo interrupted. "The one who runs your EAM bill sky high staring at exterior shots of the planet. Call her in here."

"Kyle Rabbe Arim has returned to her land," I said with truth. "She has no need of us."

Karima Le was pregnant. When the hunt began, the sisters of Arim left to live as they always had. This year they didn't farm. They had grown too rich for that. But fruit was gathered and Terry tended their stock. Haku built two new stock buildings on the land of Murd.

May came into Somule weekly to give the now nominal tithe to Rabbenu. Tina worked at the mill, not from need but because many unmarried women did. But I didn't offer that to Ricardo. "Get her in here," he demanded. "I have business with her."

I walked back to my mill quarters and changed for dinner with Ricardo. Tina brought in the dailies. "You should have gone home hours ago," I gently told her. "Listen, can you get a word to Kyle Le? We need to talk tomorrow as early as possible."

"Kyle Le was in the mill today under the veil of another."

I stopped short. "Klistina Le, take off your veil."

Without caring, she slowly pulled it over her head. "You see, it's only me. Not the one you want. Just me." She was thin and pale with a full mouth under high cheekbones.

"You look lovely tonight," I said. "Are you going to meet someone?"

"You know I cannot," she answered with a smirk. "Unless. I could go with you."

I patted her arm. "You would hate it. A bunch of old guys smoking kari root and talking delivery dates."

"I would not hate it," she said in another tone. "They say the room opens up like a cave with jewels hanging in clusters and walls that feel like a Ketiwhelp's fur."

"It's just a house with many rooms, most of them empty. Will you talk to Kyle Le?"

"Take me with you. I won't say anything. I'll leave right away."

I met her eager gaze. "I could never face May if I did a thing like that."

Later when I entered the hotel lobby, I thought about Tina's

53

description. The conscript gangs had completed their work and been sent back to the transport. Gleaming chandeliers and flocked wallpaper created a formal decor. Deep furniture and tables with polished edges awaited guests from foreign lands.

Non-Chinese Blackshirts in thigh length dress tunics with shiny insignia and white gloves emerged from elevators. With bravado and cold stares, they passed me then entered the waiting ECCAVs at the hotel entrance.

Martin Sumuki entered the lobby looking every inch the banker in his dark evening suit. "We can talk with Kyle Rabbe Arim in the morning," I said. "What does Ricardo want?"

"Netta's a natural substance," Martin said. "Kyle Le must accept his price or see it paid to another."

"What's his offer?"

"Electrification of the district."

"That's to his advantage. He would do that anyhow."

"The electricians have disembarked," Martin bitterly explained. "Appliances will arrive on the next shuttle. But cheer up. There's at least one new arrival you won't turn away."

Her name was Lucy, the athletic type as comfortable in khaki and dago t-shirts as in strapless chiffon and whalebone. She was front office all the way. She had traveled to Dolvia at Ricardo's request with her two brothers, the electricians.

Chang Lin had opted to return to the Company compound for dinner with Sim Chareon and the elite Blackshirts. I was seated next to Lucy at dinner in a hotel stateroom where we were served by three uniformed Putuki women, one of whom worked in the mill during the day. The blue-black tribeswoman nodded to me from behind other guests but did not speak.

Ricardo sat at the head of our long table and talked in low tones with Captain Ellis, an invited garrison Blackshirt of non-Asian descent. Ricardo had reason to make friends with the Blackshirts assigned to police work, I reasoned. I stared at the panda logo on Captain Ellis' black tunic sleeve. He nodded to me with a thin smile.

I turned to Lucy and her brothers, Jim and Hank. "And what will you be doing on Dolvia?" I asked Lucy to have something to say.

"I'm told Dolviets have no method for food preservation," she offered with melody in her voice.

"You're going to sell deep freezers?"

Jim chuckled. "Lucy's a chemist."

I wished I had smiled and gone along with the talk, but I bristled. Lucy was there to test netta and synthesize it. Why did Ricardo's snakes have to come so beautifully wrapped?

Martin, that consummate politician, saved the moment. "Brian got past tribal taboo and hired native women. Tell us about it, Brian."

I was on display, the Softcheeks who had turned gaucho. "The mill equipment faces away from the entrance," I began, making eye contact with each of them, a gesture Dolviets considered rude. "We paid a young girl to watch the door and sound a bell at a man's approach. The women who were custom-bound put on their body veils.

"The bell became the signal for a break. If one group of women stopped, they all wanted to stop. So I routed traffic to keep the men in another section. Now the place has all the allure of a harem." The brothers chuckled with delight.

"Plus the millhood has become popular as streetwear," I continued. "It's a symbol that the woman earns her own money. Tribeswomen refuse to marry because they have more freedom and money at the mill than on their husbands' land. So I don't know if I solved a problem or created one."

Martin added with a twinkle in his eye. "And the only man allowed on the millhouse floor in the women's section is Brian."

"Really, Martin," I said as though he lied.

"Why do the women accept you?" Lucy sweetly asked, then listened attentively for my answer. I felt like a pawn in three dimensional gauntlet. How could I say I was honored because in my six months' residence, I hadn't touched a native woman.

I suspected Lucy knew that and more. Perhaps she was instructed to soothe me where I was vulnerable and thereby learn what I might hold dear. I felt at sea with Ricardo's people and renewed my vow to trust nobody, not even Martin.

"Among the tribes it's more important to name what you want than to offer a gift," I explained. "Then you enter their system of trade which operates on indebtedness. Since I can obtain their designs nowhere else, they may receive wages with honor because, within their system, I'm in their debt."

Lucy looked at each of her brothers. "And so you gained the women's trust?" she probed.

"And so I can do business with them."

"And the one who doesn't wear a veil?" Captain Ellis interrupted from his place by Ricardo.

"Only one tribe wear veils," I explained without hurry. "And their widows and holy women go uncovered. These people are as imitative of their leaders as we are of ours. They could have all chosen to go bare-bottomed." I calmly gazed at each of them with a wide and frozen smile.

After the meal Martin and I walked with Lucy into the hotel lobby, ready to go our separate ways. Ricardo shook Captain Ellis' hand then joined us with high spirits, ruddy and grinning from the acclimation pill. "Brian Miller, the milliner extraordinaire," he said and placed a heavy arm around my shoulder. "The rains had you down for the count, but you're coming back strong. Now tell me this. Cylahi gold jewelry, how is it made?"

I saw interest in Jim and Hank's eyes. Suddenly I was tired
and wanted to go home. To my home with the Dolviets who
saved my life. "There's no gold in this district," I explained.
"The Cylahi buy it from a mountain tribe where it's plentiful."

"How can the Cylahi afford gold?" Jim asked.

"Gold isn't legal tender here. Tribeswomen more highly prize
precious stones that must be cut and polished. Gold is malleable
and shiny. The Cylahi use it for jewelry because they're lazy."

"You know that," Ricardo said. "And now we know that.
But our market doesn't know it. Can you get them to make the
jewelry in quantity?"

"You'll have to bring in the gold."

"It's already been dealt with," Ricardo magnanimously said.
I felt dirty and cheated like I had spoken a secret to the boys in
the schoolyard who then shouted it out and chided me.

"What is that?" Lucy asked with alarm.

I touched my face and realized I had a nosebleed from a
combination of the alcohol and the hotel's controlled atmosphere.

Ricardo couldn't stop laughing. "A true gaucho. Works all
day in the mill but can't breathe recycled air. Go back to your
tribeswomen and your EAM."

When I left Klistina Le came to me at the hotel entrance.
She must have waited there all evening. She probably wouldn't
have shown herself, just followed me home, expect for my
bloody handkerchief. "Did someone hit you?" she asked.

I shook my head no. She began to laugh but stopped at my
warning glare. Why did my discomfort entertain so many people?

"Kyle Rula's waiting," she whispered while we walked out
of the lighted hotel entrance.

On the millhouse floor Kyle Le talked with Fumi and Rose
by the loom computer. At my entrance they covered themselves
including Rose, a married Putuki woman who had never covered
her face before mill employment. "Aren't they carrying this too
far?" I asked.

"Where's the harm?" Kyle Le answered. "This new cloth is
wonderful. Will you sell much of it?"

"Yes, at a big profit." I controlled my pleasure at seeing her
again. "Now Ricardo wants to export Cylahi jewelry."

"That shouldn't be difficult. Cylahi will sell anything."

"But don't you see?" I hotly claimed. "He gives you pennies
for these, then sells them for twenty times that much. And once
he owns the designs, he'll give you nothing."

"Before your friend came, we received nothing for them,"
she countered, too calm.

"But you should get more."

"Ricardo has the market, transportation, distribution. All we
have is the land and our labor." Kyle Le used words in her

56

sentences that don't exist in Arrivi.

"Kyle Rabbe Arim, he knows about the EAM. He monitors everything." I leaned forward with tension. "He'll strip the land and haul it away."

"No man is greater than Dolvia."

"The land cannot save you!"

Kyle Le glanced at Fumi and Rose. "Soon we'll meet this Ricardo. He's the manatee, isn't that right?"

I stopped short then breathed a sigh. Dolviets stood naked and unsuspecting before Ricardo's avarice. I was anxious for them as though they were children in a storm. I needed a reminder that they were the more ancient and, on Dolvia at least, the more successful people.

"Brian Rabbe Miller, your center has shifted," Kyle Le quietly added. "Must I take my sister home?"

I shook my head. "I'm more focused than that."

"Unless you cannot have the one you have seen."

"I can have her. Just not the way I want."

When I thought about Kyle Le, I saw the spirit in her face, her will and deep caring. I knew she had short, round arms and small hands and feet. Like most women of her tribe, her stance was solid on thick legs and ankles. But I could not imagine her body.

On the other hand, I saw Lucy in my mind and slept little that night from what I imagined. Her limbs were long and tapered, muscular and firm. I saw bare shoulders and the long back and her navel. I saw her in many positions. I was vulnerable.

Chapter Nine

This was one meeting I wasn't about to miss. Ricardo was invited to visit Kyle Rabbe Arim's land in the shadow of the giant butte. Under an open tent just like at May's wedding, cold water, fruit and fish on patties were offered to the Softcheeks guests. Formalities went on for thirty minutes which was unusual for Arrivi. This was not an official meeting presided by Rabbenu, but rather business the way Oriika viewed business. The event included watching the sweltering Softcheeks save face.

Oriika wore an amber colored gown with no design and topaz and peridot jewelry. The sisters wore their sky-blue body veils. Kyle Le wore a hand-stitched traditional gown with a new pattern and the gold medallion. She didn't sit at the table but behind Oriika, turned partly away from the guests. A swatch of netta rested on the table between the negotiating parties.

The crowd around the open-sided tent pressed in, all native all tribes. Other Softcheeks waited in Somule. None could have tolerated the heat long enough to get a good view. I sat with Ricardo who brought the electricians and Lucy. Martin litigated.

Oriika smiled and signaled the fan moved over the Softcheeks' heads. Two small boys on either side of Ricardo's group rhythmically pulled cords. Lucy responded gratefully, but the men sat stiffbacked in their suits.

"We are honored that Martin Sumuki and Brian Rabbe Miller have brought their boss, Ricardo Menenous, to meet us," Oriika began. "We will be pleased again when Ricardo brings his bosses for a meeting."

Ricardo bristled but said nothing. In her glory, Oriika allowed a few minutes to pass. "Isn't it true that you, Ricardo, meet with Company officials? And isn't it true, the Company will bring electricity to our poor district?"

Ricardo spoke from where he was vulnerable. "I will bring electricity."

"And where is your generator large enough to light so many homes?" Oriika innocently asked. "And where is your natural gas to run the generator?"

"I brought the technical people," Ricardo insisted. "I will set up the power lines at considerable expense."

Whispering and irreverent chuckling was heard from the crowd. It was more correct for Ricardo to list what he wanted than what he offered. He gave up his best argument in the first volley.

Oriika easily deflated him. "We receive electricity. We must buy your imported appliances. The Company charges us to run them. Everybody gets something. We see this as a fair trade."

Minutes passed. Ricardo's face was ruddy and active from the acclimation pill. Jim and Hank appeared to suffer less, but they had less at stake.

Martin softly spoke into the silence. "Ricardo, and the men of the Company, are interested in procuring some quantity of netta."

Oriika acknowledged new business. "Netta is a natural substance," she unhurriedly returned. "Anyone who has land may farm it."

"Ricardo's land has no geyser activity," Martin said.

"Some land yields one crop. Other land yields another crop."

Ricardo had bought solid bedrock, a prudent choice for manufacturing. The thermal areas followed streams below the plateaus and throughout the flats on Kyle Rabbe Arim's land. Everybody sitting there knew that. What could Ricardo offer that Oriika and Kyle Le wanted? And couldn't get elsewhere?

"We desire the use of netta," Ricardo plainly said. "We do not know how to farm it."

"Who is we?" Oriika lightly asked. It was time for Ricardo to speak the truth. Even Lucy and the brothers expectantly looked at him. The people began to whisper and cluck.

"The Company desires to manufacture netta in all seasons," Ricardo began. "We have brought Lucy Kempler to study it. Then we'll export netta for use on many Dolvias."

"How will the Company manufacture netta out of season?"

Ricardo shrugged. "After we determine its makeup, we combine the elements in a laboratory."

Oriika looked around at faces in the crowd. I looked too, but did not find Cyrus who I thought must be there. Oriika turned slightly and Kyle Le whispered into her ear. Oriika nodded.

"Netta is given by Dolvia," Oriika loudly pronounced. "In your laboratory you will manufacture netta using the substances provided by Dolvia. We find this harmonious with our poor understanding of Her gifts. Kyle Rabbe Arim has sanctioned the sell of her crop to Ricardo Menenous and the Company. We encourage all those who farm netta to enter into commerce for it.

"We know that you, Ricardo Menenous," Oriika continued, "don't possess netta or know how to farm it. We suggest a fair trade. For the right to make netta in your labs, tribespeople will be trained to use Company equipment including the generators and the EAMs, so there's no machine on Dolvia that Dolviets can't operate. We ask that all manuals be printed in three dialects, a task we know is simple for your transport computers." She paused and smiled.

"In addition to free electrification, all Dolviets will enjoy free service for five years starting with the last hook-up. This is the price for the knowledge of netta."

Oriika's plan was expensive but not prohibitive to Ricardo. "For the use of netta until such time you produce enough for your needs," Oriika continued, "we invite you to farm netta in its season. In exchange for instruction, we ask that these four men attend technical school on your transport."

Four young and beardless men stepped forward in a line and stared into Ricardo's face. "These four or their replacements will study the full range of courses until such time that you no longer need to farm netta. If their advancement is satisfactory, you may send them home after the Company's last crop of optioned netta is harvested."

Ricardo quickly counted the cost. "Who says how much learning is satisfactory?" he asked.

Oriika's eyebrows went up, and she looked around as if to ask why this question should be considered. "Schools are for teaching. These men are for learning. What could be the impediment?"

"They can't even read," Ricardo complained.

"If they can read, is there another problem?"

"Transport life is different than on Dolvia. And the expense," Ricardo said.

"They will adjust to the transport just as Brian Rabbe Miller has adjusted to Dolvia. You and the Company will bare the expense as the price for netta. I have written these papers of agreement that Kyle Rabbe Arim has signed. They list the conditions of the fair trade."

"But these men are illiterate," Ricardo loudly objected. "What can they learn in a few months?"

Oriika put the large, multi-page contract on the table. As if on cue, the oldest of the young men, a dark Putuki youth known as Mula and said to be a future tribal leader, stepped forward and read in Ricardo's language. "I, Kyle Rabbe Arim, have read this agreement and have full understanding of its contents. I affix my signature and my word of honor to this fair trade."

He stepped back. The youngest of the four, also a Putuki named Ely, read the same words in Arrivi.

"I'll discuss this with my people," Ricardo quietly agreed.

"We enter into this agreement freely and before witnesses," Oriika added before the gathering. "At our next meeting, we will be pleased to greet your bosses, Sim Chareon and the men of the Company."

Seated next to Martin in the ECCAV's front seat during the ride back to Somule, Ricardo fumed. "The nerve. The arrogance!" he complained. "And those clothes. They deliberately wore solid colors so my designs mean nothing. I negotiated this deal. My idea, my enterprise. The Company has no reason to electrify. It's pittance to them."

He twisted in his seat and instructed, "Brian, you'll go with me to talk with Sim Chareon. They're going to hate this. They may not deal with these uppity women."

"The Company will deal with anybody who has the goods," Martin quietly said. "Only you are mad at Oriika."

"Yeah?" Ricardo hotly shot back. "Tell me, do they come to you in groups? Does Kyle Le always have to be on top?"

I reached forward to strangle Ricardo. Martin skidded the ECCAV onto the road's shoulder and opened the doors. Ricardo and I fell heavily onto the red dirt while I tightened my grip around his fat neck. Martin struggled to separate us until Jim and Hank hurried from the other stopped ECCAV and pulled me off him.

Martin helped Ricardo to his feet. "What the hell, Brian?" Ricardo complained, sweating and rubbing his neck. "Are you trying to sacrifice the right to jump back?"

I stopped short and stared at him with hatred. With ground duty I had felt independent of the Company, in control of my world. But I was no better than conscript. The Company twisted and yanked me with puppet strings.

The right to jump back. Raise horses in Montana. Cold, mountainous Montana with the *aurora borealis* overhead. I felt the gossamer thread of an umbilical cord extending from me through the worm hole and to Earth snap and curl away. I had no reason to jump back. I had only Dolvia and the quick, mischievous smile of goulep.

Chapter Ten

Electrification was underway. Ricardo had generators constructed on high ground north of the hotels. Lucy's laboratory where she tested the components of netta was in the adjacent air-conditioned building. The twisted electricity converters on rows of metal towers comprised the most impressive structure in the district, completely imported and surrounded by an electrified fence to keep out Ketiwhelp and migrant birds. Ricardo claimed he was glad for the fence. Curious tribespeople made the long trek to Somule to see this new wonder and dared each other to touch the oddly shaped constructions.

Jim and Hank installed electric lights along the streets and in businesses, then moved onto the nearest homes. The Council disputed what constituted a home with adequate structure to qualify for electricity. Tribesmen petitioned Ricardo to bear the expense of safety improvements to the rickety Cylahi huts near the railhead. But Ricardo had returned to Stargate Junction and was indifferent to the agreement's details.

Cylahi women who lived south of the town were given vouchers saying their homes would be hooked-up with electricity when the remodeling was complete. Council members created a municipal fund and hired colonists to upgrade private dwellings. Colonists' manhours were in high demand with so much construction. Ricardo communicated with Chang Lin who sent the gangs of transport conscripts back to Dolvia.

The hotels were landscaped and open for business. So conscript gangs were quartered in the Company offloading docks at the railhead. Chained together at night and guarded by a detachment of garrison Blackshirts led by Lt. Lebowitz, conscripts knew more freedom during their daily work details in the Cylahi community.

Cylahi tradition welcomed all guests to the comforts, such as they were, of their homes. Cylahi women understood they were not indebted to the conscript workers because of the fair trade Oriika and Kyle Rabbe Arim had negotiated. Cylahi hospitality was in addition to the terms of the agreement.

By the time Jim and Hank entered Cylahi homes for the installation, the women were pregnant by God knows who and offered only dates and dried fish to these last guests. In these upgraded huts overrun by pigs and with a single overhead lightbulb, eighteen mulatto children were born later that season.

Brittany Mill expanded into another building with another loom and a separate section for jewelry manufacture. I hired additional women for each section, unable to employ tribesmen. Those who didn't herd cattle were taken by the Mekucoo for the northern fighting.

Lam and Dak remained through the dry season, but other Mekucoo were absent as much as they were present. One day I stood in the street just outside the mill office discussing with Dak the need for a stable work force to get the product out. Terry and Tina under Arrivi veils approached us from the street of shops.

"Can you speak with Haku Rabbe Murd?" I complained to Terry. "I need reliable workers who will commit to a forty hour work week."

I realized the woman with Terry wasn't Tina but rather Heather Osborn under Tina's veil. Heather had learned Arrivi and some halting Putuki. She used more freightate words than Terry understood. Occasionally they asked me to translate some question they could not communicate together.

I stared into the thin facial panel and wondered what Heather thought she was hiding dressed as a sister of Arim. Terry moved between us as though to protect Heather, and they quickly walked to the millhouse employee entrance.

Lucy befriended the women of Rabbenu, especially Julia Le. She tried to ease feelings between tribeswomen and Hardhands and represented the Company during a tentative first contact over tea. The sisters of Arim were absent by necessity, being servants to goulep. Heather took no interest in Hardhand politics and was mostly ostracized by them. Oriika attended out of curiosity.

I was not present nor concerned with what the women did, but I overheard several comments after the failed meeting. The gathering, held in the Hardhand church basement, started on a positive note while they discussed native tea and the finely woven designs of Arrivi cloth. I cannot say where it went wrong. I can only report what was repeated within my hearing.

Apparently one Hardhand woman asked if it was true that the ghost of an Arrivi youth walked the savannah searching for his lost love, then became an angry Ketiwhelp at any approach. The women of Rabbenu were silent at that question, Julia Le in particular.

Without a prudent voice to silence them, another Hardhand

woman asked if it was true that Mekucoo warriors ate the beating hearts of their captured enemies.

Some Hardhand women attended the tea as a means to convert the tribeswomen to the one true religion. Later Oriika pointedly complained that a Hardhand woman read from a book called the Piblee about a great warrior who vanquished his enemies then buried them in a pit.

"Such an abomination!" Oriika indignantly complained. "To pollute the body of Dolvia with the evil forces She has allowed! Unspeakable!"

"What book did she read?" I quietly asked.

"The Piblee. I read Hardhand words. It said right on the cover, the Piblee."

"The Bible? The Book of Revelations in the Bible."

"Whatever," she curtly returned.

One day late in the season while we prepared for the rains, Kyle Le visited Somule. "I brought these as payment for your twelve percent." She poured several amber topaz gems from a small bag onto the table.

"Why do tribeswomen wear peridot but you always bring me topaz?"

"A man's aura is earthtone," she said simply. "I will have these mounted in a ring or a cuff if you want."

"I have no use for jewelry," I claimed. Kyle Le turned away with a sad look. "What is it?" I softly asked.

"You have much wealth but send nothing offworld. You live in your office."

"It's true I sacrificed my option to jump back."

"You don't hoard against hard times, but trust Dolvia," she added.

"Perhaps I should be more prudent."

She showed that illusive smile. "Is it true what they say?" she ventured. "A great warrior from your planet buried the evil ones in the body of Mother Earth?"

"It's just a story."

"The tale of the ghost on the savannah is just a story, yet there's truth in it."

"I cannot explain," I shrugged, unwilling to enter into a discussion of metaphysics. "The story's about the future. Sometimes after we're all gone, this timeless warrior will return and bury the evil ones in a pit."

"In the earth?"

"Yes, so it is written."

"And that doesn't offend you?"

"I never thought about it. Our traditions aren't the same."

"I see," she said and seemed to withdraw.

One evening before the rains began in earnest, I dressed in millmade clothes for a formal dinner at the Company compound.

Tina brought in the dailies but didn't beg to join me. There was a knock at the door, and I called for him to enter expecting Dak with the labor reports. But it was Lucy who entered, wearing a strapless organdy gown with her hair up to show off diamond earrings. Long legs tapered in shimmering silk stockings to her smart two-inch heels.

Tina cleared her throat. "Just leave them on the desk," I told her. "Thank you. That's all." She stood motionless. "You can go now," I added.

Lucy walked to the desk and fingered the material of Klistina Le's body veil. "Perhaps she wants to offer me a drink," Lucy coquettishly suggested.

"Don't you know what bad taste you show, coming here without your brothers?" I said.

"They're outside," she shrugged. "We came to drive you to the compound."

Tina bolted through the office and outside, then peered into the ECCAV's windows. Lucy and I followed. The brothers waited near the office door and smoked kari root. Smoking was one of many nasty habits they had picked up during ground duty. "If Klistina Le weren't present," I said in no uncertain terms, "the tribespeople would assume you sell your sister's favor."

"If we know better, what's the difference?" Hank shrugged.

"Perhaps you're here just for the job, but I live with these people," I said. "Besides, if Lucy's for sale to me, then she's for sale to anybody with money. And these days, everybody has money."

"You try watchdogging her. She'll only maim the first one as an example."

"How well does she deal with groups?" I asked.

North of Somule stood the Company compound, a windowless concrete slab building with solar panels across the back where it receded into the side of the gentle rise. Company men made no pretext of living among the tribespeople. Their hearts were where their paychecks originated. We climbed eight steps from where Jim parked the ECCAV and entered the Chinese-decorated interior. We waited to pass the first security checkpoint. I stared at the giant panda logo emblazoned on the sleeves of the officers' uniforms.

We walked down a cool hallway where windowpane panels made of rice paper and narrow wood lined one side. We passed an open panel that revealed a deep studio where Chinese Blackshirts in loose pants and open shirts practiced martial arts exercises.

At the corridor's end, two highly made-up Chinese women, long braids down their backs and wearing traditional robes with the stylized dragon design, bowed deeply to us. They slid back adjacent panels to reveal a lush and intricate Chinese garden with manicured trees and exotic orchids. Three square acres of twisted paths guarded by jade Luduan statues, the garden included breasted crane incense burners that gave off the rich, musky scent that I associated with the Company offices on Cicero.

I waited with Lucy and her brothers next to a bubbling pool with multi-colored fan-tailed goldfish. At another garden entrance, Hamish Nordhagan talked with Captain Ellis and Lt. Lebowitz, the garrison Blackshirts. They shook his hand and left. Hamish joined us, looking dapper in his dark crew uniform with his graying hair tied at his neck. He shook hands with Jim and Hank and allowed Lucy to lightly kiss his cheek. Then he came to me, very confidential, turning away from the others.

"Big mushi-mu going on here," Hamish whispered. "The Regent is about to marry off his oldest daughter to a Manchu Taipan. A good match for her, daughter of a lowly Mongolian. I'm surprised they invited a gaucho dressed like you."

"It's the netta."

"I heard. A native commodity that dehydrates anything."

"Not anything. Plus it's seasonal."

"And you discovered it?"

"An Arrivi woman used some to save my life. But she gave up the secret."

"To save your life? Not much of a trade-off," Hamish dryly claimed.

We received a signal from the formally dressed Chinese women. Hamish offered his arm to Lucy, and we walked down the corridor in another direction. In a large diningroom with a raised dais decorated in high Manchu style, ornately carved wood backdrops and weighty jade statues stood behind two cushioned thrones. Six long tables were laden with fine service of hand-painted china and crystal.

Most of the hundred or more guests were Han-Chinese Blackshirts. Company officers plus a few outland administrators already sat at the tables over wine and bread. Several Asian women in long brocade robes and white makeup moved among the tables, silently filling glasses and brushing away minuscule crumbs.

We were led to a prominent table below the thrones. I sat between Hamish and Lucy and waited while our glasses were filled and our plates piled with soft bread delicacies. I leaned over to Hamish. "The shuttle must have been doing double shifts to get all this into place."

"Make a good show for the Taipan," Hamish returned. "Notice they invited elite Blackshirts only. Can't pollute the air with barbarians."

"Except the old guard."

"And the gaucho who owns twelve percent of netta."

At the CEO table Dillan Rabbe Penli and Julia Le sat near

two empty chairs. Also Chang Lin who nodded to me without expression. Dillan saw Chang Lin's move and curtly nodded to us. He leaned to one side while Julia Le whispered into his ear.

Martin was absent. Since Company wives in long dragon surcoats with otter-trimmed wing shoulder flaps were seated at the CEO table, Martin couldn't be invited without including his wife. Company men had no taste for dinner spent with a pregnant and barefoot mother of two.

Before the fish course, Sim Chareon entered with his younger daughter who wore an elaborate dragon robe with sleeves that covered her hands and long strands of coral. They were seated in the empty chairs at the first table. Julia Le respectfully spoke to the young Chinese woman.

Four women in butterfly printed robes with sleeves that fell way past their hands paraded in to music. Behind them walked the prospective bride, weighed down with layers of brocade robes and ceremonial beads. She wore a surcoat with exaggerated shoulder flaps and a spiky hat that depicted three phoenix birds in flight plus several pheasants in a circle. She sat without greeting on a throne and the ladies-in-waiting arranged her long skirts.

The Manchu Taipan who was Regent Chareon's guest and the prospective groom entered from the other direction wearing a mandarin yellow robe patterned with flying cranes and a round Chinese hat rimmed with oversized Manchurian pearls. He sat straight-backed on the other cushioned throne and was served by two of the attending ladies. The music ended and the next course was served.

"That's Tao Chek," Hamish whispered. "Scion of the Company's strongest mushi-mu family. And the coldest-hearted son of a bitch I ever met.

"Tao Chek is Manchu," he continued, "and traces his line back to the emperors in the Forbidden City. Chang Lin is Han-Chinese. When China was first consolidated, the Manchu nomad tribes conquered the Hans but felt inferior to them culturally."

"That was in the seventeenth century," I added.

"After the collapse of Communism, many wealthy families reclaimed their royal heritage. For all its size, China's a narrow society."

"What's Tao Chek's tie to Sim Chareon?"

"I'm not privy to Company negotiations," Hamish said, shaking his head. "But I'll tell you this, Gaucho. Dolvia's important to them. The land surveys for this region far outnumber their research on other planets. They're looking for something, precious stones or uranium ore. Tonight's display confirms their intentions to invest on Dolvia."

Sitting next to me, Lucy smelled of rose petals and something slightly acrid, daisies maybe. Streamers of hair came loose and laid against her neck. Her lips were moist and soft over perfect teeth. She commented on each dish offered by the robed servants. She tasted them and smiled with pleasure, indicating everyone at the table should be served. Lucy was the only woman served before the men, the apparent hostess at our table. Company wives waited in silence and didn't show their hands while they nibbled the entrees.

Between courses Sim Chareon talked with his guests. He shook hands with Hamish and asked how we enjoyed the food. He pulled up a chair near me and began without small talk, "Tell me about the Mekucoo."

"They live farther north," I said. "I employ three men, excellent supervisors."

"I'm told they don't marry their women."

"A Mekucoo woman is married to the land," I answered. "If she's forced away from her land because of famine or bad fortune, she becomes as an old woman."

"And the women own everything?" he asked.

"Their material wealth is passed on through the woman's lineage. A brother or an uncle is more important than the child's father."

Sim Chareon quickly digested this new information. "So a Mekucoo man with no sisters has nothing."

"He has the company of warriors and the guidance of ancestors," I claimed ironically. When Sim Chareon smiled, a whole different set of wrinkles showed on his face. "Dolviets are willing to enter into commerce," I added.

"Either you are the lion or you get eaten."

"And if there's more than one lion."

"There isn't."

"But what if there were?"

"Then the people will all die."

There was a policy I could admire. Concise, clear to everyone and easy to execute. That is, if you never saw the faces of the people, or ate in their homes, or had your life saved by one of them.

The meal ended with sorbet and wafers. The prospective groom left first, then the bride and her ladies by a different exit. Sim Chareon bowed to Chang Lin and then bowed to me. He and his second daughter exited behind the bride in a slow procession.

"My god, Brian," Hamish whispered. "How much does your twelve percent yield?"

"I don't know exactly. I receive dividends in topaz gems. I haven't had them assayed."

"You don't send your payments through Company channels?"

"I don't send any of it offworld."

"The Company cannot gauge how much the Arrivi receive in barter without knowing your worth," Hamish concluded.

I smiled. "I suppose not. Listen, how long will you stay? Perhaps we can get a drink."

"Sorry, Gaucho," Hamish returned, delighted with his nickname for me. "I catch the shuttle tonight. Just stopped by the lend my support to the engagement party. But let's keep a channel open."

After Hamish left, I found Lucy waiting alone in the garden. She signaled me to join her. "Jim and Hank left with some Blackshirts," she complained. "Women are not invited. I'll give you a lift back to Somule if you like."

We left the Company compound, and Lucy took the driver's seat in the ECCAV. Western stormclouds gathered behind the tall butte. It was odd to see the savannah covered by a threatening sky that was clear blue most other times.

Lucy recklessly sped toward Somule as if to test my nerve. Red dust kicked up when she skirted the shoulder of the narrow road then looked over at me with a big grin. She slowed when we approached the buildings on the outskirts of town. "Come by the hotel for a nightcap," she suggested.

Lucy left the ECCAV parked in front of the hotel. We entered the lobby where garrison Blackshirts sat in lounge chairs over drinks and kari root cigarettes after their night of revelry. While I waited for Lucy to get her key from the front desk, Captain Ellis watched me from where he sat among his men.

Captain Ellis left his group and approached me with curiosity. "Good evening, Brian Miller," he said in a measured tone. "And how was the engagement party of the Manchu Taipan and the regent's daughter?"

"Very pleasant," I lightly answered.

"And how is the lovely Lucy Kempler tonight?" he added when she joined us. "No chaperons?"

"Jim and Hank are still at the compound," Lucy said.

"At the compound," Captain Ellis repeated. "At the luxurious Company compound. Enjoying the delights of Han-Chinese hospitality, no doubt."

"They went to a martial arts demonstration," Lucy returned.

"Or at least that's what they told you," Captain Ellis said and smiled at me.

"I don't know what that means," Lucy answered.

"Nothing, nothing at all," he shrugged. "So, you don't have to be Chinese to get invited to these functions. Isn't that so, Brian? May I call you Brian? I've been meaning to ask, Brian, aren't you flying under false colors with this native display?" He indicated my clothes then thinly smiled at each of us.

"Well, don't let me keep you," he sardonically claimed. "I'm told the view across the desert from your rooms is exquisite, Miss Kempler."

"Yes, it is," she coldly answered. "Good night, Captain

Ellis."

"Miss Kempler. Brian Rabbe Miller."

Captain Ellis returned to his group and spoke in low tones with Lt. Lebowitz. Lucy and I crossed to the elevators. "I'll leave you here," I said.

"But we were going to have a nightcap."

"I want to get back to the mill."

"Please, walk me to my door."

"I'm sure you can find your rooms."

Lucy's mouth turned down with cynicism. "Tell me, Brian, is it true what they say? That you carry a torch for that warrior's whore?"

"Were you assigned to distract me from her?"

Lucy's eyes flashed, and she reached to slap me. I caught her arm. "Is this the first time somebody told you no?" I asked.

She relaxed and sighed, then suspiciously looked into my eyes. "Take care, Brian. They're watching you. And the tribesmen, you're all being watched."

"Well, thanks for the good word. Good night, Lucy Kempler. Good night."

Chapter Eleven

It was after the rains that we entered a season of cylay in which forces expanded to bear fruit. Our test market results from Cicero were encouraging for Ricardo Menenous. Company women chose the Arrivi linen robes and surcoats with Chinese symbols for public events and business situations as well as in the home. Ricardo selected eight popular designs and ordered quantities made for the first shipment through the worm hole.

The Arrivi linen workclothes became universal wear for tribesmen, for colonists, and later for work details on the transports. The sturdy dungarees loosely hugged the body and lasted for seasons before they needed to be replaced. The double paneled sleeveless Arrivi tunic enjoyed a short market run but were not as popular as the pants.

Others in Somule prospered as well. Several colonists bought their indentureship papers, then saved enough to purchase property west of the former barracks to build small homes. Carl and Heather Osborn had a modest house across the way from the colony civic building. Their two children, a boy and a girl, played in the dry yard with its picket fence and makeshift swing. I walked past their place occasionally in the cooler evenings on my way to meetings at the hotel, and chatted with Heather about the many changes in Somule.

Hardhands of different ethnic groups disembarked in Somule, crowding the barracks where they were quartered during their indentureships. Captain Ellis had them report to his office and assigned them work details according to their skills and ability to pay his bribe demand. His men began a black market for counterband Consortium goods, especially alcohol and drugs, plus a brothel for the non-religious tradesmen, many of whom were former conscripts.

Because of Brittany Mill's fame, offworld entrepreneurs started many businesses that employed the newly-arrived colonists. One Consortium shipping company offloaded diesel-burning eighteen wheelers that soon made the run along deeply rutted dirt roads from Somule to Cylay. They left with shipments of tea, vegetables and beef then returned with raw wood and metal ducting needed for construction of colony homes. The same enterprise offloaded two-ton trucks from the transport plus military-style ECCAVs. Consortium fieldmen scouted countryside communities for untapped sources of market goods and native artifacts.

The native bazaars became a streetcorner market for vegetables and dried Kariom, kari root and clumps of herbs for cooking, dates and olives and hand-stitched cloth. Narrow teahouses competed with the Hardhand bakeries for the daily consumer coin of working colonists. Tribeswomen were outfitted like queens in their collapsible vegetable stands with electric fans and canvas covers. They displayed imported consumer goods including coffee and Consortium cigarettes in bright packs with foreign words printed on them.

The season of cylay yielded fruit from many sources. It entertained me immensely until one day I saw Lucy look at Cara. He had a beauty beyond his physical prowess, his golden skin and high cheekbones, beyond his princely bearing and self-effacing manner. Add his elusive Mekucoo activities and his fanatical deference to smaller and scarred Cyrus, and Cara was an irresistible friend who could do no wrong.

Lucy fell for him in about a minute. Her need to be near him bordered on insane. She sacrificed her status, her moral values, her occupation—everything to follow after a man who found her a nuisance, who had little time for her.

With the naiveté of a spoiled child, she made her need public without wondering how Cara might respond. It wasn't lost on the Mekucoo that the chemist brought in to find the secret of netta could not concentrate on her work. Cara was persuaded to show himself to her but offered her no place in his life. This he did as part of tribal resistance, a warrior's duty.

Barricaded in the lab, where she received only the visitors of her choice, Lucy knew there was no other chemist to call. The closest man with adequate education lived two systems away. Company men found themselves in an awkward position.

First they sent the brothers to reason with her. "What am I doing differently from either of you?" she shouted and sent her brothers packing.

Then the Company vice presidents visited. To monitor her progress, they asserted. "Let someone else have a go at it," Lucy haughtily said. "I behave exactly as a man would in my place."

How could she offer herself to this subhuman aborigine who took no care of her? How could she compare her obscene display with the latenight diversions of important men? Her abominable, unspeakable activity wasn't the same as theirs, could never be seen as the same.

Occasionally Lucy visited my mill quarters seeking a sympathetic ear since none including her brothers spoke to her. "They use tribeswomen whenever they want, often against her will," she bitterly complained. "Which one of them hasn't?"

"They don't fall in love with the women they take. It doesn't upset the balance."

"Their balance," she shot back.

"It doesn't upset their balance," I calmly repeated.

"I'm sorry, Brian. Cara has been gone for three weeks. What is he doing?"

"I'm not privy to the movements of Mekucoo."

"What if he doesn't come back?" she complained. "I'll be forced to leave Dolvia, known forever as Lucy the whore for something all the men do."

Cara returned for a short time and allowed Lucy into his presence. He gave her only his attention and his seed, honored her in no way. Better it would have been if he paid for her favor. Then at least she would have a place to go next.

Then Cara was gone again, without leaving a token of his intentions. Defiantly Lucy went native, or bald as we called it. She greased back her hair in short dreadlocks and dressed in a mixture of Cylahi and the few Mekucoo pieces she scrounged. She walked the street of shops in her ludicrous getup and spoke in the Putuki and Mekucoo words she had gleaned. She hired three Cylahi women to take her to Mekucoo land where she was determined to court her man. Before they could begin the ridiculous journey, Katelupe Le befriended Lucy and involved her in some tribal events thereby soothing her need.

"Will you journey with Lucy to the Canyon of Buttes?" I heard Tina ask.

"Lucy will not see the sacred lands. She has the mark," was Kyle Le's sad answer.

It's difficult to describe the mark. Kyle Le withdrew into sadness whenever I questioned her. A straight answer I could get from nobody. The best I gathered was that Lucy's aura carried no glow. A blankness, a grayness, no growth. Her spirit was not reinforced by Dolvia.

The rains came again, and the savannah gave forth the seasonal abundance that reinforced domestic markets. Then another dry season laid over Somule, the oppressive heat restricting daytime movement. The Cylahi women with mulatto children were plagued with amoebic dysentery, called Softcheeks stomach, from a steady diet of bad water and poorly prepared pork. The women couldn't keep anything down and had constant stomach cramps. Complications included dehydration, flu symptoms, starvation, and convulsions. First a few, then all those who kept pigs in the squalid slum by the railhead were unable to care for their children or even to keep themselves clean.

Quentin the healer was in the far north campaigning against the Softcheeks who fought to control the richest gold mines there. Oriika visited each small and mean Cylahi hut with its bare electric bulb glaring overhead. She saw no sickness in the spirit, only a rotting in their bellies.

Soon they began to die. Some Cylahi men who were their brothers and fathers returned from fighting, but were helpless in the face of this imported disease. Lucy petitioned into the Company's stony silence for medicine, hospital facilities, or relief personnel. They gave aid in natural disasters, why not for this epidemic? But the Company officers accepted no responsibility. They hadn't brought the pigs. They didn't minister to the tribes.

The Cylahi women who could still walk gathered the mulatto children of their sisters and went to the church in time for Sunday night Mass. They begged to receive communion, offering the children to be raised to serve the Hardhand god. They wanted to die in peace knowing the mulatto children were cared for by people who loved them. These were, after all, Hardhand children.

The Cylahi, naked pagans who worshiped the earth and ate raw pork, and their bastard, halfbreed children were summarily turned away. The children were judged to be foreign, fathered by conscript workers of a protestant sect who didn't believe in the divinity of the Virgin.

Their suffering was a forerunner to the suffering of all who stood by and watched the Cylahi women wither in pain and anguish for their orphaned children. As tribal myth said, a helping hand turns away much evil.

Late one night, two Cylahi women made their way back to the church steps and feebly knocked on the door. They were found the next morning, rail thin, naked and dead on the small porch under a stained glass window that depicted the blessed Virgin.

Some Cylahi men gathered the eighteen two-year-olds who were no relation to them and deposited them outside the Company compound. Company men sent Lt. Lebowitz with a security detail to force out the orphans. The crying toddlers made their way back to Somule and the street of shops.

There Lucy found them—dirty, starving, and with no understanding of why they were pushed from place to place. That day she shouted, loudly and angrily, at all parties while she gathered the toddlers and led them to her laboratory.

Lucy set up a nursery and hired Putuki women as nannies. She redoubled her efforts to find the secret of netta, working always within earshot of whimpering and rebellious mulatto children.

Ironically, this generosity brought Lucy new status among the tribes. She had committed to Dolvia, no longer waiting to steal a fortune for a better life on another planet.

The tribeswomen still avoided her with her hodgepodge of native clothes and poor understanding of dialects. But they left gifts of prior appreciation, supplies needed to raise children in the ways of their ancestors. Lucy delegated the Putuki nannies to distribute goods according to need. She took nothing for herself and kept an open jar above her desk for the many peridot and topaz gems that were given.

From under the veil Katelupe Le visited Lucy's laboratory and brought a sky-blue gown of Arrivi design with a lighter blue trim. "Kyle Le made it," Terry quietly said. "It's similar to the veils of the sisters of Arim."

"And where is Kyle Le?"

"She cannot come. You know that."

"I don't acknowledge goulep," Lucy said with authority.

"It's not for you to acknowledge," Terry gently returned.

"I mean, I would speak with her."

"You and many others."

"Then what does this gift signify?"

"Perhaps she fears you'll dress like Cylahi," was Terry's answer.

"You know what I want. Will the tribes see me as belonging to Cara?"

"Do you see that?"

"Please."

Terry sighed, then gently explained. "We see a Softcheeks who has learned that our lives are given in service to Dolvia. These are the colors with which Dolvia covers Herself. We feel you may gain strength by aligning yourself with the forces She allows."

"Thank you," Lucy said. "And thanks to Kyle Le."

"Kyle Rula does not desire your thanks. She seeks peace on the flats of Arim."

About that time Somule filled with returning tribesmen after their defeat at the northern gold mines. On the edge of town they stood in silent groups and closely monitored the Company compound and garrison Blackshirts. I received at the mill as many as I could employ. Tribeswomen came to me with low bows and slim excuses that they must return to the land, so their jobs could be given over to a brother or uncle or son.

Fumi bowed low and introduced her two sons. I could not afford to lose her services. "I will call a Council meeting on this!" I complained.

Fumi and Rose agreed to stay and operate the loom computer. I retained women at the sewing machines and to set gems in Cylahi gold, but soon the workrooms and halls of Brittany Mill rang with men's voices.

On another day the tribeswomen crowded into my quarters.

75

Oriika, Tina and Terry with Heather Osborn, obviously pregnant and seated off to one side.

"Carl has put her out," Tina explained in low tones.

"But why?" I asked. "She has made him strong."

"He believes the child is not his."

"But whose could it be?"

"Yours."

Such was the small-hearted, superstitious, gossip-ridden culture of the religious Hardhands that they believed the ugly story. Above suspicion we were, as the tribespeople knew.

That day Heather agreed to live under the Arrivi veil with Karima Le on the land of Haku Rabbe Murd. It was said that she had seen om, a blessing of mixed benefits. Whatever grievous images she saw in om, the sisters of Arim kept Heather close to them and far from the bustle of Somule.

Mula and Ely returned with the other students from the transport school. Excessive honor was given to Mula, sixteen years younger than Cyrus and untested. I couldn't make out what they saw in his aura.

Oriika argued with him as an equal. "Your time at the transport school is not completed."

"I have learned what I need to know about Softcheeks," Mula flatly said.

Cyrus visited and also honored Mula. While Mekucoo guards stood at mill entrances with their hands on their beltknives, Cyrus and Mula hunched together in my quarters discussing Captain Ellis' weaknesses.

Then Heather entered with Terry and Tina and under the Arrivi veil. Oriika gently guided Heather to a seat. "Honor to the one who has seen om," Oriika said.

"I don't share your spirit," Heather murmured. "There will be great suffering in this time."

"And glory."

"Glory to one man, not for Dolvia."

"One who Dolvia has raised up," Oriika corrected her.

"Perhaps you carry the burden for all of us," Mula gently suggested. "So we are free to act."

"What actions can justify so many deaths?" Heather asked through the facial panel.

"We must fight. It is seen."

"It's seen that you will fight, not that you must."

Mula looked around at the tribesmen. What was it about second sight that brought a slavish, resentful demeanor to the one who was blessed? "Many things will be required of us. A duty we did not choose," Mula said and drew closer to Heather.

"Move away," Heather complained. "Whatever you touch will die."

"We will all die," he murmured, staring into the facial panel.

"The question remains, what will we accomplish?"

"The question remains, who is left to remember?"

Terry and Oriika returned to the land of Murd with Heather. Only Tina stayed on at the mill. She was quite a young lady, twenty-four years old with her own income and honor gained by serving goulep. Many Arrivi and Putuki men made excuse to enter the millhouse floor and nod to her as though surprised she was there. Ely daily watched Tina, seeking opportunities to speak with her. He stopped wearing his round-rimmed glasses hoping to appear more attractive to her. But she gave him no notice.

"Ely was here earlier," I said when Tina brought in the dailies. "Don't you like him?"

"You know Kyle Le isn't for you," she murmured. "Her mantel is given to Cyrus."

"Cyrus has a wife married to the land."

"That's why they quarrel. She gives the images only as required by tribal law."

Perhaps Tina was right. I had missed Kyle Le during the season of cylay mostly because of her smile. I suppose many saw my heart. "Can Cyrus take her?" I asked.

"In this matter my sister is the same as Lucy."

"Hence the gift of the gown. It's meant as an affront to Cyrus."

"It's meant in sympathy for Lucy."

"It serves more than one purpose."

"Just the same, Kyle Le's not for you. You must seek another."

"A sister perhaps?"

"We both serve those who are for someone else. We can take comfort with each other." Tina drew near, then turned away her sour face. "Not that one either."

"What do you mean?"

"You don't know?" she asked with a nasty tone of glee. "They stopped Heather on the road two miles from here. She was trying to reach Carl."

"Is she alright?"

Tina's disdainful smile was all-telling. I was transparent to her. "That's why the tribespeople talk."

My patience had worn thin on this subject. "Where is Heather?"

"She's on the land of Murd. She lost the child."

I heavily sighed. So much trouble in the season of cylay. "You know it wasn't my child."

"I know it wasn't his. She came to warn Carl and take the other children away. The colonists will die."

"I'll go to the barracks," I said with urgency. "I must warn them."

"Tribesmen watch the Blackshirts," Tina claimed. "They will

do what's necessary."

"And what is that?"

"All is seen."

The garrison Blackshirts made their move against the colony under cover of night and dressed as Cylahi and Putuki. But all was seen, and the Blackshirts were surrounded by tribesmen before they reached their intended victims. Blackshirts who resisted died quickly. Others were stripped of their weapons and their footwear then released on the desert wearing only the stolen native garb. They were slashed across their chests and backs, not fatal cuts, just enough to let the blood run.

Mekucoo watchers monitored the Blackshirts' slow death march while insects and birds plagued them under the searing desert sun. Three walked to within sight of Somule before their throats were cut as they would have cut the throats of sleeping colonists.

The colonists were turned against the tribes, though, by the death of the priest who had refused aid to the Cylahi women. The day after the failed Company ambush, he was found in his church, bound and gagged, with his heart cut from his chest and impaled on the altar. Tribespeople suspected Captain Ellis and Lt. Lebowitz, safe in the Company compound where they ignored the death march of their soldiers.

The colonists were outraged by the priest's ugly death without knowing the history of similar events, only their own definition of the devil's work. There was no celebration for spared lives, no reconciliation with the tribesmen.

I received an offworld message from Ricardo that I was to keep an appointment with Sim Chareon. I must report on the mill's future during this unrest. The choice of media and message had a strange feel to it. Ricardo was proud of his independence from the Company, a selfmade man. What new trouble brewed within Company strategy?

"What will happen?" I asked Oriika.

"You tell me."

"The catchphrase for these events is that all is seen. Is that why I wasn't informed? Do you suspect me?"

"The season of cylay has ended. You must decide who you are in the resistance." Her eyes closely studied me while she waited. I squirmed under the scrutiny.

"If I remain with the tribes, will I always be outside the leadership?"

"Mula feels no affection for you. There's a new balance."

I felt my friends slipping away. "You have no word for me?"

"You enter the Ketiwhelp den. None can help you there."

I dressed in Arrivi linen dungarees and Mekucoo beltknife. During the early morning before the sun baked the land, I walked to the Company compound wondering what to expect. The Company had staged the massacre of colonists to gain an advantage. But why kill the colonists who they imported? Who was their audience for this tragedy? What new balance prevailed in offworld Company boardrooms?

Two Chinese Blackshirts escorted me through the silent corridor to a business office. Thin panels slid back, and I was confronted by the Company men who had enlisted me as administrator five years before. The Blackshirts silently stood at the entrance.

Sim Chareon the revolutionary, who had come to power by virtue of his energy and battle strategy, had felt too much sympathy for the tribesmen, revolutionaries all. At this formal meeting he sat on the side as he always did. Daniel Chin stood at a table near his open briefcase. Chang Lin sat in the ornately carved chair behind the desk. His look was deceptively open and engaging, as though we were gentlemen drawn into civil strife among the peasants of our homeland. *Noblesse oblige* and all that.

"Brian Miller, thank you for coming," Daniel Chin said. "We are understandably upset by this unfortunate massacre of our police garrison. The tribesmen's punishment was gruesome. No survivors to interrogate. But in light of certain blackmarket activities in Somule, perhaps it was in keeping with their crime."

"Relations between the tribes and the Company are not my concern," I gingerly began.

"Tell me about second sight," Chang Lin cordially invited.

"The ability to see future events exists in your philosophy."

"I have no wish to discuss philosophy," Chang Lin returned with an edge in his voice. "I leave that to old men. It's been demonstrated to us that second sight is a weapon of resistance on Dolvia. One must know one's enemy."

"I have no enemies on Dolvia," I said. "I have only a business."

"A business that thrives because of Company trade routes. You must carefully choose your friends." That was the second time in a few hours I was asked to choose sides.

"Now about this woman who can see," Chang Lin repeated. I glanced at Sim Chareon's implacable face. They had been ambushed on their way to ambush others. A new course must be charted. But first, eliminate the most troublesome natives.

"Among the tribespeople, there are many who can see," I explained. "No one person or one vision is taken as law. There must be reinforcement from nature or from another who is blessed."

"And do you have visions?" Daniel Chin asked. I slightly shook my head. "The students who returned from the transport, do they see?" he added.

"The gift is highly prized. Those who are blessed are held

79

close to the land."

"Like Heather, you mean?" Chang Lin said.

"Heather Osborn has seen om, as they call it. That's a temporary burden because recent events affected people close to her. Not to be confused with a lifelong gift."

Chang Lin watched me with a piercing gaze. "The Company will make a new investment," he said. "This region must be subdued. We ask that you join us as advisor on tribal affairs. Together we enter a new era of prosperity. How say you?"

"So this failed attack was for show offworld?" I guessed. "An unfortunate event cited to muster additional Consortium support. Put down the rebellious, barbaric tribes who kill innocent colonists."

Chang Lin leaned forward across the wide desk. "We expect your cooperation in this matter. Or we may start by confiscating your twelve percent," he said with satisfaction and signaled the Blackshirts at the door.

They brought in Katelupe Le without a veil and limp between the guards. Her glazed eyes regarded me without expression above bruised cheeks and a fat lip. "Take her away," Chang Lin said. The Blackshirts led her out. Terry limped heavily, and she didn't look back.

"We propose a fair trade, as the tribespeople call it," Daniel Chin said. "The flats of Arim for the life of this one. You will deliver the message." I grimly nodded and stood to leave.

"Your best guess," Chang Lin said behind me. "How will they respond?"

"All the resistance lacked was a martyr. You just gave them one. You will never own the flats of Arim."

Chang Lin smiled, cold and thin. "We shall see."

A message they asked for, and a message they got. I consulted with Oriika. We moved the manual sewing machines, the EAM and every trace of my twelve percent from Brittany Mill that same night, then blew all seven buildings to kingdom come.

Part Two

Chapter Twelve

The blossoms of the white orchid were for chilblains. The ground pupia root in tea brought down a high fever. The succulent leaves of kari calmed an angry boil. And the round tops of the flowering cumin that bloomed only during the first rain preserved and flavored dried fish. All these things I taught them, each one. Katelupe Le, Klistina Le, even three-year-old Kyle Rula, just as our Mother had taught me, the oldest.

We overstuffed Mother's pallet and placed it in the front room. She sewed our clothes and ground herbs and made bread patties. She dozed on the mat, and Kyle Le joined her, sitting like a marmoset on Mother's stomach and stroking her arm. Kyle Le brought a light into Mother's eyes who never rebuked her or pushed her away.

Mother was the first to notice the visions. Kyle Rula often told her when Father was coming home. Twenty minutes to an hour before he arrived, she whispered the news to Mother. There was no way to know. No vista down the road, no sound of footsteps.

Kyle Le showed me a picture she had drawn when she should have been doing her lessons and claimed it was of Mother. The drawing outlined a body with long hair. One side was smaller with very small arm and leg. Veins like on a leaf ran through the smaller shoulder and hip and the too small limbs.

I asked Kyle Rula what it was, and she searched my face with her upturned serious eyes. I pointed at the veins in the picture and asked what it could be. She answered that it was bad, very bad.

Three days later Mother lost the use of her left arm, leg, shoulder and hip. Father was traveling then, and I had never seen this affliction. I called for the elders, the Rabbenu Luria himself came to Mother's side. He explained that her condition occurred on Dolvia, but usually to very old people whose minds had separated from their bodies.

I sighed with relief that the problem was of the body and

not the spirit. I didn't offer Kyle Rula's drawing, but I burned it in the stove and stored the matter in my mind. What power could a three-year-old know?

Marta came, the holy woman who saw kari with her cataractous eyes. She felt Mother all over and called it a blood problem and not a spirit. I felt relieved of the obligation to speak of the drawing. Kyle Rula had not called the paralysis into existence by foreseeing it.

Marta sat at the table with her assistant called Omic. I served them fruit, fish and tea and prepared for the blessing on the household. Omic wasn't from the tribes but from a place far north. Some said she was a foundling. Others whispered that Marta had bought her, performed some service of great expense and demanded payment of the child. I knew nothing of these things.

Omic was fourteen, a chunky and round-faced girl whose breathing was labored when she ate. She had short arms, I remember thinking that. She grew into a mountainous woman with round short arms.

I stood at the stove, waiting for the water to boil, and wondered how we could manage with Mother so afflicted. Kyle Le went to Omic and turned up that serious face she had. She stood at the girl's elbow and stared until Omic stopped eating and looked over at her.

Kyle Le was three. She was three years old the year Mother died. What could she know? She had two words for Omic. She said, "Oriika" and "light." She held her hand close to Omic's arm, but not to touch it. Rather, she put her hand in Omic's aura that only Kyle Rula and blind Marta saw.

Omic's name later became Oriika. When Marta died, she disappeared for six years then returned an experienced and bejeweled holy woman who used manly words and laughed at such things as ambition and progress.

Our days were long and purposeful, grinding to make flour in the morning, lessons before the meal, sewing and embroidery in the afternoon. Then two more hours of lessons, tend the birds, clean the dishes, start the evening meal. I watched my sisters grow as though they were my daughters.

Terry, as we called Katelupe Le, was tawny and mauve. Strong, quick, pleasing without effort just from the expression of her spirit. Tina, or Klistina Le, was soft, the palest blue. Quiet and receiving, she treasured events and stored them in the liquid recesses of her heart.

And Kyle Rula was brackish orange like sediment from the steaming geysers that heralded the rains. Willful, thoughtless, undisciplined and disruptive, she brought calamity upon herself, seemed to loose the spirits as much as see them, like the plaintive call of the Murmurey bird appeared to bring disaster as much as send up a warning.

And me, earth-tone and green, Karima Le, named for the life force, the guide. I wanted to be with them, the same as them, part of the same flesh. But it was more me against them, the other mother to undercut.

Father worked for Rabbenu from whom we received the land and the pension. Father traveled to Somule and north to the capital where he attended talks with the Softcheeks about their business interest in our land. It was the time of kari when spirits stirred. Ambition, avarice, subjugating power were the words Father brought into our home. They meant nothing to us.

What was the value of having something that belonged to another? His spirit did not reside in the thing. To have the thing was not to have the man. To take the thing was not to diminish the man. One saw the man more clearly when he stood apart from the things attached to him. If you wanted a thing that I had, I gave it to you. Your courage to ask for it showed you had a greater need than I. Having served nobody.

Father explained that the Softcheeks of the Company wanted to have for the purpose of taking offworld. People who lived across the skies used things up. They had things, especially things from distant lands, to have them. Then they discarded them and wanted more things, sometimes the same one only new, sometimes different things to own because they were different. But why possess things you cannot use? What happened to the discarded things? How did storage serve Dolvia who stored all things already and brought each forth in its season?

"Softcheeks fear that Dolvia can be destroyed," Father explained.

I felt sorry for them to live every day with so great a fear. "But a force strong enough to destroy Dolvia would destroy their hoards," I reasoned.

"They believe once they own a thing, it's separate from Dolvia who gave it and can be defended even in the season of om."

"But why would they choose to defend things when spirits are dying in om?"

"Softcheeks count things to be more important than spirits. Softcheeks women store jewelry made of gold and precious stones. Rather than wear the jewelry, they put it in boxes where nobody can see it. They have more than they need, but never share. In fact, they have the some pieces made of something called paste so they need not wear the real ones. Then when one woman dies, her jewelry is sold to women who want it, not to wear, but because it belonged to someone who everybody knew about."

"But if the first owner never wore it, how did the gems draw from her spirit?"

"Owning is more important to them than displaying," Father said. "To own something that belonged to someone who everybody knew gives power, even if you don't display it."

"But how do others know that you have it, if you don't show it?"

Father laughed and said, "This is the best part. They show a paper, signed by two people, that says they own the jewelry."

"And Softcheeks are happy with that? To see the paper and not the jewels?"

"Yes," Father said. "Jewelry, land, cattle, carvings, grain, even spices. There's so much of everything in the land of the Softcheeks they don't trade in spices. Small containers of spices are set on tables everywhere. In their bazaars, rows and rows of spices and herbs are stored for months waiting for Softcheeks women to buy them for their tables for anybody to use and take."

"Softcheeks must be wonderful to trust the paper and give away spices," I said.

"But to have new to continually give away, the Softcheeks trick our tribesmen, then subjugate the people because they have been made poor."

"But what do the Softcheeks take?" I asked.

"North of us, they took a mountainside."

We all laughed. Father was such a kidder. How could a Softcheeks woman put a mountainside on her table for others to use?

Subjugation was a big word for us. Some words we heard and said, but don't know because we had no experience of them. Father said we never would know. He worked and traveled for Rabbenu so we never would be subjugated.

And Father brought home other words. Human rights, honor, spiritual freedom, and liberty. Manly words whose power was to keep away subjugation.

"What words do the Softcheeks use to lose the power of subjugation?" I asked.

"They use the same words but with different meanings."

"How many meanings can a word have?"

"As many meanings as there are men who use it."

I was glad that women were not concerned with manly words. I was glad that kari caressed us and doled out our lives in service and children. I never desired to visit the capital and hear these words or see the men whose wives hid their jewelry.

I was surprised when Kyle Rula asked to go with Father. She was ten then and wild. She roamed Father's land like a Ketiwhelp, staying out for days at a time and bringing home snakes and toads and springslugs. It was a constant struggle to keep her decently dressed. I complained often and bitterly that she was too much for me to handle, more a boy than a girl, rebellious and willful, yet dreamy the few times I could make her sit down.

Father answered each complaint more for my understanding than to agree. He said Dolvia loved Kyle Rula and nurtured her. From the land she learned lessons others had not asked to know. Her path was different than mine and more difficult. I must not resent or punish her, that she would know punishment enough without receiving it from within the family. And so Kyle Le donned the veil three years before her time, a special event before she traveled with Father to the capital to sit through the Council meetings.

Each year during the rains we sewed new gowns of linen with the finest designs, each pattern a description of the person, or that year's events, or an alignment with the spirits. Simple and open prints for girls not yet veiled. Lazy, meandering patterns for unwed young women. Structured and colorful repetitious designs for wives with status.

And then Father was home from the journey on which he had first taken Kyle Le. She was pale and emaciated with a hacking cough, her once intense face vague and blurry-eyed. I put her to bed with a hot compress on her chest and talismans of garlic.

When I went to check her sleep at dawn, she had left her bed. She sat on the rise by the house, bent over and facing east as though waiting for the sun to warm and open her like the daily work of the morninglory bud. Sad and lonely, she was burdened with a worry that was not her own.

I woke Father. "Should I make her come in?" I asked.

Her sadness was reflected in Father's eyes. "She has a warrior's heart."

"But she's only a child," I answered.

He sighed. "It's as Dolvia would have it. Do what you can for her. But when I travel again, she must come with me."

It sounded cynical and jarring from his caring lips. She was done in and shrinking, like a sapling that had not developed bark before the unrelenting dry season. Could he really want her to wane so? My bosom ached with fear and maternal love. I went outside and sat next to Kyle Le on the rise.

She turned up her child's face as she always had, her eyes liquid and fathomless. She nestled against my chest and wept for an hour, soaking the front of my gown and forever planting the ache in my bosom. I cried as well, though I knew not what for. My tears fell into her hair like a gentle rain.

Finally she had emptied herself. "I have seen evil," she simply said.

"The men in the meetings in Cylay have a look about them that sickens me. It's murky and slimy, teeming with desperate life, like the last pools in the bottomland before a true drought.

"And each man has his own look. One is gleaming, and his spirit shoots straight up. Father called that idealism and after discounted everything that man said.

"One man seems to have four arms always busy with some work, and bulging pockets where he constantly changes the goods from one full pocket to press into another full pocket. Father called him a pragmatist, whatever that is.

"The leader is dry and peeling like the layers of dry wood in a white hot fire. Father laughed when I said that, then grew silent, only to bitterly chuckle again in a few minutes."

It had started as a game between them, and Kyle Rula loved the special communication since she was veiled to other men. But Father solicited her impressions and depended on them. He became agitated and impatient, requiring that Kyle Rula sit through all the meetings and relate later all that she had seen.

The game was no longer fun. She turned away from what she saw, sullen and listless. She told him only those images that forced themselves into her unhappiness.

"One day I saw a bridge form across the table between the man with four arms and the dry leader," Kyle Le continued. "I tapped Father's shoulder, and he immediately called for a short break. I told him about the bridge and two similar ones that extended to men who were uninteresting because I could not clearly see them. Father asked, again and again, what they were like. Finally, I shouted that they always change, fade in and out because they commit to nothing."

Kyle Rula had begged to go home. Father was distracted and vague and would not meet her eye. She knew without seeing that he was afraid of how he appeared to her. She knew because he had not asked.

So that night they had dinner with the idealist. Kyle Rula was immensely cheered up. She had liked him best. She sat very close to him and basked in the warmth of his glow. His name was Martin Sumuki.

Then another man entered, and Kyle Rula understood why they dined privately. Mekucoo warriors never ate in the presence of others and could not be made to enter restaurants. He was a small and muscular man with high cheekbones and a long nose. His features shimmered like one's reflection in a rippling pond. And around him she saw the evil.

Kyle Rula shrank back and leaned against Martin Sumuki who lightly put an arm around her without taking notice. She wanted to look away but instead intently stared into the warrior's aura.

"Tongues of flame shot out behind his head like long hair in the wind," Kyle Rula told me. "The fire was mixed with blood and strife. His bones were made of a forged metal, but the muscles over them faded, were rebuilt and faded again only to grow back made of a truly different material.

"He was splattered with fresh blood. Every step he took struggled through mud and hacked bodies as though he dragged the battlefield with him. And yet there was not the first trace of mud on him."

The warrior, named Cyrus, didn't sit with them but stood near the window. Their conversation was short and full of hot flashes. "I saw sparks fly around the room and the stirring of his ancestors behind him. Curiously, Martin Sumuki's glow was constant and separate from the presence that filled the room."

Their talk ended and the warrior made a motion to leave without the usual bows and encouragements. Kyle Rula coughed, and Cyrus hesitated. He looked at her, staring as though he saw through the veil and under her youth into the deep chambers of her heart. They all waited, so she spoke the words that she was given. "You will know a deep and lasting torture almost to the death. But you will survive, and they won't be able to hurt you again."

The Mekucoo blinked at her, then left just as though her words were not heard. Kyle Rula reasoned that which she had seen on Cyrus that day was evil. But evil was black and cold and unyielding and inert. We didn't learn until much later, what she saw around Cyrus was not evil but our redemption.

Then was the day of departure. Father must return to his work in the capital. Rabbenu Luria had visited twice but came alone early that day for the sending off. It was a great honor that he returned after the talks were concluded for a moment that was not required by ritual.

From my place behind Father and under the veil, I saw that Rabbenu Luria's spirit was full of delight. Father smiled and received the honor but not the delight. I couldn't understand what I saw.

Father hadn't asked, and Kyle Rula hadn't offered, to anyone, what she saw in Father. But suddenly I had to know. I went back into the house where she waited. "Tell me about Father."

She was clearly pained by my question, but answered simply. "Father's straight backbone towers over the others. But his spirit hangs from it like several aprons filled with freshly picked herbs."

For the briefest second Kyle Rula looked at me, only to confirm what she must have known. My face fell and my spirit laid bare. I knew she was gifted and I had imagined her visions as she described them to me. But not until that moment did I accept that her visions held the active truth governing our lives.

What Kyle Rula so simply claimed was exactly right. Plus Rabbenu Luria was glad for it. As long as Father provided backbone, Rabbenu could stay on his land with his family.

Rabbenu played Father through excessive honor that he knew somehow Father desired. Perhaps he too saw the aprons of herbs ready to buy the good opinion of other men.

Kyle Rula moved slightly. I looked up and knew I was as transparent to her as Father. But I didn't have the courage to ask what she saw.

I didn't know how leadership passed from man to man. But I understood how it passed in our family that day from father to youngest daughter. Truth had a life of its own. Truth did its work no matter from whose mouth it issued. Father despised her power, and yet became desperately addicted to her visions and her truth.

The pattern of events quickly shaped like the open stitching on the edge of a young matron's gown. Tribeswomen tithed to us and visited often, especially Mesa Le, wife of Rabbenu Luria. She stopped by two afternoons a week, and often sat Julia Le, her youngest, at the lesson table with Terry and Tina.

Those were special times for me, to know Mesa Le's mind. She included me in the conversation of the wives. She brought sweets and imported fabric and sometimes fresh meat, claiming that the animal had been large, too much to consume or store.

And she arranged my betrothal. I knew Haku Rabbe Murd, of course, who had eight head of cattle, who supported his mother and younger brother to whom he would give half of his wealth on the proper day. "There will be five calves when the rains end," Mesa Le said. "Haku Rabbe Murd is a man of property, a man who can marry."

When Father returned, visitors who he chose to honor could look upon our faces. He was openhanded and allowed many to know us. Haku Rabbe Murd was twenty-six when he was honored to see the spirit in our faces in Father's house. I was twenty and Kyle Le was eleven. Haku visited with his brother Spinel Rabbe Murd who was included in the honor of the unveiling.

Once they knew us, they could see us whenever the setting was proper. Haku and I were like children. I saw his strength and his special pride in property. He brought little gifts, wildflowers and stones that sparkled. At the feast of Oria, when our betrothal was announced, he brought a small necklace of gold leaves placed end to end. Passed around for all to see before it was given, none but my sisters would see it again. Haku Rabbe Murd would not see it until our long-delayed wedding night.

Terry quarreled with Julia Le over a boy's armband that had been Spindel Rabbe Murd's. She refused to accompany us the following week when I took the mortgage money to Mesa Le. Only Tina sat with me while I communed with Rabbenu's wife. Tina spilled her drink onto Julia Le's new gown, then refused to bow in apology.

Mesa Le pretended the squabble meant nothing, was in fact entertaining. She dealt with me differently then with other tribeswomen who raised children. She gave room to my unruly sisters where she disciplined Julia Le.

So isolated and burdened with work, I didn't see that Mesa Le's solicitous ways created a jealousy in other women and especially in Julia Le. Terry shouted her anger one day, that she hated them all and would do as she pleased. I discounted it as the hot-headed answer of a fifteen-year-old and chose to not see the signs.

Each time Father returned was like a long drink of cool spring water to me. My sisters were well-behaved as though his presence was calming. Under the veil my duty to welcome our frequent visitors was less taxing. The tribesmen did not come to chat or see what was amiss in our parents' absence. They accepted the cup of tea from my hand without the pain of acknowledgment.

Plus the presence of men in the household allowed a few moments with Haku Rabbe Murd, whose gentle eye and tender understanding swept away the memory of lonely hours and frustrated beginnings. Haku allowed me to believe I had done well, worthy to be a wife. Our plans were simple and patient, built upon our knowledge that eternal Dolvia provides for all. We didn't experience, perhaps because we didn't have expectations, the tumultuous upheavals that marked the lives of Katelupe Le and Kyle Rula.

I worked my way through the patterns, stepping gingerly to not rent the fabric, when news came of Rabbenu Luria's accident. He had gone on the Ketiwhelp hunt, a foolish enterprise for an old and prosperous man. He fell into a ravine and broke his leg. The youngest of the men were charged to bring him back while the hunt continued, so slight was his injury. But the wound festered, and his limbs grew black and numb. A holy woman was called from far away since Marta was dead. She was a drooling and selfish woman who claimed more died here than just a man.

Rabbenu Luria lived for several days, long enough for the peaceful transfer of power to his favorite administrator, Rabbenu Penli. Mesa Le was as kind and motherly as ever. Perhaps she had only done what she was told, but her heart toward me seemed genuine. She assured me that Father would return, but his work detained him a few days. It immediately occurred to me perhaps his work was deemed important not to keep him away, but to keep Kyle Rula absent.

They returned the day Rabbenu Luria died. And with them came Cara, the first Mekucoo assigned to us. Tall and unscarred, young Cara was more a vision than a man. Cara didn't enter the house or discuss with the tribesmen. He remained a sentinel, sometimes within our view, sometimes apparently absent. When I brought his meals, he stared out to the west, far out over the horizon. Privately he didn't acknowledge me as hostess or servant and didn't take the food until I left.

My sisters asked Kyle Le if all Mekucoo looked like Cara. She sadly laughed and shook her head no. She went directly to bed and slept for a full day.

Cara did one thing that said it all. On the day the tribes gathered for the ritual pyre, Kyle Rula was absent. I knew where she must have gone, and everybody asked. I just shrugged from under the veil. Cara was absent as well, and reappeared one hour before Kyle Rula on the day they took their leave to return to meetings in Cylay.

My sisters hugged Father and said goodbye. I joined Kyle Le for a moment. "Did you show the flats to Cara?"

"He didn't present himself. Not even in my line of vision." I waited but she offered nothing more. She was no more than twelve but self-possessed, even cold. "Tell me about the Softcheeks," I asked.

"I see nothing on the women at all," she gently explained. "Just a concave aura with a receptive opening. The men are very difficult to see. They have divided themselves onto three planes. It's said on their world that the mind, the body and the soul operate separately."

"Do you talk with them?" I asked.

"I'm a child and veiled. But they say nothing. The words come out of their mouths and fall to the ground. Two whom I have seen have two faces both talking and their bodies go another way."

"But what causes their spirits to be divided?"

Kyle Rula shrugged. "Their love of things maybe. They notice everything in the room, down to the last detail. Then they insult a man without blinking, through ignorance I think. They pity us. By their standards we are very poor."

"Are we poor?" I asked.

"We have the flats."

I stopped her and quickly asked, "Rabbenu Penli, what do you see?"

"Don't be like Father," she complained.

"I'm sorry," I said and drew away.

She paused, and I felt her quick irritation evaporate. "Father acts on what I say and shares with the tribesmen his interpretation. He doesn't see the truth. He applies what he wants to be there to the images." She drew close to me. "I know you love Father more than anything. They take his heart from him, and it doesn't return. He's not the man you loved as a child. Give your love to Haku."

I treasured Kyle Rula's words and considered them while the

days passed. We visited Mesa Le who quietly stepped into dowerhood. I forgave her without words for her business as Rabbenu's wife, glad we could now know each other simply. She started the pattern of a new gown and requested my help. I was honored for my friendship, I felt, and gladly agreed.

Kaykay Le, wife of Rabbenu Penli and Mesa Le's successor, joined us unceremoniously. Mesa Le showed her the new gown. My place among the women was secure for Father's sake.

Julia Le left her place by my sisters and abruptly joined our circle. "What do you want?" asked Mesa Le in hard tones.

Julia Le's chin was set and her eyes defiant. "I want to sit here."

Kaykay Le was as gracious as Mesa Le had been in her time. "It's hard for her," she murmured. "A big change." She made a place for the young girl.

We leaned in to share the afternoon. Julia Le triumphantly looked back at my sisters, and Terry stuck her tongue out at the look. We chuckled as though the naughty girls meant to entertain. We did not choose to see what would grow.

Father and Kyle Rula returned in four days. There had been an attempt on Father's life. The one who Kyle Rula had feared, named Cyrus, saved Father's life by taking the bullet that was meant for him.

"Cyrus is dead?"

"No. They took him," she said.

"And Cara?"

"Cara waits."

"What will the tribesmen do?"

"Talk is all they know."

Kyle Rula was no longer innocent or eager. "I won't go back with Father. The talk brings nothing."

She became silent and sullen. I went to sit with Father. Slowly as if to confess, he explained what had happened. "The Softcheeks build in Cylay what they call a hotel. Martin and I asked that they use tribesmen for labor at wages. But Softcheeks brought in their own people called conscripts, plus some others as police.

"Cyrus took offense at the garrison. We aren't an occupied people. I didn't see it. I just couldn't see what was wrong with commerce. But we were talking commerce and getting conquest. Cyrus was right the whole time."

He sighed and rubbed his face all over with one hand. "Kyle Rula's a child. She gives only the images. It's not that easy to know what they mean. Plus she doesn't believe we can make changes. She resents our trying. We must try. There is nothing else."

On another day Martin Sumuki visited. He brought Dak, a small and older Mekucoo. They sat with Father, and Dak took a meal with them. I was surprised then and wondered why I had thought all Mekucoo were like the dreamer Cara.

Martin Sumuki asked to talk with Kyle Rula. I knew without looking that Father was deeply wounded. "Karima Le," he called to me. I was glad this one time for the veil that my sisters chafed against. I received Father's instructions without the additional expense of him seeing my face. "Take them," was all he said.

Martin Sumuki, Dak and I walked to the flats and waited. Within twenty minutes Kyle Le joined us under the veil. Martin quickly came to the point. "This is what we suggest. Another your size will stay here. One your size will travel with Len Rabbe Arim. You will come with us without covering as a Putuki child."

Kyle Rula immediately answered. "I will remain on Father's land."

"You don't understand. They're trying to kill you."

"Then I will join my ancestors here."

I sighed deeply and sat down. Who were these Softcheeks who murder children? What had she seen that she was ready to die?

With a soft gurgling and a faint rumble, the flats slowly filled from the mountain thaw. I sat quietly, barely breathing. The sun felt warm against my shoulders. A breeze rustled dry leaves high on the Acacia tree. A huge Murmurey bird left her hidden nest with the labored flapping of wings but no cry of portent.

Kyle Rula bowed to the men who left. For a long time she sat with me in silence. Shadows lengthened. Small animals moved about as though our presence was a natural part of their home. Kyle Le sweetly smiled. "Dolvia embraces you. You are made fertile."

"Come home with me," I said.

"Father's land is my home."

"You have no hearth."

"I have the sunrise over the savannah. I have cold water from the spring. I have the companionship of the butte and the plateau. Stay with me a few days."

"There are guests."

"Terry and Tina can mind them."

"Will we go to the cliff?" I asked.

"Dak watches us."

I sharply looked at her. "How do you know these things?"

Kyle Rula giggled, something I hadn't seen her do for a long time. "If you were Martin Sumuki, what would you do?"

We foraged the land harvesting the few herbs that bloom along the swelling river. We waited out the brief afternoon shower near the high wall of the caldera. We heard the underground rumbling as though Dolvia's stomach was empty. We tried to guess where the geysers would come. All this we did from under the veil and far from Kyle Rula's resting place because she claimed that Dak was on the land.

We laughed and played in the cool evening and watched both moons rise from behind the butte. Kyle Le put a dew-laden branch on the night fire and giggled when sparks flew out. "Like the ancestors of Cyrus."

"What will happen, Kyle Le?"

She poked at the fire. "It's as Dolvia would have it. You will marry and bare sons."

The sound of that pleased me greatly but did not calm my worry. "What will happen with the Softcheeks?"

"No man is greater than Dolvia."

"But what about the tribe in the north who Father told us about?"

She faced me, too calm. "They were weak and without vision. If the Softcheeks hadn't taken their land, they would have ended in another way."

"Are we also weak?"

"The men are afraid," she coldly answered. "Their fear cuts their legs out from under them. Softcheeks understand fear in others. They simply kill the ones who stand up to them."

"Will they kill Cyrus?"

"Dolvia will suffice," she said and threw her poker stick onto the fire. "You have always known that," she added. "You taught me."

But I was not comforted. "What will happen now?"

Kyle Rula glared at my question, tired of being probed for more, then more still. "For a short time we will prosper," she lightly said. "You will welcome many great men into Haku's home. Then for a time you'll live in Somule."

"Why would I leave our land?"

"To save it."

Chapter Thirteen

The fire had burned down when I awoke just before sunrise. The growing daylight extinguished the stars one by one. I stirred and looked over at Kyle Le. Her pallet was empty. I laid back and listened to my own rhythmic breathing as though I drew strength from laying back to back with Dolvia.

Birds were well into their busy day. A desert mouse poked around the small pile of branches we had gathered. The sun broke over the rise, announcing the morning like a chorus of trumpets calling us to our work.

I gathered both pallets then stirred the coals to start a morning fire. I waited for Kyle Le then decided to walk to the spring for water. I saw her standing head to head with Dak. They were below me by the big rock in the flats that was our meeting place when anyone had a message. They talked earnestly for some time, then Dak abruptly turned toward Father's house. Kyle Le came back to the campsite.

"Let's sleep in the cliff tonight," she said simply.

"Do you want Dak to know about the cliff?"

"Dak journeys to Somule where Cyrus is being held."

I reached to extinguish the fire. Kyle Rula gently grabbed my wrist. "There's nobody on the land, just our fear. We will both live for many years."

"And move to Somule," I offered.

"Yes. You will live in Somule."

The butte was always there, visible and present, even demanding in our lives. It cast a shadow over Father's home for more than an hour each day, yet it was a half day's walk at a rapid pace from our campsite on the flats. Kyle Le left me and went to a spring she knew to give reverence.

When I reached the wide and terraced base of the butte, the sun was high but partially obscured by the gathering storm clouds. I nearly jumped out of my skin when a geyser shot up at the plateau's base. On the flats I could feel rumbling that announced the colorful jets of water. At the butte the bedrock absorbed all tremors. My urge was to lay out some cloth and catch the water that makes netta. But the clouds darkened, and I had an hour's climb to complete.

I carefully picked my footing and concentrated on the brush and rocks near where I walked, aware the butte was, first of all, the year-round home of poisonous snakes. I reached the cliff and intently searched until I was satisfied no snakes had come there to pass the time of the rain. I put down our pallets and small herb sack then straightened to view the plateau for the first time since the geyser had startled me.

Rain came suddenly in blowing sheets pelting the wall of the plateau that seemed within arm's reach from where I stood within its equal and companion. Water streamed down the black plateau wall and filled the stream in the wide gorge between them. Two geysers shot up when the cooling rains mixed with the heated underground water. I had seldom been on the land during the rains. I had felt, those few times, that I should be at home to stoke the fire and see to the birds. But the view held my attention even while I wanted to busy myself to make the semblance of a hearth, a place to stow our things so our spirits could gather together.

The comforting weight of the butte over my head muffled the sound of the closest rain. The high and black wall of the plateau, the flat gorge between them that spread out to open savannah in two directions, the rushing stream that flooded the plain—they huddled together, gathered their spirits together as though before a hearth. As eternal companions they weathered all conditions in the time of rain, in the time of abundance and even as a desert. They sat knowing all things, sheltering all who came, forever fruitful.

I heard a step and saw Kyle Le carefully climb the last terrace in the pelting rain. She came in wet and shivering but strangely energetic. I gave her my veil so she could undress. She sat next to me in silence. We stared into the rain as though mesmerized by its unrelenting rhythm.

Kyle Le lightly slumped against me, and I knew she dozed a little. Always wiry and on the move, in repose she felt deflated, unjoined like an armload of dry branches for a desert fire. Such a tiny package for Dolvia to imbue with power and insight. She didn't belong to me or to Father or to the tribesmen whom she served. She was like a flower that grew along the crowded roadway and always stretched to the sun, no matter the dust or trampling of too busy feet.

The rain slowed and stopped. The sun was inches above the horizon when it broke out of the clouds. A steamy fog rose over the stream and obscured the base of the plateau.

I wondered how well Father, Terry and Tina did without me. I wondered when we would return but without the desire to start the journey. This was a quiet and precious time, gathering strength from Dolvia so that fear would not cut my legs out from under me during my time of testing.

Kyle Le stirred. We both stretched and picked up our duties. Kyle Le laid out her clothes in a patch of sunlight that lingered on the cliff. She collected them dry and warm an hour later. All things were provided as though Dolvia loved her especially and anticipated her needs.

Energetic again, she looked at me with promise twinkling in her eyes and signaled that I should follow her. She went to the far end of the cliff where it became a narrow cut in the butte side, then gingerly climbed to a ledge that was already in shadow from the setting sun.

She encouraged me to follow her and led the way to a high jetting boulder, really a butte on its own but dwarfed in company with the other. Behind the boulder and not visible from the savannah or the plateau was a chasm, narrow and treacherous, through which we saw sunlight on the savannah. "How did it happen?" I said.

"It is only on this one side. Don't go in. The snakes have found it."

I stared into the opening, a hundred feet long and not roomy enough for a grown man. It felt strange to stand in the quickly cooling evening and see the sunlit plain. I looked back at my sister and saw again the energetic promise in her eyes. What need did she have for the problems of the tribesmen when the land itself conspired to entertain her?

Later we built fires in a semi-circle and tended them throughout the night, not for warmth but to ward off the gathering denizen who came for the wet season. Kyle Le showed sulfur bombs she had made that lined a high shelf in the cliff wall, stored for use to scatter snakes. Then she displayed perhaps two pounds of netta, an abundant harvest.

"Early tomorrow we'll go back to the flats. There will be news."

"What news? How do you know?" I hurriedly asked.

Kyle Le mischievously smiled. "There's always news."

I thought again to ask what she saw on me. I could not muster the courage and the moment passed. I slept little that night by the crackling fires, but felt rested when we swept the coals past the overhang so the rain would obliterate them.

In the dawn we easily walked down the terraces to the savannah floor. The air was fresh and still cool. When the sun broke over the horizon, we stood by the swollen stream and looked back at the high butte. The butte stood tall and dry as if to ignore us and its nurturing role of yesterday. A flock of birds flew overhead, and animals stirred in the lengthening grass. I looked at Kyle Le's smile and began to giggle.

We quickly walked almost scampering, with our burdens light and our energy high in the first stirrings of cylay. We reached the campsite on the flats well before noon and saw two men impatiently waiting by the rock on the quickly flooding flats. One was Dillan Rabbe Penli, son of Rabbenu. The other was a portly, balding man who we did not know.

Kyle Rula immediately stiffened. "Leave the netta here. Take the men back to Father's house. If Dak is there, ask him to follow the bald man. That man must not be allowed to stay on Father's land."

I gazed at her for a lingering moment, grateful for the days of repose. She met my gaze and guessed. "You are rooted here like the spreading Baobab tree," she pronounced. "We will hide in your shade for many years."

News waited at Father's house. Rabbenu Penli had negotiated a contract with the Company. Tribesmen would quarry limestone for wages on Rabbenu's land. Haku Rabbe Murd and several others had work for the next day.

My sisters had served great men in my absence and proudly chattered unwilling to give the mantel over to me. I joined Haku in the moist evening air, glowing from my adventure, relaxed and unconcerned. We sat for a long time while he quietly talked about his good fortune.

I heard Kyle Rula in the dark. "Haku Rabbe Murd, hiki," she said.

"Hiki Kyle Le," he answered. "Melinga."

"I ask that my sister take this bundle that she harvested earlier. Is Dak in the company?" Haku nodded. "Send Dak to the gorge when it pleases you to join the tribesmen."

"Rabbenu has sought to speak with you," Haku said.

"He wants more than talk. Melinga, Haku."

At first cylay slowly stirs like Kariom in the mud. It springs forth suddenly, as if from nowhere, with an energy not promised in the first stirrings. Many things were decided by the end of the rainy season, not the least of which was for me to face my gripping fear.

I looked up from my work one day during a break in the clouds and saw the butte bathed in shadow and light. I remembered my stay on the cliff, especially how Kyle Le had laid out her clothes like a shed snakeskin in the last sunlight. I didn't miss the cliff, didn't long to return and witness the changes that each season brought. I was at my hearth giving to those whom I loved. The days passed without complaint.

Kyle Le keenly missed her freedom during the long weeks of rain. Whether weaving or stitching or cooking, her products were excellent and regular, but too often marred when her mind drifted at a critical moment. Where I had found her unruly and dreamy in the past, now I felt a tolerant understanding. She felt trapped, drawn into repetitious activity that was comforting but built little beyond the coming season. Some days when I looked out at the butte, I felt her gaze travel past mine as if to transport her to the serene, monumental quiet of the cliff in the tower.

She put me in mind of the bulbous red Pupia cactus flower that blooms for one day then withers, already spoiled by the scavengers who gather to steal its nectar.

Forces rose squabbling and pecking, all waiting for the bud to burst and give itself to the onslaught. Kyle Le appeared stiff and pecked, unwilling to open her shell and offer the vulnerable red and yellow Pupia to the waiting vultures.

And gather they did. Unrelenting, unsympathetic, self-serving, contradictory, peevish and ultimately sullen. Each tribesman pecked in turn to prematurely open and gulp down the unripened and acrid juice.

Kyle Rula tolerated their bickering. She occasionally gave a quiet encouragement that quickly became tribal policy. I knew so little of the affairs of men, I didn't know the messages she gave. Kyle Rula told me much later, she saw only three things during that season.

The first image was from when she had sent Dak away and we camped in the cliff. He took a message that Cyrus would be given a false friend who he must not trust. Dak told Cara who waited by the prison. Cyrus told lies to this false friend who was an inmate. Then Cara watched who reacted, thereby seeking out the power structure among Softcheeks.

The inmate was withdrawn. Cyrus was taken for a second and harrowing torture that put the tribesmen into a fighting temper.

Kyle Rula's second vision was the truth about the bald man, named Kaeuper, who acted as ombudsman for the Company, even married a Putuki woman by whom he had twins. Kyle Rula saw he was a silent assassin who believed he could walk among men with his secret unrevealed.

Kyle Rula asked Dak to follow Kaeuper everywhere which the Mekucoo did for several days. The bald man's activities were so wholesome and regular, they relaxed their guard and forgot Kyle Rula's warning that one with such a heart must not be buried on Dolvia.

The third vision alarmed Kyle Rula and sent a shaft of fear into my heart. She saw an eating disease on the hands of Rabbenu Penli that slowly covered his arms and then spots on his chest with angry, filthy sores.

"How long will he be sick?" I asked.

Kyle Le sadly looked at me. "It's not a disease that can be healed. It has one name, corrupting greed." The vision was so upsetting, we agreed to tell nobody and didn't until Kyle Rula told Cyrus on the day they quarreled.

Events were set into motion by an act from the Softcheeks' camp. Father was killed on the road one night, assassinated by a spear through his back and heart. There was a lot of blood and a surprisingly large hole. His heart was small, shriveled from more than recently emptied chambers. I stood at his funeral pyre, very close to the flame to melt the cold fear that ran through me.

What of Kyle Rula's promises then? What of the time of prosperity and the hope of having Haku's children? How could I stand firm before Rabbenu Penli's greed and the Softcheeks' conquest? Perhaps I would live in Somule as a beggar with three young mouths to feed. I was only a woman. How could Dolvia expect this of me?

I wept before the dying fire for my spent and weary father and for my sacrificed innocence. Who would care for me?

The people stirred. An excited whisper ran through the crowd. Dak walked into our circle and held forward a small package to Kyle Rula who barely looked at it. "Leave it in the flats for the Murmurey bird," she said without meeting his eyes. He stared into the fire unrepentant, then turned on his heel and retraced his steps.

Lam stepped forward in the company and deeply cut his arms and chest with his beltknife. Martin Sumuki stepped forward and took off his business suitcoat. He borrowed Lam's knife and severely slashed himself through his white shirt.

Later Mesa Le walked with me to Father's house. "Dak followed Kaeuper the morning after Len Rabbe Arim's death and caught him in the act of entering Martin Sumuki's bedroom window. Dak cut out the bald man's heart and left the body on the Somule garrison doorstep," she explained.

"I wonder if he acted rightly with such a shocking statement," Mesa Le added.

Cyrus was hung on a tripod in the yard of torture a third time. His tormentors flayed his back. The hated Blackshirt torturer swore to kill Cyrus slowly and dismember him so his spirit couldn't return to the land of his ancestors.

But the delivery of Kaeuper's body set the Softcheeks into motion. Watchful Cara knew where and which ones to take out, thereby ending their conquest.

Eight Softcheeks died that night, six Company men and two Blackshirts. The garrison Blackshirts heard the news before dawn and nervously sat in their barracks. A barrage of heavy arrows carrying burlap sacks filled with poisonous snakes landed on the dormitory's thatched roof. The men ran screaming into the yard which swarmed with snakes that had been painstakingly captured during the last weeks of rain. Legend later grew there was one snake for every blow gleefully delivered to Cyrus' body.

The dormitory was quickly abandoned. Sulfur bombs subdued the snakes. Cara walked into the prison and rescued his friend. Barely conscious, Cyrus made them wait while the Blackshirt torturer was brought forward.

The story lived forever, but I knew not how much of it was true. Told again and again, it became a symbol for both sides and matured into the very spark that brought rebellion.

It was said, and may Dolvia forgive me for repeating it, that Cyrus cut out the Blackshirt's heart, then thrust it into the flame. It cannot be true, but it was said that Cyrus sliced and ate the heart along with all the men who stood with him.

One day during the weeks of Cyrus' recovery, I screwed up my courage and asked Cara if the Softcheeks left Somule because of the snakes. He stared at the butte above the far horizon. "Which Softcheeks remains through the rainy season?" he asked.

Chapter Fourteen

I didn't know the story firsthand, although the tribesmen talked about it for two seasons. I distrusted the words. Seven men stood with Cyrus the day of his release. Seven men knew the truth. Four were Mekucoo and two Putuki, a fact that saved face for Martin Sumuki. The other man was a Cylahi who sold the story for a drink at every stopping place between Somule and Cylay.

Cara and some others brought Cyrus to the flats. With them came Quentin, a jovial Putuki man with the lightest desert brown skin and yellow eyes. Quentin had a reputation throughout the region as a healer. He had been in prison with Cyrus but bore no marks of torture. It was explained, he was told to heal the ailing daughter of a Blackshirt leader and had refused. It was somewhere in the Softcheeks' minds that starvation and isolation, but not torture, would make him cooperate.

I asked if Quentin would heal Cyrus. "Quentin's gift is to heal sickness. He is powerless to heal wounds," Dak explained.

Quentin was twenty and lighthearted. He put no store in his spiritual powers. He frittered away the time taming mongooses, learning to use weapons with Lam and Dak, composing thoughtless and silly ballads while others gathered and cooked and tended to Cyrus. I hated him.

With Father passed away, our future was uncertain. The pension that paid for the land came from Father's service. Kaykay Le assured me the pension was also intended for the family. I was anxious for four orphan girls, the youngest barely twelve, dependent upon the generous hand of a despotic leader whose greed grew daily.

We no longer trusted Rabbenu. We served instead these Mekucoo and Putuki men, albeit from under the veil. My sisters quickly took on the rhythm of their day, ignoring lessons, chores and sewing to scamper over the land like feral children with no future.

They lived on the flats, the four of them. Terry and Tina

went out each day to bathe Cyrus' wounds with water from a spring Quentin had shown them. I asked Kyle Le if she knew about that spring which was on Father's land. She impishly smiled and showed me a baby mongoose Quentin had given her.

The seriousness that had aged Kyle Le vanished just as though she was healed by Quentin. She grew plump and rosy, a bright-eyed twelve-year-old who was loving and eager to please.

The peevishness in Terry that had caused so many disagreeable scenes also became a memory. She willingly served from under the veil. The few hours she spent with me gently passed while she spoke of liberty and personal integrity, manly words from a young mouth. So idealistic, she digested the stoic fanaticism of the Mekucoo and displayed their mannerisms.

Tina spoke only of Cyrus. Enamored as only a fourteen-year-old can be, she lived for his word, his gaze, his warmth. She who had accepted Father as one accepts the house where she was born. She deserted us all, found us wanting in comparison to the heroic and quickly convalescing Mekucoo warrior.

My heart froze in my chest. I remember my resigned sighs followed by a tense and frightened stretch of time from each sigh to each. I took my worries to Haku Rabbe Murd who quietly listened then shrugged. "They're growing out of your arms, that's all."

"But they're children."

"At Terry's age, you ran the household and sat with Rabbenu's wife. Did you see yourself as a child?"

The frightful season that led to Father's death and Cyrus' release had been more telling on me than on the others. I began to store things, to build and hoard against an uncertain future. More than harvest to harvest, I wanted to own fine gowns and jewelry and stores of food and heavy pots and cutlery. I rejoiced when Haku spoke of building another room onto his home and a permanent shelter for the domestic animals. I no longer trusted that Dolvia would suffice.

I stirred the soup and stared into the pot. Cara's shadow darkened our doorstep. Terry pulled on my sleeve, donned her veil and stepped outside.

"Health to the sisters of Arim," Cara said and held his spear high with both hands. "The land of Arim knows abundant harvest. I'm glad to taste that part which you shared with me."

"Your ancestors gain honor by our sure knowledge of the spirit of Cara, the Mekucoo prince," I answered from under the veil. "Do Cyrus and Quentin depart with you?"

"Cyrus' spirit lingers by the spring. Quentin's a bachelor and at home anywhere."

"Melinga, Cara." Terry and I held our hands high with palms up and shoulders and head bowed.

"Hai!" Cara turned on his heel and sauntered off into the

heat. I was deeply saddened by his departure. What mantel covered the four orphans of Arim? I went inside and stirred the soup. I stood by the stove, I don't know how long, when more visitors arrived. Each footfall on the doorstep brought foreboding to my heart.

The wife of Rabbenu, Kaykay Le, visited with her mother-in-law, the dower, and Julia Le. Mesa Le murmured that she missed our chats and had suggested this visit. I set out tea and dried fish. We settled at the table while the afternoon cooled and stretched into evening.

They were full of news from town which set my teeth on edge while I tried to create in my heart a like mood. "Each day brings trainloads of goods," Kaykay Le said. "And more Hardhands, the new settlers. Their families have taken over the garrison building."

"Hardhands started their own bazaar in imported wooden huts. They call them shops and keep them open during the heat of the afternoon. They sell the oddest goods. Large earthen plates shaped and painted like wild birds, pieces of cloth filled with some soft material, called throw pillows. Dishes of all shapes and colors, some clear and with many sharp edges to catch the light."

I imagined sores on Kaykay Le's hands and arms, spreading to her cheeks that were hot with desire for foreign goods. Mesa Le quietly patted her arm. "We occasionally trade in their bazaar. They also allow Putuki but reject Cylahi women."

"Did Cylahi offend them?"

"Hardhands want Cylahi to wear clothes."

We laughed showing our teeth. Proud of their bodies, Cylahi covered themselves only if disease brought scars. Nobody was able to change that.

The women of Rabbenu rose to walk home. While they stood at the doorway, Haku Rabbe Murd arrived with his brother Spindel. They brought small game for our table, an acceptable gift in barter for herbs.

Even as betrothed, Haku hadn't entered our home since Father's death. In the yard he greeted the women of Rabbenu while all but Mesa Le and Kaykay Le were veiled.

Spindel Rabbe Murd stood aside and spoke in low tones with Terry about their day of hunting. Julia Le joined them without invitation.

"Will you be in Somule tomorrow?" she asked.

Spindel stared into her facial panel. "Kaykay Le told us about imported goods," Terry said to cover the moment.

"I don't need your help," Julia Le said in icy tones. "I am of the women of Rabbenu."

"By birth only," Spindel Rabbe Murd said.

"The station is mine."

"Then act accordingly," he answered.

Julia Le joined the women who were ready to leave. Once they were out of sight, we shed our veils and sat with the men of Murd. Haku had more news of the activity in town.

"Many Cylahi have settled in Somule," Haku said. "With discarded packing materials, they built huts west of the railhead. Softcheeks wood gives off a distasteful odor in the afternoon heat.

"Plus the new colonists don't burn animal dung. They chop native wood for their stoves. The whole area around Somule is denuded of trees. Now Hardhands roam the savannah in search of firewood. The Council meets tomorrow to make an ordinance."

"Will the Hardhands stay through the rainy season?" I asked.

"Their servitude is for ten or twelve years in exchange for passage. There is no return."

"How will they live when the Company leaves?"

"The Company won't move. If it did, Hardhands will stay."

"A new tribe."

"A new master," Haku said with bitterness.

"We aren't indebted to them," I reasoned.

"They will find a way. Softcheeks must rule to live."

Early the following day before the dew had burned off, Rabbenu Penli and two advisors visited. "You honor us, Rabbenu," I said from under the veil.

"My wife chatted with you yesterday."

"If you seek the one Cyrus, Katelupe Le will lead you to him."

"We request that Kyle Le lead us."

"Kyle Le forages on the land of Arim."

"Bring her to Cyrus," Rabbenu Penli curtly commanded and left with Terry.

Rabbenu talked with Cyrus and waited long into the day, but Kyle Le didn't come. "She is out on the savannah," Terry offered. Rabbenu was vexed that she didn't arrive on his word. The men of Rabbenu returned to town, late for their meeting and without counsel from a twelve-year-old girl.

Soon after they left, Kyle Le joined Cyrus and Terry near the healing spring. Terry gingerly laid a wet cloth on Cyrus' back. "Rabbenu was here," she said.

"I saw him. I have no words for him."

"You must not ignore your gift," Terry admonished.

"Like Quentin ignores his?"

"Terry's right," Cyrus quietly said. "Rabbenu Penli can take the land from you."

"It's given. For all time," Kyle Le insisted.

"Time is a loop," Cyrus said. "Only your gift covers you and your sisters."

Kyle Le stared at Cyrus cold and hard. He met her stare, the

104

only one among the tribes who didn't wonder what she saw.

"Those who walk in Rabbenu's place are polluted." Kyle Rula petulantly claimed.

"Do others of the Arrivi have the same pollution?" Cyrus offhandedly asked.

"Some in all tribes."

"Then the best we can hope for is balance. That includes you."

"I will remain on the land of Arim."

"You are needed!" Cyrus' anger flashed.

"They change the visions to serve their own purpose," Kyle Rula shouted. "They don't see!"

"Then you must tell them what it means."

"It means nothing. The images have no meaning."

They fell silent. Each stared out at the savannah. Finally Cyrus murmured, "It's not yet your time."

In her turn Kyle Le gently spoke to him. "You will return to Mekucoo land."

"I cannot help in Cylay. I must go home."

Chapter Fifteen

And now I must tell you about our shame, the event that took from us what little mantel we had gathered. On the road between the flats and Somule, without veils Katelupe Le and Kyle Rula gathered herbs. In the early morning they expected to meet nobody and freely talked without thought of propriety. They passed behind the former Rabbenu's home where Julia Le drew water from a spring and called to them. The two shrugged and waited for this one who put on airs.

They left the road and searched through the brush on the land of Murd for the purple-topped cumin that preserved dried fish. They came upon Spindel Rabbe Murd who struggled with a young calf tangled in the brush. He freed the calf, and she bounded happily to her waiting mother in the small herd. Spindel cleaned his beltknife and gathered his pack preparing to move the cattle up to the house.

Terry and Kyle Le quickly donned their veils. Julia Le remembered Spindel's insult from the other day. She approached Spindel without veil while the other two trailed behind. Spindel looked up, then quickly looked away.

"Why do you avert your eyes, Spindel Rabbe Murd?" Julia Le asked. "Do you not know me?"

"You are not properly covered."

"I have been presented to you."

"In the company of family."

"You don't turn from these two who flaunt themselves before you."

"Julia Le!" Terry cried out. "Your veil."

"I'm of the women of Rabbenu."

"You are a virgin on the road in the presence of a man," Spindel corrected her.

Julia Le gave him a hot look, then turned to Terry. "You hate the veil, Katelupe Le. Take yours off. Are you afraid?" Spindel moved away, ignoring them with all his heart. He knew the dare carried no weight if no man was present.

"Wait!" Julia Le called after him. "You know the spirits of the sisters of Arim. Is there something between you that must be kept hidden?"

The dare meant nothing, the day easily forgotten. A childish game among young people who didn't yet know themselves. Except many were on the road that day, including two Hardhand youths who cut wood for barter in town. From under the veil, Terry got her first view of Hardhands, so different in build and aura than Dolviets. She and Kyle Le made the gesture of greeting.

The Hardhand boys looked at each other and shrugged. Still unveiled, Julia Le was in a wrong posture. She stared at my sisters with her chin set in defiance. She stepped surely to the Hardhands and held her hand out in the gesture she had seen in town. They were surprised she used a gesture for men. Each slowly reached to shake her hand.

Terry and Kyle Le stepped closer to Spindel whose hand rested on his beltknife. One Hardhand touched Julia Le's hair that freely streamed down her back. She was surprised at his move and stepped away from him. He grabbed Julia Le's wrist and boldly stared into her face.

Spindel Rabbe Murd did that which was demanded by honor, although it was Julia Le's offense. Spindel rushed the young man and pushed him from Julia Le. Both Hardhand youths quickly drew knives as if glad for a fight. Spindel glanced back at Terry and Kyle Le, that they were safe. He faced the men and held out his hand, wanting to slow down and talk.

The Hardhands rushed him, and they three fell to the ground struggling with knives. Terry threw off her veil and pulled one youth off Spindel while he rolled in the dirt with the other. Julia Le joined Kyle Le and donned her veil.

Kyle Le and Julia Le ran down the road to find help, crying and calling out. When they returned with Haku Rabbe Murd, who had been working down the way, the fight was over. Spindel's blood spilled onto the rich dirt of his own land. One Hardhand was badly cut, the other still struggled with Terry who had kicked his knife away. Haku cuffed him and sent him to his friend. Haku knelt over Spindel just as the light went out of his eyes. Haku gathered his brother's body into his arms and let out one fierce cry of pain.

Startled, the Hardhand youths ran from that place. And that should have been the end of it, an unfortunate fight of honor.

Time is a loop with all things intrinsically tied together. Without covering, our lives were bound up with the intruders. The Hardhand boys' cuts were tended at the Company clinic. Company businessmen visited Rabbenu asking for details of the event. Julia Le lied to her mother and to Rabbenu Penli about what she had seen and done. Rabbenu visited us that same day and got different answers than he had heard from Julia Le.

Spindel Rabbe Murd was dead. We mourned a needless loss. We didn't anticipate Rabbenu's anger. Why must he place blame? Why blame these women who carried no knife? These who were veiled and on private land?

Rabbenu took Kyle Le aside, an innocent bystander, a frightened child after witnessing her first fight. He badgered her with questions, shook her by the shoulders and asked her again. Kyle Le went limp in his strong grasp and said nothing. Rabbenu returned to Haku with his face still red with anger.

"These girls must be disciplined," Rabbenu Penli insisted.

"They did nothing," Haku returned.

"They were alone on the road."

"They were in the company of a daughter of Rabbenu."

"They caused this death."

"They only witnessed it."

Rabbenu Penli preferred Julia Le's story that Terry had started the incident by traveling without her veil. "Katelupe Le was unveiled," Rabbenu accused.

"Only after the fight broke out."

"These questions demand answers. Where are their loyalties?"

"Terry never saw Hardhands before yesterday."

"The Council will meet to decide."

"Decide what?" Haku insisted. "An incident that you would use to control Kyle Rula's visions."

The false pride of Julia Le Luria was a poor reflection of the pride of Rabbenu, a huge and unwieldy thing. Rabbenu Penli must cover Julia Le's guilty act of provocation. But more than that, he must break Kyle Rula's will so she served him above others. This he would never have.

For two days the Council met in Somule. They discussed questions ranging from cut firewood, to prices for goods sold to Hardhands, to work contracts, to city ordinances, to curfew laws. Twice Rabbenu Penli took Kyle Rula aside and talked to her silent and veiled figure. He neither won her confidence nor pried answers from her.

Julia Le's presence was not required at the Council. There was no vote. At the last meeting, Kyle Rula was stood before the assembly and shamed by unveiling and by the mantel of goulep. Blame was attached to her for the death of Spindel Rabbe Murd, the brother of my betrothed. But it had nothing to do with Spindel's death. It was pride that uncovered Kyle Rula, pride and corrupting greed.

Chapter Sixteen

I cannot find words to convey our experience with the deep shame of goulep. Our sister appeared to be staked out in the sun of the dry season, ravaged by scavengers until only her bleached bones laid uncovered.

Nobody came forward to argue the event, to champion Kyle Rula. Nobody went on record with an opposing view. Cyrus was in the north on his own land. Martin Sumuki viewed this as a tribal question. Haku had no standing in the tribe beyond his wealth since the succession of Rabbenu was secure.

Looking back on it now, I remember a quiet, dark hum that was neverending and never productive. A spirit of apathy settled over us, and our lives slipped away into nothingness. So oppressed, we didn't leave the land even to visit Somule and knew nothing of the events there. We weren't concerned with Dolvia, and She wasn't concerned with us. Nothing was said about our absence in tribal events. No hand of apology or forgiveness was offered. The yoke of inertia remained four long years until Quentin returned from the far west with the holy woman Oriika, and a new season of cylay began.

Dillan Rabbe Penli married Julia Le Luria less than a year after Spindel's death. We didn't see the wedding, although Kaykay Le made a special trip to the flats to invite us. Without the inclusion of Kyle Le, my sisters and I felt we could not attend. Even on that day, Kaykay Le had the effrontery to ask for Kyle Rula's vision. What did she see for the house of Rabbenu?

Kyle Rula gave no answer. The answer wasn't what they wanted to hear. She privately told me during a long, deafeningly silent night we shared on the flats that she saw disgrace for the family of Rabbenu. Some day they would beg in the streets of Somule and turn to the Company for the barest sustenance. How could she offer that image on the eve of Julia Le's wedding?

Left to ourselves, we gradually shed the angry open wound of goulep, our lives overlaid with the resilient scar tissue of

109

ostracism and solitude. In truth, it was a delicious season of cylay that we spent on the land. My sisters grew out of their childish bodies and into young womanhood. Far from the punishment we were supposed to feel, we grew in strength and resolve, confident within the purpose Dolvia held for us.

Tina and I sewed new patterns into our gowns and veils. Open, swirling, structured patterns of mauve and gold, the sustaining colors of the savannah. We farmed netta in the month of geysers and gathered the domestic birds before the rain.

There were lessons and songs during the idle months, new tools and weapons to master that we had not considered with men on the land.

Without a competing positive influence to temper their thoughts, my sisters wholly digested the fanatic, mystical vision of the Mekucoo. Terry especially saw us as masters of our land, our bodies, and our fate. She and Kyle Le took up hunting to supplement our diet and were absent from the household even during the first weeks of the rain.

Terry pulled out Father's old clothes and remade them for her trim figure. "For hunting," she claimed, defiant before our questioning faces.

"It's forbidden," I said.

"Who will see?"

"Dolvia."

"I do the work of a man. I can don a veil if someone approaches."

"And if you don't see the approach?" Tina asked.

"I will see it."

Terry and Kyle Le cut their hair, allowed the long braids to heavily drop onto the floor. In another season we may have considered the value of the rich, thick braids in the Somule bazaars. But someone was sure to ask from whose head they were taken.

My sisters combed and tossed their light heads like calves in the morning sun, then trimmed the curling tresses to closely hug their faces. Kyle Le's short hair would become known to all, of course, but Terry's preference remained private under the veil.

One day toward the end of the rain, Terry and Kyle Rula returned from hunting with a string of birds and rodents slung over each shoulder. There was a new look about them, serious and resolute. "What is it?" I asked while they shed their wet men's clothing for domestic gowns.

"Locust," Terry said.

"How many?"

"Swarms throughout the dry season," Kyle Rula said. "Allow the land to go fallow this year. One of us will travel to Somule to buy grain. Soon, before the price shoots up."

"How do you know it hasn't gone up already?" Tina asked.

110

"What does Rabbenu see?" Terry answered without hesitation. I chastised Terry for her need to speak out her contempt. She made a sour face and turned her back to me.

"I'll go," I said. "It's my place."

"No, I'll go," Terry insisted. "I want to see what's new in Somule. Besides, I want to buy more tools."

"Weapons, you mean."

Tina was indifferent to our adventure. "If we don't farm this year, what'll we do?" she abruptly asked. "I know. We can dig a new cellar. Away from the house," she suggested, answering her own question.

"No need," Terry said while she busied herself preparing the fresh game.

"For the provisions," I said.

"Dolvia provides. I found a cave with two entrances."

"How did you find it?" Kyle Rula asked with a quick smile.

"I followed the Ketiwhelp."

We all laughed showing our teeth. Imagine, tracking the Ketiwhelp. Terry shrugged. "It's a young Ketiwhelp, orphaned I think. Perhaps not too sly."

"Sly enough to know the cave," Kyle Rula said.

"Maybe the den where she was whelped."

"And shares with others of its kind," Tina claimed.

"We'll encourage them to find a new home," Terry answered.

I looked at Kyle Rula and shook my head. "Terry stalks the Ketiwhelp. What's next? The Mekucoo spear and shield?"

"I know," Tina suggested from the doorway. "We can build another room. In the front, the whole length of the house and far from the cooking stove. So it's cool in the evening."

"I like it," Kyle Le said.

"When tribesmen visit, we don't need to invite them into our home," Tina added.

So Kyle Le and Tina made adobe in a pit we dug by the fowl hut. We set up long rows of planks and dumped mud into a wooden grid to bake in the sun. We joked about how high the walls must be on our return, then Terry and I set out for Somule.

"You just find a weapon that scares the Ketiwhelp from its den," Tina called after us, her legs covered with mud from the pit.

Except for Kaykay Le's prenuptial visit, we hadn't been in the company of others since the verdict of goulep. With our new gowns and veils, not even Arrivi women would know us straightaway.

We were in no way prepared for the changes in Somule. Shops lined the streets that were lit by gas lamps set on poles ten feet apart. Hardhand women strode down wooden sidewalks just as though their husbands owned land. Brightly painted signs hung over glass windows that displayed goods of every shape and use.

111

Near the Council building was erected an inviting white adobe building with a plain metal sign that read 'Tri-City Bank Corp.' As we passed, a rotund man in a cream-colored linen suit stepped outside to smoke kari root.

"It's Martin Sumuki," I whispered.

"And then some," Terry teased.

We scurried past him to the grain store. Terry lingered by three smithys all manned by Hardhands. I turned the corner, and before I could stop myself, I let out a high squeal. Terry quickly came to my side.

We stared at the two creatures, as tall as the Council building with gangly long legs and two humps on their backs. One creature turned its head on a long curved neck and looked at us.

"My goodness, it's ugly," Terry said.

We bought the needed grain and learned the creatures were called camel. In the seed store tribesmen snickered at our ignorance and our untimely purchase, even though we got the lowest price of the season. We arranged to have the grain delivered near the Ketiwhelp den and counted our journey nearly complete.

Terry went into the first smithy to order the tool she had fashioned. She was turned away like a pesky rodent. She glanced at me where I waited in the shade, then entered the second smithy, only to be quickly turned out again.

Terry joined me with question in her voice. "They open shop and refuse work."

"Perhaps they have enough work."

"One doesn't have the kiln lit."

"One more to try," I encouraged her from under the veil. We hesitantly approached the machinery shop. The painted wooden sign read, "Carl Osborn, Proprietor."

"Yes?" the burly Hardhand said. Terry held out the wooden model she had cut. "Can you make this in iron?"

"Iron would be heavy," Carl said, inspecting the tool. "In steel perhaps."

"Show me steel."

Carl handed her a steel knife, long and sleek with gleaming edges. Terry showed her tanned arm when she brandished the knife. "Yes, in steel," she murmured with pleasure. "How much for this?"

"More than you have," he claimed.

"How much?"

"Eight ounces Cylahi gold."

"In peridot?"

Carl squinted at her. "I would need to see the gem. Is this for your father?"

We stopped short. Terry stepped back a fraction of an inch. "For Haku Rabbe Murd," she lied. "We'll return for these in two

112

weeks."

"With the gem," Carl suspiciously added. We bowed, holding our hands high in the air, and hurried from the shop.

"Don't show your skin," I whispered to Terry.

"I'm not ashamed. They made us what we are."

We stopped short again, both staring at an unbelievable sight. Julia Luria-Penli stood among several Arrivi women wearing a close-fitting beige gown with a high collar and long sleeves. She wore a partial veil made of intricate heavy lace that came to her shoulders only.

"Did Dillan Rabbe Penli die?" I asked.

"She must be sweltering in that. She looks like a Cylahi whore," Terry said.

We couldn't imagine what had possessed her to display herself on the street. We clearly saw the outline of the hemispheres of her backside and the shape of her thighs.

The veiled Arrivi women seemed unconcerned with her grotesque looks. They walked with her to the Tri-City Bank Corp where Julia Le left them, curtly bowed to Martin Sumuki, and entered the building with him.

We turned away and started home, then glimpsed Oriika wearing the patterned skirts from the northern tribes and strange, gleaming jewelry. She easily talked with two Putuki men near the shops. She strutted without veil or escort, not that as holy woman she needed either.

We shook our heads and left, wondering at the many changes in Somule. Before we reached the house, we saw Kyle Le on the land. Terry hurried to her. "You won't believe what we saw in Somule."

"Oriika has returned," Kyle Le claimed.

Terry's countenance fell. "Blazes, I hate that," she said hotly and walked ahead.

Kyle Le called after her. "I'm sorry. I saw Oriika on the savannah." She turned to me. "That's all. Really."

At the evening meal, we shared our stories about the wonders of Somule. When we described the camel, Kyle Rula drew a shape on the table with chalk. "Are camel like that?" she innocently asked.

"Blazes, I hate that," Terry said. "I can tell you nothing."

"I saw the image of camel one night," Kyle Rula softly said. "But I thought I must be going mad. Can a creature be so ugly? Tell Haku, do not buy camel."

"They can go without water," I said in defense. "They come from a desert land."

"Tell him," she soberly encouraged. "Don't allow his cattle near camel, nor their feed nor their feces. The camel with all die." We nodded, such was her leadership in our lives proved one hundredfold.

"Is there talk about the locust?" Tina asked.

"Nothing," Terry said with contempt. "They laughed at us for buying."

"I hope the delivery comes before the locust," Kyle Rula added.

Chapter Seventeen

On another night, there was a step at the door. We quickly donned our veils. Tina went to the entrance. She waited until Kyle Le left the room and Terry and I were seated again.

I cannot explain this clearly, the feeling I had. Our freedom was absolute in our disgrace. We bowed to nobody, were veiled before nobody, took second place to nobody. The simple act of putting on the veil in Father's house was humiliating. My heart drew down in my chest as I knew Terry's heart had from the first day she was required to cover herself.

Oriika stood outside the door. "Health to the sisters of Arim."

"Why do you come?" Tina asked.

"Is it so strange to visit?"

Tina answered in a whisper. "Nobody has come. We are goulep."

"No, my pet," Oriika gently said while she entered. "You serve goulep. One day that will bring you great honor."

She gestured to our veils. "Take those off. You know I don't hold with that."

"We are orphans on the land," I quietly said.

"Rich orphans who don't break ground for crops. Who don't care for camel. Bring out Kyle Le."

"Kyle Le is . . ."

" . . . in the other room," Oriika finished for me.

Kyle Le immediately appeared without a veil. We shed ours, and Oriika didn't raise an eyebrow at the sight of their hair or Terry's manly clothing. Tina served while we communed at the table. "I came to talk about the land," Oriika began.

"Locust will come," Kyle Rula said.

"I know. I mean the land of Arim. I know a way it can become yours. You need to follow my guidance in this matter. This is a political game. Soon the cattle will die."

"It's the camel."

"What do you see?" Oriika asked with new interest.

Kyle Rula shared with Oriika without hesitation. "Something in their stomachs. It comes up with their mouth foam and in the feces."

"Can the cattle be saved?"

"If they have no contact with camel."

"Then it can be averted," Oriika insisted.

"Can be, but won't be." Kyle Rula's slavish resignation remained firmly in place.

"The tribesmen will come to you," Oriika cautioned confidentially.

"They always come," Terry quickly answered.

"You girls have grown mouthy in your solitude," Oriika teased. "Take care. That which is spoken in confidence often finds it way to the light." Terry didn't acknowledge my look of triumph.

Oriika had visited for serious matters, though, and got onto the meat of it. "You will negotiate for the land. Rabbenu Penli must sign the paper before his cattle die."

"But how can I own the land?" Kyle Rula bitterly asked.

"As a man," Oriika offered. "I spoke with Martin. There is a way."

The locust ate away the flowering cumin we used for food preservation. They ate the tender shoots of planted crops. They ate the tall grass the cattle fed on. All that was green or lived by eating green was quickly decimated by the flying plague.

In an act of desperation to save his cattle, Rabbenu Penli bought from the store of grain reserved for the camel. His cattle fed with the camel, an unnatural act that Oriika spoke against.

But the cattle didn't die. Rabbenu's cattle grew sleek and fat while others saw their herds strewn across the savannah, too weak to stand, with ribs showing and mouths foaming with hunger.

Many followed Haku's lead and kept their cattle from the camel's feed. Others couldn't stand to see the cattle suffer and led them to stand with this exceedingly ugly creature at the feeding troughs of Rabbenu.

It was known we hadn't planted in the season of locust. It was known we warned Haku Rabbe Murd to keep his cattle from the camel. It was known Haku's herd was thinned by starvation and locust bite. But the week before Rabbenu's visit, Haku's remaining heifers gave birth to twin calves, every one.

Our new room that Martin Sumuki called verandah was completed when Rabbenu visited. It had walls to Tina's shoulders and a high, thatched roof under which we had mounted six double ceiling paddles worked by a single rope to fan our guests.

Rabbenu came to gloat that goulep's vision was wrong. And to dispel the talk about Haku's good fortune. Rabbenu must act while his hand was strong, appear magnanimous with the orphan women alone on the land.

Without a crop to tend and unable to hunt in the clouds of locust, we sisters of Arim had ample time to care for the farm buildings, repair fences, and trim the walk. Rabbenu made no mention of the improvements when he visited with his seconds, fat men in dark suits who we didn't know. Kyle Le whispered from her hidden place that these two had sat in war council in Cylay in the days when Father traveled for the tribes.

Rabbenu Penli introduced his friends and sat at the table on the verandah. "They say the Kariom will burrow early this year," Rabbenu quietly stated.

"Our Father, Len Rabbe Arim, would know the meaning of that," I said from under the veil. "But we are poor women alone on the land."

"There's one among you who can see."

"Which?"

"Kyle Rabbe Arim."

So the agreement was struck. Stripped of her mantel as a virgin and daughter of Arim, Kyle Rula could do business with Rabbenu and other tribal members as an entity on paper, a presence that carried the rights of a tribesman. For this special privilege, Kyle Rabbe Arim must share her visions with Rabbenu before all others. The papers were signed and the pension that paid the mortgage on the land was secured. Only Rabbenu Penli, Kyle Rula and I knew that an additional amount in Cylahi gold or peridot was to be given as the tithe each month in keeping with the increase of our fortune under Rabbenu's protection.

When all was agreed and Kyle Rula was brought forward to sign, Rabbenu sat back ready to receive his reward. Not asking her, a tribesman, to sit, he said, "What do you see?"

"Your cattle will die," Kyle Rula said without inflection.

"You have said this. What else?"

"The days of locust are nearly past. When they die, people will not be able to find clean water. Tell them, store water now."

Rabbenu spoke in whispers with his guests. "This is enough," he pronounced. They left without further ceremony.

When they were out of sight, Tina asked, "Is it true?"

"The streams will be polluted with the bodies of Rabbenu's cattle." Kyle Rula said. "The flats, my flats, are on high pasture. They are safe."

The camel died first, all eight of them in one week. Their owners gutted them and tried to sell the meat, but word was out through Haku that whomever even handled the meat would surely die, and any whom he touched.

Then Rabbenu Penli's prize bull dropped dead in the middle of his corral. Rabbenu called on several tribesmen to gut and slaughter him, but none entered the enclosure. Finally Rabbenu himself put on gloves and a mask, ran the other cattle into the barn, and cut the eight hundred pound bull's throat so the quickly coagulating blood spilled out in clumps and stained the ground.

Men walked away shaking their heads and listing those who had run their cattle with Rabbenu's cattle, those who would soon be poor. Before the rainy season, the savannah was littered with rotting carcasses. Birds and predators that fed on the remains died in their nests and burrows.

It was as goulep had said. The locust were gone. The cattle died and polluted the streams. There was no fresh water except what could be drawn from deep wells. And from the flats of Arim, of course.

The tribespeople still ostracized goulep, perhaps more so. But the pension paid the bank note. Rabbenu visited to hear goulep's visions. And the people more closely watched the actions of Haku Rabbe Murd, he who was betrothed to goulep's sister.

We knew the family of Rabbenu despised us. They had since Terry and Julia Le had quarreled over the headband of Spindel Rabbe Murd, now six years dead. We knew the family of Rabbenu spread lies and rumors to discredit second sight. But secure on the land and cut off from Somule and the season of cylay there, we put little weight on the presence of the Company, the growing number of Hardhands, or even the erection of another seven story building called hotel.

One day Kyle Le came into the house singing and sashaying about in a clean gown with clean hair and her favorite peridot earbobs.

"Will there be company?" I asked while hunched over my sewing.

"More than company," she shyly said. "There will be a wedding."

A messenger arrived with a small box, a gift from Haku. It was a bracelet of leaves that matched the betrothal necklace.

"I killed and cleaned two birds," Kyle Le innocently said. "Also, there's fresh fruit. Why aren't you changed?"

I just looked at her and smiled. We were no longer children if the youngest turned such a young lady's face to me, even in our troubles. We were grown every one, of an age to marry.

Haku arrived with Oriika and Martin Sumuki as his second. He would have chosen his uncle who worked his land, but Haku wished to honor goulep on the sly by including her favorite among the tribesmen, Martin, who was once worthy of a failed assassin's plot.

They came onto the verandah and sat at the table. Haku intoned that which satisfied ritual, and we removed our veils. Terry served tea and the fruit Kyle Le had prepared. Tina pulled on the long rope that worked the ceiling fans, and we looked around at each other in the breeze.

"Where's Kyle Le?" Oriika asked.

"You know that goulep cannot be here," Tina sadly claimed.

"I have business with Kyle Rabbe Arim," Martin pronounced in a booming voice. Kyle Le immediately appeared carrying a platter laden with steaming boiled fowl, and we sat together this one time for a cheerful repast.

Martin brought a tall bottle made of dark glass and containing a deep red liquid. "It's Softcheeks," he explained. "They call it wine. Makes you silly in the head."

"Will it make my mouth foam?" Tina fearfully asked. We stopped short and looked at Kyle Rula. She blinked with surprise, then laughed, "No, it's fine."

While Tina poured a little for each of us, Kyle Le slyly told Martin, "Terry has tamed the Ketiwhelp."

"No, it's not possible," said Oriika.

"Not tamed exactly," Terry quietly said.

"How did you accomplish that?" Martin asked.

"I knew its den," Terry explained. "I knew it would feed on carrion when the cattle died, so I barricaded the entrances. At first it dug at the barricades and growled at me. Then it pissed all over the grain we stored there. I mean, all over it. I don't know where it got the fresh water for so much piss."

We laughed showing our teeth. A clever revenge.

"But the Ketiwhelp grew hungry," Terry continued. "It doesn't eat grain, you know. Especially piss-soaked grain. When it hears me approach, it comes to the barricade with murder in its eye. I just talk to it and put out food. When the rains come and river water is fresh again, I'll let it out."

"The whelp follows her," Kyle Le insisted. "She's even named it. *Farhew tucahihe*, he climbs to the stars."

"She has a starburst marking on her forehead," Terry explained while staring down her sister. "With white spots on both front legs. Like she paws at the night."

"And it comes to Terry for its meals. It won't hunt," Kyle Le claimed, having fun with news that didn't come from a vision.

"She was orphaned before her mother taught her to hunt," Terry defended.

"Perhaps it's Cylahi," Tina offered. We laughed with our teeth showing again, more from the Softcheeks wine than from Tina's quip about the lazy Ketiwhelp.

"Spindel would be proud of you," Haku gently said.

For a moment we saw the vulnerable heart of Terry as a child, the heart she had denied and worked to erase since the unspeakable events of that day which led to the mantel of goulep for her sister.

Terry asked Haku during this, our prenuptial dinner. "How did you get Rabbenu Penli to agree to officiate at the wedding?"

119

"He wants my bull that sires twins to stand stud to his new herd," Haku said. "I told him my fee. You know Rabbenu. A favor instead of barter is their motto."

"And your new friends will attend the wedding, Martin?" Kyle Rula asked simply.

Martin pointedly turned to her, "How is it you see me so clearly?"

"One need only look," she defended.

"Can you see Oriika the same?"

"There's so much of her," Kyle Le grinned. "It's hard to take her in at a glance." Oriika shook a fat and bejeweled finger at goulep while we hid our smiles.

"You have new friends?" Haku asked Martin.

"Softcheeks," Martin said. "Ricardo Menenous and one who I will meet soon, Brian Miller."

"They bring with them a large frame that has many fingers," Kyle Rula slyly said, having a game of it.

"It's called a loom."

"Loom," she repeated after him.

Haku chuckled. "Tell me, Kyle Rula, have you shared this image with Rabbenu?"

"The mortgage for this season is already paid."

Part Three

Chapter Eighteen

It was common practice in the past for the Company to sterilize indentured female colonists. Policy stated they had mining enterprises on planets where the atmosphere or labor conditions were hostile to children. They couldn't be responsible for families who were left behind when contracts ended and supply lines were severed. Of course, if no births occurred in a colony, then property rights were managed by the Company until indentured terms ended. Without land or groundborn offspring, free men and women couldn't resist Company relocation assignments.

My name is Heather Phelan Osborn, and I'm offworld born. I'm 23, married and with two living children, a boy and a girl. My husband and I signed away futures on our work for 15 years each in exchange for passage to Dolvia.

Why here, you ask? Why anywhere? We heard about the colonized planet rich with animal life, farming and minerals. And sparsely populated. It sounded like paradise to colonists and freighter conscripts without a single handful of dirt to own.

When we arrived on Dolvia I was 19, in love with my husband but unwilling to raise children on the freighter. The shuttle landed, and we disembarked onto solid ground. Well, I have no words for that day.

Sunlight was free. The air was free. A hot breeze kicked gritty dust into our faces. I stretched out my arms away from my body, turning in all directions, and did not touch another person. I ran in a straight line until I was out of breath and didn't slow or turn. We never knew such privileges.

From that first day when I breathed fresh air, when I saw the horizon through the shimmering heat, when I laughed openly and people didn't stare as though I had violated their privacy—I sent down roots here. My roots were deep and broad, seeking the nutrient rich old water that gave abundant life. My roots supported a firm base and spreading full limbs to nurture my groundborn children. Whatever the cost, whatever was asked of me—these I did without complaint. I wasn't moving. I was not leaving.

Carl's trade was building machines, and we disembarked with his tools and single destination license for importing parts and raw material. The Blackshirts led by Captain Ellis closely assessed the monthly tariff we paid plus the added 'living fee,' but we got by. We were assigned the end apartment of a long dormitory in the former garrison barracks until our indentureships ended. It was a wood frame, two room, dirt floor home with a tile roof and simple fireplace for cooking.

Carl inspected the door that could be locked from the inside. He made me wait in the yard for a moment while he tried the key from both sides. Then we entered the dusty room and secured the deadbolt. What a feeling of privacy to lock out the universe.

As much as we counted our blessings, we knew it could end within a few hours. We could be killed or evacuated, our groundborn children sent offworld as conscripts. Life was but a breath.

When colonists opened businesses in the open native bazaar on tables or stacked boxes to trade with each other, I wanted to pursue my longheld desire for an enterprise of my own. I didn't see how to compete with colonists who brought household staples and farm tools to trade. But I noticed early on that colonists excluded or cheated tribespeople who came to barter. Without a fair rate of exchange, both sides traded on perceived value, a treacherous method.

That was my opening. Near the arched gate of the garrison's high wall, I bartered with Cylahi women for gold. Soon I traded Dolviet goods door-to-door with the colonists who shunned the tribeswomen and openly insulted the men in the common bazaar. I shrugged when colonists asked how I could bring myself to address and touch tribeswomen in barter. They spoke out their prejudice while they feasted on Dolviet-grown vegetables seasoned with native herbs. The colonists' bigotry doubled the price they paid for simple toiletries and staples.

When Carl and I saw a market develop on the transport, on Cicero and later throughout Westend for Cylahi gold jewelry, even the cheapest and least skillful pieces, our bartering abilities increased tenfold on and offworld. Within a few years we bought our indenture papers and became free. Plus Carl was colony spokesperson. Not because he led the Hardhands or was adamant about their complaints. Carl's trade had no need of the Company. He was seen as independent, an impartial businessman.

By the time Carline was born, I had my shop on the main street complete with glass windows, an imported hardwood floor and secondhand showcases. These long, glassfront cases filled with imported china and glassware were my prize possessions. To own so much, to trade freely, to talk openly—these values Carl and I highly prized.

Plus I liked the tribeswomen, or some of them at least. The Cylahi were curious and easily frightened, but grateful for a kind word. Putuki women were servants at heart, broad stanced with rich black skin. Arrivi women were hard to know, hidden under veils and traveling in large groups. One family, the women of the leader Rabbenu Penli, traveled without veils displaying their long, coiled hair and peridot earbobs. They had an improprietous taste for imported luxury items of every description.

Julia Luria-Penli shopped every week but made purchases only when other fully veiled women of her tribe were in my store. She was haughty and small-hearted but innocent of true evil. She chatted with me as an equal. And she paid with Company script. I had no quarrel with her.

I ruminated on these things while I sent my son off to the colony school and carried my infant daughter through the winding bazaar to open my shop. I unlocked the front door and looked out at the day, four years and two living children since our arrival. Behind the counter, I settled Carline into the crib my husband had built. I felt the bright morning sunlight stream into my little shop covering the floor and display cases. I treasured the moving geometric shapes of shadow and light.

Our involvement with politics in Somule had begun slowly. Late one evening I saw them talking in the dusk, Carl with the electricians Hank and Jim. Carl's hands were jammed into his pockets and his back was arched. He tilted his head to the right and downcast, the age-old gesture of resistance on freighters. Company policy met the same response on Dolvia, not an attribute of a closed environment.

Hank made the pitch. Jim stood silent and lethal with a friendly smile frozen on his face. I saw the blades of long sabers swing out from their bodies and repeatedly pierce Carl's side. I blinked and looked again. But they finished their talk and shook hands. Jim and Hank strode away with their long steps in sync.

The vision of the long sabers troubled me, but I didn't share it with Carl who came in, the weight of the world on his shoulders, and sat on the floor. Gravity seemed to pound him into the earth. He was the same texture as the dirt floor he so prized.

I remember it clearly. My hair was just at shoulder length, still tightly bound under a headscarf. Joey was in diapers. We didn't have Carline yet. Carl's wide shoulders and strong arms curled in a deep circle while he hunched with Joey in his lap, inspecting a toy and tickling his son. I heated dinner and softly called his name. I took Joey from his arms when he came to the table.

But Carl stopped short. He lightly touched my cheek with

the back of his hand, then reached with both hands and pulled the scarf from my head. He ran his fingers through my red hair, gently encouraging it to hang close to my cheeks.

"Wear it down."

"I will, in our home."

"All the time. You have no reason to hide."

"What happened, Carl?"

Carl sighed and sat at the head of the table. "The Company raised the import tariff for merchants. They won't accept their own script, only native minerals."

"But the Company controls the script's value."

"And they devalued it," he explained. "Shops will close. Goods will remain on shipping platforms. Eventually, colonists will go onto the next station."

"Without their businesses?"

"As conscripts." Carl poked at his food with a fork. I sat next to him with Joey on my lap. Conscript was an awesome word for us. It meant one had nothing, no defense against the Company.

"Us too?" I asked.

"They just now invited me to stay," he sadly said. "Hank Kempler said I could continue to pay with script."

"In exchange for what service?"

"Hank encouraged me to buy the import licenses and supply contracts."

"From colonists who have no gold?"

Carl nodded and pushed away his plate. The opportunity was so valuable. But it was a Company offer. Next week they could demand the same from us or start some blackmail. "Tomorrow we'll meet with Martin Sumuki, the Putuki man at Tri-City," Carl said. "He knows some tribal people who may have an exchange rate for the script."

"I'll close shop and come over to the workroom," I said. "Greet your customers if someone needs to pick up on order."

Carl put his hand on mine. "Tomorrow there will be no retail. You'll come with me. And no headscarf. I want them to see the beauty of my wife."

"Who will be there?"

"The holy woman Oriika, Martin, Brian Miller who operates Brittany Mill, and some Mekucoo."

"Mekucoo? What do they have to do with us?"

"Dolviets listen to them in everything. We tend to think of the tribes as separate, but Martin says differently. You must be there. It's an insult if you don't attend, like I have no trust to show my family."

"You'll do just fine," I gently said.

"We will. We're a team now."

"And the colonists?"

"Some will leave. They have already decided."

Chapter Nineteen

I could see why they called him Gaucho. Brian Miller
dressed in millmade linen with a Mekucoo knife at his waist. It
was said he walked crosscountry without discomfort, even visited
Arrivi homes. But beyond the hearsay Brian Miller had a
Mekucoo escort. Two small, dry men in loincloths and sandals,
both with disfiguring scars and carrying spears and shields,
followed him everywhere. Neither servants nor companions, they
were often out of sight, way up the street. But you only saw
them when Gaucho was there, or was about to arrive.

For his part Brian spoke to them with command and only
concerning tribal questions. One felt they were not in service at
his request but assigned to him. He had no defense against the
honor of it.

The tribespeople lived for honor and debt. Their system of
relative debt was the mechanism that Carl hoped would give
colonists enough headroom to save their fortunes, or at least the
cost of passage.

I wore a scarf over my hair until we entered the Tri-City
Bank Corp. In addition to Gaucho and the holy woman, I saw
Putuki, Cylahi but no Arrivi women there. Carl encouraged me
to remove the scarf in the public room where a few tribespeople
made deposits. When I pulled it off, we heard excited whispers
and clucking. Martin uneasily looked around then invited us into
his office. Carl and I were first, being supplicants in this
transaction, and sat at the far right.

"I thought this was scheduled for outside," I whispered.

"The invitation list changed."

Brian and the holy woman sat at the far left also facing
Martin's desk. Each nodded to us then stared straight ahead.

We waited maybe ten minutes. I was charmed by Martin's
office which was native adobe and local wood painted gray and
apricot. Light streamed in the south window that looked out on
the street of shops. The desk lamp that illuminated his work was
turned off, unable to compete with the strong afternoon light. A

breakfront cabinet housed books and some collectibles. The dial of a dehumidifier was set but turned off in the dry season.

Martin came in with two others, one who I knew. Julia Luria-Penli stared at me then nodded while the men greeted each other. I realized my hair was a shock to everybody. Julia Le wore an imported long gown that hugged her form and was caught up by a wide belt. She carried as a stole the patterned body veil that other Arrivi women used to cover themselves in the presence of men.

The Arrivi man with her was introduced as Dillan Rabbe Penli. The tension in the room increased palpably when the couple sat in cane chairs between the two groups and slightly behind. Martin sat behind his desk.

"We have a common problem," Martin began. "The Company has devalued its script for commerce on Dolvia. The Tri-City Bank Corp is underwritten by mineral wealth and by the government in Cylay. Our immediate concern is the import/export contracts. By dropping the bottom out of their system, the Company more than doubled the cost of using these contracts. Their intent, of course, is to consolidate their position in traffic by buying up the contracts that default. We're here today to discuss ways to share the weight of the extra cost and avoid defaults.

"Present today are Brian Miller of the Brittany Mill," he continued. "And Oriika, the holy woman, who represents tribal interest and is empowered to take a message to some who may be able to help. Also present are Carl Osborn and his lovely, redheaded wife, Heather. They represent the concerns of the colonists who hold the contracts in question.

"Dillan Rabbe Penli represents some private interests who are willing to discuss equitable loans for the colonists who want to stay," Martin added.

"Private interests?" Brian interrupted. "Company interests, you mean. Why did you tell him about this meeting?"

"I thought you did."

Brian stood and faced Dillan Rabbe Penli. "Go back to the Company, messenger boy, and tell them no deal."

Dillan jumped up. "The Company owns you and Ricardo."

"Now, gentlemen," Martin started. "Please. Let's talk sensibly."

Dillan stepped toward Martin. "And what about Tri-City? You're their puppet!"

"Listen, asswipe," Brian shouted. "I'd rather enter a snakepit with Martin than walk across the street with you. We'll discuss nothing in your presence."

"Get in line, Company man," Dillan shot back. "Prosper when we prosper."

"Company prosperity?"

126

"What do you think you have now?"

"I'm not in any group that includes you."

Oriika leaned forward and stared past the posturing men. Her calm and deep eyes sought my face. I leaned forward and looked past my husband and past the loud-speaking men to meet her gaze. Oriika smiled, so I smiled and nodded as though I too had a secret. I had no understanding on this my first day in the arena.

Late that night a knock came at our door. Two Mekucoo roughly grabbed Carl by the arms. An Arrivi body veil was thrown over me and I was thrust with Joey into the back of a cattle-driven cart that lumbered out onto the savannah. I remember thinking I was glad for just one living child in such a frightful time.

We were pushed into a small hut that was obscured by an outcropping of rocks and brush. We heard the cart pull away. We huddled together and held our breath until a signal came to our kidnappers. The warriors relaxed and lit a small lamp on the table. One of them tugged on the body veil. I looked at Carl and let them take the veil. I quieted my son and waited while our eyes grew accustomed to the dim light.

There were three of them, two Mekucoo and Oriika, the holy woman. "We apologize for your discomfort," Oriika said. "You will be returned to your home before first light."

The Mekucoo were unknown to us, younger and unscarred. Carl stood and extended his hand to them in the gesture he had seen Gaucho and Martin Sumuki use with equals. There was humor in their eyes when they each shook his hand. Carl nodded to Oriika. "I assume this is about the contracts."

With the rustle of skirts and a muted clatter of jewelry, Oriika came into the light. Carl met her gaze with a long stare. "Do you have something to drink for my family?" he asked.

He put the Mekucoo in an awkward position. Because of her status, Oriika did not serve. Yet native protocol demanded hospitality be extended to us because of our rough handling and sudden station as guests. Carl encouraged me to come forward to the table. Mekucoo warriors must serve a Hardhand woman and child.

One warrior flung an animal skin full of water onto the table. To disarm the moment Oriika sat in one of the two chairs, took a small cup from the deep pockets of her full skirt and served herself. Then she poured water into the cup and extended it to the empty seat. Carl guided me to sit. I held the cup to Joey's lips then lightly drank from it.

Oriika nodded in her ceremonial way. "If we may speak freely."

Carl nodded back. Oriika blatantly looked into my face, a rude gesture called evil eye in freightate. "Why did you choose today to show your hair?"

"I don't know what you mean."

"Your hair. Nobody saw it before today."

Carl put his hand lightly on my shoulder. I smiled at the rude woman. "I am offworld born," I explained. "Company policy on freighters required that we shave our heads, everyone but midshippers and the crew. They claimed it was for hygienic reasons, but we knew it was to control us.

"My mother told stories of the place where she was born," I continued, "Where the water was sweet with a bright mist in the morning. She said she and her sisters had worn their hair loose and hanging down their backs. When we disembarked, my husband and I decided I should let my hair grow."

"But you covered it," Oriika said.

"At first my hair stuck out, then the color embarrassed me. My mother's hair was more brown than orange."

"Then you uncovered it for the meeting," she probed.

I looked at Carl's face that was full of mistrust. Personal questions were uncommon in freightate. "We were chosen to speak for the others," he said. "We have nothing to hide."

"You were both chosen?"

"I was chosen," my husband said.

"You have no contract with the Company?"

"I pay a tariff for parts I cannot manufacture and for raw materials."

Oriika turned back to me. "And your mother?"

I blinked at her twice, wondering why she didn't engage the business discussion. "Uh, she died before her indentureship ended," I said with question in my voice. "According to policy, I served the two extra years."

"How much longer must you serve?"

"We bought our freedom with the wages of our own endeavors," Carl proudly claimed.

"You mean with Cylahi gold," she corrected.

"It was open commerce," he defended.

"And your first child?"

"Joey is also free."

"I mean the girl," Oriika lightly said.

I audibly drew in my breath. I felt Carl stiffen behind me. Tears stood in my eyes and I looked away. Such probing was unbearable. On the transport without physical privacy, all held their personal history in secret.

"Nu delaya," Oriika said. The two Mekucoo turned on their heels and left the hut.

"Nobody knows about that," Carl said hotly when we were alone with her.

"I apologize for the question," Oriika said. "It's not difficult to see the places of children on a woman's body."

"It's alright, Carl," I said. "We knew there would be a test."

If my roots were to spread on Dolvia, I needed to shed freightate attitudes. I blatantly stared into her face as she had stared into mine. "We only want groundborn children. But I was careless. I terminated my pregnancy in the fifth month."

Oriika's implacable gaze wandered to Carl's face. "These contracts have value?"

"They give the right to buy for resale and communicate offworld," he tensely explained.

"If one has a license, what's the value of owning a second one?"

"They can be leased for a percent of the profits."

"So you will buy them?" Oriika's business questions were asked in the same tone as her personal questions.

"I wish I could," Carl said. "Most will go to the Company."

"But you can pay with script."

Carl reacted before he could stop himself. Oriika was most knowledgeable. "For today perhaps," he admitted.

Oriika smiled. "The Company will accept Cylahi gold without conditions attached."

"We have none."

"You bartered in gold before."

"It bought our freedom. We have none now."

"There is room here for a fair trade." Oriika smiled broadly and spread her fingers in an expansive gesture across the table top. She went to the door and invited the Mekucoo to witness the fair trade of gold for contract partnership. Carl would buy the departing colonists' agreement papers, at a generous price in gold, and lease them to tribespeople and new colonists in his name. He would share the profits with Oriika and show her a regular accounting. As part of the trade, Carl agreed to take as apprentices three young men of Oriika's choosing. Oriika retained all rights of expansion for imports and exports, plus all rights of communications. When the deal was struck, Carl asked, "What do I tell Martin Sumuki?"

"I will talk with him," Oriika said guardedly.

"You could have gotten the contracts from the colonists for a quarter as much," Carl added.

"We have no love of the Company. We too have seen their . . . policies, as you call them. They must believe that it's you who buys. You only."

"Why did you choose us?" I quickly asked.

Oriika's eyebrows went up. She seemed entertained by the question. "There's an image in our prophecy of fire over old water, the deep water that we receive from springs and geysers. Old water won't sustain fire, even with chemicals poured onto it. We didn't know until today the meaning of this image."

"What does it mean?" Carl asked.

"It's a vision of your wife."

That meeting with Oriika was three years ago. Carl bought the contracts for a generous price in gold. Colonists profusely thanked him and went onto the next station with dignity. Many said they would never forget him and told the story of his generosity everywhere. Carl was mostly embarrassed since it wasn't his money or his idea. But he was true to the bargain and told no tales.

When the tribesmen joined my husband at his workshop, questions ceased about the source of Carl's new wealth. People grudgingly gave him credit for blocking the Company and, I believe, privately admired his enterprising spirit. The three young men who Oriika sent, one Putuki and two Cylahi, proved to be industrious and intelligent. They struggled at first with the language barrier. Carl and I practiced and taught my son their dialects along with freightate.

But the Hardhand women shunned us at church and looked the other way when schoolchildren persecuted Joey. Only through the women's taste for the goods of my shop did their stiff judgment soften.

After Carline was born, I imported many goods and appliances. Hardhand women and tribeswomen mingled at my shop and chattered about the strange housewares. I got to know Dolviets better than Hardhands and, quite frankly, like them more. I bartered with visiting tribeswomen who came in groups and touched my hair to see if the red color gave off the heat of a campfire. They jerked away and giggled, but my hair was better than advertisement.

Our lives have been peppered these last few years by late night visits from Oriika, sometimes with and sometimes without her Mekucoo escort. She had precious gems to export and orders for farm implements. We were glad for the gems because the package was small and passed through the tariff offices without complaint. We justified the cost of imported steel but ordered some farm equipment in parts to be assembled at tracksend to confound the watchful Blackshirts.

I learned from Oriika and served her in Arrivi style in my home. An astute businesswoman, she used every minute of EAM time available to her and searched many offworld channels seeking possible markets. Occasionally I sat next to her at the EAM-12 set up in my kitchen. I learned the codes and vocabulary, but just didn't have her need to open up every file on every menu. When I looked over the EAM bills, I saw the path of her curiosity. She viewed this privilege as a backdoor to the Company.

Oriika was not communicative about the customs of the tribes except to ask about our different ways and to speak of certain things that were seen. She spoke of prophecy but her actions pointed to guile. I knew her by her actions. She had treated me as an equal that first day at Tri-City Bank Corp because I displayed that which had been covered. With other tribespeople I was honored for more personal power than my station demanded.

Oriika never entered my shop. Nor Gaucho or Martin Sumuki or his family. We saw the Mekucoo at our home on delivery dates when Oriika's imported materials were quietly carried away into the night.

A couple times while I worked late at the shop, I thought I saw a shadow at the window. But when I peered out into the night, I could discern nothing. Once when I opened the shop's backdoor to throw out some trash, I saw in the narrow shaft of light a reflective glint, perhaps against a Mekucoo spear.

We knew many stories about native myths and their revered ancestors. But we didn't know what to believe of the hearsay. Certainly we put no weight on the story of the Mekucoo warrior who ate the beating heart of his enemy. Or the tale about the ghost of one Spindel who wandered the savannah and became a Ketiwhelp at any approach. We were intrigued by the story about three virgin sisters who lived on the flats of Arim and served a goulep with second sight. I wondered which visions that Oriika followed were her own and which were goulep.

One day two Hardhand women ran into my shop clamoring about some tribeswomen on the street. We went to the store window and saw three richly veiled Arrivi women who peered into the shop windows. "There was another with them," a Hardhand woman quickly explained. "A young woman with short hair, lots of jewelry and no veil. The tribeswomen started clucking and pulled their children away. But she's gone now."

We stepped back when the three veiled women approached and studied the goods displayed in my window. The Hardhand women scurried out of my shop before these three approached the door. I waited alone when the sisters of Arim entered wearing their sky-blue body veils. They nodded in my direction and slowly circled the room, staring through the facial panels of their veils, but touched nothing. They approached where I stood behind the counter rocking Carline in her crib.

"Melinga, ladies," I greeted them. They stopped short. One of them took two steps toward the door. The tallest one steadied her and turned to me. "Melinga, Heather Osborn."

"Allow me to show you something you may like," I ventured and reached into the case for a blown glass curio. They backed away in panic.

"No, wait," I said. I put down the piece and came around the counter, but they were already out the door. "Wait! Stop," I called after them. One looked back through her facial panel while they scurried away in a tight group.

Oriika visited in the night that week, this time accompanied by a veiled Arrivi woman. Oriika waved away refreshment and spoke to Carl. "There's fighting in the north. Resistance to the mining company."

"The men speak of it." Carl answered, uncomfortable discussing business with women.

"We must be careful now," Oriika casually continued. "No more imported equipment. Restrict exports to artifacts and gold."

"What about the new contracts for appliances and some wood?" Carl said.

"These the Company condones. But I cannot visit again."

Oriika and her friend waited. We sat in silence for a long moment, then Carl stood. "I'll just see to the activity at the workshop."

That was his standard offer to oversee the shuttle delivery pick-up. Carl leaned over and lightly kissed me on the lips, as he did whenever he left our home, then grabbed his workpack and walked into the night.

Oriika and her friend visibly relaxed. The veiled Arrivi woman made a slight gesture. Oriika smiled widely. "When he brushes his face against yours, my friend wants to know, what does that mean?"

"You mean the kiss?" I answered in Arrivi using freightate for kiss.

"Why would he do that?"

I was accustomed to Oriika's nosiness. I took Carline onto my lap and kissed the fine hair on her head. "It's a gesture of affection for anyone you love. But mouth to mouth, it's also a gesture of passion between husband and wife."

The two nodded, and I put Carline on the floor with her toys. "I must present you to one who will become a friend and take my place in our business meetings," Oriika said. "This is Katelupe Le of the sisters of Arim."

With eyes averted, the young woman pulled the body veil over her head and gently folded it. Katelupe Le was lovely with short hair that clung to her tawny skin. She glanced at Oriika then lifted forest green eyes over high cheekbones and gently curling lips. "Hiki Heather Osborn. It's an honor to know you."

"Hiki Katelupe Le of Arim," I said in Arrivi. "The honor is mine. I hope we will become friends. Then perhaps you won't run from my shop."

Oriika explained. "The tribeswomen won't buy that which the sisters of Arim have touched. Terry and her sisters protected you from loss."

"Then I thank the sisters of Arim," I said and began tea service in Arrivi style.

"When we bought the contracts," Terry said, "we knew they were monitored through this machine." She touched the EAM.

132

"The sisters of Arim bought the contracts?"

"It's as Dolvia provides," Terry said simply.

"But you cannot handle the goods that you import?"

"We came to the shop more to see you and your daughter than the imports," Terry claimed.

"You mean my hair."

"The spirit in your face."

"I'm not familiar with that term. Are you saying that you see something more."

"We see no more than is there," Terry said with humor.

I drew close to her, a rude gesture the tribeswomen counted as friendly. "What do you see in my face?" I asked.

"What do you see in mine?" she countered.

"It's that simple?"

"*Merco saaba coulinay*," Terry said.

"I don't know these words," I complained.

"They're Mekucoo," Oriika said. "There's no direct translation. An explanation could be that a mystery once revealed appears small."

Chapter Twenty

Terry and I became fast friends. In my kitchen she monitored offworld inventory on the EAM, but without Oriika's aggressive curiosity. She requested the right to place some millmade pants in my shop for commission. "Perhaps Hardhands would appreciate durable clothes," she gently offered.

I purchased some dungarees and an Arrivi tunic for Carl, and ordered similar pieces for Joey and Carline. Before long all the men worked and school children played in clothes that were produced after hours at Brittany Mill.

From our share of the proceeds from the domestic trade in Arrivi linen, we saved enough to purchase a small plot of land for a house and garden. We petitioned the Company for the right to buy a half acre across from the colony civic building.

Then one Sunday afternoon the Hardhand men erected the walls of our makeshift home. Carl was greatly pleased. He promised over and over to make it better, work to add the needed improvements. The jealous-hearted Hardhand women did not applaud or offer hugs, but I didn't care. This was my home. This was mine.

Terry waited behind my shop one afternoon, wrapped in the body veil of another. She handed me a second richly-patterned veil. "Come with me to the mill."

"I have no reason to hide," I said, following the pride of my husband.

"We are watched everywhere. Why show our friends?"

The world was completely different when viewed through the thin facial panel of the long veil. We were as invisible as one got in this life. People passed by without acknowledgment just as though we weren't there. Within my hearing in front of my shop, two Hardhand women talked about me with envious and bitter gestures. We scurried across the street and approached the mill. I stopped in my tracks at the sight of Brian Miller standing in the hot sun with his Mekucoo escort.

I saw that he was a small man, only five-eight, blond and

trim. He had always seemed large to me, multi-sided. Brian looked our way without recognition. But while I watched, the many sides of his being combined into piercing attention. I felt him stare through the facial panel into my eyes and deep inside my soul. I caught my breath and stepped back. I felt Terry's hand placed reassuringly on my shoulder. We entered the mill by the employee side entrance.

"What did you see?" Terry quickly asked.

"I hadn't seen Gaucho for a long time," I rationalized.

"What startled you?"

"It's nothing."

"The visions are important."

"What visions?"

"We share our insights during the season of cylay."

Perhaps the shared privacy of the veils led to Terry's willing intimacy. "My people don't have those spiritual gifts," I said guardedly.

"It's as Dolvia provides," she returned.

Brian's office at the Brittany Mill doubled as his quarters. The crude kitchen, a table with many chairs, a sagging sofa and a bed. These were more than casual familiarity with Dolvia's standard of living. They were all that Brian Miller required.

Surrounded by mismatched straight-backed chairs, the EAM-50 and coolant cover was banked by stacks of files and a small desk where I was sure he sat to pay his bills.

After we shed our veils and looked around, Terry started tea. To my surprise, people gathered there to spend the afternoon. Brian entered with a lovely young woman who I didn't know. She wore an Arrivi gown without a veil. She went to the kitchen area but touched nothing there.

Brian sat at the table and propped up his feet. "It's about time you visited," he claimed.

"I didn't know I was expected," I lamely replied.

To avoid looking at him, I watched the women by the stove. I wondered about the uncovered woman who did no work, then remembered I had arrived under an Arrivi veil. She could be anybody.

"Kyle Rabbe Arim!" Brian curtly said.

"Brian Rabbe Miller!" the young woman called back.

The two women giggled together. Terry brought tea and fish on patties to the table. Terry smiled at some in-joke then turned to me. "You know Brian Rabbe Miller already. May I present to you Kyle Rabbe Arim who owns land and a small interest in Brittany Mill."

"Hiki Kyle Le," I said. "I'm honored to meet you."

The young woman neither spoke nor looked up. "Perhaps you misunderstand," Terry gently said. "This is Kyle Rabbe Arim, a businessman."

I looked at each of their faces. "Kyle Rabbe Arim, melinga," I said, holding one hand high with palm up in the submissive gesture that Arrivi women showed to men.

The young woman nodded to me. "Hiki Heather Osborn with the fiery hair." They giggled again. "Aren't you accustomed to my hair?" I asked, more to be included than from curiosity.

"I hadn't seen it before today," Kyle Le said.

It came to me in a flash. "You're the one with second sight."

"Like you."

"Not that old trick," Brian complained and got up. "Perhaps she'll love atmosphere." He walked to the EAM-50 and sat heavily in a rickety chair.

Without announcement Brian's Mekucoo escort entered and stood by the door. The women became serious, and Kyle Rabbe Arim left the table to stand by the stove. But Terry did not put on her veil.

The warrior named Cyrus entered wearing only a brief loincloth and Mekucoo leggings. I stared at his sheathed beltknife while he walked straight to Brian Miller who stood and shook hands.

"It's good to know your presence again, Cyrus," Brian said. "Would you meet a friend of Terry's?" His use of Katelupe Le's familiar name and the continued lack of veils gave this group an intimate feeling in spite of Kyle Le's introspective move. "This is Heather Osborn whose husband owns the contracts and supply rights for importation."

"Hiki Heather," Cyrus said from where he stood.

I nodded but did not stand or speak. In my world it was improper for me to meet men without my husband present. Cyrus went to Brian's small desk and sat languidly in the chair. I tried to avoid looking at Cyrus, but his many wicked and rippled scars were oddly fascinating in their ugliness.

"It's a trap that Oriika created," Brian began with irritation.

"We have been over this," Kyle Le wearily said. "If we hadn't bought the contracts, the Company would have brought in their own people."

"I didn't see that," Brian said emphasizing the word 'see.'

"Our lives were fine before imports," Cyrus said. "Are their goods so much better?"

"What's wrong with a little commerce?" Kyle Le asked in a strong voice.

"Better to put our energy into crops," Cyrus insisted.

"And we can't have both, I suppose?" Kyle Le shot back.

"Already the children ask for soft bread," Cyrus claimed. "And when it's withdrawn, no native skills to make bread will be survive. Have you forgotten?"

"I have forgotten nothing!" Kyle Le shouted from the stove. "We cannot stop it from coming to us. We have always known that. You would close even the mill."

"The mill's success brings more of them with every shuttle landing."

"Must we have this argument every time you two are together?" Brian interrupted while he stared into the EAM-50. "Now? In front of guests?" he added. There was an awkward silence. Each sourly remained in his place.

"You have no idea how lucky your lives are," I spoke into the silence. "To greet the sun each day on your own land that cannot be devalued or separated from you. I've never known a day that didn't depend on mercy from the powers-that-be."

"And we may sacrifice it all to our appetite for Company benefits," Cyrus sourly said.

"I'm not allowed to do both?" Kyle Le said again.

"I'm telling you, the one sacrifices the other," he said.

"There are many sacrifices, some of them fruitful," she shot back.

"Enough!" Brian shouted. "Just get to it. Then go someplace else to fight."

I turned to Brian with question in my eyes. "We want you to visit the transport," he said. His voice was gentle but his look was hooded. "We wouldn't ask except there's a need."

I felt my heart sink to my tailbone. "That's like asking me to visit Hell."

"What is Hell?" Terry asked.

Brian shook his head. "Uh . . . it's like what Cyrus lived through only acted upon your soul instead of your body. In an afterworld."

"You don't know," I said to Brian, trying to overcome my horror.

He looked into my face. "I do know. I'm the one who knows. It's a trap that we created. But you're in it."

"I created nothing," Cyrus said from his seat.

"You most of all," Kyle Le shot back.

"Stop it!" Brian shouted then turned to me. "Please," he gently said. "We want you to speak to someone, that's all. There's a crewmember who shares our interests. Use the pretext of inventory with distant suppliers."

I was close to tears. "Carl is their contact. My husband should go."

"Only you can hide the package," Brian said and looked away.

"Package?"

"It's a sample we want tested," Brian said. "We need you to smuggle it onboard."

"I'm your mule," I guessed. Brian sadly nodded. Terry stared at the floor.

"It makes no difference," Cyrus insisted. "It won't help."

You cannot know the rich feeling of horror I took back to my home. I felt pressed down, like my husband had felt by the demands of Jim and Hank. Carl was greatly angered they took me aside with such a request. "No better than the Company," he muttered.

But my feeling was different than his. I didn't talk about this before. It's difficult for me to share personal history. It's true that I was indentured with Carl when we disembarked. Before that however, my mother and I were conscript, traveling on transports throughout Westend as servants and dock laborers.

I met Carl when he boarded at Stargate Junction. He had just come through the worm hole, armed with his single destination license and his toolbag. When we married, it was said in the labor quarters that I had made a lucky match, since I had no rights to ground duty. It was also whispered that I sold my youth and virginity for a handful of dirt.

I was not from Carl's religious tradition and attended church only to protect my children from the judging colonists. I endeavored to make my husband proud of me, labored for a better life for our children. My status on Dolvia came from my husband's ability to lead. So independent, he didn't align himself with the colonists. He didn't align himself with the tribespeople either. On this matter we quarreled.

Dolviets were concerned with surviving a difficult time, with commerce that benefited the community, with the future of their children. My visit with Terry to Brian Miller's quarters had been staged. They wanted me to embrace their cause, to take their risks. I was asked to run an errand for Cyrus and Kyle Le, with risk to me only, and without the promise of a payoff. But was it so arrogant to ask? Or did they assume we had a common enemy and therefore common goals?

Early one morning Terry entered my shop while I stood in a patch of bright sunlight and savored my tea. "You never tire of that feeling," she said from under the veil. Curiously, after my own experience with the anonymity of the veils, I peered deeply into the facial panel and responded to Terry as though she were dressed the same as me.

"Do you see my enjoyment of sunlight?" I asked, emphasizing the word 'see.'

"Arrivi women were veiled hundreds of years ago so we don't betray our emotions to others," she lightly answered.

"My people believe a man's heart is known through his actions."

"Perhaps a man's heart is. But a woman's heart is more complicated."

I smiled and looked away. "Would you like some tea?"

"You know that I cannot. I came with an invitation," Terry said. "Two days from now Oriika, Kyle Rula and I will journey to the Canyon of Buttes. It would please us if you came along. We'll be gone four days and walk crosscountry. It's not a trip for children."

"Why do you journey there?"

"We glean the savannah for herbs and fruit. But more than that, we give thanks for Dolvia's gifts."

"Any gift in particular?" I asked while I studied my tea, just as though she needed to look into my eyes to know my thoughts.

"I'm not double-talking," Terry said. I looked at her with surprise. I had wondered just that moment about her motive in asking me. I looked down with embarrassment.

"There's no need to be sorry," Terry said, and I felt her smile through the veil. "We ask you to join us because we want you to be our friend, because you have status in a structure that may become adversarial, and because we need help on the transport."

"Thank you for that."

"It was not expensive," she said. "Better to stand in the honor of one's own spirit than to hide. We need to learn your customs to know when it's correct to speak our desires. From you we can learn a great deal. And besides that, I like you." She paused for a moment, then added. "I believe that's all that I feel. At least at this time."

I smiled and felt her hidden smile. "I apologize for my suspicion. I would also like a new friend in Kyle Le. I'll speak with my husband."

"We can supply food and the acclimation pill if needed. And we'll give you something to wear. Bring only that which you can carry without effort. Perhaps something to eat."

"You mean if I won't eat mudfish?"

"We call the mudfish Kariom," she said without anger. "Once he was worshiped as a god because he was the first to arrive from nowhere when the waters came. It doesn't disgust us that he burrows into Dolvia. Rather, he's more favored for Her embrace."

"But the mudfish eats carrion."

"To survive on the savannah, any creature will eat carrion, even you."

"Have you?"

"I am pampered by forces that are allowed."

"I'll eat what's customary."

"We will begin in the night. Be ready."

At the dinner table that night I told Carl about Terry's visit. He sat back and thought about it for a long time. He lit a kari root cigarette. The aromatic smoke filled our new home. It seemed to calm our nerves and help the children drift off to sleep. I joined him at the table after the children were tucked into bed. "Among the Arrivi this invitation is considered a great privilege," I began. "They are offering to show . . ."

"The sisters of Arim are called witches by their own people," Carl impatiently interrupted. "Cyrus and Quentin use Kyle Le's paranormal powers against us."

"Hasn't the presence of the tribesmen in your shop helped business?"

"I provide a needed service, that is all. Where is the need for a trek across the savannah or a return to the transport?"

"Terry said the situation in Somule may become adversarial."

"I don't care what the women say!" he loudly claimed. "I decide what my wife will do."

Joey stirred and I looked over at their bed. Carl closely watched me. "Is it this Brian Miller you want to know?"

"Why do you say that?"

"People are talking," he angrily claimed then paused. "Look, I thought having the shop would satisfy you. I thought being free was enough. But you're never done. Always there's more with you. Pushing, pushing. Without thought that you risk everything. The children, everything. Why bring down Company interest on our heads? What's to be gained?"

"This is our home! We must work to make it better."

"Our lives are as they should be now. Better than conscript."

I drew in my breath. Carl had never spoken that word accusing me. I owed everything to him. He led in our family and our community, not Oriika nor Terry.

"Besides, they don't even care for their own," he insisted. "Cylahi women are dying left and right in that slum by the railhead. No Arrivi has offered to help them. Or their bastards. They won't stand up to the Blackshirts for us."

"Of course you're right," I quietly said.

But that was not the end of it. A few days later Captain Ellis visited Carl's toolmaking shop with two Blackshirt officers. He casually looked around. "You have done well for yourself and your family, Carl Osborn. You bought your papers with Cylahi gold."

"We bought our papers through the labor of our own hands."

"And the labor of these ones, I imagine," Captain Ellis added, indicating the three tribesmen who sat at workbenches in the back. "And now you own land."

"All I have done is lawful," Carl defended.

"Yes. Yes, of course," Captain Ellis said without inflection. "I have a small request. Can you make more of these?"

He showed Carl a pair of handcuffs with wide bracelets and a long chain between them. Carl inspected the cuffs and realized they were fitted for small wrists, a child's or a woman's. "Don't you want them in a larger size?" Carl asked.

"It is of no concern to you." Captain Ellis thinly smiled, staring into Carl's face. "If you can make them just like this, I may request several pair."

"When do you need them?"

"Whenever it's convenient. I'll drop by perhaps next week. Thank you for your time," he said evenly then signaled his officers to leave ahead of him.

Carl went to the shop entrance and watched them walk down the sandy walkway. When Captain Ellis passed the native vegetable stands, people stopped their work and waited for the Blackshirts to move on.

Carl looked across the way where Cyrus stood in a tight group with Cara and Dak. He had not seen the Mekucoo together on the street before. Cyrus nodded to Carl and left by another direction. Cara and Dak walked past Carl in the same direction as the Blackshirt officers.

That night Carl instructed me in low tones. "Journey with these tribeswomen. Find out what trouble comes our way."

Chapter Twenty-One

During the first day of our journey to the Canyon of Buttes, I walked beside Oriika on a plodding and straight path across the vast savannah. Long after sunrise Terry and Kyle Le joined us for tea and wafers. Then they took off in different directions with long strides before Oriika had put away the remainder of the repast. "Where do they go?" I asked, jealous of their high spirits in the oppressive heat.

"Terry gathers herbs. Kyle Rula knows a spring where we give thanks and draw water."

"Why is she called by so many names?"

"I suppose she is," Oriika said simply and began her same heavy-footed pace.

I was pleased with the roomy and light Arrivi gown that protected me from the searing sun and trapped my body moisture. I settled into the rhythmic quick gait of this mountainous woman while the savannah opened to me its wide vistas and immediate treasures. The heat of the day embraced us and communed with our silence like a third presence.

My heart soared at the sight of the endless view that stretched to the curvature of Dolvia's side. I understood why they ascribed a personality to Dolvia as though they lived on Her body and partook of Her gifts. When Oriika stopped at a rocky outcropping, I was almost sad that the need to speak focused our spirits in our faces.

Oriika handed me a salted patty from her pack. "You have done well for your first day," she said while she munched.

"Will the others join us here?"

"They are here already."

I looked around, expecting to see the sisters of Arim walk toward us. I looked back at Oriika. "Dolvia's embrace covers all who are on the savannah," she said without returning my look. "That they are out of your view means little."

I became lightheaded as though my spirit rose from my body and hovered high over the savannah. I felt the oppressive heat lift and looked around with new eyes. My world was more than my perception. More than my concerns. I existed for this moment on these rocks, but I was embraced by a much larger reality. "Is there a spring nearby?" I asked.

"I have water here," Oriika said and reached into her pack.

"No, I mean, I thought I smelled a fresh scent like a body of water."

Oriika said nothing, only continued to munch her wafer. I climbed the few rocks there. I stood up after the brief ascent and was greeted by the hot slap of a desert breeze. My loose gown billowed, and I stretched out my arms to feel the refreshing air. I was lightheaded again as though my spirit hovered way above me like a kite. I suddenly grew afraid I would stumble. I sat heavily on the jagged rock. But the expansive feeling continued while I looked around at the endless sky.

In my mind I walked many miles on the savannah and viewed many open vistas. I knew it was impossible to remember these wide and inspiring views. I had never been on the terrain before. But images crowded into my mind of a quick turn around a high butte or a long vantage point from a plateau.

Perhaps all who journey onto the savannah have unreal sensations of communion with the heat and the sky. More than feeling small in the presence of a greater world, I felt acknowledged just as though a place was prepared for me. I gave myself over to the parade of images, then panicked when I saw Oriika resolutely striding away from our resting place.

I scrambled down the rocks and ran to her. "You wouldn't leave me to be lost."

"You are not lost. You are there already."

"I won't survive if I get separated from you," I angrily insisted.

"We are not separated."

"But you walked away from me."

"I walk to join you." Oriika pointed to the hazy blue horizon. "Where Dolvia embraces you." Staring, I could just make out the blue-green foothills that were our destination.

"If you leave me again, I'll walk straight in that direction," I resolutely claimed.

"We are not separated," Oriika repeated as if it were a joke. She continued her heavy-footed stride long into the night.

My silly enjoyment of the savannah vanished with fatigue. By nightfall I didn't look up from the path or capriciously soar over the open expanse. We dragged into the small camp lit by firelight and moonlight. Terry and Kyle Le had constructed a lean-to and opened four pallets near the stunted trees. They stood by the fire and studiously ignored my sour exhaustion when I refused food and conversation.

I wondered if I would make it back to Somule, let alone to

the canyon. I wondered why they had neglected to tell me this would surely happen. I wondered at their motives in dragging me out here. I crawled off to the first pallet and was asleep within a few minutes.

I awoke in the night aware of our campfire and a light breeze in the shrubs. I knew the others were asleep and I didn't move, laying on my back. I listened to the sounds of the night creatures. My feet tingled after the abusive day and I felt the cool earth along my spine. I felt refreshed, as though I gained energy laying back to back with Dolvia.

I heard a twig snap in the shrubs. I intently peered into the moonlit night but could discern nothing. I sighed and restlessly sought comfort on the thin pallet. Finally I snuggled under the covers and glanced again into the few shrubs near our encampment.

I saw the palest green eyes staring back at me. I saw a white starburst pattern in the rich fur around the bulging eyes and covering the long snout, so close I could have touched it. No more than four feet high and weighing less than two hundred pounds, she caused a spasm of fear through my blood.

The Ketiwhelp curled her upper lip to show gleaming fangs and rows of sharp teeth. Her strongly muscled forelegs led to wide and padded feet. She let out a growl, more like a purr. She stood tense and ready, staring into my face.

Yet there was soft question in her eyes as though wondering where the men were and why the chase wasn't engaged. The Ketiwhelp waggled her head like a housepet then slinked into the night without another sound.

So that was the creature of legend. Beautiful and lethal, the young female must have been a solitary night hunter near starvation in the dry season and attracted by our fire. Terry had said that any creature on the desert would eat carrion. I glimpsed a small understanding of the web of life they trusted to sustain them from season to season.

I awoke again to the smell of a crackling fire and brewing tea. Dawn had not yet arrived. The women moved about in their daily chores, high-spirited and smiling as though they prepared for a wedding.

I didn't tell Oriika or the sisters what I had seen during the night. It was my learning tree these few days as a native. Kyle Le smiled at my blurry-eyed reluctance. "We will arrive at Butte Canyon in two hours," she offered to start my day.

I painfully stirred and dreaded putting weight on my swollen feet. I was given a shallow bowl of water to bathe and a fresh gown, followed by tea and a patty with salted fish. The women rolled the pallets into slings where they hid their food and clothes. They dismantled the lean-to and scattered the fire ashes. They stood and stretched, then looked my way.

Of course I was coming with them. I smiled back at their wry humor then stood and stretched as they had. Terry and Kyle Le giggled and headed out of camp.

We approached Butte Canyon from the floor of the savannah. Between two facing plateaus a narrow chasm opened like a puckered mouth with sandstone outcropping and the barest of shrubs. As we drew near, the mouth appeared to open wide as if to invite us. When we entered it was nearly half a mile wide.

One towering butte squarely stood sentinel at the canyon's entrance. We walked for several minutes to get around it, then turned a corner and viewed an awesome array of monoliths of every shape and hue. They stood in groups on the canyon's floor like guests gathered at a wedding. The atmosphere was cool and moist like an empty warehouse closed to the elements of the day.

Only a few hours of direct sunlight reached any one spot on the canyon's floor. A low mist swirled at the base of the buttes in the plateau's shadow. Kyle Le pointed to the east where several smaller red buttes were warmed by the sun. "Those are your friends," she said. "They share your colors and love the morning sun."

I took a few steps to investigate, then turned back to Kyle Le. "Is there a ritual I should perform?" I asked in a whisper.

"Whatever pleases you."

I walked to the red bedrock piles. I looked around for a comfortable perch in the sun, then broke off a small branch from a shrub and cleared a place to sit. I then sat crosslegged facing these three beauties. I stared at them to memorize their shape and character. I realized there was another butte, partly hidden and a much deeper red. I shifted my seating so I could view it among its sisters.

I watched the patterns the sun made while it passed overhead. I wondered what gesture could cement the communion I felt with these ancient and lovely formations. Finally I reached way over to where I had piled debris to clear my seat. I scooped up a handful of dry, red pebbles and held them over my head. I looked up at the red buttes, then slowly poured the pebbles onto my head and shoulders. I grabbed a second handful and a third. The warm, gritty texture of the pebbles against my skin and clothes greatly pleased me and increased my sense of belonging to that place.

On the east side of the canyon, the sun rose above the plateau. I looked at where some buttes were bathed for the first time that day in the warming sunlight. I struggled to get up, painfully aware of my physical weakness, and left to find the women. I wasn't afraid to be alone although I could easily have gotten lost. I felt I was in the company of many others.

I peered around several rocky formations until I saw the women standing at the base of a tall and narrow, grey butte that

145

shot straight up into the sunlight of midday. Kyle Le heard my footsteps and eagerly looked my way. She left the others and came to me with a sly grin. "I will show you a thing."

We walked for a few minutes into the shadow of the plateau. "Do they have names, each one?" I asked.

"Do the minion need names?"

"I heard this canyon was formed when the desert floor sank under geyser activity and the bedrock didn't give way."

"Legend tells us the buttes wait here for End Times when they will march out to vanquish an enemy from far away."

"The Company?" I quickly asked.

"Would you have End Times upon us so quickly?"

We came to a spring bathed in sunlight at the base of the eastern plateau. It bubbled and gurgled, giving forth a clear stream and orange sediment. The ground around it was laden with many pieces of a coarse, natural fiber like burlap. I realized Kyle Le showed me one place where they farmed netta. I knelt to touch the water.

"You will rob the desert of one," Kyle Le said behind me.

"I don't know what that means."

"If you drink the water, it will kill you before the desert can." I quickly pulled away my hand.

"You will not die from skin contact," she added. "Some died from bathing in the springs, but I think they drank some. Here." She handed me a dry piece of the burlap.

"It's filmy."

"Now touch the water."

I scooped a little from the spring. "There's no weight or film. How can that be? How can a thing that comes from water repel water in a different form?"

"Why does the savannah that gives life bring starvation in another season?" she asked. "It's the secret of netta."

"You mean the secret Lucy Kempler seeks?"

"I don't know it to write an equation or to add chemicals in a jar."

I eagerly leaned toward her, feeling itchy on my back and legs. "What is it?"

"It's sunshine," Kyle Rula said with a grin. "To get from old water to netta, you add sunshine. But it only happens before the mountain thaw swells the streams and mixes with the old water."

"Why are you telling me?" I suspiciously asked.

"You aren't curious?"

"Well, yes."

"I saw that," Kyle Le said, flashing her mischievous smile.

We walked back to the others and I asked, "What do you see with second sight?"

"I believe we all see the same things," she said. "But some of us choose not to look. Some of us choose not to be curious.

Some of us choose to apply a previous or personal definition to events. And some are confused."

"There's nothing extra?"

"I don't know. What do you see?"

I felt the itch along my back increase. "I see a young woman who likes to have fun at another's expense."

"And I see a woman who Dolvia blesses."

Chapter Twenty-Two

On the third day of our journey, we climbed the east plateau's steep wall. We reached the ridge and looked east. The savannah stretched out in a gentle slope, hiding the deep treasures of the canyon. Yet when we looked back over the rim, the jutting buttes reached up from the shadows like long fingers ready to pull us to them.

We wore our body veils like turbans with long trains so the sun warmed our faces and bare arms. We skirted the plateau's rim and looked out over the savannah from that high vantage point. Each of us communed with the heat and sky without intruding on the others' privacy. In that monumental dry place, the very air became teacher and taskmaster.

Terry gestured rapidly for us to join her where she waited several paces ahead. We hurried to her and saw two ECCAVs parked on the savannah's floor. Four Company officers struggled with some ungainly equipment.

"What are they doing?" I asked in a whisper.

"They cannot hear us," Terry said simply. "They're surveying."

I knew about surveying from freightate. I had seen the computer's green glowing grid with maps of proposed plantsites. Symbols of buildings were added in different combinations for possible approval. But I hadn't coupled the image of the glowing matrix with men drawing perpendicular lines on the savannah.

In my mind I saw a luminous grid descend and collapse the atmosphere that had so uplifted me the day before. Winds and influences that had soared free and carpricious over the vast expanse seemed trapped, unable to break the matrix surface tension and move even to the next luminous square.

I sat heavily in the dirt. Terry leaned over me and asked, "What do you see?"

I turned up a face of tears and despair. Nobody held title to the desert, so it was undiscovered, naked under the feet of men who had the capital and the matrix to subdue it. "What do you see?" Terry repeated.

"A new force is allowed. The savannah . . . suffocates."

"And Dolvia?"

"Dolvia is tolerant even as we all die."

"These are troubled times," Terry said without expression. "You will know moments when we cannot help you or even reach you." She pressed in. "But your children will have children on Dolvia."

"What to do?" I asked with resignation.

"Only what's in your heart."

I blinked at Terry through my tears. "I'll carry your package to the transport. Any errand that I can accomplish."

"You can accomplish much. You are blessed by Dolvia."

I remembered the ravenous Ketiwhelp and felt my spirit was akin to hers. I grabbed onto the hope of securing a future for my children and steeled myself for a long struggle. We pulled our body veils over our heads and descended to the savannah floor. In the heat of the day we rested several hours, mostly I suspected, because of my exhaustion and my mood.

As the afternoon cooled, Kyle Le came to my side. "I will show you a thing," she said with her special smile, just as though our revelation on the plateau meant nothing. Perhaps she already knew, had seen it all in a flash. Perhaps she had argued with Cyrus and Brian about their response to the grievous truth.

I painfully rose and followed her, wishing only for my dirt floor home and soft bed. She led me to another spring. She knelt and signaled me to join her on the ground. I heavily fell on my bottom with my feet sticking out from under the Arrivi gown, most unladylike.

"Another spring," I wearily said. Kyle Le scooped up a double handful and held it toward my face. I sipped from her cupped hands, then reached into the bubbling water and scooped more to taste the artesian flavor. "What is it?" I asked.

"Softcheeks call it cavern water," Kyle Rula said. "It's found at the base of some plateaus where the springs are cold."

I tried to think how the men of the Company would value this commodity. "So it's not heated by the continental rift, but it's old water. And it's all over the savannah?"

Kyle Rula shook her head. "Very hard to find. Perhaps more than one pool. The springs come mostly below the flats where there's no thermal activity."

"You mean on the land of Arim."

"On my land," she said with childish pride.

"What are its special properties?"

"You must find out."

So that was why Oriika scoured the EAM records, to learn the Company's secrets about Dolvia. I looked at her with level eyes. "They'll take the flats if they can. Bring in their people and machines to rape the land."

A sadness passed over her face. She gently turned to me. "You did well on our journey of reverence. We are glad you joined us."

"I'm sorry for my bad mood today. It just seems more than we can defend against. More than the dry season."

"Brian Rabbe Miller would say more than the rainy season," Kyle Rula smiled, showing her teeth. Then she thought for a moment. "Don't be ashamed of what you see," she added. "Who can stand before the truth?"

We approached Somule with a bone weary shuffle, our body veils gritty and stained from our long trek. Terry nudged me. I looked up, shaking off my glassy-eyed mood. I couldn't allow Hardhands to see the physical toll of my vacation. I adjusted my pack that hid a quantity of netta. I shook the body veil to remove the outer layer of road dust. With square shoulders and arched backs, we strolled down the street of shops.

Nobody noticed the four shadowy figures. If they couldn't see the spirit in our faces, Softcheeks and Hardhands alike tended to discount our presence. I watched them scurry about with their self-important tasks and artificial time frame, like ants unaware of their minuscule place in the world. What Hardhands perceived as slavish resignation among the tribespeople, when viewed from the end of my few days on the savannah, was more like a tolerant humor with those who placed themselves ahead of Dolvia.

We entered Brittany Mill through the employee entrance, looking to all the world to be Oriika and the three sisters of Arim. We went to Brian Miller's quarters and started tea. Terry drew water for washing and Kyle Le sat off to one side, subscribing again to the definition others placed on her. I offered to help, but was encouraged to sit and eat something.

While the pot boiled, Brian entered and focused his piercing glare through my veil and deep into my soul. I felt frozen where I sat, shocked that he saw through the private aura. Surely he knew who was covered and where we had been. But to touch me so deeply was beyond anything I had experienced even with my husband.

Terry held her hand high, palm up. "Hiki Brian Rabbe Miller." I mimicked the gesture and said nothing, hoping he would leave.

"So you want to go bald?" he said into my world.

I pulled the body veil over my head. My face and neck were streaked with desert grit, and my hair was matted and tangled. But the exposure seemed better than his pointed accusation.

He came to me with three long strides and lifted the hem of my Arrivi gown to reveal my swollen and bleeding feet.

"Do you know the infections you could have?" he angrily

150

asked.

"She bathed with water from the healing springs," Kyle Le claimed.

"Perhaps the water heals only Mekucoo," Brian shot back and went to the stove. He filled a large bowl part way with water that boiled on the stove and with fresh water he kept in a gourd. He slung a kitchen towel over his shoulder, then knelt before me and removed my Arrivi sandals.

It felt warm but very wrong that he knelt and washed my feet. "This isn't necessary," I protested and struggled against his firm grasp. He soaked the towel and wrapped it around my ankles. "Do you have tricarbonate?" he angrily asked me.

"Yes, we have some."

"Bathe your feet daily until the cuts heal. There's no telling what entered your body through your feet." I looked away embarrassed and shy. Brian glared at the three women then stomped out, forgetting the errand that had brought him there. Terry and Kyle Le giggled together as they had so many times.

"Why do you laugh?" I asked with a measure of Brian's bad humor.

"In Mekucoo legend," Oriika innocently explained, "sex prepares the woman's body for children, but she's impregnated by the land with the soul of an ancestor."

"He doesn't think I'm pregnant," I insisted.

"Brian Rabbe Miller is Softcheeks. Have Hardhands been so served by them before?"

I just stared at them, then looked at my swollen ankles. "It's funny?" I asked in a different tone.

"It's a tribal gesture," Oriika claimed. "A husband to wife gesture. Like kissing."

Chapter Twenty-Three

That night I quarreled with Carl. But I couldn't share with him about the Ketiwhelp or how the savannah suffocated under the Company matrix. We quarreled all that week about how the garrison Blackshirts viewed my friendship with the sisters of Arim and my request to board the transport.

"Those women are using you. They have no care for our lives!" Carl insisted then added, "How can I face the colonists when you run Oriika's errands that don't serve us one bit?"

"You accepted Oriika's gold for the contracts," I said in defense.

"That doesn't make us her servants. Or anyone's!"

"We could learn about offworld business and increase our buying power. We need an alliance with the Arrivi to survive."

"We used to need only each other."

"It's more than we can stand up to alone."

"Then we should keep our heads down and not get involved."

"I already am involved. And so are you."

The night before my departure, Terry visited with a small package. She looked around the kitchen where we always met. "You don't have to go," was her nod to the tension.

"I said that I would."

"Sew these into the lining of your pack." She poured onto the table a handful of peridot gems along with some kari root stems. "If you carry gold, they will confiscate it in customs. But we have some storage in what they call midship."

"I know the place."

"Try to speak with the students while you're there," she gently instructed. "Look into their situation if you find an opportunity. Use this. The goods will help open doors."

She gave me a small key and gently squeezed my hand when I reached for it. "Time is a loop," she added. "We are often through events before we know their meaning."

With my small pack, I stood unescorted on the train platform wearing a Brittany Mill linen skirt over Arrivi sandals and a lightweight millmade roomy blouse. My husband didn't see me off or allow my children to come. Oriika or the sisters of Arim couldn't be seen with me. Brian must never see me again if I was to preserve peace in my home.

I saw the daughters of Sim Chareon, slight women with alabaster skin and slanted eyes, waiting to board the train. They traveled in rich array with many pieces of luggage. Their butterfly patterned short jackets covered roomy gowns with Chinese symbols weaved into the material, products of Brittany Mill. The oldest one named Kate was engaged to an influential Company officer and wore a padded hat with spiky birds in flight sculpted on the top.

I had served them in my shop where they occasionally browsed, mostly to stave off boredom. Except for infrequent shopping trips to Somule and the capital, their only source of recreation outside the Company compound was occasional joyrides in the ECCAVs with Jim and Hank.

On the train platform four Han-Chinese Blackshirts stood with them. The Blackshirts didn't carry luggage or cater to the women, rather they appeared to be posted at conspicuous stations watching the crowd. Kate and Susan nodded to me then boarded the private car at trainsend.

I sat in the common car with businessmen traveling to the capital and some native women who could afford the fare. I stowed my small pack under my seat and watched the savannah speed by. My view of the sandy roadside and far horizon seemed far removed from my crosscountry adventure a few days before.

Later in the diningcar to my surprise, the daughters of Sim Chareon joined me while their Blackshirt escort stood at the entrances. They sat across from me, their white make-up with rouged cheeks and lips glowing under the strong light. "We already ate," Kate said. "But we saw you board in Somule. We thought you might like to share a drink with us."

The Putuki man who had served my dinner cleared the table without complaint. An Asian woman in a dragon-decorated surcoat poured from their decanter into glasses that were brought from the private car. "I assume you have business in the capital," Susan said off-handedly.

"My name is Heather Osborn," I offered and held out my hand to shake. They glanced at each other, then offered limp hands and murmured their names, Susan and Kate.

"I'm going to the transport on a buying trip," I explained into their haughty curiosity.

"We're going to the transport," Susan said with new interest. "And from there to Cicero. They have the finest casinos and shows. Their shops are not to be rivaled. Will you order goods from Cicero?"

"And deprive you of a reason to get offworld?" I had been to Cicero many times on one freighter or another but had not disembarked there, just another offloading stop for conscripts.

They smiled at my quip then looked at each other again. "Will you join us in our car?" Susan asked. "We'll share the trip to chase away boredom."

"I have some business papers to go over," I lied.

"Business. Of course," Kate said. "We'll see you at the shuttle then."

I got off the train at Cylay in the early evening. A porter offered to secure a ride to my hotel. I smiled and shook my head. I intended to spend the night in the station and change in the unclean public washroom there before trudging to the shuttle holding area for another long wait through the breakfast hour.

I sat on the long bench and looked around at the cavernous room, unhappy with my brave decision that brought discord at home and fear of every shadow on the trip. Someone cleared his throat in front of me. I focused on a very small Cylahi beggar. "Please," he whined and held out his hand.

"I can spare nothing," I sadly claimed.

"Please," he repeated and thrust a small piece of paper into my hand. He walked to the entrance and pretended to loiter while I read the address of a first-rate hotel and Brian Miller's signature on the paper. I carried my pack to the entrance and wondered how to get around in the strange city. The Cylahi beggar stood a quarter block up to my left. He stepped out of the shadows and signaled me to follow him.

"I must be demented," I thought to myself. "Trusting strange people on a dark street." Brian Miller's signature was well-known and could easily be forged. This adventure was more deadly than a crosscountry walk on the savannah.

Cylay was lovely after dark with amber street lights and vibrant shop windows. But there were few people on the street, mostly Han-Chinese Blackshirts in groups. The Cylahi man stopped across the street from the hotel that was named on the paper. He signaled me to cross to the lighted entrance, then slipped into the shadows.

I looked around and heavily sighed. I decided to send a message via EAM to my husband, saying that I had arrived safely, then somehow get back to the station. I entered the well-lit and tastefully decorated lobby of the small hotel.

"Are you Heather?" I heard behind me as soon as I was indoors. I quickly turned to greet a rotund Putuki man with thick glasses and a newspaper under one arm. "I have a message for you. Would you do me the honor of taking a nightcap with me?"

The gallant if musky man led me into the hotel bar where we sat at a small table in the back. He put the newspaper on the seat between us and ordered drinks. "Look in the folds of the paper," he said while we waited. "There's a room key where you can spend the night. You'll also find a small tube of lipstick. Put some on. Now."

I looked at the goldish metal tube without understanding. We had no cosmetics in the labor quarters of the transport. Plus Hardhands were opposed to painting their faces for religious reasons.

The tribesman took the tube from my hand. He removed the top and twisted the beveled edge to make the red stick move upward. He handed the open tube to me. "Press it against your lips," he whispered. I did as he instructed. "Now go like this." He rubbed his lips together while he watched me do the same.

While the waiter brought our drinks, I twisted the stick back down into the tube and returned the cover. My host unfolded a set of business papers onto the table. "I hope these numbers are satisfactory to your husband," the Putuki man said. "We appreciate your time to review them with me."

When the waiter left, he folded the papers again and whispered. "Take the far elevator to the room. Open the door for nobody. Be on your way at first light."

He stood with the newspaper. "Tomorrow a woman will ask about your lipstick color. Give her the tube. I'll leave you now. Wait a few minutes, finish your drink. And above all, don't worry."

I followed his instructions and even drew a bath in the modest suite. I inspected the lipstick tube and thought about my ignorance. I put some on, then pressed my lips together while looking into the mirror. The goo tasted strangely and made my face look imbalanced. "Perhaps if I painted my forehead and cheeks like the daughters of Sim Chareon," I thought and chuckled to myself. I wondered how many clumsy mistakes I would commit over the next three days.

In the morning I arrived at the holding area refreshed and perhaps a little braver. I wore the Arrivi gown that Terry had supplied for my journey to the Canyon of Buttes. I carried the veil over one arm and intended to use it as a shawl on the air-conditioned shuttle. And my lips were ruby red.

From the observation window of the shuttle during the short ride, I watched the hated Company transport come into view. The lighted military Company ship with external cameras and a Chinese giant panda decal dragged two attached hulls through each orbit around Dolvia. I remembered the day Carl and I had disembarked as indentured colonists. I had sworn then that I would never be forced offworld.

Susan and Kate joined me by the window. "Made it here safely, I see," Susan said through her boredom.

"And dressed up," Kate snidely added. "What's that lipstick color?"

155

I felt beads of sweat form on my upper lip. All my fears came before me. What if I'm arrested? What if they search me and find something in the lipstick? What if they inject me and begin an interrogation? What if the men from last night were Company agents? Can they hurt my children? What if I can't get back?

I sweetly smiled at them. "Will you spend the day on the transport or go directly to Cicero?"

"Two days we must endure the transport," Susan complained. "It's such a bore. I can't wait for the regent to be reassigned. Someplace with a night life and people you want to know."

"I certainly value your visits to my shop," I said without inflection. "The tribeswomen buy whatever you praise."

"At least they have the sense to not rely on their own taste," Kate added.

When the shuttle docked, I disembarked with Susan and Kate and walked down the long causeway to the customs booth. We were scanned and our purses dumped. Their luggage was taken into another room for inspection. "Oh, not again," Susan loudly complained.

"I must go," I said to them. "Perhaps I'll see you later." I grabbed my pack that had barely been scanned and strolled to the exit. I knew suspicion was not attached to me because of their company. For that service I forgave the remark about my lipstick.

At the customs exit, I faced my dread. I dabbed my face with the edge of my shawl and straightened my back. I then walked into the cramped promenade with flickering blue shadows cast by the Company overhead comtech that blared offworld news.

Two Blackshirts and some midshippers stood whispering together near the labor entrance. I felt my stomach twist while I walked to the concierge. To my surprise, he was a former colonist who had sold his supply rights for Cylahi gold.

"Heather Osborn!" he buoyantly said and flipped back his shoulder length hair. "We heard you were coming. Right this way. There are several who want to greet you."

"But you left Dolvia more than three years ago."

"I have a business here. We're midshippers!"

I nodded unbelievingly. Boasting of a business in partnership with the Company was difficult for me to digest. I reached for the pen to register. "Oh, no," the concierge stopped me. "Please, be our guest."

"I have business," I lamely protested. I had never liked these people. Plus I risked missing the all important chance encounter if my freedom of movement was restricted.

"We know all about it. Inventory of supplies. My son works in that section. Come along, we can go there first."

I was trapped by his hospitality. He led me down the midship corridor to the receiving offices by the docking bays. I greeted a young man with yellow hair loosely tied at his neckline. He dropped a huge file on the counter between us. "I'm more interested in the computer files," I said.

"We have access to the hard copy only," he bitterly explained, not as happy with their lot as his father. The young blond pressed a button on the counter then spoke into the console speaker, "Passage."

Two armed guards in uniforms that displayed the panda logo entered from a door across the room. They suspiciously looked around and signaled I should come to them. "Thank you," I said to the blond and his father. Midshippers watched me walk with my pack through the door.

The Company ship was laid out in military orderliness with gleaming edges, directional icons and hydraulic doors. I felt momentary panic when the door snapped shut. In my experience conscript women were brought into this section only as servants. I reminded myself that I was a businesswoman with negotiable goods. "I'm not a slave. I'm not a slave."

I was led past several carpeted conference rooms with computer and EAM screens. The guards stopped at the communications center manned by a crew of six and took up positions at the door. I entered without ceremony. An older man wearing a crew uniform approached me. "Yes?" he blankly said.

"I have a Company pass to conduct an inventory for . . ."

"You must be Heather, Carl Osborn's wife. I'm Hamish Nordhagan."

Hamish saw my eyes wander to the Chinese giant panda in a circle of mandarin yellow on his uniform sleeve. "I'm in communications," he quietly added. "In this quadrant, that's Company only." Hamish signaled the guards who left. He led me to a monitor and pronounced for all to hear, "I'll call up the file for your perusal."

I sat in the chair he offered, and he whispered behind my shoulder. "My shift ends in twenty minutes."

The bright screen was responsive and multi-display. I stared into it, entranced more by the options than by the information I sought. Hamish lightly tapped my shoulder and I focused on the members of his shift who watched me with humor in their faces. Six more crewmembers entered for the next watch. "This way," Hamish said.

We walked to a lunchroom where they sat at one table in easy camaraderie. They ignored the Company commentator who read the news on the ceiling-mounted comtech. I sat with them and turned slightly so the flashes of colorful images from the comtech wouldn't absorb my attention. One crewman who Hamish addressed as Roger brought me hot tea and a softbread treat.

"Groundwork agrees with you," Hamish said. "You're not like the others who returned."

"I have a business and access to an EAM-12."

"So we saw," Hamish returned while the others smiled. "Some of those channels we don't even use. How many languages do you speak?"

"Dialects really. Arrivi, Putuki and some Cylahi." I waited, but they offered nothing more. "Perhaps I should go back now."

"You prefer midship?"

"Compared to what?"

"Is it better than the desert?" Roger quietly asked without looking up.

"Nothing's better than the desert," I answered in the same cheeky tone.

They were serious then, intently watching me. "You can see the far horizon and the curvature of the earth as clearly as the round muscle of your arm," I explained. "You feel one with those who have existed there for a thousand years. You can walk for days without seeing another living soul."

They glanced at each other then studied their drinks. "Your travel orders include meals and a room in the women's quarters," Hamish explained. "We dine in two hours."

"I thought we were dining now."

We left the lunchroom without his crewmembers in tow. Hamish led me to the women's quarters and motioned to a young woman there. "This is Lisa Sheridan's station most days. Lisa, get her something appropriate for the captain's table."

Lisa wore clothes of the same cut as Hamish's uniform but without insignia. Her sand-colored hair was bound in a tight coil at her collar and she wore no make-up. She glanced at my Arrivi gown and shawl and my red-red lips then opened the security door.

Hamish turned to me. "In two hours in VCC-2," he said. "And don't extol the virtues of the desert at dinner. Watch your step."

Once I had settled into the quiet room, I took many deep breaths and thought about the red sandstone pillars clustered in Butte Canyon for an eternity. What were my poor trials compared to their timeless community? I had two goals only. Pass the lipstick tube to an unknown compatriot and learn the value of cavern water. Why then did the midshippers and crewmembers treat this like a state visit? Was their world so constricted by lack of space and trust that any event created a stir?

Borrowed clothes were laid out for me, the close-fitting crew tunic plus soft, flat-heeled Chinese boots so different from my open sandals. What a temptation to wear the power-giving uniform.

My only change of clothes was the long skirt and a cream-colored pullover from Brittany Mill. My worn sandals were flat and wide, designed for long hours spent tending my shop. But I couldn't wear the Company tunic even for dinner, so contrary was Company philosophy to mine.

At the last moment, I put on the red lipstick and placed the tube in my skirt pocket. Hamish's eyebrows jumped at his first sight of my clothes, but he didn't ask about my lipstick color. I had the luxury of a second day to reach the right person.

In the spacious diningroom no Blackshirt guards were seated. Only Company men, administrators, crewmembers, and Consortium officers. Hamish and I were led to the Captain's table. Susan and Kate sat with Sim Chareon at the right of the captain and his highly made-up, traditionally dressed Asian wife. The daughters of Sim Chareon stared at my clothes, arrayed themselves in dragon surcoats and a showy display of jade and coral beads. None of the guests wore the precious stones or Cylahi jewelry designs from Dolvia. In fact, except for my millmade skirt and blouse, nothing spoke of the mineral rich land that had secured the fortunes of all at this gathering.

We were served by conscript women in brown uniforms with white aprons and headscarves. They didn't look up at the conversation but served with measured motions to erase any attention to themselves.

"Do you know Brian Miller at Brittany Mill?" the Han-Chinese captain in a dark suit and white round-collared shirt politely asked.

"The success story of Brittany Mill is known throughout Dolvia," I murmured.

"Your success story is also remarkable," Kate off-handedly claimed.

"Many here on the transport gain their living from Dolvia's wealth." I controlled my voice to carry no intent.

"But you speak their languages," Kate interjected.

"Enough to agree on a price for barter."

"And what do the women talk about?" the captain asked.

"Electricity."

They all smiled and looked around. Of course, ignorant savages fascinated with the commonplace. I didn't look at Hamish but steadily gazed at Sim Chareon. A small and wrinkled man, apparently unconcerned, he barely looked up from his meal. "I'm not a slave. I'm not a slave," I silently repeated to myself.

"The young tribesmen who study here," I said to the captain. "How are they progressing?"

"Why do you ask?"

"The questions that you ask me, they could best answer," I said, modulating my voice in the Company rhythm. "Perhaps tomorrow I may be allowed to visit the classroom. Something to

159

fill the idle time after inventory."

"At whose request do you visit them?" Kate asked.

"Just curiosity. Have they found many friends here?"

"Uh, we would have to ask," the captain said evenly.

The meal ended. The captain and his silent wife bid me goodnight. Sim Chareon turned to some officers and seemed engrossed in their conversation. Kate and Susan started a game of backgammon.

I was the evening's curiosity, the sensation of the hour. Hamish led me to his crewmates, but they were reticent in public. After a short time I turned to Hamish. "I'm tired now. Is it impolite to leave?"

"I'll walk you back."

"I can find my way."

"I'm assigned."

"I didn't realize that meant more than dinner."

"You prefer someone else?" he shyly said.

"I want to see the students tomorrow. Can you arrange it?" Hamish seemed uneasy with this suggestion. "Can you?" I asked again.

"Yes," he said and led me away.

In the corridor, he turned to me, "You know, the transport has much to offer besides business and politics."

"I would like something not political," I grinned.

"Come with me," he said and turned back another way. He led me past the married quarters to the turbo area which I had never entered. "What's that noise?" I asked.

"The engines. After a while, you don't even notice it." Hamish showed his ID to the guard, and we passed through the hydraulic doors into a different bulkhead. This was the working end of the ship, the causeway lined with ducting. We walked along a narrow corridor and entered a large room that smelled of chlorine and mildew.

"Over here," he said. We stepped through a small doorway and saw something I didn't know what to call. It was a rectangular body of clear and glowing blue water. There were ladders and several planks mounted on a structure that jutted out over the water. I walked to the edge and looked into the gently vibrating surface, so close to the ship's engines.

"It's beautiful. Like a quiet painting."

"You've never been swimming? I swear you're more conscript than Dolviet."

"I was indentured when I disembarked, not conscript. What are you doing?"

"I thought we'd go for a swim," Hamish said and pulled his tunic over his head. "Crewmembers come here sometimes. Takes away the stiffness after a long shift."

"Without our clothes?" I quickly asked. I had always worked

at manual labor. The idea of laboring for fun or for health was quite beyond me.

"You can wear a suit. Come here." He led me to a dressing room marked for women and peeked inside. When he determined it was empty, he entered and opened lockers until he found a suit for me. Then he went to the pool, stripped down to his shorts, and dove headfirst into the water.

I didn't change but sat on the pool's edge when he came up for air. "You think it's a trick," he said unbelievingly. He hoisted himself onto the edge very near me. I shyly moved away. "You think I'm going to drown you," he gently accused.

"It's wrong to show one's self."

Hamish looked down at himself. Then he laughed loud and long. The sound reverberated throughout the large room. "It's been a long time since a woman saw me that way." He thought about it and became shy. "Perhaps I did bring you here for a wrong reason."

Hamish dried himself and pulled on his uniform while I studied the water as it became calm. He easily sat next to me, surprised to see tears in my eyes.

"It's so beautiful," I said. "And you take it for granted. Like electricity."

Chapter Twenty-Four

The next morning I learned why the captain had been noncommittal about the students. With smoldering glances at Hamish, the four tribesmen and their armed escort filed into the salesroom. The students didn't know me. They were assigned to the transport before my relationship with Oriika became public. Their gray and sullen faces told me all I needed to know about their experiences in the labor quarters. They suspiciously looked at my Arrivi gown and shawl.

"Nu delaya," I said. Mula, the oldest, watched me with hooded eyes. They were ready for any Company trick. "Netta, om," I added.

"Netta," Ely answered, avoiding Mula's warning glance. Ely looked at me over his round, steel-rimmed glasses.

"Please leave us," I said to the armed guards.

The guards didn't move. "The students have been a discipline problem," Hamish explained.

"I don't doubt it. Give me a few minutes."

Hamish reluctantly left with the guards. I set out kari root stems on the table some distance from the young men. I saw desire in their eyes. To avoid embarrassment, I excused myself and left the room.

In the corridor I took Hamish aside. "Have they contacted their families?"

He shrugged. "The crew had no hand in this."

I looked at him starkly, then thought for a long moment. "If I miss the shuttle tomorrow, how long's the wait."

"Ten days."

"Ten days is a long time."

Hamish didn't like the surprises I brought him. He looked at me appraisingly. "You give yourself away with this act."

"People on the transport know about the students. But Dolviets don't yet know. The Company needn't lose face if they meet my needs today."

"What's your plan?"

I uneasily looked at him. "Uh, well, first I need to spend time with them and contact their families. And then . . . then I'll figure something out."

"You risk everything with this move," he whispered, using the same words and tone Carl had used. I reminded myself that my children would have children on Dolvia.

"Who developed their class schedule?" I asked.

"The education administrator," Hamish said. He reluctantly added, "I can bring him here. Perhaps this afternoon."

I nodded and chewed my lip. Hamish cynically watched me for a moment before he walked up the corridor. I joined the students who hid the cigarette butts they hoarded, having filled the room with the rich aroma of their culture. I put the intercom on speaker. "We'll be meeting in here for several hours. Send in a meal for six, whatever is served to the crew for lunch. Also, I need to speak to the concierge in midship."

There was a long silence on the line while they checked my credentials with the duty officer. Then the voice of a former colonist who had invited me to stay with his family came online, hesitant and guarded. "How may I help you?"

"I'll be taking rooms in midship for ten days and expect two others to join me tomorrow from the shuttle," I lied. "A double suite. Plus I'll entertain tonight in these rooms. Please arrange a cold buffet at 5:30. And, also. Is there a midship assay officer or do I deal only with the Company for gold and gems?" There was nothing like the jingle of coin to get some attention.

I was sure Company men would speak with Sim Chareon who would chew on the problem for hours. Perhaps he hoped I would board tomorrow's shuttle. I racked my brain for a way to help the students, then it came to me quiet and simple. I liked it quiet and simple.

I called up the library files for aptitude tests given to incoming students at all levels. I printed out hardcopies for language, geography, math and philosophy. I couldn't think of other subjects and had no menu to access. Each was an act of ignorance. But at least it was an act.

The four men dumbly watched the screen, then nodded to each other agreeing to complete the tests. They were nearly done when the meal was served. Either Hamish had stamped his foot or Sim Chareon wanted to draw me into some new trap. I didn't care which. The tribesmen would have a good meal before we met our fate together.

"Netta, om?" I asked when they finished their plates and papers.

"Netta," Mula answered. They expected the worst. And now they expected the same for me. They were probably right.

Hamish entered and introduced the education administrator, an aging and soft-cheeked man who clearly disapproved of our completed tests. It was his neck stuck out, but mercy was within my power.

"These students' progress is remarkable considering the number of class hours they have been able to tolerate," I began. "I think perhaps it's time to step up their involvement. I have reassurances from each of them that they'll be less disruptive to the routine."

I waited two beats. "At this time, I would like to see new class schedules. The tribesmen have much to share about the mineral wealth of Dolvia. They need class and social time with other students, especially families of crewmembers. If you would bring the new schedules to my quarters in midship tonight after 6:30, that would be most convenient.

"By the way, the students will communicate with their families today. And with Oriika who negotiated the fair trade. I'm so gratified I can report their advancement in the studies and their enjoyment of their stay in midship."

He stared at me with his mouth open, most unbecoming. Hamish tapped his arm, and they made a move to leave. "Hamish, is there a gemmologist in midship?" I added within the man's hearing. Hamish glanced at me, then falsely smiled at his nonplussed companion.

"Shall I send him by here?" Hamish innocently asked.

"I'll find his office when I take the students to midship."

Hamish firmly took the administrator's arm and led him from the room. When Hamish returned his face was stony. But then, why should he throw in with my uncertain fate? "Can an independent EAM be set up in midship?" I asked.

"There's one being repaired that I could borrow for a few days. Anything else?"

"Yes, I want to go swimming again."

He quickly controlled the flicker in his eyes. "I'll find you a suit to wear."

For several hours the students sat hunched over the salesroom EAM while their parents crowded the EAM-50 in Brian's office. We set regular times to communicate with their families, plus requested herbs for cooking and kari root for leisure. I explained that they could not smoke on the transport, but Ely gestured that they would chew the medicinal root.

Later Roger came to the salesroom door. "I'll take you to midship now."

It was a delicate situation. Crew and midshippers didn't serve the students. The former colonists wouldn't overcome their prejudice for my sake. I didn't want the armed guard back and couldn't leave the students alone. I asked myself how I had dug this hole.

"I can't leave the students."

"Then send them to the showers."

"I'm sorry?"

Roger chuckled. "When you don't want to go where you are supposed to be, but you can't stay where you are. Take a shower."

We left the young men frolicking in the airbath rooms and walked past the communications area where Hamish was hard at work and studiously ignored me. Roger paused at a security checkpoint that led to midship. I thanked him and walked past many staring faces to the concierge desk. "I'd like to see the rooms."

The concierge coldly appraised me, uncertain that my jewels compensated for the trouble I was stirring. The rooms were small and musky with no uplifting arch, but far better than where the tribesmen were recently quartered. The concierge loitered by the door.

"The dinner is ordered?" I asked very businesslike. "Oh, and they'll deliver an EAM this afternoon."

"EAMs aren't allowed in this area."

"Nobody can afford one. That's different than not allowed."

"I'll need a deposit on the rooms."

"From the colonial savior?"

"We're not on the planet. We won't return to Dolvia."

I smiled and turned away. He had vocalized my greatest fear. I rummaged through my pack. "I have three gems here with no assayed value. If you can spare the time to exchange them for Company script at ground rate, I would appreciate the favor."

He knowingly smiled at me. He would cheat the Company and cheat me and pocket the difference. But he couldn't come forward later with accusations if he engaged in their usual underhanded practices.

I hurried back to my four charges who waited uneasily at the shower entryway. We guardedly walked up the corridor, then I shrugged off my apprehension. How did I think I could hide on the Company transport? "I am not a slave. I am not a slave," I reminded myself, trying to shed my conscript traits. I straightened my back and lifted my chin. The tribesmen closely watched me and whispered to each other. But somehow the air seemed fresher and colors brighter as we walked back to the conference room.

I sat across from them. "I'm Heather," I said in Arrivi. "I must go back to Dolvia soon. We have set a regular accounting of your Company progress with your families. The hard time is past."

While I talked, I wrote on a pad and passed it to Mula. He read the Putuki words and nodded, then passed the pad onto the next student. It had instructions to say nothing in that room. There would be a better time. The last student who was Ely stripped the page from the pad, wadded it and secretly ate it while he stared at the door over the rim of his round glasses. The labor quarters must have been Hell.

"We'll spend afternoons here for the duration of my stay," I continued. "I'll work with the education director to structure your lessons. And each of you will have spending money from the profits your families enjoy from commerce on Dolvia. Right now, however, I want you to write to family members in your own dialects concerning your studies. You're all doing remarkably well. Isn't that the case?"

"Cylay," Mula said.

"I have more arrangements to make. I'll return before you finish. If others come, they must wait for my return. You're instructed to remain in this room."

I looked down the corridor both ways, then mustered my courage. I went back to midship and to the public storage. I opened a safe deposit box with the small key Terry had given me. I giggled at the sight of a cache of Cylahi gold large enough to buy the favor of all midship. I selected a few showy pieces to wear, then pocketed others for payment.

I left the secure storage area and browsed in the three midship stores asking questions about the quality of the goods. I knew their ways. I had money to spend and influence with suppliers. The prices in all shops dramatically fell each time I left one without buying.

In the next shop I ordered several sizes of men's pants and shirts of a durable material. The shopkeeper assumed they were consumer goods for the planet. He blinked when I requested delivery to my rooms in midship.

I went to three restaurants and ordered meals delivered during my stay. It would have been cheaper to buy groceries, but it wasn't good public relations. Plus the need for delivery answered midship questions about service to the students. I went to a stationery shop and ordered supplies for the students along with a small quantity of personal stationery. I snooped around in the promenade for some time, dragging out each selection while I kept watch on corridor traffic. If the one who was to admire my lipstick was from midship, she had ample time that afternoon to contact me. Another blank.

I was glad when the afternoon passed. I led the students to the midship rooms for a meal. They looked around at the accommodations then shuffled with relish to the food table.

Roger and two crewmates delivered the EAM at the end of their shift when they usually gathered in the lunchroom. The students stood by the machine ready for another lesson. I demonstrated the EAM setup and how to maintain files. I opened the education menu and let them go at it. They were enthusiastic and fast learners. Mula, especially, seemed to be a thinking person.

I sat on the bed in the other room and sighed. Ten days I had to wait. My impulse was to take tomorrow's shuttle. But I needed to secure the status of the students by routine and high profile. Or their fate was uncertain.

The education director was the only person I had identified who could ensure the students' relative comfort after I departed. What to expect from him? What reason did he have to upgrade their classes? I rubbed my eyes with thumb and forefinger. If only I could talk to Oriika or Terry. I was out of options.

At the doorway one student cleared his throat. He held out a plate of food. "I'm not hungry," I said. He entered and put the plate on the nightstand. Then he turned to me full of emotion and bowed, then bowed again. The others stood in the doorway and bowed as if to reinforce his gesture. "No, no," I said. "Please don't."

The young men respectfully sat in one corner of the frontroom until the education director arrived. They filed into the bedroom but listened through the open door. I asked the director to sit and allowed him to wait a few minutes while I pretended to continue a conversation on the EAM. I looked up from the screen.

"I'll be just a minute more. Please read these letters the students will send to their families." He thumbed through the pages, then pushed them away.

"Is there a problem?" I asked.

"These are gibberish."

"That's what I would like to discuss."

I shut down the EAM and handed him the aptitude tests the students had completed that afternoon. "Look these over. Strengths I've identified are mathematics and mechanical engineering. Plus I would like to see increased interface with crewmembers who want to learn more about Dolvia. Did you bring class schedules?"

This was it. What did the Company officially offer? He had a single sheet with classes listed that featured agriculture and mechanics. "Agriculture? These students are born farmers."

"Our methods are far advanced to theirs."

"Do you know their methods?"

"I have not experienced ground duty."

"Then how do you know Company methods are more advanced?"

"We use technology and chemicals they cannot know."

"Or have need of. This is adequate for the youngest, but I request we substitute computer classes for these afternoon sessions. Now, about the others?"

"This is for them all."

Magnanimously, I smiled at him. "I'm sure at the time of their arrival on the transport, the students were at relatively the same educational level. These most recent aptitude tests, however, point to certain preferences. Perhaps we can meet tomorrow after you've had a chance to develop a schedule for each one of them."

"What gives you the right to speak for them?"

"I'm empowered by their families and Oriika, who negotiated the fair trade with Sim Chareon, to review their advancement during my visit," I lied. "If you would like, I can call Sim Chareon since he's also visiting on the transport. We can settle this in a few minutes."

I reached to turn on the EAM and punch in a series of numbers I hoped he wouldn't recognize as gibberish. "That's not necessary," he sourly claimed. "I'm sure we can accommodate their growing needs."

At least for ten days, I thought to myself. "Tomorrow I'll visit the classrooms. You and the teachers will dine one evening with crewmembers who are curious about life on Dolvia. Thank you for giving up your evening."

After the director left, I broke out the packages. One tribesman stripped off his shirt to put on a workshirt and pants. I excused myself and went into the bedroom. I heard them angrily whispering at him.

Twenty minutes later there was a knock at the outer door. From the bedroom I heard Hamish's booming voice. Everybody in the promenade heard him, I was sure. "Lessons are over for today. Where is Heather Osborn?"

I walked to Hamish, and he stepped aside so I could be seen from the promenade by whomever passed by. His face was stern and tense. Something was wrong. "I'll take you back know. Get your case."

Mula brought my small pack from the bedroom. "I can't leave them," I whispered.

"Look around you," Hamish whispered back.

By the concierge desk I saw the same two men who had loitered by the labor quarters when I first arrived. Two young women studied goods in the windows of the closed shops plus some others, many people for late at night.

I saw an image of curling tendrils, like those of the sweet potato vine, extend from the unsavory men to Hamish, then turn gently back to caress the feet and legs of all who were in the promenade.

"The light is in her eyes," Ely whispered to Mula who stepped close to me.

"Tell us what you see," Mula quietly said.

I dropped my pack and leaned against the doorjamb. I was barely able to catch my breath, struggling against the images. Mula's hand touched mine when he handed the small case back to me.

I saw a vast battlefield, strewn with mangled bodies of men and animals, stretching behind Mula and lit up by a fiery sunset.

Hamish grabbed my arm to steady me, and I looked at him with equal disbelief. I saw an image of Hamish bearing down on me with his sexual member exposed and erect.

"She has seen om," Ely said.

"Many claim to see," were Mula's hard words.

I explained without knowing why it was important. "I visited the Canyon of Buttes with the sisters of Arim. Three red sandstone buttes hiding a fourth."

The students whispered together. I took Hamish's hand from my arm and guided it to touch Mula's wrist. "This is Mula who has two brothers. He leads the resistance."

I turned to Mula. "This is Hamish. Learn from him. He will save the tribes."

"You mean after I'm gone," Mula said.

"You will not enter the season of om."

Chapter Twenty-Five

For someone offworld born to see om was not considered possible. But these two men, the Putuki who would lead the resistance and Hamish who somehow figured in saving the tribes, were together in my presence at a time of heightened fear. The tribesmen took it seriously, especially since the images seemed to reinforce what Mula already knew.

It was Oriika's regular time to communicate with her accounts, or rather Carl's accounts. I sat at the terminal and hoped we weren't being monitored. "I have seen om," I typed on the EAM.

"You are blessed," was the answer after a long delay.

"Do you have something for me?" I asked, trying not to show our hand.

"It is as Dolvia provides," was the noncommittal answer.

To make things worse, whenever Hamish drew near, I saw the image of his sexual interest. He was insulted that I drew away, and he lent no support for three days. I bought a few clothes in midship, did the needed inventory at the terminal in his area, and ate with the students.

I planned a dinner for the students on the fifth day of my visit. The daughters of Sim Chareon had departed with their father for Cicero, and the education director was a bitter old man. No others from the Company section befriended me. I went to Hamish.

"Will you do me the honor?" I asked without looking at him.

He leaned back in his crew station chair. "I was thinking the buddy system. A crewmember spends time with each student, set an example."

"Four of you would commit?"

"If you looked up from the computer screen once in a while," he cynically claimed, "you would see friendly faces. You must shed your conscript ways."

"I was indentured, not conscript."

I realized he teased me to lighten my mood. But I couldn't

smile. The oppressive images I saw in om overwhelmed my interest in ship politics.

So the dinner for friends of the Dolviet students was paid for by Oriika's store of Cylahi gold. Held in a stateroom with fine china and silver, it was more a tribute to Hamish's influence than to my knowledge of ship's etiquette. The students gathered early and loitered by the catered trays on a buffet table. They wore midship clothes and native jewelry that I had insisted they display at all times, the source of Company wealth and midship greed. I wore my Arrivi domestic gown and shawl plus the red-red lipstick that nobody had mentioned. I greeted the students then inspected the buffet.

Mula joined me. "You mustn't let it show on your face."

"The images in om torture me."

"We all die. Few know the appointed time. The other you must hide."

"What?"

"You and Hamish. People are talking."

"Do you have second sight?"

"I have only my desire to be free."

Midshippers were excited to attend dinner in the mothership. The needs of four native sophomores were inconsequential compared to crew favors. The young tribesmen would be tolerated.

As ombudsman, I was seated next to Hamish whose voice was gentle. I smiled and graciously nodded at the few comments he directed my way, but I couldn't match their energy level.

Only official Company policy was left to overcome. The following day I communicated via EAM with Brian Miller on the excuse of negotiating a better price for Cylahi gold jewelry. "Do you know Hamish Nordhagan?" I asked watching a facsimile of Brian's face on the computer screen.

"Good man, Hamish," he answered without inflection.

If they knew something, they didn't trust the communication lines. I sat next to Hamish during his shift. "When do the students get to try out swimming?" I asked.

"You trust me again?"

He was nothing but a tease. "I have been confused and depressed," I confessed.

"Conscript traits."

Later the students, staring and chattering, walked around the swimming pool. Hamish stripped down to his suit and dove into the clear water. They stepped back amazed at his move, then gingerly sat on the water's edge and immersed their legs. Soon they splashed around and pushed each other underwater. Hamish sat next to me with a towel over his shoulders. "I wish you'd put on some clothes," I complained.

"I wish you'd take some off."

"It's wrong for me to swim with the young men."

"Then I'll send them back." He made a move to get their attention.

"No, wait. We'll come back another time."

"Later tonight."

"I don't know."

"After dinner," he insisted.

After the tedious evening meal in the Company diningroom, I waited in the women's quarters. I paced the room then opened the door, peering down the long hallway. Twice I went to the desk on the excuse of giving some instructions for tomorrow or to get a drink.

Lisa was on duty and talked with two other women dressed in dungarees and pullovers. They turned from watching the overhead comtech and politely answered my questions, then whispered to each other while I walked back to my rooms.

Hamish didn't come. I didn't have a pass to the engine area. I dozed off while fully clothed and sitting in a chair.

Early the next day I understood the problem. Sim Chareon and the Company executives had unexpectedly returned in the late evening. They brought with them a detail of Consortium officers who served a high official engaged in a fact-finding tour.

The Company executives' return meant exercises in efficiency, inspections and dry runs. Dance for the man. When the official and executives were satisfied for their own security, the alert was stepped down. A full dress ball in honor of the Consortium officers was announced to celebrate the crew's high marks on efficiency tests.

Company men loved elaborate ritual. As a young girl still in my mother's care, I had often tasted the charity plates given to the laborers so we benefited from Company power. I had glimpsed in the promenade two Company women in long, brocade dragon robes with escorts wearing dress uniforms. Now I was to attend one of these events.

Well, if I must. And why not put on the dog, a phrase my mother used when she wore her few, tawdry pieces of jewelry to callouts.

I went to the shops in midship but found nothing suitable. There were no gowns of appropriate material because midshippers weren't invited. I returned to the women's quarters and asked Lisa where I could secure a gown. Her eyes grew big, and she murmured I should approach the Company purveyor. Of course. A Company game, Company issue.

I carried my small pack to the purveyor's office. I was asked to wait for no reason that I could see. I poured some peridot gems onto the desktop and grinned. "I don't care to wait, if you don't mind."

Company shopping was like nothing in the universe. You didn't grab a likely item to feel and hold up to yourself. I was measured and asked to sit while non-Chinese styles were modeled by striking women of various ethnic groups who I had not seen before. With the haughty tailor's encouragement I chose a floor length gown with a tight-fitting bodice, no collar and slight sleeves. Shoes were secured and a clutch purse.

The fey man turned to me with his nose in the air. "And now for your jewelry."

"I brought my own, thank you very much. Have this delivered, please."

I went on my usual rounds then shopped in the midship stores, wondering why nobody asked about my lipstick color. Plus I had found no answer in the ship's records concerning the secret of cavern water. I was running out of time.

I went back to the women's quarters and opened the delivered packages. Another larger package was left with a note, "Wear this."

It was a lovely and clinging palest blue gown with many sequins and long strands of glass beads streaming from the shoulders and across the hipline. It was stylish and very daring, not at all comfortable.

I couldn't decide who to trust. I went to the desk of the women's quarters where Lisa stood with her two friends. "Excuse me, Lisa. I don't know your friends."

"This is Caroline and Billie. Their parents are crewmembers like Hamish Nordhagan."

"My name is Heather Osborn."

"We know."

"Could you help me for a minute? In my room?" Lisa looked at the others who shrugged, then followed me to my room. When she saw the two gowns, Lisa let out a squeal of delight, holding up first one then the other for inspection.

"I don't know which is appropriate," I said. "What will you be wearing?"

Her face fell. "You're invited," I softly said. "Everyone in this section."

"They always invite us. They know we cannot afford gowns."

"Who is us?"

"Mostly families of crewmembers. There are seven of us who work but without rank."

"Then we need seven more gowns."

The adventure of making debutantes was expensive and trying. The talk of the entire ship, how the Hardhand presumed to buy the young crew women's favor. I cleaned out Oriika's thoughtful cache of goods, hoping they were not placed there for some more purposeful end. I had the gold carted to my quarters in a most public manner. I found at the bottom of the safe deposit bin, wrapped in an oil cloth, the loveliest string of oval-cut peridot gems with one darker gem that would hover in the hollow of the neck.

I went to the Company purveyor, where the gown had earlier been returned, and demanded something more suitable to my age and status. The haughty men looked at each other and led me to a rack holding several gowns the same style as the one Hamish had sent. I asked to see them modeled for me. But the men weren't in a forgiving humor.

There came a knock at the door. The seven young women rushed past us to fondle the gowns. "But this cannot be," the fey man complained. "They're not intended . . ."

Unfortunately, there were only six ballgowns of acceptable style and material. The seventh girl, the one named Billie who worried about her weight and was easily deflated, unhappily shrugged. "It's no matter. I don't have to attend the ball."

"Don't you have something more, anything?" I asked the purveyor.

They brought out a matronly gown intended for some administrator's hefty wife, but that she had not selected. "We'll have it altered," I suggested.

"But you can't," one of the men said in a rush. "It's special material. There's no thread to match."

"You can use thread from the piece you cut away."

"We cannot possibly have it done in time," he insisted.

"Then I'll do it," I said undeterred. "We'll work in my quarters. Bring them. Shoes, ribbon, everything."

While we remade the gown, the young girls preened and spoke out their aspirations. I felt ancient, belonging more to the Canyon of Buttes than to this group. "Why do you wear your hair that way?" I asked Lisa, indicating the tight roll at her neck.

"Company women wear theirs the same."

"Are you with the Company?"

"No, it's not intended," Billie said mimicking the haughty tailor. Each of us got a haircut that day, one helping the other to brush and curl chin length hair.

We were late to the ball, of course. Very late. They each selected a piece of Cylahi gold jewelry for their exposed arms and handwrought gold earbobs that tangled with their freshly coifed hair. I helped Billie into her new dress and tied her hair back with a piece of ribbon left over from the tailoring. "Here, put on some lipstick."

"What is lipstick?" Billie asked.

I showed them the tube and how to apply it. "You don't have lipstick on the transport? What about the Company women?"

"They use a brush to apply color from a . . . it's like a cup,"

Lisa explained.

I thought about it for a moment. "But Kate Chareon asked about my lipstick. Are you sure?" They looked at each other and shrugged.

"Once I saw a prostitute on Cicero with some," Billie said. They starkly looked at me when I started to laugh. It made perfect sense to me. Tribesmen had no contact with Company women or with Hardhands. The only way they could get cosmetics was from women whose time they could buy. How were they to know we didn't all use the same accessories?

The debutantes waited. "Do we have escorts?" I asked.

"They're waiting."

"You go on ahead while I change."

"We'll not enter the ball without you," Lisa said.

I changed into the gown Hamish had sent, fervently hoping he was among the waiting escorts. I fastened the peridot necklace and selected a showy piece of Cylahi gold for my arm. I thought the gold band was garish, but there was no way I wasn't wearing it.

I stepped out of the bathroom and heard the young women murmur at my looks. The blue gown was different from their beiges and light yellow.

Like a gaggle of geese we rushed down the corridor. The waiting men loitered in their dress uniforms dusting their shoes and pulling at their collars. Roger stepped forward. I couldn't hide my disappointment that he wasn't Hamish, so he said, "He waits at the ball with Sim Chareon and some Consortium lieutenants."

Chapter Twenty-Six

Such a fuss. The tables were removed from the common diningroom and the floor polished to a high sheen. The young women caused a stir, arriving late and in a group, but word had already spread about what we had bought to wear.

It was their hair, don't you know, all the same style and very like my own. And the Cylahi gold they wore, perhaps overdone, competing with the glow of young, eager faces.

Suddenly there was a new force on the transport. The crew were more than so many ensigns standing to duty. They were men who had gone adventuring and whose daughters, nieces and sisters were well-educated, well-heeled and desirable debutantes. Seven young women dressed to greet the visiting Consortium officers made for an evening of romance.

I stood with the matrons and the captain's wife, looking very different from them in my revealing beaded dress. I saw Billie, my heart's favorite among the debutantes, flushed and giggling, unable to choose among the three who competed for a dance with her.

So this was putting on the dog. It had a certain feel about it.

Company women stood in a tight group near their ruling fathers and husbands. They looked Old World with their dragon surcoats and tightly wound hair. Their favor was seldom sought that evening.

Behind them were several other women, each from a different ethnic group and dress, each a beauty but somehow worn down. I recognized three of them as models from the purveyor's shop. They seemed entertained by the turn of events, but essentially bored while they played backgammon together.

Hamish stood prominently in the ballroom talking with the senior Company officers and the visiting Consortium official. He spoke to the ship's captain and danced with his wife. He nodded to the Company women and walked right past them.

The few times I glimpsed Hamish, he appeared to be showered by golden flecks, a weather condition that affected him only in the assembly. I tried to shake the image, but it came whenever I saw him among others.

Roger asked me to dance. "I don't know these steps," I resisted.

"I'll show you." We danced for a moment, then he led me back to my place where two more crewmembers waited. "I'm a married woman with children," I protested.

Hamish whispered from behind my shoulder. "They're related to the women whose fortunes you just made." I nodded and heard him whisper again. "You're either a political genius or a damned fool. Either way, you're the most dangerous woman I ever met."

As the evening wore on, the debutantes came to me with bright faces and many thank-yous, each on the arm of a Consortium officer who would later make excuses to return to the transport and pursue his love interest. Billie introduced me to her young man, a Lieutenant Blakesley, tall and broad-shouldered with a strong jawline.

The Company men retired along with most of their women. A few lingered with bitter mouths and constricted hearts. The orchestra struck up a finale wherein all marched in procession. Hamish was pushed forward to take my arm and lead the grand march. This he did with a grim face and straight spine, part of a soldier's duty.

It was my turn to tease. "Do you like my dress?" I asked quietly while we promenaded in front of the other couples, then turned and walked back the other way.

"Very much."

"Do you like my necklace?"

"Most becoming."

Such a man, controlled and infuriating. "You haven't called me conscript."

"That term no longer applies to you, or could ever again."

"Say you want to see me."

"And prompt you to buy the entire ship?"

We stood together on one side and waited for the others to promenade. "I waited for you last night," I whispered.

"You know why I couldn't come."

"You no longer care." His face betrayed the feeling he had struggled against all evening. Half a second it lived there, then was vanquished, sent someplace deep inside.

"Tonight by the pool," he whispered.

"I have no ID."

"They'll let you pass. After tonight, you could walk on water."

"I don't know what that means."

"Good. Then you won't attempt it."

Later in my quarters while I changed, I thought about Carl

and my children. Carl was the only man I had ever desired. My husband, my life's mate. The interest of other men confused me and sent me into hiding. Brian Miller's piercing look, for instance, made me feel cold and frightened.

But this was different. I trembled at the memory of our moments together. The turn of his head, the strength of his grasp, the straight-spined manner with which he conducted our business. I wanted to know what was under that. I wanted him to uncover me and discover me, to share moments that we would remember into our old age.

I waited as long as I could, then waited a few more minutes, then a few more. When I ventured into the corridor, my way was paved by many who stood sentinel ensuring safe passage. I quickly reached the pool and saw Hamish standing there in dress uniform, his back turned to me, waiting for me. Waiting for me.

"You changed clothes."

"So many people to get by."

"They think we're planning the revolution," he whispered into my ear.

"That's not what they think."

"That's what they've been told to think."

Hamish led me behind some thick pipes and noisy ducting, down a narrow catwalk to a wider area where a thin pallet was laid on the floor. I turned to him when I saw the pallet, but he looked away embarrassed by the awkward assumption.

Then I heard him behind me again, the intimate whisper in my ear. "We're not frightened teenagers who hide and rush to the end. This moment is separate from our daily lives and can come only once, but will last a lifetime. A memory to hold onto when courage flees and duty is all that we have. I want to see you, to taste you, to know all there is of you locked in my memory for all time."

Hamish's body was strong and lean, disciplined and with high stamina. He had a taste to look and tease. To treasure what was offered and heighten pleasure through gifts of patience and passion. An experienced lover who guided me to new depths of sensation, he paused and began again with a gentle touch. He encouraged me to move with abandonment under his hand and his mouth which delighted him and fulfilled our enjoyment of each other.

Much later we laid together in a shared calm. "Show me lipstick," he casually asked.

"You're the one!"

I handed him the tube I had carried around for ten days. He removed the top and turned the colored stick. "And the ore's in here?" he asked. "We got the message you were bringing it, but we couldn't decipher lipstick. We thought it was a native term."

"Why didn't you ask me?"

"This is the only place we can talk. Engine noise confuses any listening device."

"That's why you always brought me here."

"You were a frightened child, assuming the worst. Then you gave your time to the students," he complained.

"Are you part of our fight?" I quickly asked.

"Come, let me tell you the truth."

We dressed and sat separately on the pallet while he told me of wonders in the universe I had not imagined. The Company had enemies in many sectors. Some gained strength to overthrow the Company's stranglehold on Westend. Tribal resistance and the wealth of Dolvia gave courage to others who resisted without a mandate from a harmonious group.

"And you lead them?"

"The young military officers at the ball tonight will lead this battle. Now they fight for personal reasons, thanks to you."

"I didn't know about them."

"Is that what's meant to seeing om? To see more than you can know?"

"The gift of seeing is for Dolviets," I hedged. "No Hardhand has second sight."

"But you do," he probed.

"I was in the presence of Mula, who leads the resistance, and you who will save the tribes."

"A grandiose idea," he coldly said. "I don't hold with these native images."

"Neither do I," I quickly claimed. "Well, perhaps I sought it. On the savannah with Oriika and the sisters of Arim, I felt a presence that nurtured me. But then it seemed trapped by the Company matrix."

"And you miss the desert?"

"I miss the weather, patterns of light and shadow as the sun passes. Here every hour's the same. There's no rhythm in sync with Dolvia."

"And that's the secret you share with Mula?"

"You must teach Mula how Company men think, weaknesses he can use."

"Their blind arrogance will be their downfall," Hamish said with authority. "Take tonight, for example. They always invite the young crew women, knowing they cannot afford the clothes. The Company couldn't refuse this one time they made a show of it. That must have cost a deep shaft of gold."

"Gold isn't legal tender on Dolvia," I shrugged. "But I wanted to ask you. Those ethnic women, the ones with the Company men, who are they?"

Hamish bitterly smiled. "Divisions of Consortium troops have been mustered to protect business interests in Westend. Those women entertain the visiting officers for coin."

179

"I see. And you go into them as well."

"Don't judge me for what I was two weeks ago. After all, you're no longer conscript."

I slept most of the next day and missed my rounds with the students. In the late afternoon, there was a knock at my door. Blurry-eyed and groggy, I looked out at the brightly lit corridor. Lisa Sheridan nervously waited.

"Dinner in one hour. You must attend," Lisa insisted. "And where do we return our dresses?"

"They're yours to keep, part of your dowry."

"That's too generous. I collected the jewelry. Do you want it stored?"

"I want you to keep it," I slowly said. "I thought that was understood."

"Truly?" she asked with a shy smile.

"Truly. Now let me get ready."

"You must put your necklace in our safe. There's little time."

"What's going on?"

"Please," she pleaded and glanced up the corridor.

"Come in, take them."

"I'm bring you a receipt. You may have them back on demand."

The transport rumor mill was revved into high gear concerning an insurrection at a mining facility near Cicero. Conscripts knew the increased security was an excuse for search and seizure. The crew and midshippers were prepared. Everything of value had been stowed.

Appearances must be maintained. Those in mandatory attendance in the diningroom casually milled about as though it was Monday. Undue tension would have been quickly rooted out. But while we pretended, our quarters were searched for goods and information.

I was glad my fortune in this adventure was given to those who squared off against the Company over rights to privacy and ownership. I ate Company caviar and drank their wine. I nodded to the Consortium officers who were more than a little embarrassed at this ruse, another policy they didn't endorse.

I felt Sim Chareon watch me from across the way, but didn't acknowledge his presence. My mission of goodwill was a one time offensive. He couldn't block my new friendships or my departure. I was a celebrity, and Sim Chareon couldn't afford to make me into a martyr.

My stay on the transport was nearly over. That which was begun couldn't be undone. Company countermoves stiffened the crew's resolve. Company executives must have seen that and stepped down the alert. The only part left to play was my departure with far fewer goods than my arrival, a visit more of diplomacy than inventory.

Then suddenly I remembered. I must learn the secret of cavern water. Less than a day, what to do? I wandered back toward my quarters wondering how to get a message to Hamish. Roger stepped forward in the corridor. "Come with me," he said.

"We're being watched," I lamely added.

"There are ways." He led me to a janitor closet where a woman my size waited in a red wig and some of my clothes. Roger left with her while another crewmember handed me a uniform and a dark wig. "Put these on. Hurry."

I was led to a nursery in the married quarters and pushed through a door. I looked around the dimly-lit room while my eyes adjusted. There were many cribs and three sleeping babies. A recorder played baby noises and some adult voices. Hamish stepped out of the shadows. I quickly walked to him and melted into his embrace.

"Hamish, I must know one more thing," I said. "Cavern water. The Company surveyors search every spring on the savannah."

"Is there a pool of cavern water under the desert?"

"I don't know. Why?"

"The ore sample you brought is high-grade uranium."

"Uranium?"

"It traps an energy that lasts a thousand years. Dolviets call uranium the rock that kills."

I giggled. "There's no rock like that. Unless you throw it."

"Yes, there is," he countered. "And the Company wants it. But they need a substantial reservoir of pure water for uranium refinery. If there's a body of cavern water, the Company will make a large investment."

"You mean war." I felt the downward pull in my heart that I had felt on the savannah when the Company matrix descended onto the land.

"Not much of a war without an equal enemy."

"Investment," I bitterly repeated.

I had counted only what was accomplished. A second night of love was more than I dared hope. In silence on the nursery's floor while the listening devices heard gurgling babies and quiet attendants, we tenderly clung to each other so unlike the night before.

Much later we peered down the long corridor, ready to part. How does one say goodbye to one's beloved? "Tomorrow you must make your rounds to the students and the crew. Everyone," he whispered. "I won't come down to midship."

"But what will I do? How will I live without you?"

"No conscript traits now," Hamish said with emotion. "I'll remember you as you are. Smiling, demanding, foolhardy. An example to us all."

"And I'll remember your touch, the night we danced together."

"You must go now. There is nothing more."

Chapter Twenty-Seven

The next morning I hugged the debutantes and cried with Billie. Lisa gave me a small package with a red ribbon. She insisted I shouldn't open it until I was safely home. I spoke with the crewmembers and bowed to Sim Chareon.

While I waited in midship with the disembarking colonists, Mula stepped into the cramped promenade with its blue overtones from the blaring comtech. The other students stood behind and to one side while Mula's look sought my face. I curtly nodded to him, the gesture of honor toward Putuki. He nodded with humor in his face. Then Mula bowed low and long, signifying me with a gesture of great honor, especially for a Hardhand. The students left the promenade before the signal came to board the shuttle.

The shuttle flight was short and connections were effortless. Once settled in the train's common car, I stowed those things that were mine within the deep recesses of my heart.

I wasn't the woman who had disembarked with my husband five years before. I wasn't the woman who gave reverence in the Canyon of Buttes. I wasn't the woman who ran offworld errands for my friends.

I was my own woman with memories so deep they could not be shared. My first such memory was the sight of the starving Ketiwhelp on the savannah. My last wasn't yet known. "I'm not a slave. I'm not a slave," I repeated and giggled to myself.

In Somule Carl didn't meet the train. A young Putuki man helped me step down by the tracks. When he touched my hand, I stared into his eyes. "You are brother to Mula," I whispered. "He's well and more comfortable than before."

"You will be remembered for that," he whispered in Putuki and passed on.

I had claimed on the transport that I missed weather, but I was unaccustomed to it. I left the noisy train station through the revolving doors and stepped onto the tile-roofed platform extending along the street of shops. I was fairly slapped down by a blanket of desert heat. I gasped for breath and sat heavily on a bench.

Two Arrivi women stood nearby and clucked disapprovingly from under their veils. I recognized their voices. They quickly passed me. One dropped into my lap the large and acrid Company acclimation pill. I re-entered the train station and bought a drink. I stood at the concession there and waited a few minutes while my heart rate increased and my pupils dilated. Colors became vibrant.

I was grinning like a yearling in the heat by the time I walked down the street of shops. I paused by my shop that was closed and dusty. I looked forward to opening the shop to fresh air, new goods and curious Hardhands. How could Hardhands be the same when I was so changed?

On the street I saw Lucy Kempler, her hair greased back with the sticky paste that Putuki women used to repel insects. She wore Cylahi and some Mekucoo clothes and jewelry. Lucy carried a naked Cylahi toddler in her arms and held the hand of another. Several young Cylahi children gathered around her, dirty and crying, and haphazardly followed each other toward the laboratory.

Lucy angrily shouted in Arrivi to everyone, or at least at nobody in particular. "How can you have no care for these ones? Do you no longer believe a helping hand turns away evil?

"These are Dolviet children," she shouted. "Children of us all! How can you be so cold? How can you leave them to starve on the street? These are groundborn children! Do you want them to be taken as conscript?" Dolviets turned from her while she herded the toddlers up the street.

I walked through the winding native bazaar where tribeswomen covered their goods preparing for the afternoon siesta. They didn't look up or whisper behind me. They were shamed, I thought, by Lucy's chastisement.

I arrived at my own home in my own yard. Carl and my children waited by the door. He turned away when he saw the effects of the acclimation pill.

My children ran to me for kisses and hugs and demanding presents. They drew me into the house with their chattering eagerness. I looked up from their smiling faces at the bare walls and glimpsed events that would transpire there. I saw my children alone and frightened, huddled by the fire while an angry pounding came at the door.

Would I be plagued always with these unwanted images? I must talk with goulep, I thought.

That night Carl and I laid separately on our bed. I had hoped he would embrace the cause, but he only muttered, "Worse than the Company, the way they use you." The sight of his back and the sound of his regular breathing were the remnants of our marriage.

I crept into the kitchen and opened Lisa's present. I found, lovingly wrapped in tissue paper, the peridot necklace that I had worn to the Company ball. The bluer teardrop gem seemed to gather light and store my deepest memories.

I opened the shop early the next day. I dusted and swept then sipped some tea while I stood in a patch of sunlight that streamed through the display window. The Mekucoo who shadowed Gaucho were on the street. I saw Cara across the way, but only for a moment.

I rearranged some goods anticipating a delivery from the train station. When the time for delivery passed and nothing arrived, I stepped outside and looked down the long street where people rushed forward to stare and point. I quickly closed the shop door and ran to the crowd.

My delivered goods were unwrapped and scattered in the dusty street. Lt. Lebowitz and another Blackshirt searched through packages and scratched to make unfit for resale the housewares I had purchased. Hardhands and some tribeswomen laughed and pointed. Nobody stepped forward to stop them.

"Wait! Stop!" I cried out and pushed Lt. Lebowitz's shoulder. He turned to me with hot eyes and his knife poised. The crowd drew their collective breath. The other Blackshirt drew him away. They repeatedly highstepped over the lacy cloth that had cost me weight in Cylahi gold.

Martin Sumuki and his Putuki clerks from Tri-City Bank Corp hurried up the street. "Fine thing when a businessperson cannot expect safe delivery of goods," Martin complained to the Blackshirts. "I will call a Council meeting on this."

Lt. Lebowitz glared at him then walked away. Martin's people collected the goods that were strewn about and carried them to my shop.

I felt the jealous prejudice of the Hardhand women and the inert curiosity of the tribeswomen. I had forgotten how I must face them off to conduct a little business. It all seemed hopeless, so useless, compared to the hard times that were coming.

"Thank you, Martin," I murmured without looking at him.

"You will come for tea today at three o'clock," Martin said with authority. "We'll sit in a cool room and plan how to invest your money."

I forced a smile. "My money is given, and Oriika's too."

"Then we'll plan how to make some more."

"I must speak with goulep."

"Many wait to welcome you."

I arrived at Tri-City Bank Corp changed and refreshed, having closed my shop that I just reopened. Martin and I sat over tea in his gray and apricot office.

"Would you like something stronger?" he whispered with a twinkle in his eye.

"Please," I gratefully said.

Martin came around his desk and poured from a small flask into my teacup. He whispered over my shoulder. "Do all that I tell you."

I eagerly gulped the biting drink wondering at my decadent ways. I heard him announce in his public voice, "The first couple days of acclimation are the hardest. We'll move to the air-conditioned rooms."

We slowly walked in obvious parade to the room reserved for visiting Company officials who didn't care to acclimate. Martin ushered me in and closed the door behind him.

There were gathered all my groundborn friends. Oriika, Terry, Gaucho, Kyle Le, Cara, even Cyrus. Oriika came to me with an ample embrace. "You are blessed of Dolvia."

Terry also gave me a hug. "I have missed my good friend with the fiery hair."

Kyle Le nodded from her place as far from Cyrus as she could sit. We sat around the table and Oriika began. "You must tell us everything."

I bitterly looked down. "I have seen om."

"We can see that on your spirit," Terry gently said.

"How can you face your lives knowing what will come?"

"How does Mula face it?" Oriika asked.

I felt a cold chill run across my neck. "I will tell you everything," I said. "But first, there is something. It's for Cyrus only."

They looked at each other in surprise, then assented. Martin ushered me back to his office. We made small talk for a few minutes, then shook hands in the lobby for all to see. I went to my divided home and slept for several hours, too depressed to care what political move any of them made next.

Late that night Terry arrived with a soft knock at the door. I looked at my husband and sleeping babies. "It's not far," she said.

I didn't know Cyrus or care to know him. His smoldering presence, his quarrel with Kyle Le, his richly scarred body. He seemed like the dark man in a child's nightmare.

We stepped into a stifling, unlit Cylahi lean-to where Cyrus idly sat at the table. Terry guided me to sit across from him. She backed out of the hut, holding one hand high in the air and bowing. "Anyone who might be outside can hear us," I complained.

"Then they're dead before they can speak."

"There's one at least."

"How do you know?"

"I was to give lipstick to one who asked me about it. But

later I learned they had not understood the term lipstick and didn't send anyone to ask."

"And?"

"The daughter of Sim Chareon asked me on the shuttle the first day."

Cyrus slowly digested my words. "Perhaps it means nothing."

"Perhaps," I agreed. "I thought goulep could see people's spirits."

"The season of om will be difficult indeed if we depend on the visions of one reticent child," Cyrus pronounced.

There was an uncomfortable pause. Cyrus was patient with one who had sought his presence. "You were the only one I could be sure about," I complained. "I cannot face groups."

"Dolvia will cleanse your heart," he answered, showing the gentleness I had seen him display with May and Tina. "Use today's incident as an excuse to close the shop. Visit Karima Le during her term. Families of the students will also visit the land of Murd. Tell only what you want to share."

"Who can I trust?"

"Trust what you see."

"What I see is grievous."

"Then trust that it will come true. Anything less will seem like a gift."

It was like a state visit, my stay at Haku Rabbe Murd's home. Carl allowed my children to accompany me when they cried that I was leaving after being absent for so long.

Karima Le was heavy with her second, and there were many children in the yard. Sister, as Joey called Carline, mostly stayed with me. Joey was as wild and uncontrollable as any native child. From the verandah we watched them chase domestic birds and tease the chained mongooses.

"Don't you just love the children?" May asked and put her arm around my shoulder for a quick hug.

The long verandah had many ceiling fans moved by a single rope, cooling guests in the afternoon. "Bigger than the one on the land of Arim," Tina shyly offered.

With a vista up the road, the women dressed to suit themselves and donned their body veils only when the alarm was sounded. Terry wore mostly men's clothing. She practiced weapons in the yard with Lam and Dak who were on hand, I suspected, to ensure my safety.

Terry and her instructors vanished when others arrived, unwilling to spend long hours in idle talk. May invited the families of the students onto her cool verandah. Putuki and Cylahi communed with Arrivi women and knew the spirits in their faces.

Then one afternoon from under their veils, with gentle and measured gestures, May and Tina served Kaykay Le and Julia

187

Luria-Penli in a formal tea. Julia Le had persuaded Kaykay Le to dress like her in tight-fitting, high collar gowns and mantillas. The woman of Rabbenu wore many pieces of peridot jewelry and spoke of the delights the daughters of Sim Chareon had shared with them.

"You enjoyed tea with Susan and Kate?" I asked in the face of their haughty looks. "We shared the shuttle flight together. Very kind ladies," I added.

"Oh, yes," Julia Le said. "On their recent trip to Cicero. Have you been to Cicero?"

"Many times." That shut them up. I neglected to add I had never disembarked there.

"Susan and Kate have such beautiful things," Kaykay Le said. "Will we see similar goods in your shop?"

"Only if I can secure safe delivery."

"An unfortunate incident," Julia Le claimed. "The officer was punished, I'm told. Acting on his own for fortune." We smiled and tasted the bitter tea.

I slept soundly and woke before the morning light. I looked in on my children, then strolled up the long lane that led away from Haku's house. I took deep breaths and enjoyed my view of the dewladen brush. I heard a step behind me but saw nothing when I turned.

At the end of the lane a wide view of the savannah opened. I sat on a boulder there watching the patterns the sunrise created. When the sun began to beat down in earnest, I retraced my steps and found Haku at breakfast on the verandah.

"You mustn't go out alone," he admonished me with steel in his voice. "An accident could come to you on the road."

"Who followed me?"

"None would need the duty if you stayed put."

Haku took up his tool bag and walked across the barnyard with long strides on sturdy legs. He was joined by several tribesmen who left with him to tend the cattle.

"You have made a bad bargain of it then," came the musical, mischievous voice.

"I knew you would find me." I grinned at Kyle Le with her blue gown tied up like pantaloons and her close-chopped hair.

"This desert planet that you love," she said. "Your life here is spent during the hard time before the season of om. Better you should sell the licenses and move onto the next station."

"My children will have children on Dolvia," I pronounced almost as a sacrament.

"Come. I will show you a thing."

"I was just dressed down by Haku for wandering off," I protested.

"Haku lost a brother on the road. We must go now. Later there will be visitors."

"How do you know?" I quickly asked.

True to herself, true to the demands others put on her. "There are always visitors," she said with a twinkle of the mischievous grin.

We walked a short way together. "So. Tell me about Hamish," she said.

Kyle Rula didn't speak of seeing om, or about the hard times ahead. She went directly to the deeper issue that the best moments of my life were already past. "Tell me what you saw."

"At first I saw Hamish erect and ready," I quietly confessed. "I didn't understand the image, as though he would rape me. Then I saw him in assembly but with a shower of gold and silver flecks that occurred on him only."

Kyle Le laughed out loud, showing her teeth. "This image is common. In Mekucoo legend sex prepares a woman, then she is impregnated by Dolvia with the soul of an ancestor."

"I know this myth."

"The man is also prepared," Kyle Le added. "He is showered by a life-giving rain within the woman's viewing. All this is as it should be."

"Then why was I given the other, the image of him that frightened me?"

"Would you have looked upon Hamish this way without being pushed?" she asked with a motherly tone. "You caused the entire thing to happen, prompted to act upon what you saw. And now you will have his son."

I stopped short in my tracks while she continued a few steps ahead. Kyle Rula turned to me with that special smile. "Can hard times be so difficult when Dolvia blesses us so?"

Part Four

Chapter Twenty-Eight

Rain pelted the makeshift canvas canope of our flat-bottomed canoe. A shallow sea, clogged with long grass, stretched across the savannah obscuring any landmarks that could point the way. The nearest groundfog receded. The canoe's high nose brushed against orchid-filled hanging moss suspended from the lower branches of the Acacia tree.

Sitting in the bow, Marcy turned for a signal from Mula who protected a compass from the rain. Marcy's long, bare back glistened with rivulets of water. Her loincloth and simple leggings were soaked from the constant pelting she had stoically endured during the two days of our foolish adventure. The fourteen-year-old Cylahi mulatto, one of Lucy's kids, nodded to Mula then stared without complaint into the deluge. No need to speak. We couldn't hear over the sound of weighty raindrops on the canvas and sea.

I was tucked like cargo in the belly of the canoe, feverish and chilled to the bone, continually checking my arms and neck for leeches and mites. Mula stroked the paddle left then right and grinned at me, his disdain for the Softcheeks gaucho written all over his face.

I hated that sarcastic grin. The crazy chances he took over the years, the hubris. Mula didn't seek a comfort zone, knowing as he did when he would die. He led tribesmen to their deaths while he charged in with the sure knowledge that he would survive the day. Better to work in the same clutch as Quentin. He only persecuted me.

Sitting in the canoe's stern, Tommy swung his paddle over my head with measured, rhythmic strokes. A powerful and handsome lad who followed Mula everywhere, Tommy was the strongest of Lucy's kids. Nine of them survived out of the eighteen. Abandoned and betrayed while toddlers, orphaned from their stepmother at age eight, Lucy's kids were the most militant of Mula's personal guard. They went anywhere, performed any task, gave themselves at his word to any fight. And Mula allowed them to die, their lives given in the hopeless, endless fight that siphoned the wealth and strength of the tribespeople.

I sighed deeply and prayed for the season of om. It had been eight years since Oriika and I demolished Brittany Mill and I went bald. During the struggle I had killed many men. I had led men and women to their deaths. I had ordered the deaths of some. We built a few good things. The Diet of Snakes, the Fortress of Arim, the Cylahi Caves. Cyrus taught us to travel in small groups called clutches, to stockpile munitions, to speak only to one who is known to you.

Who was left to remember? So many dead, so many tortured. So many changed into something they abhorred. I no longer felt the fire of retribution in my veins. I only felt the ubiquitous, numbing rain.

The greatest threat against those in leadership was assassination. Both Martin Sumuki and Oriika were lost in the night on the road and from behind.

Disease was the worst enemy most of us faced. Before Softcheeks came to Dolvia, native diseases were not fatal. More lethal that laser cannon directed at us from the distant transport were imported goods, strange domestic animals, refined sugar, and close proximity with Hardhands.

Lucy had died six years before when cholera crept into Somule. Under Regent Chang Lin, the infrastructure wasn't maintained including the shaky water and sewer system. The street of shops was long closed, the offworld trading rights dormant. The generator and transformers for electricity were sabotaged and crippled. The tall and expensive hotels were but shells of steel and glass, some rooms never occupied except by Blackshirts and Putuki maids.

On high ground and with its own generator, the laboratory where Lucy had solved the puzzle of synthetic netta was presumed safe and clean. Cara no longer visited and Lucy hadn't bore a child. Jim and Hank had moved onto better duty, shaking their heads with shame. Ricardo offered Lucy work in his new enterprise on Cicero, but she didn't accept since she couldn't bring her stepchildren.

When the cholera spread, most of the orphans were bedridden with distended bellies and black tongues before medical attention was tardily provided by the Company. The orphans were eight years old then, each displaying his or her own cynical, psychopathic personality. Laying on her deathbed and barely able to speak, Lucy assigned them to various dutch uncles, mostly Dolviets who led the resistance. Three died along with Lucy who wouldn't leave their bedsides.

Considered Hardhand and embryo spies, Lucy's kids were not embraced by their foster parents. Honor came to them grudgingly after many sacrifices and heroic acts that belied their

191

youth and spotty educations.

Company men had not built on the flats of Arim. Dolvia's mantle there was unstable over the largest pool of cavern water. So they chose the closest bedrock formation that afforded strategic protection. The uranium refinery, constructed between the butte and plateau below the flats, became the focal point of Company investment and tribal resistance.

Three years in construction, hampered by sabotage and weather, the refinery's completion cost the Company most of its reserves, a monumental project meant to yield astronomic profit. Proceeds from the sell of synthetic netta were to cover the cost, but it never carried the potency of sun-dried netta.

It was a putrid abomination on holy ground. The windowless concrete walls and fire-spewing towers spanned the natural breach between those timeless formations. Fortified and impregnable, it was manned by elite Blackshirts, the best of the executive guard, sent to this most valuable project because of their Chinese pedigrees.

The refinery included deep wells that robbed the flats of old water. Geysers that had once towered over the caldera basin became bubbling mudpools or dry vents.

Dolviets developed several defense strategies. As far back as the time of limestone quarries on Rabbenu land, they used Company equipment to create the Diet of Snakes. With Company bulldozers, while on supposed survey expeditions, Haku Rabbe Murd and many others dug narrow trenches on the savannah. Each slanted, crude trench was a brisk forty minute walk from two or more others. Tribespeople patiently spent days to traverse the open savannah. They waited for hours within a trench's cover until the transport dipped below the horizon and they could quickly march to the next cover.

The trenches were poorly maintained, and snakes had found their cool interiors. Travelers needed to clear the area with sulfur bombs and snares before they hid for the six hours between walks. Tribesmen were so accomplished at this travel method, they carried few provisions and ate captured snakes.

The Fortress of Arim was constructed through attrition beginning from the time Heather withdrew to live under the Arrivi veil. She couldn't be protected on the land of Murd or with goulep because of her skin color and red hair. A huge reward was offered for rumors of her movements. Arrivis built a simple hut north of the flats embedded in the rocky basin wall. A second cool and secure room was added, then another. Supplies were stockpiled. Soon it felt like a palace, especially to one who had just endured the Diet of Snakes, the only route there.

The fortress was our inner sanctum, visited by Dolviets in leadership. After Heather and I married, she lived in seclusion there for six years with only intermittent communication with goulep when their visions tortured them. Cyrus and Cara came by way of the Diet of Snakes two consecutive years when some old friends gathered before the rains. I visited eight times only before Heather became ill from eating rancid Kariom.

That was a sad time. Kyle Le and I sat with Heather for ten days while she wasted away. She wasn't that sick, and Quentin was traveling to visit. But she didn't want to continue. Carl had been deported along with Joey and Sister. We guessed that Heather's family were assigned as conscripts in the bowels of some dank Company freighter in another sector or even outside of Westend.

Heather spoke of her four children, lost babes who didn't flourish. She wondered if destroying the first in the womb was a sin that she repaid with the lives of the other three. She spoke often about Terry and the orphaned Ketiwhelp who had been Terry's companion on the savannah. She reminisced about the Canyon of Buttes and her communion with four sandstone pillars there. Heather gently passed away early one evening after she asked me to send her love to Hamish. Quentin arrived before dark. He had spend the last six hours in a trench that was a forty minute walk from the fortress.

The Cylahi Caves were played-out quarry pits the Company had written off. Holy women went there to give reverence to Dolvia and pray for Her forgiveness for these scars. From the holy women the Cylahi learned the area was unclaimed and promised shelter. Over time they dug further into the pits and hid four-ton trucks and bulldozers captured from convoys that apparently vanished from the transport surveillance.

Transport cameras photographed May hanging out the laundry, so precise was their technology. Tribespeople were vulnerable to attack anytime they ventured onto the savannah. Trucks and animals in groups left infra-red trails.

The simple Ketiwhelp trick of backtracking totally fooled Company methods. We ambushed the convoys just as the transport dipped below the horizon. We drove the trucks in reverse, backtracking along their own route, where they were joined by many other trucks in a confusing traffic jam. When the transport rose above the horizon again, long-distance cameras could not sort out which trucks to follow and which were most likely empty. Trails sometimes led out onto the desert where the infra-red imprints simply stopped.

Then Mula grew bolder, capturing one convoy that carried handheld munitions. But instead of scattering to confuse the transport cameras, native drivers continued along the pre-assigned route until they reached Somule. The trucks were driven through the narrow bazaars while goods were quickly offloaded at many street corners. Family members in the Somule prison dearly paid for that day's adventure.

193

Then there was the ore itself. Company officers so often found small quantities of uranium in their quarters that Geiger counters were installed twenty feet apart. A shipment of sealed containers, intended for transporting the deadly ore, had hairline cracks ever one, a problem the transport crew claimed must have happened during the shuttle flight.

Plus there were weak places in Company defense strategy. Convoys of supplies were Mula's favorite targets. He constantly hammered away at these. The Company's most recent response to continual losses was to build a shuttle launchpad near the refinery. But not too close. If the shuttle was sabotaged, the refinery must not be at risk. The strip of ground between the new launchpad and the refinery was the most heavily guarded real estate by ground troops and transport ordinance in Westend.

The garrisons in Cylay, at the shuttle site and the railhead in Somule were islands of Company strength in the sea of resistance. Mula organized raids and assaults that captured Blackshirts' stockpiled weapons, cut off supply deliveries, and demoralized the mercenaries. Siege and starvation were impractical but, when he felt so moved, Mula kept the Blackshirts bottled up at their stations.

Chang Lin embraced the hostage system as a means to an end. Hardhand colonists had been evacuated before fighting broke out in Somule. Blackshirts moved back into the former barracks. The exercise yard in the compound was the same where Cyrus had endured three whippings by his brutal tormentor twenty-two years before.

The Blackshirts held Dolviet hostages, mostly women and children, at the garrisons. They circulated stories of torture and starvation in the hated Somule prison. Every Arrivi, Putuki, Cylahi and Mekucoo family lost loved ones at the hands of the Blackshirts who seemed selected for this duty according to their taste for brutality.

In Regent Chang Lin's time many acts of torture and execution without trial occurred in the prison yard. It was said that noises could be heard like a baby crying in the night, the mournful cries of the spirits of those who were murdered there.

Katelupe Le was the first Dolviet captured under Regent Chang Lin. Company men considered Terry a major weapon to control goulep and grab the flats of Arim. Blackshirts alternately brutalized her and nursed her back to relative health. She was shown to prisoners scheduled for release so her suffering was made known to those in leadership.

Early in the struggle, some heavy equipment the Company was moving to the uranium mines was crippled. Blackshirts took as hostage Haku Rabbe Murd and four others who had operated Company equipment in Rabbenu quarries. That they were, or were not, the saboteurs wasn't a question that concerned the

Blackshirts.

After months of isolation and interrogation, Haku was taken into a room where several Blackshirts sat at dinner. There was little more Haku could tell them. Imprisoned for so long, he knew nothing about recent tribal strategy. He was brought in for their entertainment.

In his shame Haku never told the story or acknowledged reference to it. But it was news throughout Dolvia the following day. The Blackshirts forced him, under pain of disembowelment and death, to have intercourse with Terry the Martyr, his sister-in-law, while the Blackshirts cheered. When he refused to perform, they stripped Terry and passed her around. When he couldn't maintain an erection, they whipped her. When he finished the act over her emaciated and bloodied body, she spoke Spindel's name into his ear and passed out.

There's more to this story. Lt. Lebowitz delighted in tormenting Terry. He hung her on tethers for days and read letters supposedly from her family about people who had been killed or ran away. He kept her in an open cell near the yard of torture and named those who passed by so she knew whose cries she heard throughout the day.

When it became obvious that Terry was pregnant, Lt. Lebowitz increased his abuse both mental and physical. Terry's child was stillborn at seven months, and Terry died the next day. In an effort to silence the uprising that immediately assaulted Company positions, Haku Rabbe Murd and many others were released in a general amnesty. Lt. Lebowitz was posted to the transport. Regent Chang Lin didn't rely on the hostage system after that.

Tommy rocked the boat slightly to get our attention, then pointed into the fog. My god, we made it. We nearly crashed into the plateau that housed the clutch of Murd. We stood in the boat and gingerly felt our way along the rockface, reaching into the constant run-off that pelted the canope and threatened to sink the canoe. We came to a cleft in the high wall that was deep enough for us to stand behind the downpour. We climbed onto the slippery rock and inched along the ridge, tugging the boat behind by two heavy, sodden ropes.

Finally we reached a natural cave where our friends waited. Two tribesmen grabbed the ropes and laboriously hauled the boat up the face of the plateau. We entered a narrow opening and were deafened for a moment by the absent sound of pelting rain.

The tunnel opened into a low-ceiling, wide and dark cave. The men of Murd stood with weapons ready, then recognized us and relaxed by the cooking fires. They heartily greeted Mula while Marcy and Tommy stood to one side.

Each clutch wore a distinctive uniform sewn by Arrivi and Putuki women on the iron sewing machines taken from Brittany

Mill. Haku's clutch wore loose linen pantaloons under Arrivi double-paneled sleeveless tunics. They carried toolbags loaded with munitions and mostly handheld weapons. Many in Haku's clutch were expert with demolitions having been trained by the Company during the time of Rabbenu's limestone quarries.

I drank from the steaming cup that was offered and gladly received dry clothes. I indicated the two who all ignored but got no response. I took my dry clothes to Marcy who stared me down with a stony face. What had we created to deserve such a look from a fourteen-year-old? I left the clothes near her and returned to the fire.

The cave dripped and smelled of sulfur. The fires put dancing patterns on the walls but had little effect on the cool air. I longed for the burning, purifying desert sun. That crucible was far preferable to this chilly cauldron. In my discomfort I missed the subtle signal that ushered us into another area. Lam firmly grabbed me by the upper arm and led me to Haku Rabbe Murd just as though I were Softcheeks.

Haku was much changed since the day I met him at his wedding. Imposing and strong, he was disfigured across the left side of his face and neck from a napalm burn. He stiffly carried his left side from older wounds received in the Blackshirt prison. "Hiki Gaucho," Haku said then gave me a bear hug. He held me at arm's length inspecting me like a Ketiwhelp pelt.

I wore the dark dungarees and tunic of the clutch of Quentin plus my Mekucoo beltknife. My hair was closecut and discolored, as was my complexion, from the insect repellent I used nearly year round. But I displayed stamina and understood strategy, as nearly Dolviet as they. He pointed at my wet clothes and looked around.

"I gave them to Lucy's kids," I quickly explained.

"Get him some more," Haku said.

After I had changed, Haku and Mula sat with me by the fire. "We cannot reason with the Softcheeks," Haku explained. "When he was told of Heather's death, his soul turned from his face." They looked at me as though this Softcheeks malady was universal.

"I haven't seen Hamish in years," I said into their cold stares. "I don't know what you think I can do."

"Tell him it doesn't bother you that he loved your wife," Mula offered and the others softly chuckled.

We entered a third chamber where Hamish laid on a cot with his back to us. Mula stood over him. "Get up, Hamish. You smell like a wet mongoose."

Hamish turned and stared into Mula's face with alcohol-blurred vision. "It's Mula. I must be early." My turn to chuckle. To Hamish, Mula the revolutionary leader was a barefoot student whose presence retarded the season of om.

"We will rob the desert of many Softcheeks before the season of om," Mula claimed.

Hamish swung his legs off the cot and painfully sat upright. He realized that others watched him and leaned against the cave wall. "Haku, ever vigilant," he pronounced in cynical tones. "The patient will survive."

"We brought a Softcheeks," Mula said pointing to me.

Hamish's expression was set, a soldier's discipline. "Brian Rabbe Miller. Ricardo wants to speak with you."

Haku and Lam hid their smiles. The destruction of Brittany Mill had signaled the beginning of resistance and oppression. The Company's shining example of successful commerce and goodwill became the explosion heard around Westend. I had endured the Diet of Snakes and had not communicated with Ricardo Menenous since that day.

"Get dressed. We have something for you," Mula curtly said and left the chamber.

Before he followed Mula out, Haku signaled Lam who stepped back to wait by the entrance. Hamish gave Lam a long look. "They think I'll kill myself. Or kill you."

Hamish poured water from a pitcher into a shallow bowl then splashed some onto his face. He exchanged his very soiled shirt for one that was laid out for him. He scratched himself and lit a kari root cigarette, then looked around. "Would you have a short bracer for an old man?"

I passed my small flask to him. He raised it in my direction, then drank deeply. His three word threat to kill me was the only reference he made to the fact that we loved the same woman, that she was married to me for six years, that their child was stillborn.

Hamish drank again and passed the flask to me. He stretched and belched, then stared into my questioning face. "As I see it," he began, "the Company has the same weakness they had when this began, their own arrogance. They didn't engage the ground war except for the Blackshirts. Now that the refinery's operational, they're assembling Consortium troops to occupy this area."

He glanced at me, then continued. "Consortium officers have divided loyalties. Mula's people may have a new advantage. If you can keep the Company fighting from the transport only, it's possible to bleed their resources without troop conflicts. Plus recruit more Consortium sympathizers."

"So Dolviets should allow Blackshirts to torture and slaughter them until some offworld Softcheeks gathers the energy to cut their throats," I summarized.

"I'm not the architect of the resistance," he said. "Chang Lin has been replaced. The new Regent wants to talk."

"Ha, what news is this? They always want to talk at first, to

197

feel us out. Then kill us in the night. Mula will never sit down with them."

"Regent Tao Chek wants to talk with you."

"And you're their messenger boy?"

"I volunteered. My first time ever."

Chapter Twenty-Nine

Tao Chek was a tall and fey, blanched-white Manchurian with almond eyes and long fingers. He wore the Company dark suit with a round collar and the lapel pin of the high command. Regent of Westend for six weeks and resident on Dolvia for ten days, he worked in the refinery offices of former Regent Chang Lin reviewing dossiers on troublesome natives and political prisoners.

Across from him sat Captain Ellis, the Somule prison commander. Regent Chek knew Captain Ellis as a brutal and self-serving man whose loyalty was to his stolen fortune above Company policies. "The barracks are vulnerable," Captain Ellis claimed. "We need a detachment of your troops stationed with us."

A disdainful look covered Tao Chek's face. "You were garrisoned on Dolvia to keep the peace, Captain Ellis. Now you need protection?"

"My men are sick from this fungus that has no cure."

"Give them Company netta."

"Their condition's too advanced."

"Do they still hear cries in the night?" Regent Chek said acidly, counting the Blackshirts' many complaints.

"Those cries are real," Captain Ellis defended. "I have heard them. Like a baby whimpering."

"Perhaps there is a baby."

"We had the yard searched. Now about the extra troops."

Tao Chek bristled at the effrontery of Captain Ellis' request. "My guard doesn't draw police duty. Use the midshippers."

"They won't fight."

"Then take their families hostage."

Captain Ellis paused, and the regent looked up. "What?"

"The most recent group weren't allowed families."

There was a soft knock at the tall and ornate door, followed by the implacable face of the regent's military secretary, Daniel Chin. "They have arrived, Regent."

"Have them wait."

Tao Chek signaled the end of the interview with Captain Ellis. "Use natives from another region. They have families."

"Yes, Regent. In the meantime, we're most exposed."

"I can send you extra munitions."

"We have more guns now than men."

"That's what I can spare. Leave by that door. Ask the one in the hall to join me."

Captain Ellis curtly bowed, then left by the side door. Dillan Rabbe Penli entered and easily sat in the chair Captain Ellis had vacated, wearing a dark suit of Company cut with Company-style platinum and coral jewelry.

Dillan lit a kari root cigarette that he took from a thin platinum case he carried in his suitcoat. He exhaled with relish. "Kari root is the only compensation for returning. I truly missed that aroma."

Dillan felt he was instrumental in securing Tao Chek as regent. They played handball together and spent long hours in preparation for Regent Chek's ascension. The family of Penli including Kaykay Le, wife of former Rabbenu, lived in exile on Cicero in a modest house in the high-security Company enclave. They dressed Company, talked Company and paid an exorbitant rate for services and amenities. They called themselves ambassadors and were on display at Company functions. They were watched every moment.

Tao Chek loathed Dillan as a turncoat capable of only two-dimensional thinking. He had standing orders for Dillan's public execution if certain events transpired.

"You should take Brian Miller now," Dillan peevishly claimed. "We can make him talk."

"And learn today's gossip?" Tao Chek asked with tolerance.

"I'm telling you, he knows everybody."

"Go back to your family," Regent Chek said with tolerance. "Allow me to handle things."

"But about Cyrus and Rularim."

"They aren't my primary concern. I'll call you."

Dillan stubbed out his cigarette and unwillingly left by the side door. Tao Chek pressed a button on his console and the secretary showed his face again. "Bring them in," Tao Chek said. "But first, remove that." Daniel Chin took the ashtray out with him.

Five Consortium officers were ushered into the regent's presence by Daniel Chin. They curtly bowed to Regent Chek who spoke to Captain Blakesley. "Please, make yourselves comfortable."

The officers relaxed and waited near two facing couches that were gathered by a Chinese screen decorated with black and red outline drawings of cherry blossoms. "I have arranged for you to meet our liaison with the tribespeople," Tao Chek continued. "Brian Miller may be able to answer some questions, clear the air about resistance to the refinery. If you'll wait for just a moment."

Tao Chek pressed a button on his console then, with a formal air, waited behind his desk. Hamish and I entered wearing our best military bearing and cynical faces. Hamish casually bowed to the regent, aware the Consortium officers watched. He skirted insubordination but complied with protocol.

"Regent Chek," he said. "I trust you've settled in comfortably."

"These rooms were inherited from a predecessor."

"May I introduce one you have sought to meet, Brian Miller?"

"Good of you to come." We each stiffly bowed with arms at our sides.

"I don't know if you remember, Regent," Hamish said. "Brian attended your engagement ceremony at the Company compound. How is your family?" As he had in the clutch of Murd, Hamish put adversarial parties at ease.

"My wife and son live on Cicero for now," Tao Chek said. "May I offer you a drink before we begin?"

Tao Chek came around the imposing desk and led us to the sidebar, ignoring the Consortium officers. He poured three tumblers with ice and red tea. I couldn't keep myself from staring at the ice, something I hadn't seen for years. I saw question on Regent Chek's face and felt very native. I glanced at Hamish whose expression didn't change. I disliked the role of gaucho with these two.

The regent led us to the waiting officers. "Brian Miller," he said, "please meet some Consortium officers who serve on the transport and on Cicero." I bowed to the five officers who wore brilliant blue dress uniforms with gold braids on their shoulders. A large group, it seemed to me, and not sharing the regent's buoyant mood.

"Brian has been our liaison with the tribes," Regent Chek lightly said, not meeting the officers' eyes. "His service has been valuable in acquainting us with tribal law. Brian, these men have certain questions we thought you were most qualified to answer. If you don't mind, perhaps you could spend a few minutes."

Regent Chek stepped back to the sidebar, while Hamish and I faced their inquiring looks. Hamish gestured slightly and the men relaxed. "The one Cyrus," Captain Blakesley began. "He's the Mekucoo who the tribesmen rescued by showering the garrison with snakes."

I shrugged. "Twenty-five years ago."

"Twenty-two years," he corrected. "One stripe, one snake is the legend."

"I have met Dolviets who participated," I casually said. "And I have seen his stripes."

"And does his spirit linger in the yard of torture, whimpering in the night?" a young man in the front quietly asked.

I met his uneasy look. "I have heard a similar story. Night terrors frighten only the guilty."

"Tell us about the Putuki Quentin," another officer said. "Is it true that he heals battle wounds?"

"He can heal infections but not wounds."

"How does he do that?"

"It's a spiritual gift."

I saw their disbelieving glances. "Like the laying on of hands. Quentin has a connection with spirits on the land."

"What spirits?"

I saw their interest rise. Hamish fidgeted. "There are many spirits," I quickly added. "But not ghosts, not witches."

"Is it true that Mula's a shapeshifter?" one officer asked from the back.

"You believe in shapeshifting, but not in the laying on of hands?" I asked, then glanced at Hamish who raised his eyebrows.

"It's said that Mula becomes a Ketiwhelp to escape capture," the officer defended.

"Mula's just himself. The myth of the Ketiwhelp is about a young boy named Spindel who died many years ago."

"Then why has Mula never been captured?"

"Mula knows the desert," I shrugged. "Plus he was trained on the transport, so he knows about military procedure and surveillance. I doubt he could find you on Cicero."

"Do you believe the tribespeople have special powers?" Captain Blakesley asked.

"All people have special powers. Your knowledge of interplanetary communication, your knowledge of what lies below the surface of Dolvia, your knowledge of how to make gunpowder. These are special powers to Dolviets."

"But they aren't spiritual powers."

I thought about it for a moment. "It's true that you could teach Quentin about gunpowder and not learn to heal sickness from him, if that's what you mean. But all that Mula knows, you could learn in time."

"It's said that you share in the treasure of the one Rularim," one officer quickly asked as though the interview was ending.

"The tithe to Rabbenu is your measure of Rularim's wealth, not my poor savings."

"We know this Rabbenu Dillan Penli," the one in the back said. "He has no special powers."

"That's enough questions," Regent Chek said, and I saw the

cold evil that was his heart.

Hamish moved slightly and the young men became tense. Ah, so these were his minion. The usual formalities were endured. The young officers appraisingly looked around on their way out. One glanced back over his shoulder before the door closed behind them.

"What's your assessment of the situation here?" Tao Chek abruptly asked.

"Militarily, it's impossible," Hamish reported. "A ground force would have many fronts, hamstrung by the rainy season. Transport firepower puts the planet's mantle at risk. And thereby, your investment."

"Negotiation, then?"

"How will you negotiate with tribesmen who your predecessor oppressed?"

"A poor choice on his part. An exchange for prisoners perhaps." Tao Chek looked at me.

I cynically smiled. "Drop the pretext. You know Dolviets don't take prisoners. You called me here to deliver a message. Just get to it."

Regent Chek valued straight talk. "We need an ombudsman. Someone who can travel with impunity, someone they trust. To begin negotiations."

"Negotiate what?"

"That will be decided between Mula and myself," Regent Chek said. "An end to hostilities, a return of commerce."

"The return of self-rule?" I probed.

"The natives aren't equipped to refine uranium."

"Dolviets want the rock that kills left in the ground," I returned.

"That's impractical."

"Impractical for whom?"

Tao Chek paused ever so slightly. "We have drawn up a paper and a bank draft to offer compensation, retroactively, to one Rularim. For the use of her land and the pool of cavern water. In this way, we show that we wish to deal in good faith during my rule as regent."

"Rularim will never accept," I said.

"It's a great deal of money."

"If they accept your money, they condone your activity. Perhaps you haven't understood why they fight."

"For self-rule."

"For harmony," I corrected. "Dolviets have a specific definition of harmony. It's a complicated concept to us because we don't see the land as a living being. To them it's very simple."

"The return to an agrarian society," Tao Chek concluded. His upbringing included grudging respect for those whom he must subdue, but I couldn't allow him that comfort.

"Perhaps in part," I answered. "Dolvia is alive. They must fight for Her survival and theirs in harmony with Her. The solution they seek is that you stop uranium production."

"Surely they see the futility of their struggle," he said with a sneer. "We have unlimited resources, superior firepower."

"I will tell them you said so. I recommend you don't insult Rularim with this offer of . . . rent."

I saw the ruthless flash in his almond eyes that was the true Regent Chek. Hamish had gained the only advantage. Ground forces would not be deployed. "Set up a meeting between this Rularim and myself. We may be . . ."

I chuckled softly. He stopped short. "That's funny?"

"You will never meet her. The death of Katelupe the Martyr taught you nothing?"

"I'm offering a peaceable solution."

"No man is greater than Dolvia. You can kill all the people and animals and plants. They'll fight to the last one to save their planet."

"Then they will all die."

"Sim Chareon said that before you. And Regent Chang Lin after him."

Regent Chek quietly considered me for a moment. "This has been a good meeting. I hope you'll accept our invitation to visit again when it's convenient. An open channel of communication is most valuable."

I put my drink on the table, ready to leave. "May I make a suggestion?" I asked. "If you want to talk to certain factions in the resistance, then release the traitor Dillan Penli and his family to Dolviet justice."

"To a mob?"

"To a trial attended by many."

"An interesting idea," Tao Chek conceded. "But I suspect tribal leaders have a surprise for us with such a move."

"Negotiation means concessions from both sides."

Chapter Thirty

No contact with Dolviet leadership was possible until Hamish boarded the shuttle and I disappeared into the deluge. So we braved the rain in Somule for dinner and drinks, then entered a bawdy house. "I admire your system of clutches," Hamish said while he stood at the bar. "I admire many things you have accomplished here."

"What was all that in the regent's office?" I asked. "Who were those men?"

"Husbands of the debutantes, some of them," he explained.

"Who?"

"Heather didn't tell you? When she visited the transport, there was a ball where she arranged for some women from crew families to be presented to visiting Consortium officers."

"So?" I shrugged.

Hamish thought about it for a moment. "So they remember her fondly."

During the struggle Hamish had been posted at various communications centers throughout Westend. He used rotation of personnel as an opportunity to talk with Consortium officers concerning questionable Company policies. He spoke always of a greater struggle. He saw Dolvia as a beacon for many who labored in Westend, allies who we inspired but could not know.

But once again I felt sorry for Hamish. He had known Heather for twelve days eight years before. Their child he never saw. He labored with much younger men who understood little of his tradition or his humor. Yet he met each day with discipline born of training and a personal strength that came only from moral fiber.

We parted at the Somule hotel entrance near an ECCAV that waited to take him to the shuttle launchpad. I spoke in that last moment. "She thought about you every day. Her last words were of you."

His face betrayed nothing. "I'm glad she found comfort with you, Gaucho. I'm glad it was you."

I made connections with Marcy and Tommy, changed clothes and canoes several times, doubled back on our path in continuing loops like the warrior Oria of legend, then rested in the clutch of Quentin the healer from where I had started this adventure.

Each clutch had its own character. Formed for special purposes with various leaders, the clutches displayed none of the uniformity or shared agenda of an organized army. It made me vaguely nauseous to enter the chaotic array. How could they accomplish any move against the Company from this murky wellspring?

Quentin's clutch wore dark green tunics with dungarees over boots instead of pantaloons and sandals. They were the most militant and carried the heaviest armor. Quentin's confidence as a young man had been in his gift of healing. When confronted with a force he couldn't affect, he armed himself many times over, mostly to cover his back.

After I reported to those who would report to Mula and Kyle Le, known after all this time and in her advancing spinsterhood as Rularim, I was encouraged to go into hiding. I was glad to turn away from errands accomplished in the rain. I hoped my pawnlike moves weren't needed again until the savannah was dry.

In the solitude of hiding, I considered the many forces Dolvia allowed. What had become of my friends from long ago? Where were the tribespeople who found me entertaining, my partners and employees? I seemed on a path that traveled away from them even while I labored to remain near them.

What was left? What reason to carry on? All we had once envisioned for our futures was sacrificed to the egotistical maneuvers of a maniacal leader who didn't fear his own death. Where was the voice of reason?

Marcy brought a bowl of soup and a piece of bread. I knew she ate only after others in the clutch had their fill. I took a few bites and passed the bowl to her. She stood to return it to the cooking fire.

I grabbed her wrist. "Stay with me until you finish the remainder."

She glanced at Tommy who stood aside. "They will think I serve you to have some."

"Why do you bring it?"

"Your spirit turns from your face," was her evasive answer.

"Eat it. Then put on dry clothes. You're too old to wear nothing. Lucy would wonder that I allow it. As do some of the men."

Marcy had drawn easy duty. Assigned to me by her dying stepmother, she felt her own weakness was the root cause. Too frightened or useless to follow Mula or chase after Cyrus and Cara, she must watch over the morose Softcheeks. Each act of kindness I performed increased her shame that hers was the softest station for the weakest orphan while the other mulattoes fought and suffered and died alongside tribal leaders.

So different Marcy was from the smiling Kyle Le who I had met at Haku's wedding. Kyle Le's assumption had been she was gifted and alone, persecuted by her own people. If one believed the reports, she still felt that.

Kyle Le didn't participate in the resistance, nor did her sisters. Before Terry was martyred in prison, Kyle Le made many attempts first to free Terry, then failing that, to secure prison privileges. Captain Ellis developed an appetite for Kyle Le's entreaties and valuable gifts, always demanding more of greater value or deeper sacrifice.

It was said but never proven that Rularim regularly went to Captain Ellis' quarters with gifts of another kind. Of course it couldn't be true. Any Blackshirt would turn her in for the reward. Her bribes to prison guards were small by comparison.

Karima Le lived openly in Somule with her three children. May's home was a sprawling adobe building situated south of the Council building and near the Cylahi slum. Actually it was across the street from where the Brittany Mill had been. It had wood floors, electric outlets, plus a tile roof and thatched verandah overhangs.

Haku never visited, unwilling to risk being captured again. But their oldest son Orin, now nineteen, traveled to Somule with news and small gifts from Haku. May was not harassed by Blackshirts being the sister of Terry the Martyr. She was watched, of course, being the sister of Rularim who guided the tribes through her gift of second sight.

Klistina Le ran away. She felt there was no place for her in tribal activity. She had loved Cyrus as a young girl, only to be pushed aside by the lifelong fight he knew with goulep. Then she had loved the Softcheeks who ran Brittany Mill who also foolishly loved Kyle Le. When I married Heather, Tina's face turned bitterly downward, and she went on adventure as far from us as she could travel.

I knew where she was, but I didn't have the heart to tell May. Hamish asked if he should buy Tina's contract and return her from Cicero. Since Company men didn't know her lineage and didn't care, we felt her peril was greater on Dolvia.

So Tina, by her own choice, played courtesan to officers as one of many in the Company stable. Hamish took care to add that Tina served greatly by delivering to the ears of trusted crewmembers news that Company men told while in bed. I didn't believe him.

Marcy stood before me in dark trousers and a short tunic. Her hard face regarded me with disdain, but I knew her stomach was full. "Carry a change of clothes with you at all times. If I

207

see you without both shirt and trousers, I'll insist you wear a gown." Tommy snickered from the side where he watched everything.

"Also," I added, "you will not show your body to any man, including Lucy's kids, without my approval. If you become pregnant, I'll beat you before the full Council meeting." Marcy's hateful look didn't flicker.

"Now go find something useful to do," I said. "And take your shadow with you. Is it Tommy's duty to guard you from me?" Marcy almost smiled before she turned on her heel and walked past Tommy.

Later I heard excited murmuring and the rustle of dry skirts. I looked up from my private ramblings to focus on a small woman wearing an Arrivi gown and veil. She could be only one person. The veil had been outlawed by the Company some time ago. The much smaller millhood, which tribal women had once so proudly displayed on the street of shops, was excuse enough for imprisonment by the Blackshirts. Plus wearing so many ankle-length clothes in the sulfur-laden cave was poor judgment unless it was undertaken for the effect it produced. From the dry rustle, I knew Kyle Le also wore a small section of natural netta, a commodity still prized throughout Westend.

"I'm told you turned down payment offered to me," she said from under the veil. "Considerable payment."

"Their money is paper. They need only print more. Accepting the payment includes giving up certain rights."

"My rights to give or not give."

"Plus my twelve percent."

Kyle Rula pulled her veil from her head and shoulders, then handed it to Marcy who received it like a rare treasure. Others crowded in and strained to see, so rude.

No longer an innocent child fascinated by atmosphere, Kyle Le wore her hair like May's in a thick braid down her back. She was more Arrivi than her own mother, more Arrivi than Dolviet. "I had forgotten what it's like to talk with you, Brian Rabbe Miller. Always a challenge."

Kyle Le accepted a steaming cup offered with many bows and hands held high. "Please," she said, barely nodding to their adulation. "This morose Softcheeks and I have much to discuss." Those of the clutch of Quentin the healer reluctantly drew away.

Marcy lingered, staring wide-eyed at Rularim. "Still inspiring young girls, I see," Kyle Le dryly claimed.

"They reject me when they become women," I said.

"That should tell you something."

"It tells me that women are fickle."

Kyle Le looked around for a place to sit that wouldn't soil her hand-stitched gown. Marcy quickly laid a tunic over a munitions crate. Rularim sat and arranged her skirts. "Are there any among the tribes you actually like?" she asked in the same tone.

"There's Cyrus."

The girlish smile had become a confident smirk around her eyes. "You're in luck. Cyrus will visit."

"Let me guess," I offered. "An offensive against the shuttle launchpad when the clouds break. But first ambush the convoy, assassinate certain leaders, and a jailbreak. Don't you think they're braced for that?"

"Many of these methods we learned from you," she said with humor. "Is there another you haven't shared?"

"Hamish says there is."

"Heather and the child are gone," Kyle Rula recited tribal policy. "Who is Hamish to us? Even if he wasn't placed here to learn our secrets, they can make him talk on the transport. Mula dislikes this plan."

"Mula dictates to goulep?"

I saw a faint shadow of her delicious smile while she passed the cup to Marcy. "You know it's treason to speak that word."

"I'm Softcheeks."

"You're a bitter old man," she quickly accused. "Heather could not change you, try as she may."

"Heather was Softcheeks."

"Hamish, Heather and you. Why do you strike this one note?" Kyle Rula's eyes flashed with irritation.

"Why do you wear that ridiculous gown?"

"I just finished it," she said with childish delight. "So few occasions to wear one."

"A spinster's vanity then."

"A privilege once denied goulep."

"Armor in preparation for Cyrus' return."

"Nobody speaks to me this way," Kyle Le sternly said but without anger.

"What will you do, now that your defenses are gone?"

"Don't talk in riddles," she impatiently said. But I knew she had warmed up to our game. She had sought me out to confide her feelings.

"You're no longer in disgrace," I said. "No longer too young. You and Cyrus agree on war strategy, in equal places of leadership. Hiding behind the veil has become . . . flimsy."

"Cyrus is Mekucoo."

"And this gown states you're Arrivi. So then?"

"His wife raises their children on Mekucoo land. That's immutable."

Chapter Thirty-One

I keenly missed Martin and Oriika. Their presence had afforded a layer of leadership between me and Mula or Quentin. Able negotiators, they and not me would have parlayed with Regent Chek and answered to Rularim. Plus they would have been the most public players in the trial. As it was, I became the pawn that both sides pushed around on the board.

It was the trial of Dillan Rabbe Penli who collaborated with Company men, who stole the tithe of his tribespeople, and who preferred the friendship of Tao Chek over his kind and even his family.

Dolviets had considerable grievances against Dillan Penli. While he lived in grand style on Cicero, money for munitions was scarce and medicine for wounds and disease was nonexistent. While Dillan traveled to the pleasure domes of the Company's high command, Dolviets were tortured and starved in prisons in Somule and Cylay. While Dillan and Julia Le dressed in Company finery and attended military galas on the transport, Dolviet children died of starvation without the comfort of knowing where their parents lived and fought in the resistance.

Julia Luria and the in-laws were included in the condemnation and the charges. Only Kaykay Le received the people's sympathy. It was widely believed she had agreed to accompany her daughter and son-in-law to Cicero in order to raise her grandchildren after Arrivi customs.

The trial became the event of the season. "Could it be true?" Dolviets asked each other.

"Just another Company trick."

"What a thing to see. The comeuppance of Dillan and his Company wife."

"They want us to gather in one place so they can massacre us," was their suspicion.

"Still. To see the spirit in Julia Le's face."

The trial was held in the public room of Somule's Council building. The room was shuttered and air-conditioned. Hot lights and a weighty camera on a high tripod blocked the view of many in the rear seats. Daily events were broadcast over Cicero's comtechs, on transports and freighters, and at military installations throughout Westend.

There was no jury and no judicial representative from Dolvia. There was only the Company arbitrator, a graying woman with a strong jawline and a glint in her eye.

Daniel Chin, as the Company defender, was skilled in speaking to our fears. Mula, Cyrus, Rularim and me together couldn't second guess his maneuvers. Oriika even, had she been with us, would have known her greatest opponent.

Tribespeople eagerly watched Daniel Chin, entranced by the cadence of his deep voice, straining to see the next flash of his manicured hand. He was trim and tailored, his gestures few and quick. His accent was crisp, his imagery precise. Ah, he was good. He mesmerized me. And I was his opponent.

Holy women once claimed Softcheeks were difficult to read, being divided onto three planes. But somehow Daniel Chin polished that view of himself as well. He was beautiful to Dolviets with second sight, shimmering without revealing the truth.

A small group of Company men sat behind Daniel Chin, carbon-copy faces with slanted eyes. They secured a respectable presence for Company interests without appearing to impose order on the crowd of citizens.

Also in the Company gallery sat the family of Dillan Rabbe Penli, including Julia Le in Company dress and Kaykay Le in a traditional Arrivi gown and body veil folded as a shawl. I wondered at their choice of clothes. Among Dolviets, sympathy for Kaykay Le was tempered by the sight of Julia Le's garish outfits. Offworld, the presence of a traditionally dressed parent only gave visual reinforcement to their aboriginal roots.

Some Dolviets came daily and grew accustomed to the environment. Groups of students were ushered into the back rows, and teachers whispered instructions throughout the proceedings. Students were more interested in the camera equipment than in the circular arguments and occasional outbursts.

Somule came back to life with the attention of the trial. The garrison was boarded up. Blackshirts moved prisoners to the more defensible Company compound on the high ground north of Somule. The electric generators were repaired and service restored. Reporters and cameramen checked into the scarred hotels, their first offworld guests. Tribespeople opened the newly-profitable food bazaars where offworld reporters milled about waiting for news of daily events in the Council building.

Often tribespeople were asked if they knew anything that shed light on past events. Just tell the truth. Was it true that goulep could see a man's heart in his face? Fascinated by roving reporters and cameramen with shoulder-mounted camcorders, the tribespeople stood as though frozen and stared into the wide lenses. But they revealed nothing to the offworld audience.

We communed at Karima Le's house on the main street of Somule. Over time many rooms had been added to accommodate impromptu meetings and overnight visitors. Lam and Dak were present, now viewed as granduncles who conducted lessons in the yard on taming mongooses and how to prepare domestic fowl for May's table.

Two offworld reporters with camcorders were stationed across from May's front yard. They smoked kari root with Dak and accepted a family of mongooses as mascots. We carefully monitored who entered May's home by that route.

In the back was the kitchen, the real power center. May presided over meals and laundry while she taught groups of children at the wooden table. I was given a room near the kitchen, a convenience during the trial. Some evenings we sat together on May's back porch, her private place that looked out onto the small yard where linens hung on a clothesline. While the trial progressed, I saw her grow sad that I no longer enjoyed their company.

"Is Kyle Rula the new holy woman?" I quietly asked one cool evening.

May looked at me with disbelief. "Is it not enough that she's goulep? Besides, holy women don't marry."

"Kyle Le will marry?"

"Perhaps I said it badly," May hedged. "Whatever attracts men to women, that aura doesn't exist on holy women. Men don't notice them. In this way, Dolvia covers those who She reserves for Herself."

"But everyone knew Oriika. She filled the room."

"Since men didn't see her on a certain level, Oriika displayed herself after the customs of her tribe. But you know that Kyle Le's aura is that of a woman who will marry."

I blushed deeply. "Why doesn't a holy woman come forward?"

"But there is a holy woman. She attends the trial every day." May paused at my questioning look. "When she has a word for you, it will be given."

"But I need guidance. How to handle Daniel Chin." I disliked feeling exposed at the trial where we thrusted and parried and danced for audiences from several philosophies.

May smiled with mirth in her face. "What?" I demanded.

"We all love you dearly, Brian Rabbe Miller. It was seen that you would come to us and that you would lead."

"You pity me," I bitterly complained. "I know you can see my frustration, my jealousy of Daniel Chin, my limp defense."

May laughed, showing her teeth. "You are a delight. When you become morose, you divide onto three planes, like other Softcheeks. You just named three objections, one for each plane."

"Stop laughing at me. I'm asking for help. Give me some word."

"These things are difficult to capture in words," May gently claimed. "I'll give you Oriika's word that you received before. You're effective when you act outside yourself, without considering yourself. Then you become focused here." May tapped her abdomen. "Then you become Dolviet."

Before the trial began Lucy's kids had little contact with May's children, being soldier and part of Mula's guard. They didn't sit at the table for meals or play organized games in the yard, but loitered on the street of shops waiting for a new campaign. They wore whatever was available, with adornments taken as trophies from Mula's sorties.

Marcy wasn't allowed to join the dangerous outings that Mula led, responsible as she was to me. As the weeks of the trial wore on, Marcy took up chores in May's kitchen and was even seen with a ribbon in her hair. Kyle Rula sent amber earbobs for the young woman who served Gaucho as she once had. Marcy braided her hair like May's and wore the earbobs every day, defiant before Tommy and her other cousins.

One morning I was dressing in my room at May's house, facing another day of the trial. I pulled on a millmade tunic with dungarees and laced up the round-toed boots. Marcy loitered in the backyard outside my window and glanced in when she thought I wasn't looking. She reminded me of Tina in the days of Sim Chareon, her fascination with hotels and ECCAVs.

I inserted folding money and credit cards into the pouch on my belt. That was more than Marcy's curiosity could stand. "What are those?" she asked through the window.

"Money," I said without looking at her.

She leaned in on the windowsill. "I have heard of money. Let me see it." I handed her a worn bill that she carefully inspected, then held it up to the light. "But it's only paper."

"And credit cards are only plastic."

"And Softcheeks accept these as payment?"

"Not the plastic exactly, but what it represents. It says I have wealth and agree to put a certain amount into your account."

"And how do I get the wealth free from my account?"

"With your credit card."

"Can I get money in topaz or peridot?"

"You get the promise of payment. The money stays in one account or the other."

"No wonder Softcheeks are rich," Marcy claimed with wonder. "They keep the mineral wealth. We get only promises."

213

"Marcy, you're a political genius," I said and replaced the bill into my wallet and pouch.

"Their wealth depends on the refinery," she continued. "But it's our rock, the rock that kills. We just don't use it."

"Uranium holds a power source that could bring electricity to all Dolvia."

"Can it run a transport?"

"That to," I said and finished dressing.

"You have traveled on the transport," she informed me.

"Marcy, who have you been talking to? These things didn't interest you before."

"You never told me," she said with anger flashing in her eyes. "I don't take lessons on the EAM like Ely and some others. I'm Lucy's kid."

"Have I been so awful to you?"

"No more than you were to Klistina Le."

"Ah, you have been listening to stories."

"It's Rularim you care about," she said while her cynical eyes coldly regarded me. "I watched you together when she visited the clutch of Quentin. You're different with her."

I sighed and defended again. "I don't have eight cousins full of gossip to occupy my time."

But Marcy had thought this through, discussed it with Lucy's kids. "You didn't intervene with the Hardhand church in the time of my Cylahi mother. You didn't fight the cholera when Lucy died. You never gave me lessons. You only care for Rularim."

"And with you it's only Mula."

"He made a place for us!"

"So he can see his own reflection in your eyes."

"It's better than nothing. Less than nothing we receive from you."

"You reject all that I offer," I claimed. "Karima Le's house makes you see the difference. May's caring feels different than Mula's using you."

She became contrite, then shrugged it off. "It just hurts more."

I turned back to the mirror, sparing her a bad moment. "I'll arrange some lessons if you want. Books to read, time on the EAM. Will that make it better between us?"

"Did Klistina Le study on the EAM?" Marcy peevishly asked. "You allowed her to be uncovered."

"Who's been telling you these stories?"

"Lucy's kids have only each other. And Mula."

I sighed and left for another day in the courtroom.

Company strategy focused attention on Kyle Rula and Cyrus which accomplished many things. Dillan was untouched, portrayed as a reasonable man in an impossible situation.

214

Company conquest of Dolvia and the presence of the refinery were secondary, a backdrop to the discovery of paranormal tribespeople. And all the while Regent Chek waited for an error, a report that Mula or Cyrus or Rularim visited Somule to view the proceedings.

Daniel Chin rarely mentioned Dillan. He drew us to him with honey as though he, and not the Company, held the power to pardon or imprison. In Daniel Chin's skillful hands, the trial became the indictment of Rularim, goulep and self-serving holy woman, who used her gift of second sight to build her own fortune, and who sacrificed Dolviets to her need for revenge.

While the arguments unfolded, Daniel Chin appeared to respect and understand goulep, admired her cunning and vengeful tricks played on the Company and tribespeople alike. How could I claim his version was wrong when his admiration for her maneuvers was so apparent?

And whenever interest flagged in his fabrications, as when they totally disregarded events, he reiterated that goulep was a she-devil in constant communication with Cyrus, the Mekucoo revolutionary who ate the beating hearts of his enemies. If it wasn't so, let them come forward and defend themselves.

"Madam Arbitrator," Daniel Chin began, "I offer into evidence the confession of Katelupe Le, known as Terry the Martyr, her last statement given on her deathbed."

"I object," I called from my seat.

"Who would lie in the face of death?" Daniel Chin claimed. "What could she gain by hiding the truth?"

"She protected her sisters and harmony on Dolvia," I protested.

The arbitrator pounded her gavel on its sounding block. "Mr. Miller, you're familiar with procedure. Don't interrupt unless you have a point of order."

I stood and faced her. "Point of order, Madam Arbitrator. Why is a Dolviet citizen on Dolviet soil, a planet with its own government and judicial system, being tried by a Company appointed official?"

"Sit down, Mr. Miller," she irritably said. "Your objection has been noted before. You must take that up with Regent Chek along with the right of appeal. In the meantime, these proceedings will continue."

"In her final confession, Katelupe Le said this . . ." Daniel Chin said, focused on his gentle concern for the truth.

"I object," I said and jumped to my feet. "This confession was gained as a result of brutal and continual torture. It cannot be considered true."

"Do you have proof of torture?" Madam Arbitrator asked.

"I have eye witnesses of Katelupe Le's treatment in prison."

"Do you propose to offer the testimony of condemned

criminals as your argument?"

"Political prisoners who were not tried for any crime."

"It's not a crime on this planet to destroy property and assassinate people because they're different from you?" Madam Arbitrator lightly asked.

"What they witnessed concerning Terry the Martyr is still fact. She was tortured."

"Where's your witness who was present at her death?" Madam Arbitrator asked. "Can you produce the body?"

"The body was not returned to her family."

"Then your objection rests on hearsay. I'll allow the confession into evidence."

Daniel Chin was too good at what he did to show pleasure at the victory. "Kyle Rula Arim, known as goulep," he began, drawing us to him with the warm, deep voice, "also known as Rularim, refused to serve Rabbenu or the leader of any tribe as far back as Rabbenu Luria. She refused to share her visions of second sight with Rabbenu Penli, Dillan Rabbe Penli's father, concerning the cattle blight which decimated many herds throughout the region."

"It was Rabbenu Penli who took her mantel and made her goulep," I loudly claimed.

"Madam Arbitrator," Daniel Chin quickly countered, "Kyle Rula Arim caused an event some years ago in which a young tribesman named Spindel Rabbe Murd was killed in a struggle with some colonists. She received due punishment from Rabbenu Penli, Dillan's father. That which was required by tribal law."

"That's not true," I insisted. "He took her mantel for his own reasons, to serve his greed!"

"Then she refused to share her vision of the cattle blight," Daniel Chin quickly added.

"She told Oriika," I countered. "She told Haku."

"My point exactly," Daniel Chin quietly said. "Kyle Rula kept her vision a secret from all who owned cattle. All except Haku Rabbe Murd who was betrothed to goulep's sister."

"Everybody knew," I insisted. "They didn't believe it from her."

"Mr. Miller, please," the arbitrator said. "The prosecution will have its turn to speak."

"Madam Arbitrator," I spoke loudly, "Rularim isn't on trial here. What does this have to do with Dillan Penli's crime against his people?"

"Sit down, Mr. Miller," she said with finality. "It's part of the confession which has been allowed."

"Operating under the masculine persona of Kyle Rabbe Arim," Daniel Chin tolerantly continued, "she sold a natural substance called netta to Dolviets at an exorbitant price without sharing the knowledge of how netta forms in nature or how to farm it. Further, she entered into an agreement with Ricardo Menenous, now under indictment on Cicero for collusion, to trade the secret of netta for personal gain, once again bypassing leaders to whom she was responsible according to tribal law."

"The people received electricity for the sell of netta," I explained. "It was a fair trade."

"When tribal leaders objected," Daniel Chin said, "she secretly hired an assassin, a bald-headed man named Kaeuper, to murder Rabbenu Penli, Dillan's father."

"This is outrageous," I shouted. "The assassin killed her father, Len Rabbe Arim, years before and would have murdered Martin Sumuki except Kyle Le saved him by having the assassin followed."

"So you admit she knew the assassin."

"I admit nothing. You can't prove this."

"It was confessed by Terry the Martyr."

"Who you tortured to death."

"I arrived on Dolvia three years after Terry died," Daniel Chin said simply, savoring my open look of jealous admiration. "I'm only here to fulfill a role for my people. Unlike you who argue for people to whom you're not related."

He turned back to the matter of the confession. "Kyle Rabbe Arim also managed to gain a monopoly of offworld trading right granted to colonists, known here as Hardhands. She bought these rights for a handful of gold, causing the colonists to move onto the next station because they had no livelihood on Dolvia. She used these rights of commerce to import munitions and export jewels for her personal treasure held offworld."

"She saved the colonists from becoming conscripts."

"By taking their trading rights?"

"The Company had devalued its script," I insisted.

Daniel Chin faced me from across the prosecutor's table. "She took advantage of a depressed market for profiteering."

"She was helping the colonists move on with dignity," I claimed, unable to control my anger at these trumped-up accusations.

Daniel Chin leaned across the table toward me. "She wanted them to leave Dolvia. She thought she was better than them," he claimed with rapid-fire delivery, "just like she thinks she's better than tribal leaders."

From my seat I looked past his shoulder. "Madam Arbitrator, every act for which he condemns Kyle Rula was an act of generosity and inspired leadership."

Daniel Chin stood tall and disdainful. "Of course we hear this from you, Brian Miller," he said with satisfaction. "You own twelve percent of all that belongs to Rularim. And tell me, what service do you perform for this gratuity?"

They knew my pressure points. They knew from Ricardo

that I saw red whenever they smeared Kyle Le's honor. Before the cameras and with fists flying, I went for Daniel Chin just like I had jumped Ricardo years before. Red-faced and eager to kill, I rolled with him on the floor with my hands grasped tightly around his neck. Security guards and Company men pulled me away. My rage was beamed to millions of viewers who believed nothing I said for the remainder of the trial.

Chapter Thirty-Two

Mula, Haku and other leaders of the resistance were not mentioned at the trial, creating in Somule an atmosphere of relative security. Tribespeople were released from prison, others not arrested. Commerce grew with the return of civic services. The balance of power shifted with familiarity. Tribespeople asked themselves, if goulep has profited from the presence of the Company, why shouldn't they?

Who was Kyle Rula, anyway? A goulep, an unmarried woman who shared her visions and whatever else with the outlaw Cyrus, the scarred and brutal Mekucoo of legend. And where was this Ketiwhelp killer when she needed a champion? Was Gaucho the only one who cared enough to step into the arena? Did Brian Miller defend goulep or his twelve percent?

I couldn't be conjoled from my self-hatred. I wanted to regain my place as Softcheeks, perhaps travel to the transport and sit at the captain's table, swapping stories of past campaigns with Daniel Chin, military secretary.

I felt old, older than Hamish, older than the tall butte that flanked the putrid refinery. I was unequal to this task. How could I anticipate Daniel Chin's maneuvers, counter his stratagems with the truth?

I sat on May's porch and went over Daniel Chin's strategy in my mind. I sighed and looked out on the savannah, now cooling in the late evening. I remembered when I had first arrived on Dolvia, a Softcheeks without landlegs. I remembered when Martin Sumuki had brought Kyle Le after my encounter with Quentin, and her mischievous smile given so seldom.

I remembered the day she had understood atmosphere, and the time she came to me with gems for my twelve percent plus questions about a Bible story. So long ago. So much sacrificed. Who was left to remember?

The need to defend the past became a constant ache in my heart. We knew the confession wasn't accepted as valid by Daniel Chin's audience. Yet it acted as a mechanism to level accusations

219

with no proof which were entered into the record because they were on the paper that Terry supposedly signed. People believed what they heard without believing that Terry confessed it.

I needed to establish that Dolviets had the right to self-rule, had a relationship with Dolvia that outsiders cannot grasp. I needed to make it understood that the visions of holy women with second sight were a communion with Dolvia and not the sinister power of witches. What could I offer as a memorable demonstration to refute the confession of Terry the Martyr, beloved Arrivi and sister to Rularim?

"I thought this mood was seasonal with you. The savannah's dry." Kyle Rula spoke from inside May's home without showing herself.

"Are you trying to rob the desert of one?" I angrily said without turning, unwilling to expose her. "They're waiting for you to come here."

"No man is greater than Dolvia."

"The land cannot testify on your behalf."

"As the desert trenches are full of snakes, so their words are full of deceit. Have not tribespeople been nourished by the Diet of Snakes? The days of the trial have their value."

"If you mean the return of electricity, don't get used to it. You play their game for your reasons, but it's still their game."

"Prisons are no longer full. Cyrus travels."

I softly chuckled. "You visit me whenever he's about to arrive. I cannot protect you from him either."

"You're too concerned with my reputation," she whispered. "What do I care about the public goulep? What do I care about the spinster Rularim? When have these ever been understood? They lashed Cyrus to the tripod three separate times, yet his spirit remained untouched."

"Would another do so well?"

"Your caring says more than your arguments."

"It doesn't play well offworld."

"Oh! That's why I'm here," she said, suddenly cheerful. "Hamish has arrived from Cicero. With some colonists."

"The Company hasn't sanctioned more settlers."

"These are former settlers, Joey and Carline. Hamish secured papers for them to travel. Carl was killed, I'm afraid. Something about a brawl when some conscripts said disparaging things about Heather. That's how Hamish found the children, when he heard about the fight.

"Hamish and some officers are with Regent Chek," she added. "I wanted you to be prepared."

"Prepared for what?"

"They offer to talk only when they've lost ground. But you cannot see your success."

"Do you have a word for me?"

220

"The holy woman does. She says, Dolvia gathers all those who gather."

"That means nothing. I need instruction. How to answer Daniel Chin."

Kyle Le softly chuckled and I twisted to glimpse her smile. She withdrew into the house as though to hide behind a body veil. "Please," I said softly. "Give me some word."

"You voiced three objections for the three planes of Softcheeks. Your actions speak loudest when you act as Dolviet. Find your center."

"I cannot while I'm influenced by Daniel Chin."

Kyle Le was quiet for a long moment. "Perhaps this is the time for explanations," she quietly offered. "Doesn't your philosophy say that to control a demon on the land, you make a place for it in religious ritual?"

"Buddhists believe that," I answered, wondering why she asked. "By making some demon that torments them into a deity, the demon becomes trained to their structure of offering and supplication. He performs for them to keep his place. How did you know that?"

"The Fortress of Arim has many Softcheek books."

"Are you seeking contingent clauses?"

"I don't know those words," she quietly said.

"No matter. You were saying, Daniel Chin's a demon on the land."

Kyle Le blinked twice, then patiently began again. "It's as Dolvia would have it. Daniel Chin doesn't care for what Dolviets think about him. And he feels disdain for Regent Chek whose placed was gained through nepotism. He seeks an equal for the contest. He has become enamored with your admiration for him. If you weren't you, he wouldn't be so easily captured."

"Easily captured?" I nearly shouted at her. I sighed and waited for a long moment. "And that's what the holy woman says?"

"That's what anyone can see."

"But now that you've told me, the picture will change."

"As you withdraw from him, Daniel Chin will seek the warmth of your admiration."

"And that's enough?"

"You don't need to defeat him. He'll defeat himself."

Chapter Thirty-Three

In front of the hotel Hamish emerged from the ECCAV followed by two sallow teenagers with shaved heads. Joey watched me with cold eyes, and Carline stared at the ground.

We made our way to May's house, escorted by Mekucoo warriors with shields. They pushed aside offworld reporters and cameramen who shouted questions from behind the warriors' advancing line.

May's fenced-in yard was full of children. On the verandah Lam and Dak smoked kari root. The cameramen stationed across from May's yard switched on their equipment, recording every departure and arrival as part of their workday. When we approached, crowded by the clamoring reporters, our Mekucoo escort formed a cramped semi-circle by the gate.

Joey balked at being herded into the aborigine dwelling. He looked to Hamish for a signal. Hamish smiled and looked at me. "Your first experience with fatherhood?"

"He's not my father," Joey hatefully said. "And neither are you."

"This is worse than conscript quarters?" Hamish said with steel in his voice. Carline became uneasy, and Joey touched her arm.

Just then May emerged from the house and came down the steps to greet us. Cameras focused on her as though she were a queen descending the palace stairs. She wore an Arrivi gown and peridot jewelry with a thick braid down her back. May was always serving, always teaching children. I clearly saw her for a moment, a big woman, amply built with olive skin and high cheekbones.

"Karima Le," I said. "May I present Hamish Nordhagan, a crewmember on the transport."

"Mula speaks of you sometimes, how you helped the students," May said. She looked him up and down, taking in his lanky form and military bearing. "And you're Softcheeks?"

"There are as many nations of Softcheeks as there are

Dolviet tribes," I explained.

"Naturally," she graciously smiled. "And these are Heather's children, Joey and Carline, who visited the land of Murd. You don't remember, Joey, how you chased mongooses in the yard?"

"I thought you had to wear a body veil to meet new people," he said.

"The body veil was outlawed by the Company," she gently explained. "One of their few positive moves." Joey's expression softened, and Carline drew closer with hope in her eyes.

"Come in, Hamish, and share a meal with us," May said.

"My duty ends here," Hamish claimed with formality. "It's part of my tradition, however, to bring a gift." He took a small package from the jacket of his uniform and passed it to her.

"What is it?" she asked in a pleasant tone.

"The transcript of the trial," he whispered.

"Transcript?"

"From the cameras. You do have a monitor to play it back?"

May looked at me. "Ely will know. Now, you must come in. We don't want these Softcheeks to believe I turn away friends of Gaucho who pays rent for a room in my house."

She gently led Carline past the cameras and past the staring children, just as though it was Carline's first day at school rather than her third cultural family. On the verandah, May handed the package to Dak who immediately left.

It was quiet in May's house that night. Two Softcheeks were no longer a curiosity but an invasion. The younger children were sent to stay with friends. Hamish and I sat in the kitchen and shared tea with May, a familiar ritual not often extended to Softcheeks. But then, Hamish had that way about him. People took him in wherever he went.

"Tell me about the trial," May said. "What do they say on the transport?"

"That Brian Miller loves Kyle Le."

May glanced at me. "But Brian married Heather, the colonial savior."

"He married a divorced Hardhand whom he pitied," Hamish corrected. "And they didn't live together. Nor did he keep her children on Dolvia."

"Wait a minute," I protested. "Am I on trial here?"

"The trial was Daniel Chin's show until you went for his throat," Hamish explained. "At first people questioned why you were even there, the Softcheeks who caused the explosion heard around Westend. Do you remain for a native woman's love?"

"I was asked to prosecute," I complained. "I would gladly give the duty to anyone who steps forward."

"You misunderstand," Hamish said shaking his head. "People are interested to know about the paranormal powers of Dolviets. But they don't want to visit a war-torn desert. You're their conduit. Your future is set. Write a book, go on the lecture tour."

"What is lecture tour?" May immediately asked.

"It's like when Cyrus visits, only you talk more," I explained.

"So Brian Miller need not stay on Dolvia no matter how the trial ends," May said. "I hadn't thought about you that way." May picked up some dishes from tea and stepped to the stove.

"May, I'm not leaving."

"But you could leave, retire in comfort," Hamish said. "That changes the balance. Rularim could be killed or reject you for another. Suddenly Gaucho isn't so native as he was yesterday."

"Because I jumped Daniel Chin."

"Many in the audience wanted to deck him."

"What do Softcheeks see?" May asked confidentially.

"Nothing," Hamish said with question in his voice.

"But they reacted to him," she probed from her place by the stove.

"He's a little snob, better than anybody in his own mind. Including Regent Chek."

"That's what they see?"

"Not in your sense of seeing, I believe."

"Why not?" she asked.

"Is it so simple?"

"Is it so difficult?"

After a moment, Hamish turned back to me. "Now people ask why it took you so long, since Daniel Chin maligns the woman you love."

"It's a trick to draw out Kyle Le," I said over my shoulder to May. "It changes nothing."

"Your need to protect her plays well offworld," Hamish continued. "The absence of Cyrus plays well. But there's this problem about your future. There are so few chances for advancement. Administrators and conscripts alike believe you would take whatever opportunity presents itself. It must be made clear that you will remain on Dolvia when the trial ends."

"So you want Joey and Carline to attend the trial as my stepchildren," I concluded.

"Also the one assigned to you, Marcy," Hamish said.

"And what will that prove?"

"That there's more to Gaucho than your taste for exotic women."

May softly chuckled. Hamish added, "The husbands of the debutantes defend you to their superiors. They want to believe your motives are pure."

"Who are the husbands?" May asked. "How many?"

"Seven. They're . . ."

"Blue and white uniforms with gold braids on the shoulders."

"That's their dress uniform."

"And they have children?"

"Mostly on the transport with the families of their wives."

"The debutantes?" May guessed.

"What is it, May?" I asked. "If the holy woman has seen an image about Hamish, you should share it with him."

"Seven young men are seen," she quietly described. "Family men all dressed the same as Hamish but not what he wears today."

"Seen doing what?"

"The image means nothing," she quietly added.

"Ah, Kyle Rula saw this," I said to Hamish. "That's her answer," I spoke over my shoulder to May. "Seen doing what?"

"They are seen watching Heather's fire."

I glanced at Hamish but saw only the soldier's face. "Heather's fire is past," I pronounced.

"It will come again."

I went to the stove and faced her with hard eyes. "What else is seen? What do you keep from me who must prosecute at the trial?"

"The children will gather around you."

"And that's what it means, Dolvia will gather all those who gather?" I softly asked.

She nodded and waited. I returned to my seat at the table. "Well, Hamish, it seems your guess about me is correct. At least it can all end soon. The children are here."

"Most of them," May said from the stove.

"There are more?"

"Yes, two more."

Marcy showed herself from outside the kitchen window and cleared her throat. "It's time," May immediately said. "You gentlemen must go out. Make your rounds to the bawdy houses like you always do when Hamish visits."

Later I sat with my back against the wall in the third backroom bar we visited that night, drinking steadily, fuzzy in the head and remorseful. I was an aging, childless man far from my birthplace. I lived among people who daily watched me for signs of mixed motive. I spent time with the man who my dead wife preferred. I prosecuted in a publicized trial where I really defended a tribeswoman who I had never been able to protect. And she had told me to stop striving. Who cared? Who was left to remember?

Hamish returned to the table from where he had stood drinks and toasted everyone at the bar. "Come along, Gaucho," he whispered. "We've been invited to the movies."

We went out the back and down a narrow passageway to a dark entrance. Tommy stepped from the shadows and pulled back a smelly blanket. We entered a dank and cramped Cylahi hut where three men stood with their hands on their beltknives. "Nu delaya," Tommy quickly said. The Softcheeks were allowed to live.

"Thank you," Hamish ironically said to Tommy.

Ely stepped forward. Light glinted off his round-rimmed glasses. He was twenty-eight and Mula's first minister, no longer the young man who loitered in the mill hoping to glimpse a sister of Arim. "You have a different look than Blackshirts, Hamish," he explained. "Plus we knew you were coming. These men wait for a word from Mula."

"Mula would have given it. You've filled out some," Hamish warmly said. "And the other students from the transport, do they serve the one who retards om?"

"You well know they fight in the north. Come, Brian Rabbe Miller. We have something for you."

We viewed the trial transcript on an eight inch monitor. I hadn't realized the camera was stationary and pointed at our backs, a bird's eye view of the proceedings. And this was what everyone in Westend ached forward to watch?

The first few minutes were nothing really. Evidence was submitted and accepted. Daniel Chin read from Terry the Martyr's confession. The arbitrator called for quiet from the crowd.

Ely saw my look. "Most of it's like this. No witnesses have been called for the camera to draw close. Daniel Chin turns often to show his face at just the right angle, but you just sit there always showing your back. Then you jump up and shout at the judge, and she tells you to sit down. But look at this other piece."

The room went dark while a tribesman changed cassettes. The courtroom view was very like the first one. Daniel Chin enunciated clearly while he claimed that Rularim was a turncoat who traded with the Company for profit. I saw myself jump up from my seat with my back to the camera. "Madam Arbitrator, every act for which he condemns Kyle Le was an act of generosity and inspired leadership."

"Of course we hear this from you, Brian Miller," Daniel Chin said leaning in on me. "You own twelve percent of all that belongs to Rularim. And tell me, what service do you perform for this gratuity?" I went for his throat and was all over him, rolling together on the courtroom floor. Several people hesitated before they separated us.

The tribesmen who viewed the transcript with us, and who must have seen this piece several times, chuckled and poked each other with satisfaction. Ely signaled the monitor be turned off. Someone lit a lamp.

"You stole his thunder," Hamish said. "That's the same reaction everywhere."

"Now you must take advantage," Ely added. "What is said means nothing. It's all visual, a pantomime."

"The trial isn't about me," I claimed. "That incident had nothing to do with Dillan. It looks dishonest to capitalize on my celebrity."

"Three objections," Ely said. "You're still divided."

"You could turn to the camera occasionally," Hamish suggested. "And spend time with Joey and Carline in May's yard."

"To use the kids, I don't know."

"Is it more dishonest than the confession of Terry the Martyr?" Ely harshly asked.

"It puts Joey and Sister in jeopardy."

"Heather's children will have children on Dolvia," Ely answered. "It is seen."

I looked at each of them and nodded my agreement. "Speaking of children," I said. "Is it possible to arrange lessons for Tommy and Marcy?"

"These are children?" Hamish asked.

Ely smiled slightly. "Tommy's no scholar. Marcy has a quick mind, though. Perhaps a benefit she gained from serving Gaucho. I'll look into it."

It was late when Hamish and I returned to May's house. Tommy walked behind a few steps, more casual during the forty minutes the transport dipped below the horizon. We relaxed, glad to be free of the Mekucoo escort and noisy reporters.

"Did you talk to Joey about attending the trial?" I asked Hamish.

"Who can talk to conscripts?"

"His family was free when they lived here."

"He saw his father killed in a brawl. I found them with their heads shaven, huddled on a ratty mattress in the corridor."

"You think they're glad for this duty?"

"Any conscript would commit to ground duty. What you offer them is freedom, a new life with people who embrace them."

"Dolviets embrace them?" I cynically asked.

"As much as they embrace you."

"And your Consortium audience will see that?"

"They'll see a family much like their own families, seeking the right to build a new life."

The reporters by May's yard had closed up shop for the night and returned to the hotel. May waited by the gate. "Come in, Hamish. We have something for you."

Tommy joined Marcy on the verandah but within earshot. We entered May's frontroom to find a new revelation. Lam and Dak stood with a twelve-year-old Mekucoo child dressed in a tunic and leggings. His face was smeared with grease, and his

227

hair slicked back and matted. He was strangely plump with long mats of hair down his back in a way Mekucoo hair doesn't grow. The boy turned cold blue eyes on us and tensely stood with his hand on his beltknife.

"Kyle Rula wanted to be here tonight," May spoke defensively, prattling on so unlike her. "Cara and Mula won't allow it, to be present with a Softcheeks."

She stepped back, and Dak brought the boy forward. "At the end of her pregnancy," May continued, "Heather was weak and suicidal because of what she saw in om. It was Kyle Rula's most difficult decision twelve years ago, when she sent him to be raised on Mekucoo land. Cyrus agreed that one time, but Kyle Rula felt she must be wrong after Joey and Sister were deported.

"Later when Heather fell sick at the Fortress of Arim, we prayed and sought a vision. Oriika, too, looked to Dolvia for a sign, but there was none. What sign is given for Softcheeks?"

Hamish stared at her for a moment, then stepped close to the boy. He knelt and wiped some grease from his cheek.

"We couldn't protect him at the Fortress of Arim," May continued apologetically. "His coloring and hair. It was too dangerous for them together. Heather died without being told. Kyle Rula wanted to be here tonight. Speak of it herself."

Hamish gently took the boy's beltknife and cut a lock of matted hair near his neck. Hamish roughly spread the dreadlock until the knot relaxed and separated. The boy's hair was orange-red, the color of Heather's fire.

"What is this? Why wasn't I told?" I asked May.

"He's not your son."

Hamish dropped the knife on the floor. He grabbed the boy and stood, held him high in the air and laughed with a great booming sound. Hamish held his son close and turned to May with tears in his eyes. "How is he known?"

"His name is Hamish," she said softly. "The Mekucoo call him *Dacupitte*, he who waits with angry eyes."

Chapter Thirty-Four

It was decided to shelter Heather's children along with Marcy at Karima Le's house. Joey was nineteen, the same age as May's oldest son Orin and only seven years younger than Mula and Ely. Carline was seventeen, three years older than Lucy's kids. Young Hamish was born less than a year after May's third child, a girl known as Kat but named Katelupe Le after her aunt who had suffered in the Blackshirt prison.

Young Hamish, who Carline dubbed Pete, was bathed and given the trousers and tunic worn by those in the clutch of Quentin. Without the protective grease, he quickly freckled and burned. He wore his thick orange hair braided down his back in a public statement after being kept so long a secret. Pete drew away from his strangely-dressed father who returned to his duties on the transport a few days later. Lam and Dak were ever watchful, almost fatherly with this formerly Mekucoo boy.

Joey and Carline were given the lighter tunic with pantaloons and Arrivi sandals that were from the clutch of Murd where Mula spent the dry season. Carline wore a scarf tied over her shaved head in conscript fashion until her auburn hair grew past her ears. She was reserved, even hermetic, and watched Marcy's impulsive activity from the safety of May's kitchen. But Carline had a place in her heart for young Pete, sympathetic toward her halfbrother who had many families of different cultures. Carline was seen to share her sweetbread and braid his long, orange hair so like their mother's.

It was a large group and daily mixed with the children of other tribespeople. May taught the younger children at the kitchen table as she always had. But now her backyard clothesline was taken down and a long table set up there. Ely taught the older native and Softcheeks children, all groundborn, patient and repeated lessons on how to repair Softcheeks equipment and run the EAM.

So I became responsible for four young people who understood the purpose of the trial and their roles to play. Each day of the trial Joey, Carline, Pete and Marcy sat behind me in a long row. Pete, who perhaps understood best, tolerated without complaint the long days with nothing to do in the torrid courtroom while the camera was trained on the braid down his back.

Joey knew the offworld impact of Pete's flaming red hair. Joey explained it to me when I asked if he had any questions.

"We were conscripts with my father, but we were different from the others," he explained while we sat on May's back porch one quiet evening. "Extra rations and easy duty came our way. We were on three freighters altogether, but each time our transfer was anticipated. It was the husbands of the debutantes, don't you know."

"No, I don't know."

"The resistance is more than on Dolvia. Consortium officers object to Company policy, especially the hostage system. Plus some officers met their wives through . . ." He paused, seeming to swallow his words.

"Through the colonial savior," I softly finished.

Joey nodded. "The officers were present when Hamish danced with her. The news of Hamish's son raised on Mekucoo land changes their impression of who fights on Dolvia. And especially of Cyrus."

"Cyrus?"

"Conscripts never believed he deserved those beatings from long ago. They don't believe his spirit cries in the yard of torture. But he was seen as a warrior with special powers, a demon in battle who melts away into the night. Now he's more like Dak, a dutch uncle to Hamish's son. The demonic mask is stripped away."

"So you're willing to be used for this show?"

"You mean the cameras and all?" Joey shrugged. "Me and Sister are nobody. When Carl was killed, we had no covering. The guards . . . did things. I don't want to be uncovered like that again. If sitting exposed to the cameras for a few days helps end Company rule . . ."

"I doubt the trial will settle anything," I cynically claimed.

"You don't know, do you? Tao Chek is the head of the snake."

I shook my head. "They won't sacrifice the refinery to the trial's outcome. There are other methods of conquest."

"All of which depend on the military, and that means the . . ."

"Husbands of the debutantes," I finished his sentence.

Joey slowly smiled. I felt encouraged by his look. "About Heather," I began.

Joey grew uncomfortable. "It was long ago." We hadn't been family enough days to share on that tender subject.

"About Carl," I said in a different tone. "Hamish told me how he found you."

Joey was more open to discuss recent events. "On the freighters, it was bad for us among conscripts because Sister and I received special treatment. We shared all we had, but the situation was always desperate. And they talked about Carl behind his back, how he turned Heather out. It wasn't like that, don't you know. None of it was like what they said."

Joey made a face, then continued. "Finally Carl just struck out at someone, like you did with Daniel Chin. He got into it with two guards who had bought their places with Cylahi gold. They said Carl had used her, even though their places gained through Heather were higher than his.

"That's the conscript way. Conscripts can't stand to see any good fortune. They think maybe we're stuck in this hellhole together, but I have thus-and-so that you don't have. The attention we received from the husbands just made it worse.

"With Carl gone, the guards felt that no honor should come to us, I guess. It was a bad time," Joey paused. I waited, unwilling to probe into his painful story.

"We didn't realize who Hamish was when he came for us," Joey confessed. "Just a crewmember in the labor quarters, very unusual. Then on the transport under his protection we met the husbands, don't you know. Hamish wanted them to see what could happen to their families."

Mula visited late one night, and Ely deferred to him in every way, as much his second man as Cara was to Cyrus. But Mula's leadership brought different results than Cyrus' brought. Mula's arguments for resistance were all true. And they were all destructive. Even before the time of gathering began, their friendship was strained. Ely wanted to build, labored to find a better life for himself. And for the young students at the lesson table in May's backyard who looked up at him with eyes full of wonder and trust.

Perhaps the trouble was always there, as students on the transport when Mula chided Ely for completing his studies with Softcheeks who would murder him in the night if they could. Perhaps the trouble began during the time of Brittany Mill when Mula drew Ely away from his infatuation with a sister of Arim.

But the trouble came to a head early one morning when Mula loitered by the back gate of May's house while the transport cameras dipped for forty minutes below the horizon. Mula stood with some Putuki men who always followed, then he called to Tommy. It was time to take Ely's students for the line of fire.

Ely blocked Tommy's path and faced his old friend. He peered over his steel-rimmed glasses and told the leader of the resistance to move on, find others to fight. "Not these ones!

They're not for today."

Mula stopped short, his charisma easily melting away. "For the season of om then? For when I'm dead?" With bravado Mula strolled down the lane and bitterly called back, "You'll miss me when I'm gone."

"Who is left to remember?" Ely answered in an unsteady voice.

There were no more lessons that day. Lam and Dak took the young men out to hunt. Pete and Kat played with some chalk at May's kitchen table. Marcy joined Ely where he sat alone at the lesson table in the hot sun, hating himself for betraying his friendship with Mula. Marcy gently touched his arm and listened to boyhood stories from the days of Martin Sumuki, Ely's tribesman.

From the window of my room I watched the couple and sighed. I heard May's step in the hall where she put away clean linens for her many houseguests. She joined me for a moment but offered nothing. She was like that, always waited for others to speak.

"I feel old today, Karima Le," I said. "Older than Hamish who has a son."

"You lost another young servant to the man she'll marry."

"I suppose that was seen. What else is seen? Please," I begged shamelessly. "Something to give me comfort."

May shrugged. "When I was young, I spent time on the savannah with Kyle Rula. I was frightened by the avarice of Softcheeks. I asked goulep for a word of comfort. She told me I would live for a time in Somule, leave the land of Arim in order to save it."

"Can it be saved? How will the trial end?"

May shrugged again, then offered, "In those days, goulep knew about Dillan too. She said the family of Dillan Rabbe Penli will be uncovered on the streets of Somule and beg Company men for the barest sustenance."

"Tribespeople won't allow that. Their crimes aren't so great."

"All their crimes aren't known."

"And that's your word for me, to draw out their crimes?"

"You have done your part in the trial. You need no longer strive."

I looked into her sad eyes. "I can go on lecture tour, you mean?"

"I see that you consider it," she quietly said.

"I'm just feeling old. The best part of my life is past."

"Time is a loop. Our poor understanding of events often comes during a later cycle. Now is the time of gathering before the season of om. Many things will come to light." She sweetly smiled and patted my shoulder.

"The secrets of Kyle Rula?" I asked.

"Ah, we'll never know all those."

"And there's a secret about me. Please, May."

She sadly watched me. "It is seen that young Hamish will marry your daughter."

"A daughter? Truly? And if you knew this, why not tell me?"

"The season of om is upon us before we begin. Don't wish it speed."

Chapter Thirty-Five

My stepchildren and I descended May's front steps while the camcorders beamed our images throughout Westend. With their shields raised, Lam and Dak struggled through the crowd as we made our way to the Council building. These were Mula's followers. Many tribesmen waited in Somule while Mula lurked in the shadows and stroked their need to be near him. I was almost glad to reach my seat facing the Company arbitrator, my space that wasn't overrun.

So confident, the Company called Captain Ellis to testify before the cameras. "Captain Ellis," Daniel Chin began, savoring my jealous look. "What's your position here on Dolvia?"

"Commander of the military garrison in Somule."

"And what are your duties in that capacity?"

"Maintain law and order for this region." There was a low clucking from the crowd. Madam Arbitrator pounded her gavel several times.

"And tell us," Daniel Chin said, "did you have occasion to meet with Rularim?"

"Not in an official capacity," Captain Ellis moved uncomfortably in his seat and glanced up at the camera.

"Informally, then?"

"She approached me with a business proposition."

"A business proposition with the officer who held her sister?" Daniel Chin asked as if surprised.

"She wanted to avoid official shipping channels."

"Kyle Le wanted to smuggle something offworld?" Daniel Chin prompted.

"I object," I said from my seat. "He's leading the witness."

"Madam Arbitrator," Daniel Chin explained. "Captain Ellis has come forward with the admission of his own guilty actions in cooperation with Rularim." There was murmuring and insistent clucking from the crowd. Madam Arbitrator shook her head but left the gavel alone.

"If I may continue," Daniel Chin loudly pronounced over the

crowd. "I will bring to light the events surrounding the confession of Terry the Martyr."

"Allow the witness to answer in his own words, Mr. Chin," she tolerantly said.

"Captain Ellis, tell us in your own words, how you came to know Kyle Rula Arim."

"Terry had been detained for more than two years," Captain Ellis began, glancing darkly at the crowd. "Kyle Rula learned that Terry was in poor health and pregnant. Kyle Rula came to me with bribes to release her sister."

"And did you agree to release Terry."

"My duty was to hold prisoners for trial." At some clucking from the crowd, Captain Ellis glared at them with his jaw set.

"A considerable reward was offered for Kyle Le's capture," Daniel Chin said. "Why didn't you turn her in for the reward?"

"I felt sorry for her, and her sister." Tribespeople in the courtroom no longer clucked or murmured. They glanced at each other in shame and shook their heads.

"And this was when Kyle Le asked you to smuggle the gems and netta to Cicero?"

"Yes, she frequently brought them."

Cynicism covered faces in the courtroom. Marcy looked at me, then looked away. There was no defense that could explain away contact with the Blackshirts. "It was risky business," Captain Ellis continued. "She said it was needed to get her family offworld."

Dolviets had stood together against an overwhelming enemy. No tribesman had stepped forward to testify at the trial. Each remembered a family member who suffered in prison. The temptation for celebrity and the promised release of a brother of father or son was resisted because they believe all tribal members resisted. But goulep acted outside tribal harmony. Kyle Rula conducted business with Captain Ellis.

"And then what happened?" Daniel Chin blandly asked.

"The prisoners learned that Kyle Rula visited the prison," Captain Ellis claimed. "It was a shock to Terry that her sister didn't stand with the others but resorted to smuggling. Terry wrote the confession because she felt betrayed. Her suffering was for nothing." Captain Ellis looked around with satisfaction.

"And you were present when Katelupe Le signed the confession offered here in testimony?" Daniel Chin asked with his back to the camera, shuffling papers at his seat.

"Yes, I saw her sign it."

"Your witness," Daniel Chin graciously said and sat down with finality.

There was no defense for collusion. There was no defense for hoarding treasure offworld. There was only the truth. All the truth. What did I care what they thought about the public goulep? Or about the spinster Rularim. All things must come into the light.

I stood and calmly turned, allowing the camera to capture my profile. "Captain Ellis, did you have carnal knowledge of Kyle Rula Arim?" I stiffly asked.

The room was deadly quiet. The specter of Rularim as goulep, an uncovered spinster, a women with special powers who refused to serve Rabbenu, rose again. No man of honor could be concerned with her fate. She was without covering.

Captain Ellis shrugged. "All the native women want it. They beg the officers, show themselves and tell what they will do. My soldiers are only men after all."

"All native women? From all tribes?"

"Mostly Cylahi, I guess."

"Other tribeswomen who are held in prison?"

"Sure, they're all willing."

"Don't you mean desperate? For food, for medical care?"

Captain Ellis squinted at me. "The women like it. They beg for it."

I squinted back at him. And this time I remembered to turn toward the camera while I controlled my revulsion. "So you had carnal knowledge of Kyle Rula Arim. Where did you carry on this activity with her?"

"She came to my quarters."

"On how many occasions did Kyle Rula visit your quarters?"

"Many times." There was no movement in the courtroom. You could have heard Kariom breathing.

"And this treasure that was smuggled out because of your pity, what became of it?"

"It was returned."

"Returned to Kyle Rula?"

"Returned to Dillan Penli, Rabbenu of the Arrivi."

And so there it was. I stripped the sisters of Arim of their dignity, pulled away what little covering they had gathered. I used them up, just like Mula led Lucy's kids to their deaths. Mula and I were the same, the very same.

The next morning May shook my shoulder. Without caring I looked up from the hot pillow. "Rularim says, it's as Dolvia would have it, what you did. You gave Daniel Chin the keys to the verandah."

I turned away from her, uncomfortable under the rumpled sheet. She roughly shook me again. "Rularim's proud of you. You acted as Dolviet."

The news of Captain Ellis' testimony had gone out before we left the courtroom. Kyle Le must be nearby for a reply to so quickly arrive.

"Leave me alone," I complained and tightly shut my eyes. What did I care? My energy was spent, my resolve evaporated. I wanted rest, only rest.

The keys to the verandah, another riddle from the holy woman. I was tired of riddles, tired of flashes of *deja vu*. I couldn't face them again. I couldn't bear Marcy's look.

I wanted sure knowledge and routine duty. I wanted a vault of Cylahi gold to spend during a holiday gambling spree where I didn't have to know about barefoot tribeswomen abused by Blackshirts who believed they wanted it.

Joey roughly encouraged me to dress for the courtroom. It was his look as much as his curt gestures that pushed me forward. I avoided their glances. Lam and Dak, Ely and Marcy, Mula's twisted smirk. Why didn't they step forward, answer the Company defense attorney, offer strategy planning to diffuse the impact of goulep's actions? Three objections, ha.

Servile to a word from the holy woman, inert in their passive resistance, resigned to the fate Dolvia held for them. They seemed aboriginal and essentially foreign to me. And I was Softcheeks, never transmuted into something else. I belonged to neither group and was covered by neither philosophy. I didn't stand like Hamish Nordhagan, serene in his own tradition separate from the warring factions.

On the street that day, tribal anger took on a personality. No longer curiously enjoying the sideshow, the crowd was hostile, ready to act without direction from any leader. While we struggled toward the Council building to endure another torturous day of lies, Dolviets surged forward with raised fists and angry words. "Goulep, goulep," they chanted.

That day in the courtroom the Company pressed their advantage. Julia Luria-Penli was called to testify concerning the money trail of Kyle Le's supposed bribes. Julia Le demurely sat in her highneck and belted foreign dress, her short hair fashionably brushed back, wearing coral and platinum necklace and earbobs instead of native peridot.

"Julia Luria-Penli," Daniel Chin began after Madam Arbitrator called for quiet in the courtroom. "How well do you know Kyle Rula?"

"The goulep was a neighbor and tribeswoman. We knew each other as children."

"Isn't is true that you were friends as children?" he gently asked.

"Our mothers visited together. I was more friends with Katelupe Le."

"And did your friendship with Terry the Martyr last into adulthood?"

"No, when Kyle Le took on the mantel of goulep, they withdrew from community."

"How long were they isolated?" Daniel Chin asked.

"Kyle Le refused to serve Rabbenu, even before goulep.

Afterward, they were friendly only with Oriika and Haku Rabbe Murd," she explained without inflection.

"But the tithe was paid each week."

"The tithe of Arim became nominal," Julia Le said in whole tones. "We knew the sisters received more for netta than they tithed against." There was low clucking from tribeswomen in the crowd.

"Isn't it true that Kyle Le's visions became part of the tithe to Rabbenu?"

"By tribal law she must offer what she saw," Julia Le easily answered, coached to expect certain questions.

"And did Kyle Le follow the law in other respects?"

"They were most resistant."

"By they, you mean the three sisters?"

"Four sisters. Karima Le was the oldest and responsible to deliver the tithe to Rabbenu," Julia Le recited.

"That would be Dillan's father, Rabbenu Penli."

"That's correct."

"Just to be clear, at what time did the tithe become nominal?"

"It's hard to say," she sourly shrugged.

Daniel Chin smiled at her, ever patient. "Was it at the time Kyle Le was judged as goulep? Or was it later during the sell of netta from Brian Miller's office in Brittany Mill?"

"At the time of the sell of netta," she answered while staring at me.

"And how many years ago did netta become available to tribespeople?" Daniel Chin asked while he noted her acknowledgement of me.

"Sixteen years ago."

"Before that, how many people had the knowledge of netta?"

"Arrivi women knew."

"All Arrivi women?"

"How to harvest netta was known to Arrivi women," she hedged. "But only a few families owned land where it appeared in nature."

"Who specifically owned land that yielded netta?" Daniel Chin asked, showing his patient face to the camera.

"The sisters of Arim."

"But Arrivi women don't own land," Daniel Chin blandly said.

"They received a mortgage on Len Rabbe Arim's land during the time of the cattle blight. Four years after the goulep trouble."

"All the sisters received land?"

"Kyle Rula only. But they all farmed it."

"And isn't the mortgage payment separate from the tithe to

238

Rabbenu?"

"The sisters received use of the flats of Arim by writ of Rabbenu Penli," she explained with a brittle tone. "He was being gracious toward four orphan women of no estate. The mortgage and the tithe are within our system of goodwill, which you call prior appreciation, that underpins tribal law."

Daniel Chin nodded to her, appreciative of her willingness to share the knowledge of her station. "So the sisters of Arim farmed land that was mortgaged to Rabbenu. But the tithe that was made in payment became nominal, even after Kyle Rula refused to share her visions of second sight with Rabbenu."

"That's correct."

"So in effect, they defaulted on the mortgage."

"Yes, Kyle Rula defaulted on the mortgage for the flats of Arim."

"Was restoration payment made for the flats of Arim?"

"No further payment was received after the time of Brittany Mill," she clearly pronounced and surveyed the crowd with her chin held high. Tribeswomen murmured but lent her honor.

"Now, as for the recent visits to Captain Ellis," Daniel Chin said while he checked his notes. "How did you learn of Kyle Le's activity?"

"Lt. Lebowitz reported when he was posted to the transport that Captain Ellis had in his possession a section of natural netta," Julia Le recited. "The captain was questioned since there are few sources for netta. At that time, the bribes Captain Ellis had received were transferred into our account."

"Captain Ellis has testified that he took no bribes."

She glanced down. "I meant, the treasure that was smuggled offworld."

"How was it transferred?"

"I don't get your meaning," she suspiciously looked at him.

"In what form did this treasure exist?"

"Mostly as precious gems, peridot and topaz. Also some Cylahi gold and natural netta. It was found in safety deposit boxes on the transport and on Cicero."

"Under whose name was it deposited."

"Numbered accounts traced back to Captain Ellis."

"I see," Daniel Chin looked at me and nearly winked. "And the contents of the safety deposit boxes were transferred into Dillan Rabbe Penli's account?"

"Actually, most of it was auctioned by our solicitor, and the proceeds deposited into my husband's account."

"Why auctioned?"

"They brought a good price, more so because of the notoriety."

"Because they had been Rularim's?"

"Because they were from Dolvia," she stiffly corrected.

"Thank you for coming forward, Julia Luria-Penli. No further questions," Daniel Chin calmly finished and sat down.

"Mr. Miller," the arbitrator prompted.

I strolled the length of the courtroom, then looked at Julia Le from a place far across from her. I could barely believe my luck. Here was a tribeswoman I wanted to uncover. And she offered me the opening, blinded by her own arrogance. A Company trait.

"Why were the proceeds from the auction of the treasure of Kyle Rula transferred to Dillan?" I quietly asked.

"I'm sorry?" she asked with anger.

"Why to Dillan? Why not to Mula or to Haku Rabbe Murd."

"My husband is Rabbenu." From the crowd irreverent clucking started in unison. The arbitrator pounded her gavel and angrily stared at specific audience members.

"By what writ is Dillan named Rabbenu?" I calmly asked.

"His father was Rabbenu before him. And my father was Rabbenu before that."

"So leadership is hereditary among the Arrivi?" I asked.

"What is this? The payment was for the mortgage on the land," she explained.

"Then the mortgage on the flats of Arim is no longer in arrears?"

"The mortgage defaulted," she nearly shouted.

"You can't have it both ways. Either payment was made or it wasn't," I said, modulating my voice.

"The deposited money was recovered from the resistance," she explained. "Not as payment."

"So why was it deposited with Dillan?"

"She owes us!" Julia Le angrily said.

"Kyle Rula owes you for what? For Spindel's death?"

"I don't know what you mean," she said, gathering herself.

"Isn't it true that you were the one who traveled without covering on the road that day when Spindel Rabbe Murd was killed? Isn't it true that you loved Spindel even though he preferred Katelupe Le? Isn't it true that you caused the event that led to the goulep trouble?"

Julia Le jumped up and shouted, "No! Goulep did it. She got Spindel killed. All of it. She caused all the trouble! She owes us that money."

"Why does she owe the money?"

"She took Spindel from me. He didn't want Terry. Spindel fought for my honor. I was the one!"

"The one who stood uncovered on the road before Hardhands."

A lifetime of lies and marriage to the wrong man welled up inside her. She sat again, straight-backed in her foreign dress and with her jaw set. "One of the Hardhands touched my hair. It was wrong to touch me. Spindel fought them to defend me. Me! Only me."

Julia Le caught her breath and looked around in anger. "Terry threw off her veil and joined the fight," she continued. "She got into Spindel's way. He didn't see the thrust of the Hardhand's knife.

"But Kyle Le caused it, all of it," she angrily confessed. "She thinks she's better than us, better than anybody. But she's not, see. And she's going to pay. I'm going to make her pay." Clucking and murmuring broke out again. Julia Le glared at their faces.

"Pay for Spindel's death?" I asked over the din.

"Yes! Yes, because he's dead." After a lifetime of denial and secret revenge, Julia Le had admitted the truth. She covered her face with one hand to hide her sobs.

Kaykay Le left the Company viewing area and walked to Julia Le. The clucking stopped and everybody waited. With elaborate ritual, Kaykay Le unfolded the body veil that she brought each day to the trial. She tenderly placed it over the head and shoulders of her sobbing daughter, then helped Julia Le from the stand.

Time is a loop, the last events connected to the first ones. How different our lives would have been if as young people Julia Le and the two sisters of Arim had not encountered some Hardhand youths on the road. Spindel Rabbe Murd was Terry's future mate, he who was meant to lead. He been sacrificed, leaving a vacuum for Mula to fill.

So had begun the long thread of lies that entangled Julia Le's life with Terry's and forced a wedge into tribal harmony. Spindel's death was the first event that led to Kyle Rula's taking on responsibility for their sins.

Arrivis knew this story. The shame of goulep was tempered by Kyle Rula's service. The end of the cattle blight, the sell of netta, the fair trade for electricity. These had transmuted her shame into the legend of Rularim. By comparison, Julia Le's truth seemed tawdry, benefiting nobody.

There were moments in life when something happened to you, and you weren't even present. Watershed events that people talked about for years. Mostly you were doing something mundane when your world changed outside of your control. At the end of that day's arguments, I gathered my papers in the silent courtroom while Marcy and my stepchildren waited. News came to us in a flash, almost over peoples' heads so quickly it spread.

From the crowd on the steps of the Council building, Mula had rushed Dillan Rabbe Penli and Julia Le. He easily stabbed Julia Le. Blood stained the front of her body veil over the foreign dress.

Mula strong-armed Dillan and held him with the knife at his throat. Mula faced the camcorders with that twisted smirk, then slashed across Dillan's throat before anyone moved to separate them.

A Blackshirt, wearing the uniform of Tao Chek's personal guard, discharged his weapon. Mula sank to the ground with his arm still around Dillan's chest. The three of them laid there in a heap, appearing to the Westend audience as aborigines who acted outside of the law.

Kaykay Le knelt and gathered her daughter into her arms. Julia Le struggled for breath, causing the facial panel of the veil to bow into her gaping mouth. Kaykay Le looked up with pleading eyes, her image beamed to millions. "Please," she begged. "Please, help her breathe."

Kaykay Le turned to the officer of Tao Chek's personal guard who stood over the bodies. "Please," she begged. "Please stop the bleeding. Help me."

Julia Luria-Penli went limp in her mother's arms. Kaykay Le cried and prayed to Dolvia for mercy. And so the visions of Rularim were fulfilled. The family of Rabbenu begged Company men for the barest sustenance. And Mula did not enter the season of om.

I never understood why Mula did it, although Karima Le explained it to me more than once. Mula knew his time was short, she patiently claimed. And he knew the show was over. He captured one final moment of glory before the camcorders were packed up and sent back to the transport.

What was left for Mula? Ely no longer followed. Mula's talent for defense strategy wasn't needed with this new form of resistance. It was generally said the time of gathering before om had begun. With this act Mula chose when to die. He chose the time and place. Not at Company hands, not on the road in the night and from behind.

And Mula choked out the root of the goulep trouble. He ended the greedy hoarding of Arrivi wealth, held for one man's comfort while others suffered. He, and not I, focused attention on the accused of the trial, Dillan Rabbe Penli. Mula, and not I, provided covering for Rularim.

Chapter Thirty-Six

While talk about Dillan's trial died down, I prepared myself for something I couldn't name. My stepchildren and young Hamish moved with May to the land of Murd. I lived in the sulfur-smelling cave that housed the clutch of Murd, the deepest cover.

I no longer objected to their unstructured organization. I no longer felt outside their revolutionary zeal. We acted as one unit, a single heart to a single purpose. It was as though Julia Le's confession started all Dolviets down the path toward harmony. The old sense of harmony that had once directed their lives, that we glimpsed again, that we followed like a Ketiwhelp after the scent of game.

Without knowing what the future held, I wound down affairs, conserved my strength, steeled up my heart. Each day I greeted tribesmen with a quiet nod and burning eyes, aware they also felt a stirring.

The hotels emptied when the media corp packed up after the trial. Written off as a venture capital loss, the steel and glass buildings quickly deteriorated. The Cylahi didn't enter as squatters, afraid the buildings would collapse under that season's unusual earthquake activity.

Captain Ellis and his Blackshirts were sequestered with the remaining political prisoners at the Company compound. The Han-Chinese Blackshirts lived at the refinery. Company men closed ranks and fortified the strip between the refinery and the shuttle launchpad.

When the dry season came to a close, tribeswomen anticipated the replenished streams would fill with northern mountain thaw and bring the first geysers heralding the rain. Although streams on the flats of Arim gurgled with cold, fresh mountain water, tribeswomen noticed the geyser vents were dry. Company men had siphoned the rich reserves of old water for the manufacture of heavy water, an important component in the refinement of uranium.

As the water level of the deep subterranean pools fell, cold mountain water emptied into the caverns under the flats and quickly heated, killing the fragile plankton and microscopic bacteria on which the food chain depended. Dolviets daily felt underground rumblings when the new water volume entered super-heated dry vents and evaporated before geysers formed. The terraces of geyserite on the flats shook and steamed but gave forth no high jets or colorful sediments of algae and bacteria.

Holy women gave reverence at many sacred geyser sites, then entered Somule to give the blessing from Dolvia. Except there was no blessing. Holy women spoke of famine for the migrant wildlife and crop failure and starvation for the tribespeople.

Ely communicated directly with Tao Chek. "Stop the manufacture of heavy water that robs the desert of many." But Tao Chek refused to meet with the tribesmen. The fire-spewing towers at the refinery belched forth their odorous discharge day and night.

Within the clutch of Murd, Dak approached from behind me. "Come, Brian Rabbe Miller."

"I need to talk with Rularim."

"Dolvia knows your need. Come."

I was led down a slippery cave passageway to another firelit chamber where Kyle Le sat at a makeshift table over tea and dried fish. She looked up and gestured that I should join her.

She greeted my long stare. "Your center has shifted," I said.

Kyle Le laughed out loud, a new sound for me. "A true gaucho," she said with humor. "You're more Dolviet than any of us."

"I have a plan," I said with enthusiasm.

"So does everyone it seems," she said, relaxed after so many weeks of exposure at the trial.

"Will any of it work?" I asked, suddenly unsure.

"Cyrus says the visions are each part of one plan."

It was like music to hear her speak his name with honor. "Cyrus is here?"

"I mean, I heard Cyrus said that," she corrected.

"I want to go on a lecture tour. Or say I will. On the transport."

"To what purpose?"

"To bring Klistina Le home."

Kyle Rula reacted with an angry squint. She looked around to assure herself nobody was within earshot, then leaned forward. "I have seen my sister."

I knew better than to rush her with impatient questions. Never doubleminded, she slavishly offered the vision, knowing it wouldn't change my resolve.

"I have seen her separate from Dolvia," Kyle Rula sadly confessed. "She drifts in a coffin. Only it's shaped the same as she, with a huge bubble around her head. And she's utterly alone. That's her fate."

"No," I rushed in. "That's her escape route."

"What do you know?"

"It's called an extra-vehicular maintenance suit, an EVMS. Crewmembers on the transport wear them while they repair damaged equipment outside the bulkhead."

"Tina cannot operate such a thing."

"She will be adrift," I admitted. "That part's true. With the proper bribes, the shuttle's pilot will rescue her."

"This is a desperate act," Kyle Rula objected.

"They know who she is now. More than . . ."

"An exotic whore." She exposed brittle truth with manly words.

"You have confirmed my plan with your vision."

"To see is not to control."

"I'll bring Tina back."

"Brian, know this. I see her drifting, not on the shuttle. You're not part of the image."

"I will make it happen."

She seemed pained, as though I had pinched her. She sighed with resignation, an act that tribespeople have resented since the days of her long dead father, the negotiator. "May Dolvia honor your need," she pronounced as ritual.

I stepped into the same trap we all knew. "What do you see?"

The old barrier slammed down between us. I had not realized she clouded my view of her as an act of will. I had always assumed I was limited. "Please," I quickly added. "I'm sorry."

She peered at me from behind hooded lids, her childhood defense against the avarice of adults. She smiled slightly, and a glimpse of Kyle Le came to me. "You mustn't learn the plan. Company men will ask you."

"I have nothing for them. The offer of lecture tour is to rescue Tina."

"Are you ready for what you must do?"

I shrugged and resisted the temptation to stare into her face. "You know."

She waited for a long moment. I hung on her words. "You will be tested beyond what you are willing to give."

My jaw ached with a hunger to know her mind. I wanted to shake knowledge from her. Perhaps my resolve was a romantic dream, born of the desire to belong to people of a different blood. I sat in silence, my need for answers screaming at her from every pore. I wanted to leave, to bathe, to gather myself.

"Do you remember May's wedding day?" Kyle Rula asked out of the blue.

My third day on the planet, my first view of her spirit. My

association with Martin Sumuki whom I keenly missed. "We knew Brian Rabbe Miller as soon as you arrived," Kyle Rula added. "We knew that you would come."

"You and May always talk like this when you pity me. I must try," I pleaded.

"Then you need nothing from me."

"I need to know it's not destructive to the plan."

"Dolvia has provided."

"Is there something I can take, or do there that will help?"

"You mean destroy the transport? Disable their weapons? Break their cameras?" These had all entered my mind. I wanted to shout at her. I sighed and looked away.

"It's essential that you and I agree on nothing," Rularim said. "The men of the Company will ask you."

"I'm not trustworthy again."

"You enter the Ketiwhelp den. None can help you there."

While I prepared for the shuttle ride, Ely joined me with Haku and Dak. Tommy served us in Arrivi style, and we settled in for a long talk. "We have a request," Ely said simply.

"The Company abandoned the garrison in Somule, as you know," Ely explained. "Holy women gave many blessings in the yard of torture. Cylahi women moved from the slum into Captain Ellis' quarters. Tribespeople visiting for the weeks of the trial intended to stay in the apartments, the former indentured colonists' homes. But the holy woman said no, there was a pollution."

"From the Blackshirts?" I asked.

"Captain Ellis' group moved Dolviet political prisoners to the Company compound," Ely continued. "They reinforced it with iron bars, firewalls and heavy ordinance pointed at Somule. All this was accomplished while you prosecuted. Why distract you, concerned with Daniel Chin and the confession?"

I tried to imagine Captain Ellis and the Westend Blackshirts taking tea in the formal Chinese garden. "It was known even before their trek to the compound with the prisoners," Haku added, "that many guards suffered from fungus and mites. They wrapped thick bandages on their arms and legs, even during the dry season. Some Dolviet prisoners also wore medical bandages. They drew away in mortification when family members called to them along the road. We believe radiation burns from exposure to uranium plague them."

"We have evidence the Company detailed prison Blackshirts to dump toxic waste on the savannah," Ely softly said. "They were exposed to the waste material. And they exposed prisoners from contact."

"You mean the tribeswomen they abused?" I asked. Ely nodded and looked away. "That's why they didn't release all Dolviet prisoners during the trial," I guessed. "They couldn't risk the offworld media learning about the pollution."

"It's possible that Han-Chinese Blackshirts also suffer from radiation burns," Ely added. "There may be more than one toxic dump."

"They pollute Dolvia's body with their toxic run-off," Haku said evenly.

"You must learn if Blackshirts posted to the transport are treated for radiation burns," Ely said. "Perhaps Hamish Nordhagan has seen some unusual activity."

"I'll do what I can." We stood and Ely offered his hand to shake. "You will visit Dolvia again before the lecture tour?" he asked.

"There will be no tour."

"Have you seen this?" Ely said. They chuckled, along with Tommy, at the Softcheek's expense.

A few days later on the transport, Hamish waited in the corridor while I shook hands with my solicitor and left his office. Hamish fell into step with me. "You didn't sign anything, I hope."

"I'm holding out for more money."

"You? With the second largest personal fortune in Westend."

"With only twelve percent?"

I was surprised how much life on the transport had changed. Without the Company's stranglehold, daily routine followed different initiatives, mostly dictated by the needs of children. The entire place was a nursery.

Security protocol between the three sections was bypassed. In the promenade, conscript women with scarves over shaved heads minded the children of crewmembers and midshippers. Hamish smiled at my unbelieving stare. "It's like this on every freighter. People believe in the future again."

"And the conscripts?"

"They're responsible to the Company. But where is it written conscripts cannot have decent food and decent hygiene? So crewmembers set policy and charged the Company."

"Payment you'll never see."

"Payment made with Cylahi gold."

I starkly looked at him. "It can't be."

"It can, and is. But it won't last."

Captain Blakesley's wife and two children waited in the corridor. "Hello, I'm Billie," she said to me. "These are my children, Carl and Heather."

"Carl and Heather?" I asked with raised eyebrows.

"I met my husband through Heather Osborn when she attended a ball here."

"You're a debutante."

She smiled. "We're no longer called that."

"But the officers are called husbands," I objected.

247

"They practice husbandry with many resources."

Spurred by my poor understanding of harmony, I made restitution to Ricardo Menenous, even sent a small section of natural netta. All discreetly handled after my deposition concerning Ricardo's non-involvement in the netta enterprise.

I set straight my affairs and stood in the light of my own spirit without borrowing strength from Hamish or Cyrus. The source of my new energy was difficult to explain, even to myself. Hamish gently approached the subject. "You see them, don't you?"

"I see many changes," I hedged.

"I tried to tell myself it was culture shock," he said. "But Heather had the same experience. And now you."

"You can see them?" I starkly asked.

He shook his head. "It goes away after a few days."

I saw Softcheeks as Kyle Le had described, divided on three planes and sometimes going in opposite directions on each. Energy easily dissipated from their auras, leaving them pale and without purpose. "No wonder Kyle Rula always laughed at me."

"I never met goulep," Hamish said. "Only May and Haku. And Mula."

"And Ely who now leads."

We entered a wardroom where seven men in formal military dress milled about over coffee. They wore blue and white uniforms with gold braids on their shoulders, exactly as May had described. I stopped short, struggling to face off their spirits. They appeared bright and centered, with set jaws and steel muscles in their hands and arms.

Captain Blakesley languished in his chair, seated off to one side, seemingly unconcerned, then looked up with flames shooting from his eyes. I walked directly to him and held out my hand. The steel muscles of his face stretched into a wry smile. "Is there a formal event?" I asked after we shook hands. "Your uniforms."

"We stood honor guard just now for a Consortium ambassador from Cicero," he explained. "Ambassador Davidovich will disembark with you on Dolvia."

I nodded and continued to stare into his face, a gesture considered rude on the freighters. With question in his eyes, Captain Blakesley looked at Hamish.

"Culture shock," Hamish murmured over my shoulder.

Suggestions for strategy planning were postponed until after dinner. I dined with the ship's captain and his wife plus their honored guest, the Consortium ambassador, a burly and older, straight-talking former military officer. He wore the dark suit of his new occupation like a starched uniform. He squinted at Company arrogance but kept his own counsel.

"I'm conducting a fact-finding tour in this section,"

Ambassador Davidovich confided to me. "We have reports of impending crop failure and famine on Dolvia. I thought I would have a look for myself. You know the tribespeople. Can you arrange a meeting with Rularim or Cyrus?"

"You want to meet Ely," I offered. "He has information you should know."

"I'm glad we have this time on the transport. I also invited Hamish Nordhagan. I'm told he has disembarked before."

"Yes, he visited Dolvia during negotiations with Tao Chek that set the trial of Dillan Rabbe Penli," I said diplomatically.

"Ah, the famous trial. And we heard about your lecture tour. Besides Cicero, where will you speak?"

"It's not decided yet. There are several offers."

I stared into his active face. It was like a game to me, this heightened sensibility. I gained confidence through the reinforcement of images mentioned in passing by May and Kyle Rula. I was intoxicated with a sure knowledge I couldn't have ascertained by trying. I acted as Dolvia's vessel apart from my goals. Mula must have felt the same headiness, leading to his hubris.

The ship's captain bowed to me from his place across the table. I chuckled, thinking that time was a loop. But I grew strangely sleepy during the meal, unable to concentrate on their talk. Later I woke up in my bed in the crew quarters. My memory was blank concerning several hours after the meal.

Why didn't I discern their underhanded trick? Kyle Le had warned of my vulnerability. Spiritual strength required more than a few, poor flashes of heightened vision.

That morning I voiced my suspicions to Hamish. "They have drugs, you know. I must have told them everything about defenses on Dolvia. All of it, from way back."

"I've seen those drugs work," Hamish calmly said. "They only reach top of mind."

"That's plenty."

"What? A lot of babble about the need to cover Kyle Le?"

He saw my cutting glance. "About Klistina Le," I said.

"That's true," Hamish returned. "I'll look into that part."

We decided to implement plans, then drop them at the last minute. Hamish changed the guard around Tina where she waited for the shuttle to return from Cicero.

"About the Han-Chinese Blackshirts with radiation poisoning. We'll never get the evidence now," I complained.

"There may be a channel."

We visited the communications center where two husbands reviewed their monitors, halfway through their duty shifts. Captain Blakesley gestured that we join him. We watched a monitor that tracked the starboard camera view of the plateau concealing the clutch of Murd. I caught my breath.

Captain Blakesley smiled. "Now look at this one from last week." He switched views, and the record disc revealed people and munitions on the savannah below the plateau. "Now today's activity again." He switched to the first view.

I stared into the screen. Only a Murmurey bird returned to feed her young in a nest on the high plateau. "Do you think Dolviets abandoned their strongholds because of your visit here?" Hamish asked.

"I wasn't taken into their confidence. As usual."

"Here's the best one," Captain Blakesley said. The luminous screen entertained us with bleeps and shadows, infra-red trails across the wide expanse, representing people with hopes and dreams. The forward transport camera focused on the Cylahi caves. Captain Blakesley pointed to a faint infra-red trail that led into the wide opening. "That's weeks old," he claimed. "The Cylahi abandoned the area before the trial."

"The Company could recover some equipment," I offered.

The young officer shook his head. "It sets off a Geiger counter like solar wind." He switched off the monitor and sat back in his chair. "We believe that's the main dump. The deep caves mask radiation trails. There's no telling how much toxic waste they stockpiled."

"How close to the water table?"

Captain Blakesley shrugged. "They cannot be connected. There would be more sickness. Perhaps they stored the waste in reinforced drums."

"So there is evidence of dumping," I concluded. "Does the Consortium ambassador know?"

"Ambassadors can die, or be discredited," Hamish said. "What you need is a public scandal. Ambassador Davidovich travels with media. Some are cameramen who covered the trial. But they haven't obtained permission to undertake documentaries concerning Somule and the tribes."

"Now we know why," I added with cynicism.

"Their Consortium networks dispatched them to follow the ambassador. Return to Somule."

"And you want a meeting with Ely," I guessed.

"We want videotape of Dolviets with radiation burns," Captain Blakesley flatly said.

"The Company will claim it's from a natural source," I shrugged.

"That's why it has to be Westend Blackshirts and prisoners," Hamish said.

"That's all?" I asked. "Why not give me something difficult to accomplish?"

The next day Ambassador Davidovich waited to board the shuttle. When I approached with Hamish, reporters with camcorders reached to shake my hand. I recognized some faces.

250

They boarded the shuttle with their considerable luggage and Blackshirt escort. Captain Blakesley stood in midship and casually saluted Hamish, then we walked down the causeway.

During the flight, the ambassador explained his goals into tape recorders held by the attentive media audience. Hamish befriended a cameraman and inspected his camcorder. Blackshirt guards sat next to me in the crowded compartment. I excused myself and went to the portal.

I saw the extra-vehicular maintenance suit, supposedly carrying Tina to be rescued by the shuttle's pilot, drifting in the cold blackness of space. The shuttle drew near it, then flanked left. The EVMS pushed away and quickly spun off until it disappeared from our view, endlessly drifting in dark and cold, unfeeling space. I reacted as I was slated to, then sullenly sat in one corner. Blackshirts glanced at each other, then forgot the native girl who had been a Company whore.

We disembarked at Cylay and waited to board the train for Somule. I stood near the common car of the long train. I nodded to Hamish and Ambassador Davidovich when they entered the Company car at trainsend, followed by reporters and Blackshirts.

During the quiet bumpy ride, a young Putuki man, a friend of Ely, entered the common car. He looked at me and blinked twice without expression, then passed onto the next car. I sat back and enjoyed the ride, sure in my heart that Tina was released from her hiding place in the reporters' baggage. She once again communed with Dolvia.

Chapter Thirty-Seven

It was said that the Mekucoo measured time by cycles that could last half a season or twelve seasons. With the death of Mula, we entered the season of om, the only such cycle we expected to know in our lifetimes.

Cyrus walked through the shimmering heat of the savannah, dressed in the Mekucoo loincloth and leggings with shield and spear. He wore an amulet on a strap around his upper arm. He walked alone up the long lane to Haku's home where the extended family relaxed under the cool fans of the verandah.

"Hiki Haku Rabbe Murd," Cyrus said with feet planted wide apart and his spear held over his head. "Health and prosperity to those who dwell on the land of Murd, where it's said the cattle all bear twins."

"Hiki Cyrus, Melinga," Haku said. "You know the spirit of my wife, Karima Le of the sisters of Arim."

"Hiki May," Cyrus gently said. "I seek shelter on the land awarded for all time to Rularim."

Pregnant May slowly smiled. "You're welcome throughout the region, but especially by the spring of old water that healed your lashes from long ago." Word went out that same day, the gathering had begun.

Later May pressed Kyle Rula to say why Cyrus had come. Why at this time after so much was ended. Kyle Rula sadly shook her head as though grieving for a lost family member. Finally she forced the words, "His tribal wife has died, she who raised *Dacupitte*. The amulet's a token of mourning."

And so it was. Cyrus no longer belonged to Mekucoo land. He was free to belong to the people. Kyle Rula had never lent her mantel to him. I had assumed it was because of the goulep trouble. But they both knew it was Cyrus who wasn't yet ready. She had resisted giving herself to a man who couldn't give himself to her.

Cyrus didn't linger on the flats like an uncertain beau, telling stories of his past prowess. He didn't call for a personal treasure chest or a Council to discuss strategy. Much was learned by what he didn't do.

Cyrus sought out silent men with hot eyes and strong hearts. We steeled ourselves for the fight without calling forth the words of battle that were so often in Mula's mouth. Years of compounded wrongs were righted. We were unbound from the cult of personality.

Carrying Company prison drawings, Quentin and Cara joined the leaders. It made sense to me. Capture Captain Ellis and the sick guards with radiation poisoning. Put them on display before the Consortium ambassador.

But Cyrus' vision was clearer than mine. He labored to release only two prisoners. For the purpose of standing before one Arrivi woman.

During the bustle of preparations, Ely met with Ambassador Davidovich in the hotel stateroom where I had once displayed bolts of textured cloth from Brittany Mill for Ricardo and Chang Lin. Separate bundles of microphones were mounted on the table in front of the ambassador and in front of Ely where they sat across from each other.

In dress uniform Hamish sat next to the former Consortium commander and tolerantly watched the scrambling reporters. At Ely's shoulders, Quentin and Cara stood with imposing spears and shields. They gave no ground while the reporters maneuvered to get a better view. Cyrus and Haku were absent, busy with plans for the next day's events. I was allowed entry by reporters who solicited recap interviews.

Hot lights glared and the camcorders whirled. "The Consortium was made aware during the much-publicized trial of Dillan Penli that the Company refinery may present a danger to the ecosystem of this region," Ambassador Davidovich pronounced in whole tones while he looked into shoulder camcorders, playing to the offworld audience. With raised eyebrows Quentin and Cara exchanged looks over Ely's head.

"Because of refinery needs," the ambassador continued, "the water table of this region has dropped dangerously low during the dry season. We meet here today to give voice to Dolviet concerns. To find an equitable solution for the best use of the rich mineral wealth of this land."

He looked around at the faces in the room, signaling that his opening remarks were complete. "Company presence, and especially the refinery, have helped Somule become an interplanetary center of commerce," he said, making eye contact with Ely. "I can see that mixing such divergent cultures may have led to some misunderstanding. Perhaps during the next few days we can find solutions to immediate problems. Map out a plan for the future that is agreeable to all parties." He paused and smiled at Ely.

Ely put one elbow on the table and leaned forward to the mics. "We want the rock that kills left in the ground," he said without humor.

"That is impractical," the Ambassador gently claimed.

"Impractical for whom?" asked Ely. Quentin and Cara hid their smirks.

"Has your investigation," Ely continued, "looked into reports that the evacuated Blackshirts have radiation poisoning?" The reporters murmured and looked at the ambassador with question.

"Company internal problems are not part of today's meeting," he insisted in a loud voice. "We are meeting to discuss the lowered water table."

"Dumping is not an internal Company problem," Ely broke in. "They pollute the land with their toxic run-off."

"I have no evidence of toxic dumping."

"And if we bring you evidence? Will you broadcast the truth? The Company kills their own through negligence!"

That night Cara and Quentin joined Cyrus and his men on the rise behind the Company compound. They dropped down between the solar panels and entered the trashed Chinese garden from the roof. They scurried up one long corridor to the ornate, teak-laden private chambers that had once housed Tao Chek as the prospective groom to Sim Chareon's oldest daughter. Captain Ellis laid sick and drooling on the brocade pillows. Cyrus put his spearhead on Captain Ellis' throat.

"Go ahead. Finish it!" Captain Ellis begged.

"Tao Chek has killed you already," Cyrus said. "Get up. You will come with us." Captain Ellis painfully swung his legs off the bed and sat up. His arm was wrapped with stained medical bandages. He pulled on his uniform trousers and gingerly laid his black tunic with the panda logo over his shoulders.

Quentin handed Captain Ellis' keys to a warrior who left to release Dolviet prisoners. Quentin opened a case near the bed and showed the goods to Cyrus. It contained peridot and topaz gems, Cylahi gold jewelry and natural netta.

"The treasure of Kyle Rula," Quentin said simply.

They heard metal clanking against metal. At spearpoint they encouraged Captain Ellis to walk between them into the other room.

Cara angrily hammered his spearhead at a pair of handcuffs secured to the metal headboard of a military cot. Quentin pushed Cara aside, easily unfastened the cuffs, then handed them to him. Cara made a sour face.

"Let's do it here," Quentin said.

"She wouldn't find it fitting," Cyrus balked.

"Such was done after your bad time. You would do less for Rularim?" Quentin asked.

"It means nothing to her," Cyrus claimed.

"It means something to all others," Cara said and sealed Captain Ellis' fate.

Quentin cut out Captain Ellis' heart and left the body on the cot where many prison women had suffered. They looked down at him, white and thin, with festering sores. Captain Ellis was no longer imposing without the black shirt and shiny insignia.

"Those who have suffered must be allowed to see," Cara said. "We are blacker than they."

"Strip the ones in the garden," Cyrus instructed. "We'll not expose Kyle Rula's shame."

Blackshirt guards were disarmed and herded into the Chinese garden. The healthy ones removed themselves from the six unlucky Blackshirts who had been detailed to stockpile barrels of waste inside the Cylahi Caves.

Dolviet prisoners were released from their cells. Some insisted the rescuing warriors step back. They carried a leprosy they were loathe to pass to healthy Dolviets. In the garden five Cylahi and three Arrivi women crowded together near the sick Blackshirts. They wore makeshift bandages on their hands and arms. Their prison garb concealed other burns, the loose tunics and baggy pants that conscripts wore. They cursed the guards and spat on them, but wouldn't allow other Dolviets to approach.

With tragic faces the warriors and healthier Dolviet prisoners watched the suffering women. One Cylahi with an open sore on her cheek spoke out in anger. "You pity us? Pity them! Nobody rescues them. Their spirits will not return to the body of Dolvia."

"You are the heroes of the resistance," Quentin said in a loud, clear voice. "Your names will live forever in the chants taught to Dolviet children."

Tears ran down her cheeks. She struggled to keep her chin from trembling. "That is enough."

"This must be made public," Cara quietly told Cyrus.

They opened the compound front entrance and easily walked down the steps. Between them two warriors carried the case that held the treasure of Kyle Rula. Cyrus handed a small package to Dak who turned and sauntered toward the flats of Arim.

A cheer went up from waiting family members who rushed forward to embrace the released prisoners. They were held back by a wall of warrior's shields and complained at being kept from the reunion. When it was made clear that some who suffered could not be embraced, the crowd's jubilation evaporated. Many other prisoners passed the barricade of shields and quietly joined their loved ones.

Haku and his two sons arrived in a confiscated jeep. Haku joined Cyrus and Cara then looked with horror at the polluted Blackshirts. "We've been watching the refinery," he reported. "There's no counterattack. They don't come out of the fortress to defend their own."

Hamish brought forward the young cameraman who he had befriended on the shuttle. The reporter quickly loaded his camcorder and hoisted it onto his shoulder.

"Can Quentin heal them?" Hamish asked.

"It's a mineral burn, not a virus," Cara explained. "The same as a battle wound."

"How many Dolviets?"

"Eight women," Cyrus quietly said. Haku stared at the ground with disgust.

The warriors formed a wide circle around the three groups. The doomed women looked away and pulled their clothes over their shame. The healthy Blackshirts stood in their black tunics with the bright panda logo on the sleeves, aware that Dolviets didn't take prisoners. The sick Blackshirts listlessly sat on the ground. "Tell them to remove their tunics," Cara said.

The healthy Blackshirts reluctantly complied and threw their black shirts into a pile. Dolviets jeered them with shouts and loud clucking. The cameraman with his camcorder was allowed into the wide circle and focused on the sallow and sick Blackshirts who sat on the ground.

With both hands Cara held his spear high above his head. The shouting stopped. "It is enough that Tao Chek has abandoned these ones. They will be exposed to the Consortium audience who witnessed the trial."

"Where is Captain Ellis?" Hamish asked Cyrus.

"He has been punished for his crimes."

Tribespeople heard a loud screeching noise. They looked up, then hurried onto the savannah in all directions when the compound shook from a refinery ordinance blast. "That son of a bitch is firing at us!" Hamish complained. He grabbed the cameraman's arm and guided him to Haku's jeep that Orin quickly drove away.

The warriors hustled the Blackshirts and sick women northeast toward the protection of the rise. Heavy ordinance exploded with billows of smoke, destroying part of the compound wall and leaving heated craters. Dolviets later claimed they felt underground rumblings from twenty miles away, just as though Dolvia complained at these latest blemishes inflicted on Her body.

Another bomb exploded near the compound entrance. Cyrus and the warriors nearly lost their footing when the ground quaked from the aftershock. "They anger Dolvia," Cara called to Cyrus.

Escaping tribespeople were thrown to the ground that opened into long fissures and wide, dry trenches. A geyser shot up from one trench. The Company attack abruptly stopped. "They cannot risk an eruption so close to the refinery," Cyrus shouted.

256

"And they won't leave its protection to fight," Cara called back. "We have won the day!"

In Somule the polluted Blackshirts were put on display before the Consortium camcorders. Behind closed doors Ambassador Davidovich met with Hamish. Later he made a public statement and shook hands with Ely before the whirling cameras. With the media corp the ambassador boarded the shuttle without communicating with Tao Chek.

Rularim's fortune offered in shameful clandestine meetings for the relative comfort of Terry the Martyr was returned. The remainder of Captain Ellis' hoard was distributed to families of radiation poisoning victims. Captain Ellis' heart was carried to the big rock in the flats and left for the Murmurey bird. It was said that so putrid was the offering, no bird came to feed.

Chapter Thirty-Eight

Cyrus traversed Haku's land a second time, with a fully veiled woman and veiled child walking beside him. Orin Rabbe Murd tended cattle near the lane and saw Cyrus and company. Orin dropped his work and ran to the house calling out that Cyrus would arrive. Hamish and I sat with Haku and Ely under the long paddles of the verandah fan.

On the wide porch of her husband's home May stood without veil and big with her fourth child. Marcy and Tina were in the place of service. Kyle Le waited at the steps of the verandah but not under its cool fans, as goulep was never welcome. Kat and Pete sat on the steps. In the yard Joey and Sister came forward with Tommy. Only Terry was gone from us, returned to Dolvia's bosom.

Cyrus and his two companions stopped ten paces short of the verandah. The traditionally veiled figures lent formality to an uncertain moment. "Hiki Karima Le, sister to Terry the Martyr," Cyrus said. We looked around, surprised that he first addressed a woman.

"Hiki Cyrus," May said with ritual. "Melinga. May we know the spirits of your companions?"

Cyrus removed the veil of a young Putuki woman, very dark-skinned with bowed heavy legs and a ring in her nose. "This is Lula, Martin Sumuki's daughter who, except for the gift of netta, would have died as a young girl from a fungus on her ear and eyelid." The young, blue-black woman with a disfiguring scar near her eye stared at the ground.

Feelings came to me that cannot be articulated except perhaps in Mekucoo. Relief from the fungus, the years of prosperity, the street of shops in Somule shimmering with electricity to illuminate the desert's edge. All these resulted from goulep's sale of netta.

"Hiki Lula," May said. "You're welcome in the home of Martin Sumuki's friends."

Lula nodded and looked at Cyrus for reassurance. She

removed the veil of her companion. We saw a six-year-old girl, too young to require covering in assembly. Lula uncertainly glanced at Kyle Rula then led the child to stand before May.

"This is Hakulupe Le," Lula said. "Daughter of your husband and your sister. From a union forced on them by pain of death in the Somule prison." There was perfect silence. You could have heard Kariom breathing.

"Terry died after her birth," Lula continued. "As your mother was diminished bringing forth Rularim. Terry told us it's a sign when the daughter steals the life of her mother."

Lula gathered her courage and continued. "I lost me three-week-old son sired by a Blackshirt guard. We switched my dead son for Terry's premature daughter. I hid Hakulupe Le in the causeway leading to the yard of torture. I visited her as often as I could, as did others who risked their lives to bring her food and comfort. It was her lonely cries in the night the Blackshirts thought they heard."

As the presentation of Lula had healed wounds, Hakulupe Le's presence set our hearts to a single purpose. A child raised next to the yard of torture with only dying screams for comfort, Terry the Martyr's daughter.

Against all sense, against the bonds of kinship and rightful birth, against the possibility of discovery and brutal torture to death—this child stood before the sisters of her mother. Chin held high, her forest green eyes flashed with a sure knowledge that was matched in Kyle Rula's eyes. Here was the equal who Rularim hadn't found among the men. Here was her reason to work within the assembly. This one, this one child only, must live.

"To the battlefield then," Rularim said in a whisper.

The Night of the Hunt wasn't a state dinner in this cycle. Rather, a simple communion among people with a single heart led by clear vision. Men of purpose went into their wives, perhaps for the last time, with the hope of fertility in the face of death. New and vital songs were heard about the former prisoners who were the heroes of the resistance. About om and that which must live on into the new cycle.

Later the gestures were frozen into myth and ritualistic repetition. Not a wrong thing, the only season of om we expected to know in our lifetimes.

Fresh meat was slaughtered, fresh fruit and herbs gathered. Houses were cleaned and set straight. Men bathed and wore their best. The sisters of Arim and their guests wore skyblue body veils until they closed the door, shutting the world out from the family hearth.

At the ceremonial fire in Haku's yard where the bachelors sang and danced, Hamish and I were served by Joey. Hamish shook hands with Pete, a new gesture for the boy, then showed

Pete how to load and use the shoulder camcorder.

Quentin performed feats of magic, occasionally glancing my way but without malice. Ely sat with Orin and the other bachelors in leadership who were served by Tommy. Cara stood apart, ever waiting for Cyrus who was honored in the house of Murd.

And what passed between Cyrus and Kyle Le? In the house of Haku Rabbe Murd all ritual was observed. From under the veil Kyle Le served the ceremonial tea. She brought gifts of remembrance in the form of bracelets for her sisters Karima Le and Klistina Le. She honored Lula, the daughter of her friend Martin Sumuki. And she embraced Hakulupe Le, officially under May's guardianship, then sent her to play with the other children who Marcy and Carline minded.

Kyle Le asked that Carline step forward. Kyle Le officially passed onto her the teardrop peridot necklace that Heather had worn at a ball during her visit to the Company transport.

"I cannot accept this. It's too valuable," Carline said.

"Care for it," Kyle Le encouraged. "Give it to Pete's wife on the proper day."

The meal was short and lovely. Lula sang a song from her tribe. Haku recited the size of his herd and acreage, as a man facing battle is wont to do.

Cyrus asked at length, after all ceremony was satisfied, to know the spirit of the virginal sister of Karima Le, the only one there who was veiled. May was glad this one last time to present her youngest sister to the Mekucoo warrior. She lifted Kyle Le's veil showing the light blue underside to the men. "I present Kyle Le, who hasn't been among us since she was a young girl on the flats owned by our father, Len Rabbe Arim."

The shame of goulep was transmuted by legend into glory. The anger of the despotic leaders no longer stood between her and this Mekucoo man. The avarice of Softcheeks, the resentful opinion of the tribespeople, the presence of older family ties, the edits of tribal law. None of these separated them. She was a grown woman, counted as a virgin, available and vulnerable to his advances.

"Hiki Kyle Le," Cyrus said simply.

"Hiki Cyrus," she said with eyes averted. "Hiki Haku Rabbe Murd. It's an honor to know the spirits of the family of Murd."

"You are sister and former employer to my wife," Haku said with formality. "Your visions have served the tribes for twenty years. You honor us with your presence."

Cyrus crossly looked at him, then turned to Kyle Le. "Who has claim on you that I must ask?"

Kyle Le stared at the floor. Cyrus turned to Haku. "Who has claim on this woman of your household?"

"Rularim is a grown woman of property," Haku said, "who

has given her mantel to no man. She's an ideal among women."

Cyrus quickly stood, square before Haku, nostrils flaring. Since the truth about her visits to Captain Ellis was known, Cyrus could follow Kyle Le into the hospitality of her room. Nobody there would resist him. It was an avenue open and natural. But Kyle Le had not stated what was in her heart. Between these two all ceremony must be satisfied.

Haku held his ground as his position was right. Cyrus gathered his shield and spears, all traces of himself in that house, then left without a word.

At his appearance in the yard, a cheer went up among the assembly which by then included families whose ceremonial dinner had ended. Cyrus joined Cara near the bachelor fire.

Many Dolviets gathered to watch the antics of Quentin who was in his element on the Night of the Hunt. He danced and did magic tricks for the young men, his armaments laid aside while he returned to the lighthearted ways of his youth. People laughed and joined in, chanting and slapping their thighs in unison.

The tribespeople fell silent when a woman in a shimmering white body veil was led from the back entrance around the side of the house by two others, Tina and Carline. Members of the extended family of Murd stepped onto the verandah to watch.

Cyrus stepped forward and pulled off his tunic, exposing his Mekucoo brief leggings and the many scars on his back, chest and arms that were the stuff of myth. He walked without escort to the veiled woman and held out his hand. After a long moment, Kyle Le shyly pulled the veil back from her arm only and placed her hand on his.

Cyrus and Kyle Le created ritual with every gesture. The crowd went delirious with cheering and congratulating each other for being present at this moment in tribal history.

Cyrus removed the heavy braided band that secured Kyle Le's veil. He handed it to Lula, then gently tugged on the veil. Kyle Le stepped back a fraction of an inch. Cyrus lifted the veil to show a vivid apricot underside like the lining of white clouds at sunset. He pulled the veil from her and placed it into Tina's waiting arms.

Kyle Le wore a loose, light apricot gown, styled like those worn by the women in Brittany Mill. She also wore a millhood that covered her head and mouth, made of the same apricot material. The crowd murmured while Cyrus stepped close and waited.

Chin high and eyes flashing with the defiance of a lifetime, Kyle Le pulled the hood over her head and let it fall to the ground. We saw the gold medallion on heavy chain that Oriika had given her at May's wedding. Kyle Le slipped the chain over her head. She murmured to Tina that it be given to Hakulupe Le as part of her dowry.

Cyrus made the gesture of belonging that May had described to me eons before. He lightly put his hand on Kyle Le's shoulder and neck, then moved his fingers slowly down her chest to cover her heart. It was a daring and provocative gesture before the company. Everyone in the crowd strained to see her response. Kyle Le put her hand on Cyrus' neck and moved it down his chest in the same manner.

The barest smile crossed Cyrus' face. He held her wrist firmly against his chest. Without taking his gaze from Kyle Le's face, he held out his other hand. Cara handed him an exquisite peridot bracelet with oval cut stones, the most difficult craftsmanship. Further, the stones were set side-to-side so several additional stones of exactly the same size and color completed the length of a bracelet. Cyrus held the bracelet aloft for all to see, then clasped it onto Kyle Le's wrist.

Again Cyrus held out his hand. Cara gave him a beautiful, vivid blue peridot necklace of the finest workmanship. Cyrus released Kyle Le's wrist and held the necklace before her. He ignored the crowd and gathered his spirit around her. Kyle Le waited while he gently reached behind her neck and clasped the necklace ends together.

Kyle Le allowed Cyrus to place her hand upon his arm. With long, ceremonial strides, he guided her three times around the bachelor fire, displaying her jewelry and his scars before the assembly. When they returned to their place, Cara stood before them.

"Who challenges the union of the warrior Cyrus and Kyle Rula of Arim?" Cara demanded. A spear came out of the shadows and thudded into the ground inches from Cara's feet.

"This union is under the protection of Quentin, the Putuki healer," Quentin spoke from the crowd. "Anyone who harms them or their progeny will die in fear of me."

The men looked at me and waited with honor. I had no spear and no gift. The best I could offer was a toast. "May the old water that gurgles through the flats of Arim make you fertile."

A cheer went up. Cyrus leaned down and grabbed Kyle Le around the knees. He lifted her over his shoulder, as one does when the wife is a virgin, and quickly walked out of the firelight and around the side of Haku's house to her private entrance.

Cara held his spear above his head and gave one loud shout. Tribespeople turned back to their revelry.

Chapter Thirty-Nine

Battle strategy was long-planned. We had one objective, one battle to fight. We must lay seige to the fortifications of the refinery and end Company rule over our lives. We knew it was a hopeless effort. But the savannah was choking. We could die in battle or die of starvation.

While we made preparations for the offensive against the refinery, Tina journeyed to the Canyon of Buttes to give reverential offering and beg for a cleansing. With her traveled Marcy, Carline, Lula, and Hakulupe Le who was too young for the journey but who wouldn't be separated from the only mother she knew. I don't know what happened during their time on the savannah, it's not manly to wonder what the women do, but Tina later told me some of it.

Tribal leaders devised a three-pronged offensive. Cyrus' men would attack the shuttle launchpad in force drawing fire from the refinery. Quentin's group would climb the butte's sheer back wall and fire down on the Blackshirt defenders. Haku's clutch would plant plastic explosives into the ridge of the west plateau that protected the refinery buildings. While the other two forces kept the Blackshirts at bay, Haku planned to detonate the charges and send a shower of rock down onto refinery armaments. Then all three forces would engage the Blackshirts on their ground.

"The Chinese Blackshirts won't dispatch men to save the launchpad," Haku said. "They never defend their own."

"It's Tao Chek's offworld escape route," Cyrus said. "He won't choose to die with us."

After the toxic dump scandal, Tao Chek couldn't leave Dolvia without losing face. The Consortium ambassador had made sure the regent looked responsible for negligence toward his polluted men. If Tao Chek traveled to Cicero just before the anticipated battle, his Chinese descent Blackshirts would become demoralized.

Plus he must defend the refinery with the resources at hand. Offworld Company directors saw the trouble on Dolvia as a local matter, worrisome but simple to counter. Tao Chek held the high ground with superior firepower and Consortium backing. Subdue the tribes and get on with the export of Dolvia's mineral wealth. What could be the problem?

And so finally Marcy was allowed to participate in a suicide mission. With Ely and Tommy and under the cover of night, she climbed the outcropping of the butte's back. They approached a cleft in the butte that Kyle Le had described to Cyrus. A small person was needed to climb the last twenty feet, wiggle into the cleft, and plant the charges. Armed with a toolbag of plastic explosives plus sulfur bombs to scatter resident snakes, Marcy grinned at Ely and scurried up the sandy embankment.

Ely and Tommy waited forty minutes past the time Marcy was to return. Ely prepared to climb after her. Then she joined them, covered with grit and her hands bleeding. "Blackshirts filled in the cleft with concrete," she complained. "I had to dig some out to situate the charges."

"Should we try again?" Ely asked.

"Whatever good Dolvia will deliver is in place now."

Many people called on Dolvia in those days. Many watched for a sign that She reinforced their efforts. A steady stream of petitioners visited Rularim, requesting an insight that each would live on while the savannah suffered and died. Kyle Rula was gentle but not encouraging. Resigned to the truth in her secret tortured images, perhaps not even shared with Cyrus during their private time, Kyle Rula seemed weighed down with the troubles of many tribespeople whose courage ran hot and cold.

But the young people laughed and danced and made love under the stars. And Ely grew in stature. With Marcy at his side, his presence shored up the courage of many others.

One day Hamish and I worked with Haku taking bore samples on the savannah. Hamish showed Orin Rabbe Murd how to drill the thin barrel into the ground and pull up deep samples which we inspected for water and bacterial life.

We four stood with our heads together when Ely returned with Marcy and Tommy from their adventure at the butte. Orin labored over the strange equipment, then boasted to Tommy that he had mastered Softcheeks technology.

Marcy wore dungarees and the dark tunic of Quentin's clutch and carried a heavy toolbag. Her hands were bleeding. She held her chin high and stared into my face. "You see," she claimed. "Lucy's kids have value. More than as a servant to Gaucho."

"I should have spanked you more when you were younger," I returned.

"Ha! You would not feel safe receiving food from my hand after," she called back.

Hamish and Haku chuckled then examined the bore sample Orin brought them. Ely handled a small section that was from ten inches deep. The dirt crumbled and scattered in the hot breeze. We stood silent and pensive under the burning sun. Would there ever be enough rain to restore the balance?

Tina and Carline joined us with a package containing fruit and bread patties. Carline inspected Marcy's hands. "Come back to the house. We'll put a salve on them."

Tina drew close to me, her bright face sunburned from her days walking uncovered on the savannah. "We are on the land of my ancestors," she whispered. "Once owned by Len Rabbe Arim."

"It's good to see you in communion with Dolvia," I said with ritual.

"Thank you for bringing me home."

Haku and the others collected the equipment, ready to move onto another site. "We'll test the ground under the high Acacias on the flats," Haku said. "Water lingers there."

The men walked away, and Tina drew me to one side. "I will show you a thing," she whispered. Hamish looked back, but left with his steps in sync with Haku and Orin.

Carline and Marcy left in another direction with Ely and Tommy. "Beware, Tina," Marcy called back. "Gaucho uncovers the sisters of Arim." Marcy and Carline giggled together and ignored the men.

"Why do they laugh?" I asked with irritation.

"It is seen."

"What does Kyle Rula see?"

"Why do you continue to petition her?" Tina asked with irritation. "Hasn't she suffered enough?"

"You brought it up."

"Not Kyle Le's vision. My vision from our journey to the canyon."

"Tell me," I gently asked. "What have you seen?"

"Come and sit with me here on my father's land, and I will tell all."

We sat under the low shrub. The dry leaves that clung to the branches shivered in the breeze creating a light melody. Tina spun a simple story about the many tribeswomen at the canyon who petitioned the army of buttes to rise up and defend them against the Company.

"The land is dying," I said. "How can suffering Dolvia help you?"

"You are too impressed with the forces She allows."

I wanted to ask what was seen. I wanted to be included in their vision and their plan. But I didn't badger her for answers as I often had Kyle Le. I looked around at the land of Len Rabbe Arim.

Tina drew close. Her perfume was intoxicating, her smile fathomless. Her touch was exhilarating. And as Marcy predicted, that afternoon I did uncover another sister of Arim. But then she dressed and walked away as though it meant nothing, our last days spent in idle talk and desperate action.

Then one night when all the preparations were made and we rested in our respective clutches waiting for the signal to advance, I saw Hamish standing by the campfire. Pete lingered with him, dressed in Mekucoo loincloth and leggings with his hair matted in long dreadlocks. With indolence in his bearing, Pete shook Hamish's hand and left with the other young men. I joined Hamish and watched Pete walk down the slope with Ely, Orin, Tommy and Joey in the jaunty steps of young men eager for the testing of battle.

"This is a young man's fight," Hamish quietly said.

"I thought I would have one more go at it," I returned.

And now I must quickly finish my story, for the time is short. As part of Haku's detachment, Hamish and I watched through field glasses from our cover on the plateau's sloping back. Through the glasses we saw Cyrus and Cara lead their men against the shuttle launchsite with heavy casualties.

Quentin detonated the charge Marcy had planted in the high butte. We heard the explosion and felt the earth tremble, but the butte tower held firm.

Quentin's advance forces scaled the butte's sheer back to the cliff in the tower. They reigned down fire on the Blackshirts who operated the heavy canons that decimated Cyrus' forces.

Quentin's main group approached from the savannah floor, but came under attack from the Blackshirts who manned anti-personnel guns from inside the refinery walls.

"We must act now," Hamish called to Haku.

We moved to a ridge position and readied detonators for the planted charges. Rifle fire scathed the ground nearby. "What the hell?" I called to Hamish.

"Snipers on the butte top!"

"How'd they get up there?"

The land trembled again, and we saw the ancient Acacia trees by the flats splinter and fall. "Perhaps the charge in the butte had some effect," Haku hopefully said.

"The land cannot save you!" I angrily called out.

A geyser shot up near the refinery wall between the Blackshirts and Quentin's men. Their ordinance report ceased. The tribesmen resumed their attack under cover of the steaming waterjets.

Haku showed me his scarred and aging face, then turned to the young warriors. "We'll set the other side," Haku commanded. Tommy and Orin strung the last wires to our detonators then scurried after Haku's retreating form.

Hamish and I waited at our station for the signal to blow the ridge. Through field glasses we saw Cyrus' men take the worst of it. "We must do something!" I called out to Hamish. Suddenly firing from the Blackshirt forces stopped. The deadly quiet sent a cold chill down my spine. "What is it?"

"Can't tell from here," Hamish said. "I'll have a look."

He left the cover of shrubs and sandbags that we had built during the night and cautiously crawled to the plateau ridge. He laid on his stomach and stared through his field glasses.

"I can't make out anything unusual," he called back to me.

"Close your blind eye and look again!"

Rapid fire hit the dirt by Hamish's leg, and he hurried back to cover. A narrow trail of bullets raffled the wires that led from the detonator to the charges. We looked at each other and shook our heads. The detonators would have to be reset closer to the ridge.

"I'll go," Hamish said.

"I'll go. You have a reason to live through this."

"You can't twist the wires with those arthritic hands," he acidly claimed and stood to make the dash. I tripped him so he fell hard on the ground next to me.

"At least I can stand and run," I said and hurried up the slope.

I grabbed the frayed wires and tested their connection to the charges. With my beltknife I quickly cut away the ends then twisted them onto another detonator. But I needed to wait in that position for the signal to blow our side of the plateau ridge.

"Can you see anything?" I called back.

"Just a horse's ass!"

I edged up and peered over the ridge. The refinery big guns were silent. Cyrus' men invaded the launchsite fortifications and fought hand-to-hand with defending Blackshirts. Tao Chek didn't show himself, perhaps more willing to die than lose face in retreat.

Suddenly fire belched up from the refinery center. A geyser shot up along the stream at the windowless rampart.

The snipers got a bead on me and opened fire. "Shit," I complained and crouched forward. I was pinned down by the pelting bullets.

"There's only two of them!" I called out to Hamish. "Can't you pick them off?"

"You're the damned fool with his ass in the air!" Hamish shouted back.

"Sight with your other eye and take them out!"

The whizzing bullets pelted the ground next to me. Two clipped my leg. "Ah, hell," I muttered. "I'm blowing the charge!" I pressed the detonator and scrambled back to cover. We felt the earth quake under the exploding charges that had been placed deep in the plateau wall.

We crouched along the outcropping of shrubs, then scurried

down the plateau's back. Something punched me hard in the side, and I passed out before I hit the ground. I came around quickly, I think, to focus on Tommy's face while he roughly pulled me down the slope. Great, saved by Lucy's kid.

Orin took a slug in the shoulder. Hamish slung his weapon over his back and pulled the young warrior to cover. We mostly slid down the plateau to Haku's position.

Tommy wrapped my waist with thick bandages. Hamish put a tourniquet on my leg then inspected Orin's wound. "Get them down to camp," Haku commanded and turned back to the work at hand.

"Don't let this old man get in your way," I admonished Haku. "He's the Company's best weapon against us."

"One night we'll tell lies about today over a bottle of Kiam gin," Hamish offered.

"You're buying," I said and winced from pain when they lifted me.

And so the rest of this I must tell as the news came to us at Haku's camp. I rested on a thin pallet near the entrance of a narrow cliff on the plateau's back. Runners reported to May while she dressed my wounds and hid her tragic face. She instructed Carline to make her way to Cyrus' camp and ask Kyle Le to quickly come.

The ridge of the plateau broke loose and sent slabs of rock down onto the refinery buildings. One section plus the fire-spewing towers collapsed under their weight. Inside the refinery buildings, widespread wildfire was obvious with the thick walls demolished.

Quentin's forces broke off their offensive and moved to reinforce Cyrus' position. Captured Tao Chek was brought before Ely and Cara. They held Tao Chek and his personal guard tied together with ropes until Cyrus came to them from the battle.

Tao Chek begged to know the death given to honored enemies. But Cyrus said no, Tao Chek's heart would continue to beat in his chest while he knew the disgrace of deserting the battlefield.

I may have dozed a little. May sat next to me and dabbed my face with a cool cloth. "How goes the battle?" I asked.

"Dolvia has saved us," she said simply. "The earth between the butte and the plateau opened and Dolvia swallowed the refinery buildings. The butte tower splintered at the cleft and one section fell into the wide trench. A great fire burns over the cavern of deep water."

"You're telling me a story because you think I will die." May sadly turned away. Tears rolled down her cheeks.

"It is enough," I said through the pain, "That my stepchildren will have children on Dolvia."

"Dolvia never lies," May pronounced with ritual. "Come

forward."

Smiling and wiping away her tears, Tina came to my side. "This one will have your daughter," May whispered. "Mated to young Hamish who will lead the tribes in a new cycle after Ely."

"That's what was seen!" I said to Tina.

"I saw you in a shower of golden flecks," Tina claimed. "The only moisture on the savannah in a season."

"Does May tell me truly? We have won the day?"

"Dolvia has swallowed the putrid refinery," Tina said with jubilation in her voice. "She didn't need to call forward the minion from the Canyon of Buttes. They are for another time."

Many warriors returned carrying their heavy weapons. Hamish greeted Pete with a grateful bear hug. Gritty Joey with lacerations across his cheek quietly approached Hamish. "You must see this."

Joey led Hamish and Pete around a corner to where Haku watched the chemical fire belch up from the new crater between the plateau and the shattered butte. "What do you see?" asked Haku.

"Company rule over Westend has ended," Hamish said.

"It's Heather's fire," Haku said simply. "The image was given to us by the holy woman before Oriika. We didn't know until today its meaning in our lives."

"What does it mean?" asked Pete.

"The season of om has passed. Netta has settled on the savannah."

Kyle Le rushed into our encampment, wearing an Arrivi domestic gown with the bas-relief designs once produced at Brittany Mill. She came to me with a sweet smile and tears in her eyes. "Are you alright?" I asked.

"Netta covers the savannah," she claimed. "There will be no dividends on your twelve percent."

"Twelve percent of famine?" I asked. "How will you live?"

"We will visit Mekucoo land and wait for a new season of kari." She waited a long moment and added. "Gaucho, do you remember when you first came to us?"

"You pity me," I whispered. "You and May always start with this when you pity me." She sadly looked away. "What?" I asked. "What secret of Kyle Rula do you keep from me now?"

"We knew that Brian Rabbe Miller would not survive the season of om. That's why we never wished it speed. And now I must tell you one last secret."

She smiled and whispered into my ear. "I have always loved you." The image of her mischievous smile stayed with me until the end.

About the Author

Raised in Indiana Stella Atrium lives in Chicago where she has completed work on her second science fiction novel *Seven Beyond*.